Go To Hell □ □ □

Go To Hell

CHARLES ATKINS

Charles Atkins:

Go To Hell

ebook ISBN 9780786753833

Print ISBN 9780786753826

Distributed by Argo Navis Author Services

ISBN 9780786753826

Also by Charles Atkins □ □ □

ALSO BY CHARLES ATKINS
The Portrait
Risk Factor
Cadaver's Ball
Barrett Conyors forensic psychiatry thrillers
The Prodigy
Ashes Ashes
Mother's Milk
Lil Campbell and Ada Strauss mysteries
Vultures at Twilight
Best Place to Die
Non Fiction mental health books
The Bipolar Disorder Answer Book
The Alzheimer's Answer Book

Preliminaries □ □ □

To Liz Fitzgerald

Acknowledgements

GO TO HELL has been a long time in the making and owes its creation to many hands. I am deeply indebted to my agent—Al Zuckerman—for his masterful guidance and editorial expertise. Likewise, Liz Fitzgerald—editor extraordinaire—has been there every step in helping me stay on task and keeping me focused on both the forest and the trees. I'd also like to thank Mickey Novak and Katie Zanecchia of Writers House for helping to shepherd this project through the digital wilderness. I'm also grateful for the beautiful cover art courtesy of Paul Johnson.

As always I am thankful for the support of my partner, family and friends who invariably have to read the early drafts and say nice things. And finally, to you, my reader, thank you for purchasing this book, I hope you enjoy it.

"I call heaven and earth to witness
against you this day, that I have set
before thee life and death,
the blessing and the curse;"

–Deuteronomy XXX; 20; 19

"Him the Almighty Power
Hurled headlong flaming from the ethereal sky,
With hideous ruin and combustion, down
To bottomless perdition; there to dwell
In adamantine chains and penal fire,"

–John Milton
Paradise LostBookI; — 44-48

Part One: The Shell Game

□ □ □

Chapter One

□ □ □

Alone in his room, six-year-old Spencer, already in his X-Men PJ's, held his breath, aware how the slightest wrong movement could cause the death of thousands of tiny creatures. Bracing his right hand with his left, he let loose a drop of murky pond water from the slender glass pipette. It landed in a perfect circle on the slide. "Please let there be one," hoping there'd be more as excitement bubbled in his belly. He gingerly pried loose a paper-thin slide cover from the stack and let it fall onto the drop of water, squishing all it contained across the surface, like a glass sandwich with a pond-scum center.

With the slide between two fingers he placed it on the stage of his spectacular—albeit second hand—Leica microscope, a birthday gift from Father. He'd been four the first time he'd looked through one. It had been a bring-your-child-to-work day, and father had taken him to the Beth Israel Hospital in Boston where he worked as a cardio-thoracic surgeon. Father had been called away with an emergency bypass and Spencer had spent the day in the lab with a chatty pathologist, who'd shown him magic worlds under the microscope. And now, clamping the slide into place, adjusting the light and mirror, he leaned in to the eyepieces. In perfect focus, he zoomed from 10X to 50X magnification, like traveling to another planet. Under his breath he ticked off names of tiny organisms, "Ciliate... blue-green algae, brown algae, more algae..." and then finally, as he'd started to think that maybe this drop was no good, he spotted a bit of movement at the top of the field. Careful to not overshoot his subject, his right forefinger nudged the slide back. "Oh... you're perfect," centering the swirling blob of cytoplasm, "and look at all your nuclei," feverishly ticking through the different species this might be, "possibly *proteus*, although they usually just have one nucleus, but you're big, maybe *Pelomyxa palustris*, they can have multiple, but you're not that big... *Chaos carolinensis*?" And as he shifted to 100X, he caught the shimmer of a single-cell ciliate coming dangerously close to his wonderful Amoeba, yes definitely *Chaos carolinensis*. The ciliate bumped against the microscopic behemoth, and sensing something was up, its synchronized hairs and single whip-like flagella quickened, trying to escape. Spencer pulled back and looked down at the slide, wishing he'd added a second drop—too late now. "Please don't dry out." He leaned in as the Amoeba mobilized and part of its swirling interior pressed out to form limbs, "Is that one or two pseudopods?—still could be *carolensis*." Like an army encircling its enemy he stared, mesmerized by the morphing Amoeba, as it cut off the north and south for the now-frantic ciliate. And then the top pseudopod twisted down as the bottom one curved up to meet it, like the jaws of a shark.

Rapt by the world-inside a drop, his heart skipped at the sound of Mommy shouting shrill from downstairs. "James, why? Please don't do this! I'll forgive you, just stop seeing her. Don't do this to me! To us!"

Spencer didn't want to listen, her voice high-pitched and desperate. Like the trapped ciliate, all escape gone as the Amoeba's now-joined pseudopodia squeezed down; the trapped organism's flagella beat against the tightening noose of the Amoeba's cell wall.

"Maybe if you weren't a self-absorbed prima Donna this wouldn't have happened! There's a reason, Lila. There's a reason I go to her! She gives me what you don't...what you never have. And make no mistake; I don't want to stop! And I don't need anyone's forgiveness. Certainly not yours! All I want...is out."

"No! Don't leave! I can't take this."

Spencer didn't budge, his attention split as the Amoeba ripped open the ciliate, and he heard Father storm out...again. Mommy sobbed, he wanted to go to her, but he never knew what to say or do when she got like this. Would she yell at him, or hug him? Like she was different people, the Mommy in the picture over his bed with her long silken hair brushed back, eyes twinkling, and a smile that melted his heart. Then there was the Mommy who could sing like an angel in front of thousands of people, and finally this one, who'd lock herself in the bedroom or in her recording studio out back for days, not talking to anyone, barely eating, crying without end.

He heard a bay door of the garage go up, and the growl of Father's shiny black car. He felt sick, his gut knotted. He hated the fights. And lately, they happened all the time.

Tears squeezed from his eyes, making it hard to focus. Wiping them back he looked in the scope, seeking traces of the ciliate inside the swirling Amoeba. Yes, it had just been eaten, but it seemed different from how other animals ate, more as though it was now a part of the Amoeba, but even though it had lost its own identity... *its nucleus still seems intact... what does that mean?*

And then he heard the piano from below, one of Mommy's angel songs from her new CD. The knot in his belly eased. *Maybe she'll be OK.*

Through the microscope lens, Spencer's Amoeba started to tremble. The tiny creature's world was drying out. He sat back and looked across his work table, past his threadbare red-velveteen Danny dog perched on a stack of scientific articles that the librarian at the Brookline library had said were too hard for him. She'd insisted he also take two large picture books from the children's section–OUR TINY FRIENDS, and HIDDEN WORLDS–now buried at the bottom of the stack.

He undid the clamps and pulled the slide off the micro-scope. It was warm. Probably too late to save the Amoeba. Even so, he grabbed the pipette and, holding the slide over the red plastic beach bucket of pond water, flushed saline across the surface. The slide cover slipped off and he soaked the connecting surfaces with fresh liquid, letting it drip into the bucket.

All the while, his ears riveted to Mommy's playing; it sounded OK, soothing, *but not quite right, too fast and too loud. Wait till she starts the singing part, then you'll know.* He focused on the rolling waves of the angel song, Mommy's fingers strumming cords like on a harp. *Maybe she's OK.* He stared past the microscope at the tree outside. A pair of crows, possibly ravens–*no, the heads too pointy*–perched there, staring at him. Something weird about these birds. Always the same two, and strange because he saw no light around them unlike other animals–and certainly people. Living things gave off lights that Spencer had always seen, a fact he could not mention around Father. *"Don't make up stories boy. No one likes a fibber."* These birds, with their glinting black eyes, were surrounded only by the growing dark, their feathers shimmering in moon glow. And why were they always there?

And then Mommy started to sing, high and pure, like a stream trickling through intricate piano cords. It swelled as her playing pounded hard and fast. He bit his lip, and grabbed Danny dog as she hit the keys, no longer sounding like a harp, but like waves crashing. He clutched the plush toy to his chest and stuck his thumb in his mouth. Her singing now loud and ugly, like she was in pain, screaming.

"*I stand on the moors, tears flow to the sea*
    "*Pray please sweet lover return to me.*"

He slid off his chair and opened his bedroom door. In the hall there was a stink, like incense and rotten eggs. *Please let her be okay,* knowing she wasn't and that this was going to be an awful night. At the top of the stair he peered through the curved baluster into the arched opening of the living room. The pocket doors were half open and he glimpsed Mommy's legs, one bare foot pressed down on the loud pedal, as she wailed, while around her swirled a glow of shiny green and yellow light.

"Oh, no!" paralyzed with fear, he saw that she wasn't alone; *it* was with her. He crept lower, knowing she needed him, but the thing that sat beside her, all glittery and gold, scared the crap out of him.

"*Return to me, return to me.*
Goddam it you bastard return to me!"

Step by step he forced himself down. The music and her screams hurt his ears. "Mommy!" he cried out. "MOMMY!"

The pounding and the screaming stopped. Their echo rang in his head.

"Go to bed, Spencer," she gasped. "I don't want you here."

Frightened so he could barely move, he forced himself across the patterned marble of the foyer floor and into the living room. She looked awful, her dark hair falling across her face, her eyes bloodshot and black streaks of makeup down her cheeks. Her nose dripped and her mouth contorted as she cried. "Go to bed, Spencer."

He couldn't speak, and shook his head, as he stared at the glittering thing that sat by her. It looked like an angel–beautiful, with gold wings that touched the floor behind it, and its face like a statue at the Museum of Art, with curly hair and a wreath of gold leaves. It grinned at him.

"I'm not kidding, Spencer," Mommy said, stifling her sobs and sounding mad. "Back to your room."

The angel creature nodded and winked. Its eyes were not gold, but black like shiny stones. It whispered into Mommy's ear. Puffs of yellow smoke swirled across the living room. The smell was stronger now, like bad eggs and something sweet and woody. Spencer's eyes teared as the yellow mist climbed around his ankles, his knees. He was getting woozy. It was hard to stand.

"Don't go with it," he begged, as it helped Mommy up from the bench.

"Go to sleep," she said, as the creature led her from the living room back toward his parents' bedroom. "I'll be fine," she lied, meeting his gaze. "I'm going to bed and you should too."

"No!" but the smell made it hard to think. "Don't go with it." Salty water flooded his mouth, like he might throw up. She wasn't okay, and that beautiful creature was bad. He knew that he had to do something, but the smoke and the smells were making it hard to think. His legs wobbled and he fell to his knees. He saw the phone by the couch and crawled toward it. He reached for it, barely able to keep his eyes open. He punched in 911.

He heard a woman's voice, "Brookline Emergency Response, how may I help you?"

He tried to speak, but what was he supposed to say? He pictured a silver-haired woman with soft gray eyes–Mommy's best friend and singing coach, Joan Shift. He clutched Danny Dog as he tried to remember what Joan had told him. She knew about the golden angel and knew it was a bad thing. She called it names—*Abomination, The Adversary, Lucifer.*

"Hello?" the woman's voice. "Hello? You've called the Emergency Response Line. Hello? If this is a prank you need to know that all calls are traced."

Spencer couldn't speak. He thought of the ciliate, swallowed whole by the Amoeba, then of oatmeal-raisin cookies fresh out of Joan's oven, and her fat orange cat–Fido–and of standing backstage at one of Mommy's concerts, his heart filled with pride as she sang. He thought of all those things, but not of the one thing that might have saved her.

And when he awoke to screaming sirens and breaking glass, his mommy was dead.

Chapter Two

□ □ □

At Lila Cartwright-William's memorial service on a white-sand beach off the tip of Cape Cod, Joan Shift held tight to Spencer's warm hand. He'd left his shabby red dog that she'd patched numerous times in the car. He'd not wanted to, but knew it annoyed his father. She glanced down at the little boy in his navy suit, white shirt and tie, so smart and strange—*Lila should never have had him.*

Standing there, her sandals sinking into the soft sand, she felt so old. Her eyes were dimming and her hips and knees ached. She knew that to anyone who bothered to notice, she'd seem nothing more than a thin woman in a dove gray suit—late fifties to mid sixties, silver hair in a bun, straight spine and pale eyes. They'd find nothing odd or weird, unless they really looked at how she had to remember to blink to keep her eyes from drying, and how she would stare deep and see exactly what made a person tick. And when she spoke, the truth and only the truth passed her lips. What they'd never know was the depth of her sorrow, and the weight of her failure as she looked across a sea of mourners—all nationalities, many in native costumes, paying their respects to this woman whose music and whose crusade for women's human rights had enriched so many. They'd known that Lila was special, only sensing what Joan knew explicitly—that Lila Cartwright had been chosen at birth by the Creator. Her path had not been apparent in the beginning, but as she picked up speed, she was spectacular—a lone woman with a glorious gift bringing hope to millions of women in cruel and despotic nations, where even in this late century they were virtual slaves. It was a trial she'd seen before, the lone warrior standing up to a much stronger opponent, armed with conviction and righteousness.

It sickened her how it so often ended like this. But to question the Creator's purpose was not an option. She'd lost count of how many times she'd been called to guide a chosen one—*maybe a hundred.* And each time beautiful Lucifer, in his role as adversary, would be sent to tempt him or her. After, they would both be dismissed–Lucifer screaming and cursing his way back to hell and Joan to peaceful bliss, until the next time. Lucifer's awful fate, and that of his siblings—the first brood—was a cautionary tale as to why angels were not to question the Creator. *So why am I still here? What is going on? Something is terribly wrong.*

A sound system gently played one of Lila's best-loved recordings. The arrangement was ethereal and on top of gorgeous harmonies floated her voice, other worldly and out of time, pure soprano, notes hanging in the air, her tone rich with emotion–the woman on the moors awaiting a lover's return, the mother singing to the child, the girl in love for the first time. All around, people wept.

Joan looked down at Spencer, his hand in hers, so small. A few feet away stood his father, James, a man Lila should not have married, but who she did love. And who proved the truths of human attraction–opposites attract, but with love not nurtured, they repel. Handsome with dark hair gone gray at the temples and in a black suit, James held the pewter urn with Lila's ashes. As the music swelled he looked toward his son, and held out his hand.

Spencer let go of hers and went to his father. The two were flanked by a diverse group of religious leaders, and together they walked toward a temporary pier, decorated in snow-white lilies.

Joan shielded her cataract-clouded eyes against the sun as she looked around. *Why am I still here?* The question hounded her, as did that final horrible scene of Lila, naked and floating in her own blood, her wrists slashed open, and her hair flowing like water weeds on the surface as a grinning Lucifer—first born of the first brood–whispered lies into her dying brain. *But not really lies,* she corrected herself, cruel distortions tinged with truths that plucked like the strings of a harp on Lila's greatest fears— *"James never loved you, just your fame and your talent, but never you. You were a trophy, Lila, and now he has another; she's two months pregnant with his child. No one has ever loved you, they just want you for the things you can do. You're tired, aren't you? Always fighting for others, when all you ever wanted was to be loved. And now he's gone—he said so. Not coming back, never coming back. So alone, so empty, so tired. Isn't this better? Just rest. Give in. Give up."* Joan had been too late, and as she'd done dozens of times— as was her particular duty–she'd hurled Lucifer back to hell. It had been horrible; his taunts as he'd stood over Lila's lifeless body, making Joan know how completely she had failed. Not only was Lila dead, but she'd taken her own life—the unforgivable sin–her soul dammed and cast into the tortures of hell. Now, she searched for Lucifer's presence. He wasn't there–no shining angel who could cause her spirit to ache, nor any of the other seductive guises he could wear. His ability to transform shape was beyond anything she and her generation—the second brood–could do. He'd done his worst with Lila. For thirty years they'd battled over her, as her music brought light into some of the most brutal corners of the world. She'd held harsh spotlights up to despots, making the world take notice, often placing herself in jeopardy. She was a stunning exemplar of what humans could achieve. But in the end, Lucifer had won–had broken her too-tender heart, using her husband's infidelity.

She watched as James emptied Lila's fine-gray ashes into the waves. She trudged down the beach, away from the crowd, and then turned back to look. Three woman in flowing batik dresses and colorful turbans sang at the end of the pier. Spencer had let go of his father's hand and was watching her. He caught her eye and shook his head, almost like he knew she was about to leave. He tugged on his father's sleeve, said something, and then walked off the pier and hurried toward her.

She waited as a wave brushed across her sandals, tickling her toes with sand and chilly water. *I shouldn't be here. Why haven't I been called back?*

He caught up with her, and slid his soft hand into hers. "Joan, please don't leave. I need you to stay with me."

A child's simple request. It took her aback. Her work was done; she should be gone. And if the Creator had forsaken her–and based on this failure, with reason–then she would find a place to hide herself and wait for the next to be chosen, maybe in twenty years, maybe a hundred. The body she was in was old and tired; she'd be glad to be rid of it.

She was about to tell him that his father would take care of him, but before she could get the words out, he stopped her.

"No," he turned back to look at the people on the beach. "Do you see her?"

Was the boy talking about his mother? She knew the child had visions, saw auras and had seen the Creature, but what was he talking about now? "Who?"

"The blond lady in the black dress with the big hat. I don't want to point, because she'll feel bad. Do you see her, next to the big lifeguard chair?"

"Yes," Joan's clouded eyes could barely make out the figure in black, but what surrounded the figure, the woman's aura, gave her pause. *How could the child possibly know?*

"It's her," he said. "Father will marry her; I don't think she likes me, although she'll pretend. She'll say she does, and she's not being mean or bad, but she wants Father and she wants other things, like the baby that's inside of her, but not me. She doesn't want me."

Joan shuddered as Spencer looked up at her with his trusting brown eyes—*his mother's eyes*, "How can you know this? Have you met her? Has your father said something?"

He kept staring toward the woman with the big black hat, "I can see it, and I can smell father's lies, and how bad he feels over what he did to Mommy. You see it too, can't you?"

"Yes," she said simply, wondering what the hell was going on? Could she have been mistaken–after all the Abomination loved to play tricks. "Do you still see the gold angel?" she asked.

"No, he's gone. I think he was there just for Mommy. And again he asked, "Will you stay with me, Joan? I need you."

She looked at the boy, and then at his father on the pier. The man was watching the two of them, his guilt and remorse evident but also a shameful relief over being rid of his temperamental wife. *Too much*, she thought, the boy's trusting hand in hers. *Is this what it's to be, some kind of punishment?* And while that made some sense, going to one of the human truisms she loved so well, *'if you make a mess you need to stick around and clean it up,'* she thought it wrong. The battle had been lost, she'd cast Lucifer into the pit—*too little too late*–and she should not still be here. All she could think was *something is wrong, very very wrong.*

*

Two years later Joan–now a de facto parent of an eight-year-old–found herself in the all-too-familiar situation of knitting while waiting outside the Vice Principal's office at Spencer's school.

"Joan?" the red-headed secretary came to get her.

"Hi Denise," Joan looked up, noting how much clearer her vision had become since the cataract surgery. She'd made peace with staying in this sixty-eight-year-old body–which had originally belonged to a piano and voice teacher who lived next door to Lila's parents—and decided she'd better take care of it. The fact that she needed a human host and Lucifer, or whatever he was calling himself, didn't was just one of the many mysteries she'd never pierced. It seemed horribly unfair to be set in a playing field where the combatants were so clearly unmatched, but these things were not for her to question. *And besides,* she mused, noting the secretary's pleasant blue-green aura that curiously matched her skirt set, *fairness is a human concept and has no bearing outside of them.*

"Mr. Flanagan is ready for you."

"Thanks, I know the way." And stuffing the half-finished scarf into her big red bag she crossed the waiting area and knocked.

"It's open," a man said.

Joan took a deep breath, and found herself in Kevin Flanagan's tidy office with its windows overlooking a baseball diamond. Spencer looked up anxiously as she came in; his red-and-white striped shirt was filthy, mud caked in his shoulder-length hair and a wad of bloody tissue in his left nostril. She shook her head, what had today's fight been about? She looked at Kevin—early thirties, fit, sandy hair starting to thin—whom she knew from PTA had two sons and a pretty wife named Kate. "What did he do?"

"Same song, different verse," the administrator said, trying to keep his expression stern. "Seems Spencer came upon a couple fourth graders trying to shake down a younger kid for his lunch money."

"It wasn't fair," Spencer shot back. "They were bigger. He was crying and they were being mean."

"Spencer," Joan coaxed, "we've been through this so many times. You need to tell a teacher. That's their job, not yours."

"I know, but there was no one around and he was crying. They'd knocked his books down. It wasn't fair."

Joan turned to Flanagan, "So what's the damage?"

"As you know, it's a zero tolerance policy for any kind of fighting."

"But it was..."

Before Spencer could finish, Joan shut him down. "Stop it! Respect your elders. You need to listen to Mr. Flanagan...as you were saying."

"Two weeks detention, but the next time it's a suspension."

Joan sensed Spencer wanting to erupt. She looked at him, her eyes boring into his. "You can't keep doing this," she said, while part of her marveled at how clear he was in knowing right from wrong–no ambiguity–and the part that made her so frightened for him–*he has no fear—too much like his mother.*

"Joan," Kevin said, "I'm going to have Spencer wait outside; there's a couple other things we need to discuss."

"Of course," How did parents ever survive raising a human child?

With Spencer gone, Kevin launched right in. "Joan, I'm really torn with him."

"Which part?"

"I wonder if we're doing him a disservice by skipping him another grade. His brain is off the charts, but he's eight years old. We've got him with ten year olds and his teachers are telling me they still can't keep him occupied. He zips through an entire semester's curriculum over a long weekend and then asks what comes next. He got perfect scores on the mastery exam in all but one of the subsets, but he's not making friends. The kids tease him, and they can be cruel, which strangely doesn't seem to be where he gets into fights. It's always when he thinks someone else is being taken advantage of. It's admirable, but one of these days it's going to get him badly hurt or worse."

"His mother was like that, 'leap before you look.' So what do you suggest? I can't tell you how much it worries me."

"If we go by his scores, we should bump him up to at least sixth–but I don't know if developmentally, he'll able to handle that. Where's his father weighing in on this?"

Joan pictured the stern doctor–now remarried and with a new baby and a second on the way. "He leaves it to me," she said. "Let me give this some thought, and see what Spencer wants."

"Thanks," flashing her a grin, "and please see if you can't do something about the fighting."

*

Five years later, in the cozy candlelit living room of her two-story Craftsman bungalow on a tree-lined street in Brookline, Joan watched Spencer. Now thirteen, and shooting up like a weed, he sat cross legged on a midnight-blue carpet, his eyes closed, his focus inward. He reminded her of his mother, and she took a moment's dangerous pride, knowing that he would grow tall and handsome, with thick wavy brown hair and Lila's doe eyes, and long lashes.

But watching him put her on edge–especially at this age. The mother had clearly been The Chosen, that lucky—or cursed depending on your point of view—individual around whom the great conflict between the Creator and his Abomination continued. Experience had taught Joan that at thirteen a quickening occurred, where the direction of the particular battle would be revealed. For Lila, it had been her fierce intolerance for any injustice, a dangerous trait that ran strong in Spencer. Her downfall, and what the Abomination had used to destroy her, was a heart that loved too fully and broke too completely. Joan often wondered if that was the trait about humans that caused the Creator to spend so much time on them—their ability to love. But Lila had been chosen; her son–albeit special–was not. And if she needed proof of this, Lucifer–*so beautiful, so proud*–was nowhere to be found. No lurking angel, no celestial portents, just a strangely gifted child, who daily reminded her of his sad and lovely mother. Bottom line, if he were chosen, Lucifer would be here—unable to resist, doing his damnable best to tempt and to pervert.

"Slow your breath further," she instructed, trying to shake off ancient memories–*proud angel, how many times has it been? Locked together in this never-ending tango*- "keep it rhythmic like the waves on the shore, rolling in and rolling out." She watched as the boy deepened his trance, a state that allowed him to hone those strange talents he'd been given.

"What do you see? Put it in words."

"It's fast," he said, as images formed on the back of his eyelids– an ancient practice call Skrying. "One thing tumbling over the other, I'm sitting with Fido reading X-Men–darn!"

"What?"

"They're making Wolverine have a new girlfriend. Why do they have to waste a perfectly good comic on that?"

She chuckled, "Let it pass. What else?"

"You don't want to know," his words breathy as he kept focus, his mind clear, his attention split between his inner and outer worlds.

"Another fight?"

"Yeah, but I don't have a choice," anger twisting his mouth.

"You always have a choice," she said, "don't ever forget that. It's what makes humans special. You can choose. You can choose not to fight, Spencer. You can choose to walk home a different way."

"They're torturing a litter of kittens," on the verge of tears. "They've killed the mother."

"Or," she said, "You can choose to beat the hell out of them."

"I bring the kittens home," now perfectly still, a hint of the smile he'd use to get his way.

"Of course," She'd grown accustomed to the steady stream of wounded strays. The first time, inadvertently revealing another of his gifts, he'd soothed a dog with a broken leg, which as soon as he'd stopped stood on all fours and ran after him. At the time—he'd been nine–his ability to lay on hands had disturbed her. As she often did, she'd cast her vision as far as her human vessel and dim eyes would allow, seeking out the Creature's glitter, wondering if It had crept back from the pit. Had the Creator opened the portal once again, as happened each time a Chosen was selected? But she found nothing. And yet, too much wasn't making sense. With always the most basic question, *Why am I still here?* The only answer she could find–penance. Was she too being tested? Cast out from the Creator and made to live in the world of the humans. She stared at the boy. *Am I being tested? But why now? Why with this boy? And with two dozen angels in my brood, why does this fall to me?* But even with those bad thoughts there was another, much stronger. *Yes, cast out,* but feeling such love for this beautiful boy, *is this what it's like to be a real mother?*

Spencer was silent and she saw him wince as if in pain. "What is it Spencer? What are you seeing?"

"I'm in jail, or maybe it's a hospital where the doors are locked. I'm in brown pajamas with writing on them, and something's wrong with me. I just stare at the ceiling and count the tiles over and over."

"OK, listen to me. Imagine the most fragile robin's egg, and handling it gently, let your mind turn the image of that beautiful egg back in time, apply no pressure, just softly let it spin back in your hands."

"Okay, now I'm in a doctor's office and then in the waiting room. Father's inside with the doctor, I can hear them."

"What are they saying?"

"Father says I'm crazy," his voice dipped, "like my mother. He says I'm hallucinating." He went quiet.

"What is it?"

"I'm going back before that; he's here and he's yelling at you, saying you filled my head with lies, that you did the same with my mother. He's dragging me away, forcing me into the car. I don't want to go with him. He says you're hurting me. You're making me psycho."

Joan was awe-struck, then a favorite line from Dickens'

A *Christmas Carol* sprang to mind, the point where Scrooge, haunted by the Ghost of Christmas-yet-to-come realizes that if he continues in his miserly ways it won't end well. *"Men's courses will foreshadow certain ends, to which, if persevered in, they must lead, said Scrooge. "But if the courses be departed from, the ends will change. Say it is thus with what you show me!"* "Remember Spencer," she said, "you can always choose. You can turn left or you can turn right. These images are just one path. Spin back further in time; find how this started," she urged.

"I'm trying, it has something to do with my stepmother, something I did to her... Father's coming," he opened his eyes.

"When?" she asked.

The doorbell rang.

"Now."

Chapter Three

□ □ □

The doorbell rang a second time. Spencer uncrossed his legs, "I'll get it." A tight lump gripped his throat, his stomach queasy. Even before he opened the door he sensed Father's mood, anxious and uncomfortable.

"Hey Dad," taking in his unsettled aura, the subtle ambers and red Spencer had come to associate with guilt, like little flames licking his shoulders. It was Saturday and the plan was for him to go off with Father and his new family for a weekend in the woodsy countryside of Dover, half an hour outside of Boston.

"You ever going to cut your hair?" Father asked, taking in his son's shoulder length wavy brown locks.

"Sure," Spencer said, wishing he didn't always feel so edgy around him.

"Would you like to come in?" Joan asked, "have some tea?"

"Another time," he glanced back at the dark green Volvo wagon, his pretty wife Allie in the passenger seat and little Tabitha and Michael wide-eyed and excited in the back.

"They're all welcome to come in," she offered. "I just made oatmeal cookies."

"Thanks, Joan, but we should get moving. You ready, son?"

"Sure," Spencer grabbed his knapsack and wondered why Father needed so many lies. Truth was he didn't want to come into Joan's house; it made him tense and forced him to think of Mother.

But five year old Michael and six year old Tabitha were another story, and Spencer grinned, as they pressed their faces against the window. The light that shone out of their faces was bright white–almost silver–like Joan's, only without the sparkle. "We're going to ride the merry go round," Tabitha—a bubbly blond who loved anything Mickey Mouse, from her red-glitter sneakers, to the bright pink clips in her hair–announced as Spencer wedged his backpack next to a large red cooler.

"I'm going to have a candy apple," Michael, who looked a lot like Spencer with dark hair and big brown eyes, offered, pulling back one finger, "and cotton candy and popcorn."

"Cool," Spencer said, sliding in between them. "And then you're going to throw up?"

"Noooooo!" Michael laughed, and continued to tick off food items, one for each finger. "And a hotdog...and a hamburger."

"How are you?" Allie asked, turning back in her seat, the blond woman's smile strained, but always trying hard to have him like her, to have him not think how she'd betrayed his mother, already pregnant with Tabitha at the time of her death.

"I'm good," he said, knowing that these weekends went best, the less he said. But as he looked at her; he knew immediately that something was wrong–something inside her–in her chest; it was alive and growing; it smelled like pond scum and if he listened close–a squishy noise. *Cancer...and she doesn't know. And how the hell can I tell her?*

"And we're off," father said, putting the car in gear.

At the amusement park, an old one with a rackety wooden roller coaster, and merry go round with brightly painted horses and chariots, Spencer was pulled from ride to ride by Tabitha and Michael, thrilled to spend time with their older brother. A classic family afternoon, but he couldn't relax. Every time he'd see Allie, his vision was pulled to the dark spot inside her chest, knowing that if she didn't catch it soon, it would kill her. *What should I do?*

Hours later, at their rambling house set back in the woods, the kids were asleep and Spencer came down to find Allie reading a paperback in the family room. A gas fire burned orange and blue in the hearth and sent weird shadows around the comfortable room.

"Allie," his voice tentative.

"Can't sleep?" she asked.

Joan's warnings rang in his head, *'don't tell them about the auras, or about skrying, or about seeing things that haven't happened yet. They won't understand. It'll frighten them.'* "You need to see a doctor," he blurted.

"What are you talking about?" putting the book down, her pale blue eyes wide, her expression between amused and concerned.

He put his hand on the left side of his chest, "here," he said, holding her gaze. "Feel here."

Color drained from her face as she put two fingers on her breast, pressed in, and felt the lump. "How could you...?"

"You need to get that taken care of before it's too late. Please, they need their mother." He felt something else too. In that moment he knew that if he placed his hand on the growing lump in her breast, he could kill it. A critical choice, Joan would call it *"do I go left or do I go right?"* she'd say. *"Do I fight this fight, or not? Do I give in to fear, or not?"* So he walked away from her. To lay on hands would plant the final nail in any chance of being a part of this family. Or worse, was this the event that would have Father rip him away from Joan? He knew Allie now would go to a doctor and have this taken care of. It was early enough and she'd be fine.

"Spencer," Allie called to him as he headed up to Father's book-filled study that served as his room for these weekend visits.

He stopped and looked back. He saw fear in her eyes, and the monster growing inside of her.

"I don't know how you know these things," she said, "but thank you."

"You're welcome, and if you wouldn't say anything... about my telling you, I'd appreciate it." And feeling good that Joan would have approved of his choices–*"Tell the truth or tell nothing"*–he went to bed.

*

One year later, not yet done with his growth spurt and already over six feet, a gangly fourteen-year-old Spencer strode across the auditorium in black cap and billowing gown and received his high school diploma. Everyone clapped even though few of his classmates knew him, the last two years having been an arranged curriculum of college courses at the Boston campus of U Mass, where he would enroll as a junior in the fall.

He took the cardboard tube from the principal, "Outstanding," she said, as she shook his hand.

"Thank you," knowing she was sincere, her broad face aglow with pleasure.

"You're going to do great things," she whispered, in the brief seconds they had before she let go of his hand and the next student came up.

He walked across the stage and saw Allie—cancer free, following a partial mastectomy and brief course of radiation—holding a small camera and snapping his picture. He smiled and did what the others did, held his diploma over his head in his right hand,

and made a corny thumbs-up with his left. As he walked down the stairs he caught sight of Joan, next to Father, Michael and Tabitha all clapping as loud as they could.

Later at his celebration dinner at Anthony's—Boston's landmark surf-and-turf restaurant on the piers—he savored the feel of being part of a real family. It felt normal, even if it was mostly make believe. For the moment he imagined he was like everyone else and not such a freak.

"You were the youngest one to graduate," Tabitha gushed—she and Michael seated on either side, their backs to the windows with the panoramic view of the harbor—cargo ships with foreign flags, the pulse of a distant lighthouse and dark water.

"But shouldn't you have won some awards?" Allie asked, as she pulled apart a steaming popover and slathered it with potted butter. "I mean you clearly were the top student in math and science."

"No," Spencer said, his hair tied back in a pony tail, the end tucked under the collar of his shirt to give a conservative look. He glanced at Joan in a vivid periwinkle dress, her hair in a bun, knowing that he was the only one in the room who could see the soft silver sparkle that illuminated her, like beams of light through a forest clearing. "I just wanted to graduate, I didn't want awards. Those should go to students who actually went there. I kind of escaped—thanks to Joan and Father."

"It was either that," Joan chuckled, "or I'd have had to take up permanent residence in the discipline office."

"I just don't get that," Allie said. "You're such a gentle soul, why all the fights?"

He squirmed. It's not something he could explain. "I've got a bad temper I guess."

"College is going to go by fast," father said, stepping in. "You're halfway through before you begin. And then?"

"Medical school," Spencer said. "An MD/PhD program."

"So that's still the direction then? Like father like son?" James Williams glowed, his pride in Spencer overshadowing all his concerns about his precocity.

"Yes, I'm mostly done with the pre-med requirements, just one more semester of core physics and that's it. I'll take the MCATs in the spring, and ride out the last year with upper-level micro, advanced physics and there's a new professor in the math department who's doing theoretical calculus; I need that. I also want to get into this genetics class, but that's reserved for graduate students. I desperately want in because there's a lab attached where I could learn to splice and sequence DNA."

Joan took a sip of wine and smiled across at Allie, "See what you've been missing. It's gotten to the point where I don't understand half of what comes out of his mouth."

"I always enjoyed school," James Williams said, "but Spencer, you take this to a new level. I remember the first time I caught you looking through my old medical texts. You were five. I remember thinking 'there's no way he's actually reading them'... but you were." Father laughed, "After you'd stay the weekend with us I'd check, once I discovered you were going through all my old textbooks one after the other–Cecil's, Grant's, Kaplan and Sadock, the unabridged Topol cardiology, Merritt's neurology. You'd leave a bookmark, and I'd watch it walk down one shelf and up to the next. It's like you're madly racing through. I guess the question is, what are you racing toward?"

Spencer looked at his father—so obviously proud of him—it felt amazing, and for that second he didn't want to think how fragile Father's pride was, how easily it could vanish. Joan's constant instruction—'tell the truth or tell nothing' was a clarion in his head. Then again, I'm not Joan. By fourteen he'd learned that simple truth wasn't always what people wanted. Sometimes it had to be massaged. "Okay." He eyed Allie's wine.

"Go ahead," she said, "you're the graduation boy," sliding it across the table.

"Thanks," he took a sip, letting the merlot's bouquet roll across his tongue. "There's so much knowledge you have to understand before you can get to anything new. It's like a wave that's cresting. Until you make it through all the background sciences, you can't find the new thing that's coming. I have got to understand all the science that's happened till now. And not just the modern stuff," he flashed a look at Joan, aware he was headed in a dangerous direction. Tell the truth or tell nothing.

Joan shook her head, but didn't stop him. "If you must," she said, her face aglow in the silvery light.

"It's like this," marveling at how bright she shone. Maybe tonight he'd ask her again—what are you? "We don't believe something exists until we can see it, feel it, touch it, taste it, or measure it. It's limiting, like even electricity before Ben Franklin. It only became real after he proved it? Of course not. Everything is witchcraft and magic until we can pull it out of the invisible world and trap it in wires, or measure it on a spectrometer, or watch it collide in a nuclear accelerator. But what about all the stuff science hasn't nailed down?" He would have loved to talk about finding the science—the proof—behind skrying, or how he could see people's auras, or know when they were ill, or sometimes catch snippets of their thoughts, like scenes on TV, but to do that would have been to see the approving light go out in Father's eyes. "Does that mean it doesn't exist? Or we just haven't been able to see it yet? This is the path of the scientist." Maybe it was the wine, but Spencer felt like he was on fire, perched on the verge of an epiphany. He thought of two things Joan often said. *"The distance between a thought and a deed is the blink of an eye."* And her most-frequent chestnut, *"Tell the truth or tell nothing."* "That's it!" he said aloud.

"What's it?" his father asked, face flushed with pride.

"How a thing goes from not existing to becoming real. It's born with a thought, spoken as word, written down on a page, then expressed as a blueprint or a model, then the first experiment, the collection of data—what worked, what didn't, go back and do it again. Don't miss a step, don't ignore results— especially bad ones. Find the truth. Work out the kinks. And before long what was unimaginable is real. Everything that can be considered is possible."

"Wow!" James said, and, completely out of character, he reached across the table and tousled Spencer's hair, "And this is my son, who will one day win the Nobel Prize. I could not be prouder."

*

At sixteen Spencer—now a college graduate, six-foot-two and still growing—finished packing at Joan's Brookline house. He'd applied to and been accepted by six medical schools, and in the end had chosen not to remain in Boston, but to go to Chicago's Gray University on a full scholarship. Outside his window he saw the familiar pair of blackbirds high up in the ancient silver maple, where apparently they nested. He flashed on that horrible night so many years back, the memory still fresh. What would his mother think of him now? He glanced at a half-packed carton; her face stared back from the cover of a CD, "Would you be proud, Mom?"

"More books?" Joan asked, coming up the stairs and standing in the doorway of the nearly empty room.

"They're my friends," he said, "Don't want to leave them

behind." As the words left his mouth, he regretted them—*you're leaving her behind... will she be okay?*

"It's time," she looked down at an unsealed box. "The unabridged *Golden Bough*. Do you remember how excited you were to find that."

"I was nine," he said, "I really am a freak."

"Don't say that."

"It's true, and you know that better than anyone." He put the box between his knees to hold the top together and taped it shut. He looked at Joan, with her aging body, and the silvery spirit that animated it, a subject that she would not discuss, although he'd tried many times. "Will you stay?" he asked.

"For a while." She looked around, her head cocked as though listening.

"What determines that?"

"You wouldn't understand."

The frustration when she did this was familiar and annoyed the hell out of him, "Hey, if you explained, I'd probably get it."

"Yes, I suspect that's true. I will miss you terribly, but you're right to go away."

"You're not even human are you?" he blurted, voicing his long-held suspicion. "You're something different."

She looked through the window at the two birds. Her gaze narrowed and they flew off. "Strange," she whispered, walking over and opening the window.

"You mean Heckle and Jekyll?" noting how quickly she changed the subject. "They're always there. Always the same two. Although I've never been able to locate their nest. And crows usually hang out in bigger numbers—you know they call it a murder of crows when there's a bunch of them–but it's always just the two."

She leaned out, "How do you know it's the same pair?"

"Because they have no light, although lately I can see the faintest purple glow, so maybe it's just a dull aura, or part of the spectrum I can't see."

She stared back at him and said nothing. A shadow of worry crossed her face.

"What? What's going on Joan? You look like you've seen a ghost."

"No," she shook her head. "It's nothing. You've grown into a remarkable man, Spencer. Your mother would be proud."

He laughed, letting go of his earlier annoyance—it was point-less. "Years ago I told you that I needed you to stay. Do you remember?"

"Of course," she glanced back at the window, searching for the birds. *All living creatures cast light.*

"I still need you. You've been my mother. Please don't leave."

She turned back and put a hand on his cheek, "You are so sweet, but it's not true. And you know how I feel about lies, even thinking something false, because it can so easily be turned to action."

"Yes," holding her gaze, "it's my mantra, although I think it means something different for me than for you—'*the distance between a thought and a deed is the blink of an eye.*' Of course some of your other little sayings...not so clear, like, '*say it three times and it is so.*' I've never figured that one."

She stiffened, "it's for bad things, Spencer, to make them go away," again glancing at the window.

"Like what?"

She was about to speak, and then stopped herself. "No, not today." She smiled sadly, "You should get these last boxes out of here. Your father's waiting." She pulled him into an embrace and whispered, "Make your choices carefully, know when to go right and when to go left. Know who you can trust, and who you can love, and always trust and love yourself. Know that there is good and there is evil too. Know when to go right and when to go left." She hesitated, "and always know that I love you dearly." She kissed him on each cheek. "Now get out of here."

Part Two: Let's Make a Deal

□ □ □

Chapter Four

□   □   □

Karel Von Graff awoke beneath the massive gilt-framed painting of Prometheus bound—the struggling naked demi-God chained to a rock as a giant raptor dove, its talons outstretched to rip into his flesh. Von Graff lay still, savoring the sensation of floating between two worlds. In dreams he could be all powerful–raise mountains, create species from the sand. The waking world was another matter, a constant race filled with anxiety and fear, like in an airport knowing you've missed the last flight, but worse. Not just running forward, but fleeing, knowing the great "It" was out there, ever eager to cast him back to hell—no rest, no stopping to catch his breath.

He let his body soak up the new day and took inventory of his senses, cool Egyptian linen against naked flesh and corded muscles, birdsong through open French doors that looked onto a vista of manicured gardens and the rolling silver expanse of the Atlantic and Long Island Sound. He breathed in mingled scents of fresh-cut lawn, spring blossoms, frankincense and the tiniest hints of sulfur and bitumen. The bedroom was massive, coffered 20-foot ceilings, and walls covered with stunning allegorical paintings—*The Fall* by Raphael—Eve's face twisted in shame, Adam anguished and pleading for forgiveness, a hand covering his sex–*The Flood* by a student of Michelangelo, the arc tiny on a raging sea as cities burned and sank beneath the waves. A Rembrandt, *Passion of the Christ*, the Carpenter fallen under the weight of the cross on the Via Dolorosa, blood dripping on his upturned face, the painter having captured the light inside the man, one of the Chosen who would not be tempted–*And just see what that got you*. Between the canvases that told of prior battles were several HD TVs, turned to different stations, and Internet feeds with the volume muted.

At the far end of his chamber, as they always did, knowing the exact moment he awoke, entered Minnie and Ian—dark, young and beautiful—like Prada models, dressed in black with flourishes of white–athletic and graceful.

Minnie settled on the edge of the bed; she wore a tight mini skirt, white ruffled blouse and aubergine stockings, her lustrous blue-black hair in an asymmetric bob with long bangs that fell forward as she placed a hand to Karel's cheek. "It must be getting close," smoothing cool fingers across his cheek, pushing the flesh up and back.

Ian stood at the foot of the bed in his Dolcé shirt, two buttons open over his hairless chest, skinny jeans and his latest love— alligator cowboy boots. "A little droop," he told Minnie, "and less gray, just around the sides–a touch on the right temple... Yes, that's the way it was yesterday."

"Did you dream?" Minnie's lavender eyes searched out his.

Karel pressed back against the leather headboard, "Yes, it's time to move forward. I need him."

"And the angel? Do you know where she is?" Ian asked.

"She's not with him. I'd know. But check anyway."

"So you think it worked?" Minnie stepped back, cocking her head from side to side to examine Karel's face from every angle.

"Yes," but immediately he felt doubt and a shiver of fear. How many times had this gone wrong? *Did you really trick her?* "The angel Joan is still in Massachusetts. She cared for the boy out of respect for the mother, but I'm convinced she believed and still believes that it was only the mother who was Chosen. Why would she think different? It's never happened before where first the parent and then the child is Chosen. Joan's eyes cannot see what mine do, in this I have the advantage. I could tell at birth that Lila's son had been touched by The Creator. His glow when I neared was unmistakable." As he spoke, his anxiety ratcheted further, just mentioning his nemesis Joan–not her given name but the one she'd taken for the last 1100 years, a tribute to tragic little Pope Joan–*that one had been fun.* Remembering the brilliant woman who'd hidden her sex and risen on her talents to become pontiff. Her fall–quite literally–had been from a horse while in the throes of childbirth. All her good works, her crusade to open learning to all–male or female–undone in a horrifically comic scene, with mother and bastard child stoned to death, her naked body tied to the horse and dragged through the streets, and her name obliterated from the official histories after more than two years as sitting Pope–*good times.* But now, tasting the raw edge of fear, and something more, the strangeness of this new game–one

Chosen immediately following the next; it was unprecedented, *and what does it mean?*

"Well," Minnie, who could follow the line of her Master's thoughts, drew her lips together in a crimson bow. "I'm skeptical. Don't you think your proximity to the boy when the mother was alive would have let her see? Isn't that how it works? You plus the Chosen equals some kind of homing beam for the angel?"

Karel looked at Minnie and then at Ian—this pair was the best he'd ever had, but something about them was different from those who'd come before–not insubordinate, but fearless, beautiful and cruel...and unafraid to question. Minnie in particular, with her love of dressing like a Jazz age vamp, read his doubts and gave them voice. "True, but the mother was alive and what the angel saw, she will attribute to her. As soon as poor Lila died, much as it pained me to leave the boy–and it still does; it was the only way—and out went your homing beam. Tied to her human body, Joan could not see that Spencer too was Chosen."

"Perhaps, but after so many times," she glanced around at the glorious allegorical paintings, "is the angel so stupid not to suspect a trick?"

"It's not stupidity—it's her nature to see things as either truth or lie. So either I was there or I wasn't. She's ill equipped for subtlety and you, my beautiful little demon are starting to annoy me. You were outside his window, you watched him grow. Is there something you've not told me?"

"Of course not. The mother, the songbird, she was pretty and had talent—they all fell in love with her voice. But is that really the best the Creator could do? Too weak, too flawed."

"Of course they're flawed," Karel pulled the velvet duvet from off his long legs, not caring that he was naked. "That's part of the equation, what is their potential greatness, what is their weakness and how will they transcend it? What will they choose? It's always the same. Our glorious Creator pointed Its finger at pretty little Lila, and sent his champion; she guided her, loved her, watched her die and felt defeat. My victory was absolute."

"I suppose," Minnie said, unconvinced. "You broke her heart and she killed herself. La-di-da! What's so victorious about that?"

"It's the context, my pet. Lila was a crusader, waging a war to liberate oppressed women and their babes. Yet in the end she was a slave to her own emotions. She loved her husband

and I found a better woman for him; one who could give him what he wanted, one who wasn't constantly on the road, or more successful than he. How sad, watching his affection, his love for Lila, snuffed out, while he fell in love with the pretty O.R. nurse who was always at his beck and call, and in whose sparkling blue eyes he saw reflected his own greatness. It's the subtle cuts that wound. But what was different, and what I could see and Joan couldn't, with her human vision, was the boy—it's strange and weird–a gamechanger–but at least I caught it. Lila's son is Chosen, and that's never happened; there's always a break between the battles. And this–a mother/son duo? But who am I to question?" He glared at Minnie as she was about to interrupt. "Don't even think it. This was too good an opportunity and I made certain the angel never saw it. You have no idea how hard that was, watching from a distance, sending you two in my place. But now, finally, the game begins in earnest, only I have the field all to myself."

Ian, not to be overshadowed by his sister, popped in, "To make the saint the sinner."

Minnie added. "Why bother with them at all? You could do anything you wanted, go anywhere."

Karel leaned back on his arms and stared up at the desperate Prometheus. "You know that's not true."

"What can't you do?"

"I can't create."

"You made us." She shot back. "You could make thousands more of us if you wanted. Why stop at two?"

"You're not real. You're not flesh. And besides, you two are enough. Any more and the angel would notice." He watched her expression cloud and thought of the children's story Pinnochio— 'But I want to be a real boy.'

"What's the difference?" she asked. "I mean really... Yes, I know our limitations, but in this age does it matter? No, I can't pick up a hammer and build a house, but I could easily find any number of willing males, screw that—females too—that would build me a mansion. Look at you, in this house, and at the head of an ancient corporation that spreads like an octopus around the planet. You pop in and out as its head, take on the shape of the current leader, and have an army of willing humans to do your will. You don't lift a finger... and you don't need to."

It was fascinating to Karel how these servants had changed... evolved. Minnie was angry and sad and confused, more and more human, not like the early ones, great lumbering giants or scary night creatures that fueled stories of werewolves, succubi, and vampires. And certain skills, like their ability to mimic the talents of humans, were unprecedented, like the day he awoke to the sounds of the Tchaikovsky Violin Concerto in D and found her on violin and Ian on piano giving a flawless performance having just watched a YouTube video of Itzhak Perlman. "But there is a difference and you know it. You have no soul," he said. "You can't procreate, you don't age unless I want you to...you cast no light, and that's why you were the perfect trick—the angel couldn't see you, and the boy wouldn't notice." He was about to add, *"and you don't have real emotions, you can't know love,"* but with these two, Minnie especially—that seemed no longer true. *Yes, she was imitating Itzhak Perlman that day, but why did it sound better–more passionate–than the original? How is this happening?*

"I know all this," she said, selecting delicate bottles of precious scented oils from a cabinet, "but there are things I can do that they can never. Change shape and get inside their heads, make them believe whatever they most fear or desire. Get them to do the things they long to do. Let's face it," cocking her head and letting a smile spread across her pouty lips. "I'm a catch."

"Hey," Ian spoke up, having let his attention stray to the antics of three red hawks who had caught and killed a squirrel and now played with its bloody tail high up on a spruce, one bird dropping it as a second swooped down and caught, and the third gave chase. "What about me? I'm a catch too."

Minnie smiled at her counterpart, as she dripped perfumed oils into two ancient Tibetan foo dog censors. "Of course you are, brother..." and then back at Karel, "Why do you care about humans so much more? Why can't we be enough?"

Karel inhaled, smelling the fragrance of vanilla, frankincense, myrrh and the hint of sulfur they were meant to conceal. "Because they're human, they have souls and they have free will." He was about to add, *and because the Creator loves them best—and for this I loathe them and will destroy them.* It was those thoughts he found most dangerous, the searing hatred...the jealousy. The Creator had made one species—his—and then cast them aside, as though they were little more than unwanted playthings. And when he, the first born, had questioned, complained, demanded an explanation, he'd been brutally cast out. His siblings—twenty-four angels of the first brood—had been torn apart, and the lie of their immortality revealed. Angels can and do die, but there's worse. He and six survivors were cast to hell, a dimension of tortured souls and endless suffering, but that was going to change. "They come to me of their own choosing, the chains that bind them are of their own making."

Minnie wanted to say more, when the buzzer for the front gate sounded.

"Company," Ian chimed, making his voice boom deep to match the electronic bell.

"That will be your girlfriend." Minnie grabbed a brocaded Prussian blue robe from a closet.

Karel stood letting her dress him, enjoying the sensations of the velvety fabric encasing his flesh, the belt cinched around his middle. But mostly his thoughts were on brilliant Dr. Lara Nash driving past the gate house in her white Lexus convertible, top down, her wheels crunching on the oyster shell drive, blonde hair mussed by the wind as she pulled up to his front door.

"I'll get it," Ian headed toward the bedroom door, puppy dog excitement at the arrival of company.

"No." Minnie raked Karel with a glance that bordered on hostile. "Let me."

"Be nice to her," Karel ordered, his tone firm.

"As you wish...master," and mimicking the Barbara Eden character from the seventies sitcom *I Dream of Jeannie*, she crossed her arms, blinked and vanished in a swirl of yellow mist.

*

Lara Nash put the indulgence that was her new Lexus SC convertible in park and turned off the engine. Her cheeks were flushed as she flicked down the visor and checked herself in the mirror. "What the hell are you doing?" she whispered, letting her brain register the salt air and the bouquet from the stunning gardens–vivid with coral, hot pink and periwinkle azalea and bearded iris so purple they appeared black. She didn't want to think about what it meant to show up at her boss's Westport mansion on a Saturday morning. Yes, he'd invited her—*"We'll have breakfast, and talk about this."* Like a line she'd give her bad-boy-soon-to-be-transformed-by-love Harrison James in the romance she was currently writing. Her life as a romance novelist was a secret–and increasingly lucrative–sideline that had started in high school and continued ever since. Like clockwork, she shipped an 80,000 word manuscript every year to Bantam, under the pseudonyms Adelaide Adams—for the contemporary working-woman series–and Eloise Fletcher–for her regency page turners modeled after Jane Austen, albeit with at least five steamy sex scenes. It was her private world, between four and six a.m., caught up in heart-throbbing fantasies—something that she'd never actually experienced–at times feeling something of a fraud for promoting the dream of unconditional romantic love.

But the last three weeks had sent her on-track and soon-to-be-wed existence out of orbit. At the center of it all was Karel, the emperor and CEO of Global Pharmaceuticals, and she was its...his...recently promoted Vice President of Research and Development. Daily she'd reminded herself that this was a promotion she deserved. In her five years at Global, as director of the New York research facility, her unit had pushed through three major and innovative new drugs, cleared impossible regulatory hurdles and fast-tracked approvals—one for female arousal disorder, one for Alzheimer's, and the most recent, Viralon, a blockbuster pill that shrank enlarged prostate glands while enhancing potency. Any or all of these might well have languished in development for ten years or more, but through her savvy, a morally flexible team of epidemiologists willing-and-able to massage the data, and Global's clout, they'd all received FDA approval in near-record time. Her day job—unlike her books–was all reality: aging men who couldn't get it up, the ravages of time, the paralyzing human fears of pain, growing old...death. People wanted these drugs, needed them. So what if she had to cut a few corners, bury a bit of questionable data, or let a few well-placed politicos know that their annual campaign donations from Global were contingent on a drug's safe passage. Everyone did that, but her greatest achievement, and why she was so hot, was her making hay with the relationship between physicians and the drug companies. As she'd tell her staff, "Doctors are the ultimate gatekeepers to any medication. Without them writing our drug's name on a prescription pad, we are nothing. So understanding every variable of what will make them write our drug down versus someone else's is paramount. We need to be inside their heads, their hearts and their souls." And she'd then say what others would be too timid or PC to put in words, "Appeal to their vanity, let them know that our drugs are the ones that work, that will make their patients grateful, that will make them feel like the Gods they so want to be." It wasn't that she despised doctors; she understood them.

She smoothed back her tousled, shoulder-length, ash-blond

hair and was pulling open her purse to fish out lipstick when she saw the door open. The shapely raven-haired woman in a slinky black mini who stepped out and smiled at her made her breath catch—she looked like a model or an actress. Karel wasn't married; *who the hell is this?* She'd seen her before, at corporate parties here; she'd just assumed the beauty with porcelain-doll skin and lavender eyes was someone's trophy wife or girlfriend. *So what the hell is she doing here? Was this a servant? Girlfriend? Those shoes... that dress.*

"Dr. Nash," the woman said, walking to the car, her fashionable heels sure-footed on the oyster shell gravel. "Karel's expecting you. Would you like to freshen up before joining him on the patio?"

"That would be great," Lara said, getting out of the car—*she called him Karel, not Mr. Von Graff,* "and you are?"

"Minnie," she said, and then she winked, "Don't worry, I'm just the hired help. Here, come with me."

Lara had been to the mansion three times before, and while she was from a well-to-do Westchester background, the opulence—the foyer that shot up three stories to a magnificent Tiffany-glass skylight, the larger-than-life Carerra marble sculpture of a winged Cupid and Psyche in front of the double staircase, the paintings, the inlaid floor—"It's like a museum," she commented.

"He loves beautiful things," Minnie said, as she led Lara to a cozy powder room. "Is there anything I can get you?"

Lara felt like saying, *information,* but said, "No, I'm fine."

"I'll come and get you in say... ten minutes?"

"Thank you," Lara felt relief as the door closed behind the stunning woman. She let out a breath and put her purse on the rose marble vanity and stared at her reflection, as her nose registered a strange perfume—almost incense. "What are you doing here?" she asked herself again, as she had throughout the drive up. This wasn't business. At 32, athletic and pretty damned-good looking, Lara had always felt that she was in the driver's seat—at least in the work place. She'd graduated first in her high school class, been summa at Yale and then whizzed through med school intent on a career in research, graduating with her MD, PhD from Gray at 28. She'd churned out several important papers, and jumped at the opportunity— and the money—when offered a position at Global to head up one of their research divisions. It had felt so right, and she'd taken to the corporate world in a way she'd never expected, her talents no longer stifled in the everyone-has-to-pay-their-dues stranglehold of academia. Like a fledgling taking flight, she found that people would follow her and that it became natural for her to influence, cajole and inspire her researchers. And great things happened. With them came huge bonuses, that coupled with the advances and royalty checks she'd squirreled away from her novels, bought her a spanking new condo on the Upper West Side, complete with doorman, private patio, a Hudson River view and a walk-in closet bigger than most Manhattan studios. Then, seemingly out of the blue, three weeks ago came this huge promotion—*I'm an actual VP.* Yet all of that paled against what was making her heart pound. Yes, she had always thought Karel Von Graff was a hot ticket, but in the way she might admire any powerful and handsome man in a *Fortune Magazine* profile, or—if she were being honest–like the bigger-than-life, albeit flawed, hunks with whom she populated her novels. It scared the hell out of her. Not just because she was currently engaged to Paul, a truly hot guy with a high-six-digit salary—seven if you included stock options and year-end bonuses–but because writing her romantic escapes was just that—fantasy.

Three weeks ago, Karel had shown up unannounced at her office. She remembered every detail from how his navy—almost black—suit moved without a wrinkle, how she found it impossible to think when he took her hand, looked her in the eye, and told her, "I think you are amazing. It's time you moved to a position where you can achieve your full potential. Global needs you...I need you."

She put a hand to her chest—like a bird fluttering, as she remembered what it was like to feel the firm touch of his hand—his fingers strangely cool–and look into the depths of his gray-blue eyes. Her insides felt like they'd turned to liquid, her throat dry. He was smiling, and so close she could catch his scent—a kind of musk, but something else too, like in this room. He was candid and warm and encouraging, as though every bit of self-doubt she'd ever had was ridiculous. This perfect man was telling her that she was amazing, no hidden irony, no sense of anything other than absolute faith...in her.

Lara startled at a knock, "Yes?"

Minnie opened it, carrying a crystal flute filled with a pale fizzy peach cocktail. "I hope you don't mind, but you looked like you could use something."

Lara swallowed, "Thank you," and took the glass. She sipped it, tasting something cool and fruity with the subtle fragrance of Kirsch and the tickle of champagne. Over the glass she watched Minnie in the mirror as she slid a chair up to her.

"Sit...relax, let me do this," Minnie said, as she opened a drawer under the vanity to reveal a tidy array of brushes, combs, cosmetics, even perfumes. "I adore your car, but convertibles can wreak havoc."

"It's new," Lara said, thinking how impulsively she'd bought the ninety-thousand dollar roadster, walking into the dealership and paying for it in cash with the bonus she'd just received. She looked straight ahead as Minnie efficiently brushed out her hair, getting it to fall smooth and silky around her neck.

"You have gorgeous skin," Minnie remarked, as she selected a sable brush. "You don't need foundation, do you?"

"I don't like to wear a lot of makeup," Lara said, comparing her own tanned complexion to Minnie's alabaster skin, arresting lavender eyes and impossibly long lashes. It was a look she'd never give an ingénue, but just right for the other woman.

"Can't blame you," Minnie said, "it just sucks up time. Here, look up," and she deftly applied a hint of rouge, freshened up Lara's lips and stroked on mascara.

"Have you worked for Karel...Mr. Von Graff, long?" Lara asked, feeling the first warm tingle of the drink.

"Years," Minnie said, and then she smiled, "what do you want to know?"

Lara coughed and nearly choked as champagne fizzed up her nose.

"Oh, please," Minnie said her voice light, "You're his new V.P. of R&D; he obviously trusts you. You've got to have questions. I'll give you two."

For the first time since Karel had invited her down yesterday, Lara felt herself start to relax, something about the softly lit room, the drink, Minnie's humor and slightly wicked smile—like playing a game with a girlfriend. "Okay...does he have a wife and kids secretly stashed away somewhere?"

"Absolutely not," Minnie said, "and no ex-wife either...that one's for free."

"Where's the girlfriend?"

"Doesn't have one."

"Boyfriend?" Lara shot back, before she could think better of it.

"Sorry, you just get the two."

And then another knock and a man's voice, "Are you two coming out or what?"

"It's okay," Minnie said, "we're decent."

Lara turned as the door opened and the most-beautiful young men she'd ever seen stepped in and cracked a smile, "You two starting a revolution, or what?"

Lara turned back at Minnie, trying to make sense of this. First this raven-haired beauty answers the doors, and she's his what? Assistant? Aide? And then Mr. Italian Vogue steps in with his cowboy boots, 3% body fat and face straight off a classical statue.

Minnie caught her questioning expression, "Okay, but now you'll owe me one. Yes?"

Maybe it was the drink, but something about this was fun and sexy. "Sure, why not?"

"Dr. Lara Nash meet Ian...my brother. We both work for Karel."

"Oh," she said, getting up from the chair, her legs a tad unsteady, "So he's not..."

"That will be two you owe me," Minnie cautioned.

"You keep track?" Lara asked.

"Always," Ian said, his smile infectious over luminous white teeth.

"Then two it is," Lara said, wondering what other rules this game might have.

"Nope, no girlfriend and no boyfriend, either." Minnie said, checking her reflection and twirling a finger through a bang so that it curled casually across her forehead.

"I have no clue what you two are rambling about, but Karel's on the patio," Ian said, holding the door. "Should I tell him you'll be a few more minutes?"

"Absolutely not," Lara said, trying to steady her breath, while she churned through the information. Getting the skinny on Karel had not been easy, ever since her promotion she'd Googled and Binged the hell out of him. And while there were tens of thousands of hits, and thousands more about the not-always glorious background of Global Industries and Global Pharmaceuticals—like some unsavory experimentation with concentration camp prisoners in Germany's Ruhr Valley during WWII, and a subsidiary implicated in third-world child labor abuses—there was nothing on his personal life, basically what could be found in the three biographical paragraphs in the quarterly prospectus. But this...no wife, no ex, no girlfriend...boyfriend. She looked back in the mirror and caught Minnie staring at her. Something in the dark-haired woman's expression was spooky—maybe it was the dim lights—but Lara had the creepy thought that Minnie could tell what she was thinking.

"Don't worry," Minnie said, as they left the powder room and trailed behind Ian "everyone gets nervous around Karel. You'll be fine." She put a hand on Lara's shoulder, and whispered into her ear, her chilly breath tickling her neck, "He's talked about you. He thinks you're brilliant, but here's another you get for free...he really likes you."

Lara longed to ask, *in what way?* But thinking of the earlier game, got the strange feeling that owing this gorgeous woman another question was not in her best interest.

*

Karel, dressed in khakis, a white shirt open at the neck, the sleeves rolled back and sandals, sat in a high-backed rattan chair angled so that he could watch the goings on in the house, or stare out at the calm steel-gray surface of the Sound. The earlier interchange with Minnie had given him pause. Was it just that this pair of servants had grown up in this marvelous age of technology? Where science had mostly buried religion, and quite wonderfully made belief in angels and devils something to be ridiculed. Yes, they were odd, Minnie glued to five or six television shows and old movies simultaneously, as Ian whizzed through every new video game and gaming system, his fingers a blur of preternatural dexterity, his attention riveted to bouncing Mario, or destroying armies in *Mortal Kombat*, or bowling a perfect game on Wii. Maybe that's all this was, animated sand absorbing the imprints of this new world and its technological magics. Minnie just playing at being human, but her petu-lance...her questioning? Her moods—turning into quite the little bitch.

As if to dispel all doubt, in came Ian followed by Lara and Minnie. The difference was clear, his beautiful Lara, encased in light—human and alive and filled with ambition and hunger and confusion, and this other most-powerful desire—a longing to be loved—how could he hate a one such as this? His mouth went dry as he stood, a smile on his lips. His thoughts reached to her. "Thank you so much for coming," extending his hand, "I know you probably had better things to do with your Saturday."

Her fingers warm in his, sky blue eyes meeting his. He noted every detail of her outfit and appreciated how she must have agonized over what to wear, finally settling on a pressed pale-blue blouse belted into a tan pencil skirt with matching pumps. He read her thoughts and knew that she'd brought the suit jacket but had left that at the last minute in her new car, thinking it was probably too formal, too much like a day at the office. "Please, sit. Have you had breakfast?"

"I'm fine," her gaze drifted across the gardens down to the water.

He knew she was struggling to not look at him, that she felt embarrassed and confused and attracted to the point she ached. "Don't be silly. You drive all the way from the city at your crazy boss's whim, because he's too paranoid to discuss things on the phone...at the very least let me feed you. Minnie, Ian could you whip up something nice? I'd also love a Bellini, in fact, bring a pitcher."

"My sense," Lara said, trying to get right down to business, "is that you view Spencer Williams's research as more than just a theoretical long shot."

"Correct," Karel marveled at her bravery. No matter how twisted up her emotions, she intended to forge ahead and figure out what exactly he needed from her. *Good girl.*

"I have to agree," she said, turning in her chair and looking him dead on. "I've reviewed his articles, and also managed to get my hands on his raw data."

"Really?" Karel said, raising an eyebrow. "Anything illegal?"

"Close, but no," she said. "He's at my alma mater. I have connections. Most of what I've been able to get that hasn't been published is material he had to submit to the peer-review journals to support his conclusions. It might be considered public domain."

Karel chuckled, "and then again it might not. I knew I made the right choice in giving you R&D. So what's your *conclusion* about the young Dr. Williams's work?"

Lara leaned in, her elbows on the travertine-topped table that separated them. "I'm going to talk out of both sides of my mouth," she said, "because on the one hand I don't want to overstate things, but on the other, I'm fucking excited as hell." She glanced up nervously.

"Go on," he said, needing her desperately, but knowing that everything would have to be of her own free will. He—like the Creator's bitch angel Joan—could influence, try to get them to do his will, but at the end of the day they always had choice.

"Okay, his compound XU472 is the result of a novel synthetic process that for the life of me—and the few people I trust implicitly in the New York R&D bureau —none of us can figure out even half the steps. I mean clearly it involves manipulating amoeba DNA—some kind of splicing and/or resequencing, but there's something more, which so far I haven't been able to get my hands on—no surprise there. But the net effect—unless he falsified the data—is that the rodents given this compound are fundamentally changed—hardier, less prone to the negative effects of protracted stress, more able to adapt to novel situations."

"Find the cheese in the maze?"

"Exactly—press the right button and get a cookie, or don't get a shock. And while it's hard to extrapolate from the data we do have, I've had my...our...numbers people run every regression, on every variable I could think of and some of the stuff that's popping is mind blowing."

"Such as?" Karel prompted, savoring the blush in her cheeks and how her pupils dilated and nostrils flared as she became more excited.

"I can't blame you for not wanting to talk about this stuff on the phone. If these early animal studies can be pushed forward, for starters the XU472 rats appear to be aging slower—far slower–than the placebo groups."

"Why wouldn't he publish that?" Karel asked. "I mean the last article was something about, 'improved stress response in Norwegian rats' or something like that."

"You know I've spoken with him?" she offered.

"I assumed when I told you that his work was a priority you'd catch the drift. Tell me everything, because if I haven't made myself crystal clear, we need to get the good Dr. Williams out of his tiny labs at Gray and set up fully operational at Global. That compound needs to get to market."

"Again, this is where I assumed you were going."

"Of course. I shouldn't have doubted. It's just that your predecessor..."

"Was clumsy," she spat out, "and may have screwed things up."

"Yes, and this is why he no longer has his job...and you do." Karel's anger surged like fire under his mortal crust. He remembered his frustration at not getting Spencer hooked on the first go round, as Minnie and Ian appeared with a linen draped breakfast cart.

*

Lara startled at the dramatic mood swing in Karel. Even the bones of his face had subtly shifted, his prior good humor and flirtations replaced by something hard. She reminded herself that despite these congenial trappings, Karel was the head of a multi-billion dollar, multi-national corporation; every minute of his time worth tens of thousands of dollars—maybe more. She wasn't here for chitchat. And she needed to wipe out any schoolgirl fantasies she had about him. *For God's sake*, she reminded herself—*you're going to be married in less than three months. You're an employee—nothing more.* Part of her railed against that, the part that had written similar scenes countless times—the governess in love with her boss, the servant girl from a noble family fallen on hard times secretly in love with the laird/baron/earl.

"Ian, Minnie, leave us," he said abruptly. And to Lara, "I'll serve, but what were you saying about Duane? I knew that he botched things, I'm not certain of the extent," referring to Duane Short, the recently 'transferred' ex head of R&D.

God, she'd struck a nerve. Well, maybe the best strategy was to lay everything out. "I've had two conversations with Dr. Williams, the one I'd mentioned yesterday and one a couple weeks back when he tentatively agreed to meet. I told him that he could name the time and the place and I'd be there. He wouldn't commit, and there was something in his tone that made me pull back. So I left it that my assistant would contact him."

"And?" Karel prompted, placing a plate of blueberry crepes brushed with confectioner's sugar in front of her.

"I have a fabulous assistant—Russell—he's been with me since I came to Global, and for two weeks he's been trying to set up this meeting. Williams mostly didn't return his calls or emails. My first thought was that we're not the only suitors."

"So who's the competition?" Karel asked, coming up close behind her and placing another of those heavenly champagne drinks by her plate.

A shiver thrummed down her back, "It's not so simple. I spoke to Russell and he was getting the same weird vibes, like we'd somehow offended him, but for the life of me I couldn't figure out how. So I called Dr. Williams yesterday, insisted on talking to him, would not take no. He told me that Duane Short had contacted him over a month ago and that he'd been so disgusted by him he wanted nothing to do with Global. And that yes, he was getting other offers, but not to worry because at this point he had no intention of leaving Gray, that he'd just gotten a large grant and that, 'thank you but no thank you'."

"What exactly did Duane do?" Karel eased back into his seat, never once lowering his gaze.

"At that point I was just trying to keep him on the line and didn't think opening old wounds was the way to go. So I apologized."

"Smart." He leaned forward, a hint of a smile over perfect teeth.

Her stomach felt like it was falling through the floor, "I told him that I was genuinely sorry for whatever Duane had said or done, and that I had tremendous admiration for his work—which I do. And that of course, I wanted to recruit him for Global, but if that were not even a remote possibility I would still like to take him to lunch and see if there was any way we could support him and his work... even if it meant his staying in academia."

"Which of course we would never do," Karel said.

"Of course not," she agreed, unable to suppress a grin, glad that his anger had passed.

He chuckled.

"What?" feeling left out of a private joke.

"You stroked his ego... played to his vanity."

"And..." chancing a look into his dark eyes, "I find that usually works with men in general and doctors in particular."

"Quite true. And his response?"

Lara took a long sip of her cocktail, and whether it was the drink, the gorgeous day and setting, or Karel's obvious approval and... admiration, she felt euphoric. *If this could only last.* "He said yes, I'm meeting him on Wednesday." And she found herself again staring into the stormy centers of his eyes, and a new and entirely alien–at least for her–thought formed. *I am in love with this beautiful man,* followed by the equally shocking realization, *I would do anything for him. Anything.*

*

"Excellent! I can see," Karel said, "you will succeed where Duane failed so miserably." His senses–human and other–reveled in this delightful Dr. Lara Nash—her waves of excitement, the chaos of her thought, the confusion she battled, having surely never felt an attraction as strong as what she felt for him. Even her secret double life as a romance novelist—she was too delicious. "Come with me," he stood, and extended his hand. He felt her fingers soft and tentative, gripped them—not too tight. "Let's walk," and holding her hand led her toward weathered marble steps that opened onto acres of park-like gardens that ended at a breakwater and lapping waves. "I sometimes talk too much in riddles, but with Dr. Williams and his compound we need to be clear. I view this as the single most important development in bio-pharmacology that has ever, or will ever, come along."

"But, how can you know?"

"Call it a well-informed hunch. Let's stop calling him Dr. Williams, as I know you will succeed..." he took her other hand and stood still.

"Or die trying," she said, trying to make her voice light, when she was struggling to keep enough saliva in her mouth to speak.

Karel shuddered, and felt the ground lurch subtly beneath his feet, a hiccup that only he could feel. "Don't say that," but his attention was split between the tiny lines around her eyes and the sudden knowledge that her death would come swift and violent—a high-speed car accident...an oncoming truck. She would be ripped from him—at least in body if not soul. More than that, he knew without doubt that he would be the cause of her death. "We'll call him Spencer, as I've a feeling we will all be friends. It's imperative that you learn everything about him. Who he loves, what he wants, what he believes, what it is he thinks he has created." He let go of her hand and felt her sense of loss as the connection broke.

Lara, like a star pupil giving a book report, spoke. "His father is a cardio-thoracic surgeon and his mother was Lila Cartwright."

"The singer?" saddened at the recollection of the lovely diva with her ethereal music. Destroying her had been bittersweet, *but*, he mused, *no one likes a happy artist.*

"Yes, very new age, made a series of gorgeous CDs with indigenous musicians, the proceeds going into a foundation she'd established for third-world women. She gave concerts around the world, made quite a bit of money and kept none of it. In the end—while it was hushed up in the press–she killed herself, but left no note, no reason why. There was speculation that she'd been murdered by everyone from a Columbian drug cartel to the Taliban. On more than one occasion she'd been thrown into jail and had to be bailed out by our local embassy—usually for speaking out about women's rights. She was remarkable; I can't even imagine having that kind of courage. Some of the stuff about her on the Internet is absolutely wild."

"For instance?"

"Some people thought she was a saint and they'd go to her concerts to be healed, or that listening to certain tracks on CDs she'd made with an Amerindian shaman could cure everything from...you name it." She looked out at the ocean, "It was Spencer who called 911. He was six. God only knows what he'd seen. His childhood had to be beyond strange. Before her death Lila was mostly on the road, and after, from what I can tell, his father likely had little time for a young son, especially one that reminded him of a wife he was cheating on."

Karel was impressed, "You're quite the detective."

"It's an old story," she said, "Doesn't take a lot to fill in the blanks. Spencer didn't even live with his father and stepmother, but was raised by his mother's music coach—a Joan Shift. Academically, he was an-off-the-charts wunderkind, graduated high school at fourteen, did his undergraduate in two years and finished medical school—with both an MD and PhD–by 23. He started publishing his first year of medical school, and it was clear from the get go that he was going for the big guns—cutting edge genetic manipulations—splicing, resequencing."

"A young God."

"Excuse me?"

"He wants to create something new, something different. That's why getting him to sign with us is beyond important. It's everything, the only thing."

"Where exactly do you see it going?" she asked.

By now they'd wandered to the edge of the lawn, the air salted from the gently breaking waves. Gulls shrieked overhead, diving for prey. Like déjà vu, Karel had had many such conversations. It was always a matter of how much to tell, how much truth she could take. "Do you believe in God?" he asked.

"Not so much," she admitted, "although I suppose from the sense that all of this had to come from somewhere, I believe there is something."

"What about evolution?"

"As a theory to describe the development of species, I think it's mostly accurate." She gave him a questioning look, "And this relates to Spencer's work. . ."

He sat on a flat boulder and waited for her to join him. "I'll tell you what I believe. Evolution, one cell becoming two, becoming fish, lizard, plant, gecko. . . gull, man, woman—this is the hand of the Creator. With each advance, each articulation, evolution is like a flower that's opening, and what controls the whole damn thing is the DNA. Each new mutation moves things a tiny bit forward, but to what end? Does anyone know? The blossoming of the human forebrain over the past fifty thousand years is the most-stunning advance—consciousness, creativity, artistry, all encoded in the twisting, changing strands of DNA."

"But things can also go backward," she interrupted, "you have that whole survival of the fittest part. Miss-steps in evolution, things that don't quite work out."

"Of course, but what I sense our brilliant Spencer has found is the key to moving this forward at tremendous speed. To take human evolution and push it into the future, but not over the course of millennia. . . now."

"So how do you fit God into all of this?"

He reached across and again took her hand, "There are no coincidences. Evolution moves with clear direction from chaos into ever-higher levels of structure and organization. Doesn't that seem to fly in the face of basic physics where everything falls to chaos?"

She let out a stream of breath, choosing her words carefully, not wanting to contradict him, "Mr. Von Graff?"

"No Lara, we're beyond that. It's Karel."

"Okay, Karel. . . I think you're mixing scientific metaphors. Systems run to chaos—to entropy—when there's nothing supplying energy to keep them going."

"Absolutely. . . so where's the engine that's pumping energy into life and the progression of life?"

She looked up, "the sun, of course, massive amounts of energy, every day streaming down. And if we're talking specifically about DNA, it's the sun's radiation that causes all of these subtle mutations and cross linkages. Some work out, some don't. If that's God the creator, then so be it."

And this need of hers to cling to the rational, now feeling such overwhelming tenderness, was why he was so drawn to her. Here she was sitting in the presence of a God, albeit an earth-and-hell-bound one, and all she could think of was how to make everything make sense. Anything that couldn't fit into a world of logic would have to be eliminated. "So if I told you that Spencer was working on a Holy Grail..."

"I'd say you were more poet than scientist. But I do see great possibilities in his work, maybe not as grand as what you see."

She was gazing into his eyes, he could feel her struggle, part of her screaming to look away because she knew she was crossing a line, just like the pretty governess in her current novel. *Let me be your hero, Lara. I will be the man you hunger for. Submit to it. Be my love. Love me. Love me. Love me.* "So you'll do whatever it takes to bring him to us."

"Yes."

"Offer him whatever he wants. Let him know how important he is to us. Understand what it is that drives him, what it is he believes his work will accomplish." He let his hand drift up to the side of her face; his fingers trailed gently down her cheek.

"I think I know what that is," she said, her voice barely audible.

"Tell me."

"It has to do with his mother," she swallowed. "He runs a mental-health clinic three days a week, mostly for men and women with severe depression. It's a research clinic where the entry criteria include having had at least one serious suicide attempt. He takes the patients that scare the crap out of other psychiatrists. Why would someone work with people like that unless, he thought he could save them?"

"Say it," he whispered. "Say what you're thinking."

"He has a Christ complex." She was trembling.

"And back we come to God. Lara, if I told you that I very much want to kiss you, would you let me?"

"Yes."

His hand drifted down to the small of her back and he leaned in and drank that first exquisite sip. As lips touched and parted, the flicker of tongues, he groaned. She was so sweet, *so tasty.*

*

By noon, he'd sent her back to the city. Like one of her romance heroines—and yes, he'd read them all–he'd let her fly on all the heady 'what ifs?' of a new relationship. She was falling in love, and a quick spin around her cranium let him know it was for the first time. He'd peeked at her thoughts of her fiancé—a handsome and thoughtful investment banker, who was apparently only one in a long line of men who'd proposed to her over the years. He noted how all of those memories were closely linked to images of her mother, Vivian. "We're not so different," he mused, strolling back through lush and fragrant gardens. His ears tuned to the distant crunch of tires.

Heading toward his paneled study, filled with priceless marbles and old-master paintings, he thought how for him, love was a curious thing, his greatest weakness. It made him vulnerable and confused the hell out of him. How on the one hand he clung to his hatred of this puny species, yet just the thought of lovely Lara... *quite the conundrum.*

His thoughts clouded as he heard voices in the entry—an older man's Austrian accent and Minnie. Of course he saw the irony—him a God—on edge, waiting for his latest shrink.

"And here he is," Minnie said, dressed in a form-hugging black cat suit à la one of her favorite TV heroines–Emma Peale from the hip sixties series *The Avengers*, her voice light and playful, as she opened the study door.

"Doctor," Karel crossed the space, his feet silent on the Persian silk. His eyes on Werner Beitersmann, a venerated Freudian in his late seventies, a dying breed from his trimmed silver goatee, pale gray suit, wire-rimmed glasses to his starched white shirt and plaid bowtie.

"Karel," his watery blue eyes making clear contact, in the dim light. "Shall we get started?"

"Of course, doctor, can I offer you anything?"

"Not necessary, and your lovely assistant has already asked," he glanced back at the shadowy doorway where Minnie, teeth glinting, waited.

"You can go," Karel instructed, wondering what the sanguine analyst would make of the true nature of his servant. With Minnie gone, Karel watched Dr. Beitersmann settle into one of two massive tufted oxblood leather armchairs. The diminutive man dwarfed by the high back, his eyes bright, his mind calm with an attitude of waiting, like a baited trap. After only one session Karel knew that the Doctor would say nothing—at least not at first. He'd let the tension build in the room. *Why am I even doing this? What's the point? And why am I so afraid?* "Like I told you the first time, I have so much anger... and fear, I want them gone." He looked at the doctor, "you'd think that as time goes by they would get less, but no."

"When you think of your anger," Beitersmann prompted, "what's the first thing that pops to mind?"

"My Creator... my parent... s."

"Hmm."

Karel, looked across, as the infuriating silence grew. He felt his rage, never far, start to flow. "You want me to talk about that."

"As you said," his German accent thick, "it's why you bring me here. If you don't you're wasting money and time."

"Of course," he settled into the chair across from the doctor. "What fucks me up the most is that I know I was loved—at first. Completely, absolutely, I was the first born, a golden child, and there wasn't anything I couldn't have. And then," thinking how to translate his fall from grace without losing the meat, *think human*, "my parents had another child; it was clear that I was no longer special, no longer loved." As he gave voice, he felt the pain of the Creator pulling back, he gasped "like something being ripped out of me. I was still with... them, but... the confusion, the betrayal." His fists balled. *Be careful*, remembering how freaked the last shrink had been when he'd made the house shake. "My world became consumed with anger, and a jealousy you can't imagine, like a burning hole inside of me."

"Toward your parent's new child... children?"

"Children," Karel glanced at Beitersmann, easily seeing past the calm façade to a nimble mind rapidly forming and discarding hypotheses. "A whole new family... one that I was not a part of, quite literally. The new kids were in a different house." *Shit, how to do this without making the whole thing too fantastic? Keep it simple.*

"It sounds like quite a large family, how many exactly?"

"No, just a boy and then later a girl," Karel said. "Although... "

"What?"

"I don't think it's important but before there was another girl—Lil. She didn't last."

"She died?"

"Yes... but really, she's just a footnote, no sense in dwelling." Although as he said it, he had a pang of grief, remembering the exquisite Lilith—a creature, who like the archangel Joan and the angels of the second brood, could wear human flesh—how differently it would have gone had the Creator let Its new playthings—Its humans—breed with the divine. Maybe it could have worked—just one happy family.

"Hmmm. I'll make the comment that a dead child is no small thing, but respect your wish to move on. You felt left out?"

Karel shook his head, and felt a tremor as the mansion creaked and the crystal tinkled dangerously from the Baccarat chandelier above. "This isn't working."

"Of course not," Beitersmann replied, "it can't without truth. You're filtering and changing the story to make it acceptable to me. Telling me what you think I can handle."

"How could you know that?"

The psychologist sighed, "I'm old Karel; I've done this for over fifty years. Nothing shocks me, and unlike the new generations, everything... everything you tell me is in confidence."

"Really?" Karel was intrigued, "if I'm a mass murderer?"

"Not my first."

"Or if I told you I was going to slice open my wrists this afternoon?"

"You're not the type and I'm a firm believer in people making their own choices. If you choose to kill yourself—while clearly a waste of a most interesting life—your choice."

Karel detected the hint of a smile over the goatee. "You don't care what I say."

"Of course I do, but the truth. Otherwise, this is a waste, and I'm too old for that. Perhaps we could get back to your parents... or rather, let's go with the word you first used. Tell me about your *Creator*."

"Interesting," Karel took careful measure of the man who'd spent his life mucking in the psyches of others. "So there's nothing new under the sun?"

Beitersmann stayed silent, his hands in his lap, gaze steady, expectant.

"OK, my original name was Lucifer. I changed it when I was kicked out of my home—out of heaven, and I continue to change it as the situation suits. I've been Karel for a while. Before that I too was a Werner. I wonder if that had something to do with my picking you." He stared back at the analyst, sniffing for the acrid tang of fear. He could, if he wanted, read the man's thoughts, but to do so would alter them. It was infuriating the way nothing fazed him. He also didn't want to spend too much time talking about the mechanics of his earthly existences, and how slipping in and out as the head of Global Industries—an organization with roots in ancient times–was an accomplishment that gave him tremendous pride. "You have to understand that what is considered heaven is nothing more—or less—than being allowed into the presence of the Creator; it is euphoria. To be banished, to have known total happiness and then have it taken away, is unbearable–torment without end. Please, say something."

Beitersmann hesitated.

"What?" Karel asked, "Now it's you who's not forthcoming. Why are you holding back?"

The therapist nodded and sighed. "I don't normally do this, but in this case..." looking around the magnificent room, at the paintings, which included a Raphael rapture and a darkly lit Goya of a witch coven around a Sabbath bonfire that should have been in museums, the carved marble fireplace, the intricate mahogany paneling transported from a Loire Valley chateau. "There is a disconnect—fallen angel or not." His right eyebrow arched. "You live well for someone in unbearable torment. True, money does not equal happiness, but still..."

"Touché, Doctor Beitersmann, and if I'm honest, my existences on earth are not unpleasant; far from it. This is certainly not the giddy euphoria of heaven, but I've come to love it here...everything about it–but what makes it so horrible is it never lasts. Soon I'm hurled back to a pit of despair. It's like telling a man on death row that he can have one day of freedom and then must return to prison to rot with no hope of parole and the threat of execution. My every moment is hounded by the fear that this is my last on earth. It's a constant torture, wondering when it's coming." He felt the gripping fear never far from the surface.

"I see. So why were you banished from your Creator?" The therapist's expression was neutral.

"Because I questioned," he said, remembering how confused and hurt he'd been as the Creator formed his new world and gave it life. All of the angels–the ancients like himself and those that came later, like Joan–had watched as the atmosphere developed, with clouds, volcanoes, lightening, a giant crucible, and that first horrifying spark of life. "None of the others would question. They didn't understand, or were too scared to see the purpose in all of it. I had to know. Why was It doing this? Why wasn't heaven enough?" His breath hot, his mind clouded, human tears welled.

And on a whisper the doctor asked, "Why weren't you enough?"

Karel nodded, "I had to know, because I could see in this creation that something, like a seed being planted and watered, would come to fruition."

"What did you fear?"

"We were being replaced," he said gasping, "and I wasn't wrong. The Creator had birthed a new paradise, one of substance and flesh, with new children. It loved them more, these children of man, and I didn't know why. I demanded answers, and received silence. The bliss was gone. I was still in Its presence, but I felt new emotions–hatred, jealousy. I would destroy this new world, and these naked little creatures." Karel cracked a smile, and looked at the doctor. The man's face an emotionless mask, his mind whirring like a Swiss watch.

"You smile, because?" the therapist asked.

"Because you must think you're sitting with a nut case."

"Hmm. I am curious why you're retelling Milton's *Paradise Lost*. But please continue, as I think this is closer to the truth."

"Yes, much." And while his sorrow and fury had such a clear starting point, it made him pause to go back to that beginning.

"What are you thinking?" Beitersmann asked.

"Something's changing...I hated what It had done," the screams of his murdered siblings still fresh as they were ripped apart, exploding into light, "and I thought I hated this new world and its creatures, and I did in the beginning. But now...I finally understand what's happening and why It created this world and humans." He thought about his conversation with Lara, the Creator *had* planted a seed—Its own seed—and what eventually grows from a seed is the parent. *How obvious. How could I not have seen this?*

"Put your thoughts into words," the Doctor prompted.

"Not today," Karel said, "You've led me to an interesting insight, and I need to consider it."

"As you wish, but remember that to do this kind of work, you must trust me."

Karel inhaled. "I do, Doctor," and finally he let his mind search out the old man's thoughts, not caring that they'd get muddled in the process. The doctor viewed his story as metaphor, as if he were really talking about a withholding father, and a mother who showered affection on her younger children. Terms like *Oedipal triangle* and *fantasies of patricide* bounced in the foreground, along with a lecherous recollection of Minnie's shapely calves and spike heels and a less flattering assessment of Karel— *whining rich nut case.*

"Then same time next week?" Beitersmann asked.

"Yes." A knock at the door and Minnie reappeared in a black chauffeur cap and her skin-tight suit with stiletto boots that perfectly matched the doctor's libidinal musings.

"Would you like to use the facilities, before I drive you back?" she asked, offering the analyst a view of cleavage that seemed primed to burst from her zippered suit.

"Thank you."

Karel watched as Minnie sauntered away. She turned back at the door. "You still need him?"

Lost in thought, he nodded. It was a moment of clarity. After all these millennia his hatred of the human race had vanished. All of his misery and rage had a single author, and the doctor was right. It was the Creator who was at fault, and while patricide might not be possible, revenge against the author of all his pain...yes, that would be sweet. But how? He knew the answer had to be tied up in all of these stupid games around the Chosen one, but even when he won a battle—like with Spencer's mother–the result was the same: he was dragged screaming back to hell. "But not this time," thinking about Spencer Williams and his strange new drug. "I will figure this out; I will not go back." His thoughts buzzed as he paced in furious circles around the room. If humans had been present they'd have seen a cyclone in the middle of the study. The doctor had made an important observation. *I like it here.* No, more than *like.* This was heaven, better really, with all of these beautiful things and charming humans, and him a God among them. He felt none of that stoned-out bliss, but alive and powerful. A line from Shakespeare's *A Midsummer's Night's Dream* flew to mind, *"Were the world mine."* And he stopped dead.

Chapter Five

□   □   □

Spencer Williams stared through the iron-barred basement windows of his lab, and mused how spring in Chicago was about as good as it got. Of course, buried in the frigid basement of the Wentworth Research building you'd never know it. It had been an awful morning. He'd just caught his assistant—Brad Harris, a balding, soft-in-the-middle doctoral student supposedly finishing his dissertation on the use of lasers, instead of enzymes, to splice DNA—attempting to hack into his password-protected files.

"What the hell are you doing?" he'd asked, shocked to find Brad in the dank lab that smelled of rat droppings at five a.m.. Harris had no notion that Spencer, who ever since he was a kid had miserable insomnia, often spent the night there.

The man had stammered, "I was just checking some figures. Thought I'd get a jump on..."

"Don't," Spencer hadn't let him finish; his lies reeked—literally—and his aura spasmed with plumes of acid yellow and bile green. "Get out now!" The man stank of deception. Spencer was puzzled–*why* didn't *I see this?* He'd held back, his fists clenched, but years of scrapping his way through the Brookline schools, with months on end in detention, had taught him the hard truth that being right doesn't always matter.

After the creep had left, Spencer combed every inch of the large cement-floored room, with its two walls of floor-to-ceiling cages of Norway rats, and the stainless tables with state-of-the-art sequencing equipment he'd bought with his last grant. In hindsight, he wished he hadn't been so quick to throw Brad out. *What was he up to?* Was he working alone? Or for someone else... like one of the many pharma companies that offered ridiculous salaries and perks to go work for them? It was clear from the computer screen—tables of carefully coded data–that Brad had managed to crack one of his pass codes—but not both. *What exactly were you looking for?* He had a good idea; it was what everyone wanted to know, how to synthesize XU472, a secret that he'd shared with no one. A secret so bizarre he wondered if he'd ever divulge it. *And that's why shit like this keeps happening to you.* Imagining what his colleagues and professors would say if they knew he'd gotten the final brainstorm for XU472 when he was skrying—*Yes, it came to me in a vision. Let me tell you all about it.* "And, nut boy, they'd lock you up if they knew what you actually did. So deal!"

Feeling angry and betrayed, he knelt and ran a finger under the surface of one of the stainless tables, hunting for any kind of recording device or camera. He glanced across at the caged rats and his eye caught one he should have sacrificed after the last experiment. He'd been a hopeless softy and broken the cardinal rule of animal experimentation—lab rats are not pets, do not get attached to them and whatever you do, don't name them. As he looked at Jimmy the rat, he realized that the sleek brown animal with its snow-white underbelly was watching him. "You think I'm paranoid, don't you? What was he up to? You were here...I bet you know." And then a knock at the door and a woman's voice.

"Spencer, it's Neri, open up."

He glanced at the clock—12:15. "Shit," *the whole morning shot.*

"I heard that buddy, and yes you were supposed to pick me up fifteen minutes ago."

He unbolted the door, and saw Neri's brown smiling face with a tiny emerald stud in the side of her nose. Her aura a calm blue with threads of lavender. Her dark eyes looked him up and down and then scanned past toward whatever he might have been doing. "You look like shit. And I used to think you were cute. When's the last time you slept?" She walked to the wall of test animals.

Spencer watched his short friend, her glossy black braid swinging across the back of her labcoat, as she surveyed his space. "So what exactly has you locking yourself in? If it was anyone else I'd think you had a girl in here." She lovingly ran a hand over one of his shiny new tabletop sequencers. "And can I have one of these? You've got two."

"Sure, for the reasonable price of $92,500."

"Bastard. So what's going on?"

"I think my assistant was trying to rip me off."

"You got proof? And not just one of your fabulous hunches. Cause if you don't, it can get ugly."

"That's what I was doing when you came. I know he cracked the first level of my computer code, but I don't know what else."

"Show me."

For the first time that morning Spencer started to relax. He and Neri had been friends from the day they got assigned as lab partners in first year medical school microbiology over ten years ago. They were the youngest in the class—he a wunderkind of 18, and she having also skipped three grades–both outcasts. While their classmates sweated through the core sciences, their attention more drawn to the Chicago night life and who was dating whom, Spencer and Neri lived in the lab, running their own experiments and trying to see firsthand how theories that were taught in books got played out in real life.

He led Neri to his desktop, "When I came in he'd hacked into one of my databases."

"Maybe you didn't log off."

"I always do, and it's on automatic shutdown after ten minutes."

"Right," she stood in front of the computer, "so the question," turning slowly, her eyes raking every inch, "is how did he get your code?...what the hell is that?" she pointed at the ceiling, to a spot where the duct work vanished into the wall.

Spencer walked over, something had been attached with foil tape to blend in with the aluminum duct. He dragged over a chair, reached up and ripping the tape, yanked it down. "Son of a bitch!"

"What is it?"

He held a tiny camcorder, no bigger than a credit card, in the palm of his hand.

"Well, the good news," she said, "you got proof. I'm so sorry. How bad do you think it is?"

"It's just data," he admitted, as he opened the back of the camera and fished out the battery. He felt a wave of despair. "I don't sleep, because there's too much to do, and whenever I get someone to help...even just taking care of the animals, this shit happens."

"You can't keep this up forever," she said. "Despite evidence to the contrary, you are human."

"I refuse to accept that," he smiled, "like you I am a mutant nerd"–A nickname that had been hurled at him as a kid, but it did fit and he didn't mind—actually liked it. His favorite comic book had been the X-Men, all mutant superheroes against a world eager to destroy them. Spencer knew he was different, like the way he could smell the fear and lies on Harris, or even now see the swirling blue aura, like lighted silk gauze, that floated around Neri.

"So what do you say," she suggested, "we skip lunch and see what other little bugs have been planted. We can grab something from one of the vendor carts on the way to clinic."

"Neri, that's sweet, but this is my mess."

"And you're my messy friend and I don't have many...just you and Jeff and my nightmare of a wedding that I wish were over already."

"How is Jeff?" Spencer asked, referring to her good-natured fiancée, currently on junior faculty in Gray's Education department.

"He's not the problem," she offered while crawling under a metal table.

"Your parents?"

"Bingo. To be fair," she said, not caring that the back of her white labcoat was getting smudged as she scooted on the dingy linoleum floor, "they got over the 'he's not Indian' thing, but they're dead set on a traditional wedding, with an army of relatives coming over and staying...for a month."

"A month? Oh my, God."

"And in among all the aunties and uncles will be several eligible Indian bachelors—mostly doctors or engineers—just in case I'm not quite certain that Jeff is the one."

"Serious?" thinking back to the one night years ago, when, after hours plating bacteria in the lab they'd gone to a bar and then back to his apartment. An awkward fumbling experience that left them clear they would be great friends, but no romantic spark.

"Yeah," she said, getting back to her feet, "but that's my own weird cross to bear. And when I'm not so overwhelmed with my mother's constant calls, about the saris or the cake, or what color the linens should be, I do get it. I'm their only daughter. I'm breaking with tradition in a way that's upsetting to them...it seems so weird, but they had an arranged marriage, and they made it clear to me from the get go that they'd be so happy to do the same for me...Spencer," her tone suddenly grim, "you know there's a reason why this shit is happening to you."

"I know, and I can't think straight enough to figure out what I'm supposed to do. I know my research has crazy possibilities—

that it's different from anything else out there, and that I have to be so damn careful in how I proceed."

"Right there," she said, "is the problem, you're like a fucking fan dancer—you show a little bit of skin and then before anyone can figure out what they're looking at, you've covered it up again."

"You calling me a tease?" He joked, noting the flare of red that shot up behind her neck—she was getting mad.

"Mutant nerd tease to be exact. Let's take your last article, 'The Effects of compound XU472 on the Mammalian Stress Response.'"

"What about it?"

"Don't give me that crap. It's not what you put in the article, it's what you left out. On the surface it's a basic double-blind placebo-control study looking at a compound—maybe something that down the road would make a nice antidepressant."

"What's wrong with that?"

"Spencer, don't piss me off. I'm not stupid." She stared at him, a hand on her hip, the calm blues of her aura ablaze with red and orange.

"Hey, I have to publish something, so I'm trying to look at what parts of my work I can make public without creating too much interest, but enough so that I can keep getting grant money."

"Thank you," she said, and like the burner on a gas stove, the reds turned back to blue, "I know you've been hurt over this stuff, but don't lie to me."

"You know, I just wish I could hire you away from Clay," he said, mentioning the department chair, for whom Neri was under contract for the next two years as his chief epidemiologist and statistician.

"That makes two of us," she said, "and I pray to God this isn't being taped. But Clifford Clay is the biggest malignant narcissist I've ever met. He's aware you're on to something major, and trust me, he wants a piece of it."

"I know...can I show you something?" and he headed back toward the cages.

"A bit of thigh?" she quipped.

"A bit of rat." He opened Jimmy's cage, and hefted out the shiny creature with its chestnut pelt and snow-white belly.

"He's big for a Norway rat," she commented, patting Jimmy's

head with two fingers. "Aren't you the cutest thing?... and look at how he just lets you handle him. How much does he weigh?"

"Almost a kilo," Spencer said. "I've never had one get this big and it's not fat. He's almost two years old. Grab some cheese from the fridge." He waited as she took a cheddar cube out of a plastic container. "Okay, now hide it in a hand... don't let him see and then put your two hands out."

Neri did as instructed, and Jimmy, his whiskers twitching, bumped his snout into her left hand. She opened her fist and let the rat have his prize. "So what? They've got great noses."

"Okay," Spencer said, "I wanted to establish a baseline, wash your hands to get rid of the cheese smell and then just grab anything off the table—like that pen cap. Do the same thing and don't let him see which hand it's in." And he waited as she soaped and scrubbed in the lab sink.

Again Neri held out her two closed fists and the rat gently placed a paw on her right. She opened it to reveal the cap. "Okay," she looked at Spencer, "I guess the first question is why would he even bother?—it's not food, but what's the big deal; it was a fifty-fifty shot?"

"Do it again."

And Jimmy again selected the correct hand.

"Okay," Spencer said, "we've now gone from even odds to a one-in-four shot that he picked it by chance alone. Do it again."

And for a third time, Jimmy placed his tiny paw on the correct hand.

"Now it's one in eight," Spencer said. "Again, just keep going."

For the next five minutes, Neri hid the pen cap, and each time the rat found it. As she went through this Spencer kept track of the probability, "one in sixteen, one in thirty-two, one in sixty four," until eventually he said, "with greater than 99.9% certainty we can now say this is not happening by chance."

"How the hell is he doing this?" she asked. "Can he smell it? Or... they have terrible eyes." She looked at Spencer.

"To be honest, I don't know, and this is just the tip of it. Jimmy's the only one left from his cohort. I couldn't bring myself to sacrifice him. He's got quite the bag of tricks."

"It's freaky," she said, "but that's not your big omission; we both know it—more like a footnote, but I'm serious Spencer, you don't have to tell me... if you don't want."

His email alert dinged. They both turned—it was from Dr. Clifford Clay. "Speak of the devil," Spencer said. He clicked on the message, knowing in his gut it would be bad news. "Damn damn damn."

"What is it?" Neri asked.

"Here..." and he read aloud, "'*Dear Dr. Williams:*

I regret to inform you that your request for additional laboratory space has been denied. While I am aware of the importance of your work, I must balance that against the equally legitimate requests of those with more seniority.

That said, it might be possible to free up your requested space—possibly even more—should you consider reconfiguring your current work to have not just a single primary investigator but to open it up as a partnership with a more-senior and tenured member of the faculty. Should that be something you would consider, we should discuss how such a team might be assembled.

Sincerely:

Cliff

Clifford Clay, MD, PhD

Professor

Chairman Department of Behavioral Sciences

Gray University'"

Neri glanced around, Spencer smelled her fear. "Let's get out of here," she said. "Something's wrong."

He said nothing, enraged at the sleazy suggestion that he include *a more senior member of the faculty* in his research. He nodded, and fished his keys from his pocket.

Neri stared at Jimmy, who was watching them from the edge of the table, his long black whiskers twitching. "That is one strange little rat. Do you want me to put him back in his cage?"

"No need," Spencer whispered, his jaw clenched trying to keep his anger under control, "he likes to be out." Shaking his head, he locked and bolted the door behind them.

"That's new," Neri remarked, looking at the heavy brass lock.

"Yup, and now I have to change it," his voice low, "And I used an outside locksmith. Why does this kind of crap have to happen? Shit!"

They took the stairs up two flights and then out into the crisp spring day. The air was scented with budding pear trees and spicy purple and yellow iris all picture perfect in front of the weathered brownstone structures of Gray University. Most of the buildings were constructed at the turn of the 20th century, but with anachronistic architecture part Tudor, part gothic and part anything else the founding fathers considered stately and in keeping with the aspirations of a world-class university: slate roofs, red mullioned windows and a wacky assortment of gargoyles, flying buttresses and carved griffins.

Leaving the ersatz Oxford behind, they turned west toward the bustle and excitement of Michigan Avenue and the Miracle Mile with well-stocked stores selling everything from design-your-own-jeans to the hottest electronic gizmo. Spencer caught their reflection in a plate glass door, and realized what an odd couple they made—him six-feet-three, rail thin, with long dark hair in a pony tail, a threadbare gray corduroy jacket, button-down blue shirt and chinos and her, barely five feet and still in her labcoat. She was right—he looked like hell. At least he'd shaved.

She glanced at her watch, "That was strange," she said as they headed toward Lakeview.

"Which part?" still seething, he slowed his long stride to match hers.

"That email from Clifford, like he was watching. You said it was a new assistant. Who sent him to you?"

Spencer nodded. "Who do you think? I feel surrounded. I do want to tell you about the work, but I'm afraid to," and quickly added, "not that I don't trust you. You're the only one I do, but by telling you... first I'm not entirely certain that my conclusions are accurate, and second if they are—or even partially—you could become a target for all this crap. I'd love to think I'm just paranoid... but we did just pull out a hidden camera."

"Spencer," she said, as they stopped and waited for the light. "The problem as I see it is that anyone with half a brain who reads your most-recent papers will know that XU472 is unique. The question is how unique?"

Without looking at her, he whispered, "It alters DNA in a live mammal."

"Excuse me?"

"You heard me."

"How?"

"Strengthens, makes less prone to mutation, degradation, and that's only what I've been able to actually test. When I sacrificed Jimmy's cohort—the animals that were the basis for the last study—there were changes throughout. I'm still sitting on most of that data and have to figure my next move. I need more lab space, more animals, I need to do a primate study—and Clifford's basically shutting me down. It's so fucking unfair. I have worked so hard to do this right, not missing a single step, no shortcuts..." But as he said that, something tugged at his gut, *is that really true? Or does an act of magic—possibly black magic—count as a short cut?*

"Back up," she said, as Lake Michigan, a vast sparkling inland sea came into view. "What changes did you see?"

"Larger brain mass, changes to their immune systems with much higher circulating levels of immunoglobulins, big thymuses, small adrenals—extremely hardy animals. Killing them was one of the hardest things I've ever had to do. Rats are rats, but these seemed to know what was coming. It was awful. You know how they make those funny little chirping noises that you can barely hear?"

"Sure."

"They screamed." Spencer believed he had long ago made his peace with the necessity of animal studies—hating the brutality of it, but knowing that before you could try something on a human, you had to determine the likely impact on lower species. It was one of the foundations of careful research—never take short cuts; do the work.

"And so you decided to keep Jimmy."

"Yup, and now I really need to push this forward, do a multi-generational study—I could start tomorrow, but without the space, how can I? I need at least three generations of rats, double blind, and to get those numbers we're talking over two thousand animals."

"At least," she said. "Which gets us to the next point—Clifford's not exactly shutting you down; he wants in. That's what he's about, and that's why your stooge assistant probably went running straight back to him. Jesus, if you've developed a compound that can positively alter DNA in a living mammal, this is huge, like Nobel Prize huge."

Spencer's attention was suddenly grabbed by a young woman, with a riotous mass of dark curly hair, on the other side of the street. He squinted as she readjusted her vibrant purple fringed scarf and headed up the stairs into the ornate granite-fronted building that housed Gray's School for the Performing Arts.

Neri followed his gaze. "Friend of yours?"

Something caught in his chest, "I wish."

"Really, the mutant nerd boy has a crush?"

"Met her a few weeks back—she's a student in the opera program."

"Name?" Neri asked, as she steered them toward the row of vendor trucks along the lake where they frequently grabbed lunch.

"Madeleine Forest and out of my league."

"What league is that?" cutting a path for the deep-dish pizza truck. "I didn't think you were even in the game."

"Cute," he said, as they bought dense slices of the multi-layered pizza, diet Cokes, and found an empty bench that over-looked the Navy Pier with its brick and terra cotta towers and prominent Ferris wheel. "So here's the deal," gazing north at the white marble belvedere in front of the Shedd Aquarium. "The whole point of XU472 is I believe it will cure severe suicidal depression—not just treat, but actually make people stronger, make them able to deal with all the horrible things that life does to them. Like my clinic patients, most have been through all sorts of trauma and abuse. At times I almost lose it when they ask me if they'll ever get better, feel less hopeless, less desperate."

"I know," she said, picking out mushrooms and putting them on her napkin "if I was that miserable, what would keep me from ending it? I mean if you can see no hope, no future, why bother?"

"I've got this one patient," he said, "Sharon, huge blanks in her memory, probably a defense to block out the abuse she endured as a child—awful stuff. Raped, assaulted, a step father who did horrible things to her and a mother who wouldn't believe her—the whole thing. But even with all that she has the resiliency to stay in high school, to graduate, to go to college, but she hangs on by a thread. Every day wondering if this will be it, when she finally takes the fatal overdose, or gets so desperate that she jumps from the overpass, or buys a gun at the pawn shop two blocks from her apartment. She's been on every antidepressant, in every combination, had three courses of electroconvulsive therapy—which just made her memory worse. And now the one thing that kind of holds her together—being in school—is about to end. It's her last year in a graduate program and she can't see beyond that. She has an appointment this afternoon and part of me dreads it, always worrying if she's safe to go home, or do I need to send her into a hospital, not that it will help, but at least keep her safe for a few days."

"You really think your drug could help her?"

"I do, not to sound like an egomaniac, I really do. But I'm stuck in preliminary rat trials, and getting from here to something that's FDA approved is years down the road—maybe ten, and if I can't even get this started....Forget about my frustration, people like Sharon, can't wait that long. Maybe I should just bite the bullet and go to Clifford...but something about that makes my skin crawl."

"Don't you dare!" she said, "He'll steal it, stick his name on it and get your Nobel."

"Does it matter?" He pushed his slice away and tried to block the image—always a hair below the surface–of his mother's suicide—the sirens, the breaking glass, a glimpse of her covered body being wheeled out the front door. "If it can help people, does it matter who gets the credit?"

"Yes," she said, "it does. There's got to be another option."

He took a deep breath and told her about his upcoming lunch with the woman from Global Pharmaceuticals. He saw quick changes in Neri's aura, shifting patterns of orange and red–a volcano set to blow.

"Why are you meeting her? They're even worse than Clay. All of them!"

"It's just lunch, Neri. She said there might be a way of working a deal with the University, where I wouldn't actually become a Global employee."

"Again, bringing you right back to Clay. You are so screwed. Can't you just take your grant money, hire lab space, employees? You got half a million with the last one; it should at least get you through most of the study you're talking about."

"I can't. The grant is specifically for work I do here. All our grants are. They all go through the university's legal department."

"Shit!" tomato sauce dripped on her white coat. "We need to get going. Let me think about this. There's got to be a way, without you becoming Cliff Clay's whore or some drug-company stooge. And by the way...and I'm not taking no for an answer. Jeff and I are going out to the Improv tomorrow; you're coming."

"I can't," he said. "I've got rats to feed and cages to clean."

"You can," she said trying to suck the tomato sauce of her coat, but only making the stain worse. "You will."

Chapter Six

□ □ □

Lara Nash stared out the north-facing window of her corner office in the Global building on Park and 55th. She took in the unobstructed view—soaring skyscrapers in all directions—a view to kill for, but not what had her mind spinning in overdrive. For the last two days all she could think about was Karel, and their Saturday. The kiss by the ocean, like gas on smoldering coals, had ignited something she didn't know she possessed. The drive back to Manhattan, top down, her brain feverishly replaying each moment—she couldn't have made it up, but how very like her potent boy-meets-girl scenes—the meet-cute. Such a fucking cliché the secretary and her boss, the governess and the handsome rake, the ambitious blonde executive and the powerful CEO of... *Stop it!*

That evening—he'd called—"Lara, I have to see you." His limo parked outside her building, Minnie in chauffeur hat and tight black uniform–opening the door, Karel inside... waiting. His smile, his smell, "I had to see you."

They'd ended up in his bed, the French windows wide open, the sea breeze fluttering the curtains, his two gorgeous servants politely knocking between rounds of love making, bringing drinks, trays of cut fruit, aromatic cheeses, pastries and delicate sandwiches—like a dream. She'd stayed the night, confused and drunk on everything about him, his strength, his sadness that seemed just below the surface... his scent. Even now, trying to picture his face, she looked at the new photo on her desk—the one that graced the back cover of Global's organizational chart– as though the details of his mouth, his nose, the shape of his jaw were too hard to imagine. His body had surprised her, hard and smooth—he had to be in his late forties or early fifties, but like an athlete, even the wisps of hair on his chest—silky. "Girl," she whispered, staring at his photo, now surrounded by three boxes of Italian silk ties she'd asked her assistant to bring, "You are in trouble." But thrilled to the core—*this actually exists*–having always felt hypocritical for all that head-over-heels stuff in her novels. "It's real and this is what it's like." Humming, she reached into one of the boxes, peeled back the tissue and stroked the rich burgundy and Prussian blue fabric. The blue, she mused, would pick up his eyes—*but are they really blue?*–more like a hazel that changed with his mood and surroundings—sometimes blue, almost black in the darkness of his room, green in the sun, gray by the sea. Her scalp tingled as she remembered that first kiss. A thrill shot down her spine, "What have you done?"

Her intercom buzzed—it was Russell. "Lara, I've got your mother on the phone. Do you want to take it?"

Like a pin in a balloon her blissed-out mood collapsed. "Not really," trying to remember when she'd last spoken with her mother—Vivian, "but put her through. If I'm still on the phone with her in ten minutes, interrupt me."

"You got it."

"Lara?" her mother's tight-jawed voice—a mix of Girl's Latin and four years at Bryn Mawr.

"Hello mother," her buzz replaced by a knot in her gut.

"Please tell me that I'm mistaken."

"About what?" Lara heard her mother's intake of breath.

"I just got off the phone with Paul. What happened? He was sobbing, Lara. What did you do?"

She stared at Karel's photo, "I broke it off," remembering the painful breakfast she'd had with Paul yesterday.

"Have you lost your mind? You're 32, Lara. Paul is a wonderful man, who adores you. What the hell? Do you think men are going to keep proposing to you?"

Lara flipped open a tie box—this one held a rich paisley with an emerald background and swirling lozenges of gold and blue. "I don't love Paul, Mother. I've been trying to tell myself that I did, or I would eventually. It's not fair to him and it's not what I want." Almost exactly the words she'd used at breakfast with the handsome venture capitalist who was to have been her husband. It had made her feel awful, he'd seemed so wounded. But she'd had other feelings too, like *why the hell didn't I do this month's earlier?* and *thank God*, like a massive weight lifted.

"I am so angry," Vivian Nash continued. "How can you be so selfish? The invitations have already been sent. For God's sake our friends have bought you gifts." The words spat fast and angry, "Paul could have any girl he wants...and he will. Don't think he'll wait for you to come to your senses—not for long anyway. You need to call him, tell him you were having cold feet, that you'd lost your mind...anything."

"I'm sorry you feel that way, Mother. As to the wedding, I'm sending a note to everyone we've invited. So please, by the end of the day this will be taken care of."

"Paul asked me," Vivian continued, "if there were another man. He said you wouldn't tell him. Is that what this is about? Are you having an affair Lara?"

"Of course not," and wondered what her mother—who was obsessed with appearances, and the trappings of wealth–would say if she knew her daughter had spent twenty-four hours of ecstasy with a man who had a net worth in the billions. "Mother, I have an important meeting and need to get off the phone. I'm sorry Paul got to you before I did, but what's done is done."

"What is wrong with you, Lara?"

"Not a damn thing. I just came to my senses, before I made a horrible mistake. Goodbye," and before her mom could launch another assault, Lara hung up. She was shaking and put her hands over her face. "Damn her!" It seemed like her entire life had been spent trying to please her mother—an impossibility. When she got straight 'A's' it'd been, 'but you need more extracurricular activities.' Her excitement at getting her first book published 'Romance novels—not exactly literature and I hope you don't intend to use your real name'. Graduating second in her Wellesley class was, 'well that is second place, isn't it?' Even her recent promotion, 'Dear, men don't like it when woman make more money than they do, and you are getting older. You do want children. You need to focus on that, not these silly promotions.'

But shit—Vivian was right too. Yes, she thought, I do want to get married and I do want children, but not with Paul. Or any of the other half dozen men who'd proposed to her over the years–easily conjuring their expectant faces, ring box in hand wanting her to say "yes." Letting them down gently, but always wondering what was wrong with her, nice guys, she'd liked them all, but no love, isn't that supposed to be part of the equation? She'd told herself that Paul was different, desperately wanting to believe that, but in her gut...there was no passion. He was without doubt the gold standard of prime marriage material. She'd rationalized that it was the right thing to do; it was time. All the bitter truths telling her to 'shit or get off the pot'–you're not getting younger and by age 30 ninety percent of your eggs are gone and *the risk of having a Down's Syndrome baby goes up and up. Tick tock, Lara.* She looked at Karel's photo—he was confusing the hell out of her. This promotion, his visionary expectations, and just him, his eyes, his body, the way he made her feel—confident, smart, powerful. What did he want from her, is this just business, sex? But one thing was clear, *you've never felt like this for any man before*—certainly not Paul—and what she wanted from Karel, damnit, was the whole enchilada, body, soul... wedding ring and kids—the whole damn thing.

She pressed the intercom, "Russell, are they in the board-room?"

"Yes," he said, "and right after I've got a limo waiting to take us to the airport. I also found quite a bit more on Spencer Williams. I'll brief you during the flight."

"Good, and did you find out what Duane was up to?"

"Some, and be careful. Duane's a snake. He'll do anything to get back into Karel's good graces, not to mention his old job. I've got maybe two hours before we fly out, and some leads to track down, but something smells bad."

"Russell, if I haven't told you lately, I think you're amazing."

"Feeling's mutual boss, anything else you're going to need before we head out?"

"Luck," she said, about to play a gambit that could cost her job and the man she so desperately... yes, loved.

*

Karel, in a capacious leather chair, gazed across a bank of flat screen monitors on his study wall, one per executive in the conference room at Global's 55th Street headquarters. He loved all of his intense men and women in their tidy gray and navy suits, trendy haircuts and glowing faces—like pieces on a chessboard. He knew all their likes and dislikes, secrets, fetishes and fears. How easy to fall in love with these humans, even to understand why the Creator was so partial to them, as they fumbled along, falling in and out of love, making and breaking promises, and always wanting more. "This is a good day," he said aloud, realizing that something had changed—his jealousy of humans was gone. "This wasn't their fault," looking over his busy-little executives, "none of it," and with that came a radical shift in his thoughts.

Without turning from the monitors he sensed Minnie in the doorway. She pointed at the center screen, "I like that one," as Lara, tall and blond, dressed in a beautifully draped navy skirt suit with a slit up one leg called the meeting of Global's top R&D people, to order.

"Ssh," Karel leaned forward and pressed the button that zoomed in on Lara's face—so determined, so skilled. He watched as she looked around the table making eye contact with each of the executives and then stared into the camera at the back—knowing he was there.

"Ladies and gentlemen," she began, "we need to keep today's meeting brief and focused, as you'll see we have a single agenda item."

There was an expectant rustling of papers.

"This is also going to take a leap of faith," Lara said, "and I need you all to jump with me... Over the past few years, Global has kept ahead of our competition by avoiding the safe, and "me too" drugs that make no major advances. We have become the undisputed leader, for the novel, the new, the important... the next. So, it's in keeping with this vision and mission that I can now give you some basic but sketchy information about what I—and Mr. Von Graff–believe will be the single greatest contribution of ours to the health of mankind. We are about to rapidly push the development of a new compound—its initial indication will likely be to completely remit severe depression–it will eclipse everything else on the market or in development. We are confident," she continued, "that this new agent will ease suffering and improve quality of life... for millions, possibly tens of millions. To make this happen, and happen fast, we need to make changes."

There was an anxious murmur, and Karel watched side conversations sprout around the table.

"Oh oh," Minnie's tone mocking, "somebody's about to rock the boat".

"To start," Lara said, "Over the next two weeks we will re-purpose the Carlos Key facility."

"But," a thin man's hand shot up.

"Yes, Greg," acknowledging the R&D director for Global's east coast facilities including the high-security Carlos Key laboratories south of Miami, a short plane hop to the southern-most point in the continental U.S.—Key West.

"That's our largest biotech facility." He took a nervous sip of water, "Are we just going to shut down a dozen active projects?"

"No, they'll be relocated."

"What?" he continued, as others began to fidget, "You're talking dozens of scientists, over two-hundred support personnel, their families, active experiments, tens of thousands of test animals, equipment...how am I supposed to just tell them they've got to pack up and pull their kids out of school? And what project could possibly require that kind of space?"

"Greg...stop please. This is going to happen, and the new staffing model for Carlos Key will be based on the needs of the lead researcher, whose identity I'm not yet at liberty to divulge. This project will be sealed, with details on a need-to-know basis. What all of you now need to know, is we've got to reconfigure, and quickly. I expect detailed plans for all of the moves on my desk by the end of the week. Reassure our people that their jobs are safe, we'll cover all expenses for the relocations, make it as smooth as possible, but we must have that facility."

"Lara," a man's voice from the far-end, "much as we all love a leap of faith, and believe in your abilities, what you're proposing—this chaos—will cost tens of millions, maybe a hundred. Not to mention setting back existing projects by months or even years. You haven't considered the fallout. Your enthusiasm is...admirable, but this isn't realistic."

Karel's head swiveled far to the left to get a clear view of Duane Short, a handsome little Napoleon in a dark-gray suit with perfect hair, his Boston accent rich with sarcasm, barely able to hide his anger and contempt—so much fun.

"Duane, at the end of the day this project will cost no-more than our average. So yes, not tens of millions but well over a hundred—maybe two–before we get FDA approval and move to market. Our key concern—as you're aware," she stared straight at him, "will be potential leaks or outright piracy. Carlos Key was specifically built and situated with those concerns in mind."

"Does the board know about this?" he continued, a vein popped in his neck.

"It of course has the full backing of Mr. Von Graff. What he chooses to present to the board is for him to decide." Karel watched the color rise in her cheeks. "What Global needs from you...from all of you...is to work together, to come up with excellent alternate space so that disruptions are minimal. Our researchers need to know we value them, and their vital work...now if you'd look into your packets I've prepared a timeline with a list of the support people who will assist you with the details. If you run into problems, or delays, I expect to hear about them, but bottom line, Carlos Key will be cleared and ready in two weeks."

"She has power," Ian remarked, having silently entered, he and his sister still as statues. "You can tell they're scared, all trying to figure out how to do what she asks, wanting to please her."

"Yes." Karel replied. "She is spectacular."

"So now she becomes your hands," Minnie added.

"Yes, and quite capable at that."

"What happens if she doesn't bring him over? Or if the angel stops her? She has to know that something's up. She's not stupid."

"Don't!" his voice hard. "I can hide a bit longer. Meanwhile, it's time to send out the bait, let the young doctor bite and then reel him in."

"But what if Lara fails? If you fail." Minnie persisted. "What then?"

"No! Not this time. This Chosen is nearly ours." He was unable to shake the sense of crossing a dangerous line, if he failed, what would the punishment be? But there was something more, a thought struggling to be born. He knew what would help. "What day is this? Is he coming today?"

Minnie rolled her eyes, "No, but for what you're paying I'm certain he'd make an extra visit. I don't understand what all this therapy is for. It's just talk."

"Of course you wouldn't."

"Then please explain it, maybe I should have some."

He chuckled, "No, I think it might be dangerous for you. But if you must know, it makes hidden things clear. And right now there's something I can't quite grasp, something of the utmost importance. Call him."

Chapter Seven

□ □ □

Normally Spencer's anxiety when seeing patients in his research clinic stayed in check. And if it didn't, there was only himself to blame. His colleagues joked about his insistence on working with the most depressed and most dangerously suicidal patients. Behind his back they quipped about his *Sylvia Plath* clinic, but all were relieved when he'd take their most-difficult patients. The ones who scared them, who they truly believed would end their own lives, and stir up angry families hungry for wrongful-death malpractice suits.

But today his gut was sending danger signals as he watched Sharon Lahey struggle to regain control in his eight-by-twelve office. He knew not to push the fragile grad student when she got like this—overwhelmed and flooded. She clutched the arm of the faded blue upholstered chair. Tears streamed, her mascara bled, her mouth twisted in anguished gasps beneath her frizzed out bird's nest of bleached blond.

She was in meltdown, each day a struggle, where she desperately yearned to cut herself, or worse. He focused on her aura, a swirling mingle of sick yellows and blood red—like a half-healed bruise. But it was her emotions—leaping across the few feet that separated them—sickening pulls of desperation and hopelessness, a bottomless well. He could see images too, and these he needed to block out, scenes of Sharon's childhood, of a drunk and sexually sadistic stepfather, a cousin who would hold her down and force her to do things, and a mother—drunk and passed out–who refused to believe her daughter's stories of incest and rape.

"Can I get you some water?" Spencer asked, knowing that if he just let her be, she'd eventually pull it together. He felt a guilty twinge as he glanced at the time on his monitor. He felt pulled in different directions—*is she okay enough to go home? Do I need to send her to the hospital? And will I be able to figure this out before my lunch meeting with this woman from Global?* Then his mind played a zippy round of anticipatory dread about the meeting that would soon follow with Clifford Clay, where he'd have to pull a rabbit out of the hat to get the support he needed to push his work to the next level. And that thought brought him straight back to Sharon, and why it didn't matter who got the damn credit for XU472—she needed this drug—*she needs it now*—end of the day, nothing else mattered.

Sharon shook her head, "I'm sorry. I'm so sorry," she tried to slow her breath, her lips counting, trying a technique he'd taught her. "Shit, I feel like I'm in freefall."

"Flashbacks?"

"Every day...awful and nightmares. I don't sleep. It's like anything can set me off."

She grabbed a fistful of tissues from the box by her chair, wiped her eyes, blew her nose loudly and smiled. It was her greatest defense and how she'd learned to get through the day and not have people suspect the hell inside of her. *"If you look happy,"* she'd once told him, *"people leave you alone."*

"No sleep?" he asked, hoping to find some thread of a positive response to the shopping list of medications he had her on.

"A little," she admitted. "It was better than the last sleeping pill, but the thought of gaining weight because of it, just freaks me out. I feel Clyde pulling away, and if I balloon out like a cow..."

"Has he said something?"

"No, but I can tell, or I think I can tell. I don't know, I get it in my head that he's going to leave me, and it makes me frantic."

"What about the group, have you been going?"

"Yes, and the Yoga class and the gym. And you're right those help a little, but only before I lose control. Not after...I've started to cut again."

"When was the last time?"

"This morning," she wouldn't look at him.

"Do you need stitches?" he asked, feeling her guilt pulsing, her shame, her fear that she'd disappointed him and that he'd no longer work with her.

"They aren't deep," and she pushed back the sleeves of her embroidered purple jacket and turned her wrists to show him the tidy rows of superficial lacerations, like railroad ties tracking up her forearms. Beneath those he glimpsed layers of older healed scars, most—but not all—from shallow swipes of a box cutter.

"Walk me through everything going on, everything you were doing, thinking and feeling before you cut."

And for the next fifteen minutes he dragged her through a painstaking behavioral analysis, bringing her back to the point at which she had lost control and viewed cutting as the only solution. "That's the crossroads," he said, "up to that point, you had some control." He thought of Joan, and her words spilled softly from his lips, "you can go left or you can go right."

"I know," she said, "it just doesn't feel like it, and after I got off the phone with my Mom, I felt like shit. I mean how can she stay with that man after everything he did to me?"

"Is that something you have any control over?" having been through this before with her.

"No, but that doesn't stop me from trying."

"And that makes you feel better?"

"Are you getting tired of me?" she smiled, knowing they'd beaten this particular horse until it was way-past dead.

"No, and what were your options? Did cutting get you anywhere?"

She stared out the small window that looked out on a courtyard, "It makes me feel like I'm not losing my mind, but after, I feel pathetic. Like here I go again. I'm never going to get better. What's the point?" Suddenly distracted "...Are they always there?" She leaned across the arm of her chair.

"What are you looking at?" he asked.

"Those birds, those two big crows...or are they ravens? They're always there, aren't they?"

He got up beside her and looked out at the massive beech tree that mostly filled the tiny courtyard. On the branch closest to his window two shiny birds their feathers an oily blue-black were staring back.

"There's always two of them," she said, "which is weird cause crows usually come in threes."

"They're there a lot," he admitted, "maybe something about the tree."

"Or maybe they like listening to all the therapy," she offered. "They're a little creepy. Did you know that a group of crows is called a murder?"

"I did," having a weird déjà vu—those birds so like the ones outside his childhood window, "but back to you," he returned to his chair. "How are you going to get through the next few days?"

And for the session's last fifteen minutes he helped bolster her, got some reassurance that she wouldn't do anything to hurt herself, and made slight adjustments to her medication that might ease her surges of panic and depression. "And you have my card?"

"Yes, and the number for the crisis center." She fished it out of her giant embroidered bag. "See."

"Give it here," he said, "I don't generally do this," he scribbled his cell number on the back. "I can only work with you if you're still breathing, Sharon. If things get bad, you must call me. Understood?"

"Okay."

After she'd gone he sat in front of his computer, closed his eyes, slowed his breath, and let images form on the back of his eyelids. They came fast and were hard to hold, some little more than flickers, like fast-moving frames of a movie. As Joan had taught him years ago, he formed a question, *"will she be all right?"*

The phone rang, shattering his concentration, before he could get an answer.

"Dr. Williams," Marie, the clinic's grandmotherly secretary said, "Your noon appointment is here."

"Right," and unable to shake the sick feeling in his gut, he grabbed his worn corduroy jacket and went out to meet the persistent woman from Global.

*

Lara Nash had seen pictures of Spencer, but was pleasantly surprised by the tall, handsome man with his long dark hair and slightly hooded eyes that made him seem like he needed a good night's sleep. His clothes were standard junior faculty–chinos, a chocolate brown corduroy blazer and loafers that should have been ditched years back, but were probably insanely comfortable. He crossed the small carpeted waiting area, "Ms. Nash?"

"Lara," she said, getting up, and meeting his gaze. While not essential that top researchers be fashion plates—most were far from it—having a good looking face to put on the project would be a bonus. "And thank you so much for taking the time to meet with me..." she smiled, "plus it gave me a great excuse for a trip to Chicago. I love this city."

They shook hands, "I'm afraid my afternoon is pretty tight," he said stiffly, "We should probably get a move on."

"Of course," *yes*, noting his polite brusqueness, *this one will take work.* "I'm open to anything, food wise. So if you've got any favorites let's do it. Plus," dipping her tone, "it's all on the company."

"I figured," bordering on rude. "There's a Thai place around the corner."

"Sounds good," her tone light, as she tried to keep a lid on her anxiety. It was clear he did not want to meet with her, and was doing it only because she had pushed so hard. On the jet she'd brainstormed with Russell, trying to figure what made Dr. Spencer Williams tick, and also what had Duane done that had so pissed him off. As they headed out of the drab cinderblock clinic, "I really miss Chicago," she said.

"You were on faculty here."

"Yes," she said, encouraged that he'd at least taken the effort to Google her. "I had my lab in the same building you do—fourth floor."

"Well," he said, looking down at his feet as they walked, "then somebody liked you. I'm in the basement."

"That sucks, but as I recall the whole scramble for lab space was hateful."

"It hasn't changed."

Lara sensed he was preoccupied, something, or things were distracting him. "Are you feeling okay, Dr. Williams?"

He stopped outside the red and green front of the Siam Garden, and looked at her. She got the strangest vibe as he stared and said nothing. Her mind, flitted through possibilities, including several psychiatric diagnoses for this intense young man. Maybe it wasn't rudeness, maybe autistic, or Asperger's, and this was just how he handled social interaction. *No, too much emotion, what the hell is going on in his head?* She felt him studying her, but not in the way she'd come to expect from men, who'd size her up as an athletic good-looking blue-eyed blond, and wonder how hard it would be to get her in the sack.

"It's a weird day," he held the door.

A thin Asian man in a red and gold brocaded vest greeted them.

"Your quietest table, please," Lara asked, and they were led to a corner booth with a window that looked out on the shady tree-lined street. The host handed them menus, and was followed by a busboy who filled their water and left a basket of crispy rice noodles and peanut dipping sauce. "Weird how?"

He stared at her, "What made you decide to leave Gray?"

It was a blunt question, like a test. "A few things," realizing he was analyzing her every word. "For starters, I'm ambitious, and it didn't take long to realize that of the hundred or so full professors attached to the medical school, only six were women. The salary was pitiful." She grabbed a noodle and dipped it in the savory peanut sauce, "the politics..."

"Say more about that," he urged.

"Okay," she thought back to when she'd made the huge switch from a life in academia to taking that first big job with Global. "You've Googled me."

He nodded.

"Then you know I was doing clinical trials with immunotherapy for Alzheimer's and other degenerative brain disorders."

"Yes," he leaned forward, his gaze not wavering. "Important stuff."

It was too penetrating the way he stared at her. "It was...it is, and it was obvious. There's a huge race going on with that research—it's eventually going to lead to major new drugs and everyone wants a piece of it...even if they haven't done any of the work. I mean think about it, treatments that will actually reverse Alzheimer's, Lewy Body, maybe even Parkinson's and Huntington's."

"I see...so every time you published, people wanted to attach themselves to your work."

"Yes," wondering what the hell he was groping for.

Finally, he leaned back, "And that bothered the hell out of you?"

"Yes," feeling exposed, like he was trying to get inside her mind. "I'd feel used, when someone who could control my access to lab space or equipment would insist on being the second or third author. They'd even jockey for first. It made me sick."

"It's not fair," he grew silent as their waiter appeared.

"No, it's not, and I couldn't get beyond that. I mean I don't mind sharing the credit when it's deserved, but this was just..."

"Sleazy?" he offered, cracking a smile for the first time. "I noticed how Cliff Clay's name crept up on most of your work, usually as second author. Somehow, I can't imagine him by your side in the lab."

"No," she stiffened; this was too close and still painful. Clay was a snake, and she'd pissed him off when she'd up and left. If he were now to find out she was trying to do an end run and steal Spencer and his work...*serve him right*. She leaned in, her voice a whisper, because even in a big city, word gets around, "the extent of Cliff's input was to give me adequate space—that's why I wasn't in the basement. He'd read the articles and then try to give the general impression that he was the principal author, but let me have it as a way of helping out a member of the junior faculty. A lot of people believed him." She searched his face for a response, sensing she'd struck a chord. "Sound familiar?"

"Yeah, but all the work you do at the university, they pretty much own it. What did you..."

"I walked away from it...and it was the hardest thing I've ever done. My papers were out there so the information was free for the taking, but I would never be the one to bring it to fruition. At that point I'd gotten good offers from half a dozen companies to go into R&D, and Global's was the best."

*

Spencer knew he was being rude as he stared at the polished blonde in her chic navy suit that showed rather than hid her curves. But he didn't want this meeting. Sure, she was attractive, even beautiful with her sleek haircut, minimal makeup and tanned legs he couldn't help but admire through the slit of her skirt–*but that's all packaging.* Ever since he was a med student, attractive drug reps had been a constant, offering books and free meals, all-expense trips to conferences in exotic locales. He could only imagine Neri's take on this athletic beauty in her outfit that probably cost more than he made in a month. Yeah, she was mostly telling him the truth, but not about her motives. *Just spit it out*, he thought, *you think you and your company can make a truckload of cash off XU472.* Still, there was something about her. She had passion and that wasn't faked, but what in hell was she hoping to get from him? He couldn't have been clearer, he and XU472 were not for sale. "You no longer do research," he said.

"I don't. I help set others up, make sure their work's moving along, get them the support they need. It's in everyone's interest, that our projects progress smooth and fast."

"Makes sense, but don't you miss it?"

"Not really," she pushed back as the waiter came with their lunch, refilled their water and tea and left. "I get to do more now. I hope you don't take this the wrong way, because clearly I'm here because I think your work is amazing, and I'm hoping we can do something together, and what I'm about to say may come off as trite."

"Try me," he said, seeing deep surges of blue in her aura, and knowing now that she was pulling from her core.

"I'm like a talent scout for research. I get to look at everything that's going on out there and try to figure out what has real potential. Your compound, Dr. Williams, is the real deal. But the hitch is you're still in early animal studies, they've got you stuffed in a basement lab—and I know the basement of Wentworth—damp and so hot in winter you've got to keep the AC going in the middle of January—not good at all for the test animals, creating all sorts of uncontrolled variables. At this rate what could be a life-saving compound may not see the light of day for a decade or more—or it might get killed all together."

"You can call me Spencer," his thoughts now back on the awful session with Sharon, and felt his earlier wariness soften. "When I said I was having a weird day, part of it had to do with a patient I just saw. Have you ever had a patient keep you up at night, worrying about whether or not you'd done the right thing?"

"Of course."

"My clinical practice is set up with mostly women, who are mostly suicidal, most of the time. But this one, she's in so much pain, I never know if she'll still be alive for her next session. And sometimes when she goes into the hospital it's more for me than for her."

Lara nodded, "Because you know she'll be safe."

"Yeah," he felt his throat squeeze shut.

"That's who your compound's for," she said, keying into his thoughts.

He nodded.

"Her and a whole lot more who so desperately need it," Lara said. "I don't know what to tell you, Spencer, other than I agree, and I will do whatever I can to help you get this moving forward."

And that's when he saw it, the subtle spikes of a harsh yellow flickering about her neck and ears. "You're not being honest with me," he stated. "And I need to get to my next appointment, so please tell me the truth quickly."

"You're right," she said, daring to look him dead on. "Yes, I want you to sign on with Global, but if that's not possible I still want to work with you—true—but also it might not be possible."

"There's more," he was noticing something else, a rose halo, and the faintest whiff of something he could only describe as essence of 'in love.' Not with him, but Lara Nash was a woman in that first heady thrall of being in love. *Good for you*, he thought. *Maybe that's the approach I should take, leave Gray and maybe get a life.* "I just can't trust you. I apologize for my bluntness, and I don't yet know if it's you or the company you work for."

"Why my company? What happened?"

He stared. She was being sincere; she didn't know. "Your predecessor made me a similar offer, actually a better one. Huge salary, unlimited resources, all the space I could want, technical support, a team of statisticians and epidemiologists to work on the old and new data." As he spoke, he softened his gaze. There were layers to this woman, like peeling an onion. *Why was she so anxious? And how was that connected to the man she loved? Or to getting him to sign with her company? And why did he keep seeing a bookshelf filled with paperback romance novels?*

She picked at the crunchy wrapper on her spring roll, "You said 'no'...can I ask why?"

"For the same reason I'll tell you 'no'. I've seen how the big drug companies operate. It makes me sick. I don't want to be a part of it, all the lies and half truths. The whole system of getting a drug to squeak by the FDA when it's not any better—or maybe worse—then what's already out there. And then comes the big sell, throwing billions of dollars at advertising, at seducing physicians and at getting the public to believe that this minimally effective—and expensive—drug will ease their pain. It's a con, and it has perverted medical research to where it will never recover. Like here," and he reached for his tattered brown briefcase, pulled out a handful of journals and tossed them on the table. "The whole thing has turned into one huge fraud! These are supposed to be the top peer-reviewed journals. Over fifty percent of the pages are drug ads. And then," angrily flipping through a recent *Journal of American Psychiatry*, "Let's look at the actual articles. Here, lead researcher has affiliations with two drug companies, and this one...only one—good for him. And here, this one's received funding from five different companies, and what do you know? One's yours. Is that good, bad? Or is he just one big whore, who'll take money from anyone? These are my respected colleagues. This isn't research. It's hype, but what makes me furious is that it's considered normal. Even you, look at you; have you ever seen an unattractive drug rep—do they exist? All beautiful women and handsome men, visiting the doctors in their territories, leaving coffee and donuts for the staff, taking everyone out to dinner, persuasively explaining why their new costly drug is the best on the market—and 'Gee, we're offering a select group of physicians the chance to go to the Caribbean and we'll even give you a thousand-dollar stipend to answer a few questions about how you prescribe antidepressants."' He could see her stiffening with his rant, "I don't mean to spew, but it reeks. Is it even possible to do research free from bias?"

Seemingly cool now, she responded, "I don't know, but does all that have to be a bad thing if the work is valid? I mean why shouldn't you get funded, or receive a salary that's commensurate with the value of your work? At least if you're working in the industry, it's the inherent value of the work that determines whether or not it moves forward. There's little of this other politicking. Your work is your work."

"No, I'm sorry but what you and, and that Duane guy, represent has turned medicine into a whorehouse, and not that there's anything wrong with being a hooker—just be an honest one...I'm sorry," and he pushed toward the edge of the booth, "I have to go."

"Wait! There's more, what else did Duane do? You didn't tell me everything, and I'm not disagreeing with what you said, but you've got to look at the new drugs I've helped develop—Viralon, Desirex, Memeron. Admittedly, we made the Oprah circuit with the whole 'female arousal disorder' but those are good drugs— none of them 'me toos.' They all help millions of people."

"There is more," getting up and feeling bad that this sexy and brainy woman had come all this way for no reason, and that his rejection was causing her anxiety to spike, much as she tried to hide it. "That Duane wouldn't take 'no' for an answer. He went behind my back to Cliff Clay, tried to cut a deal for my work directly with the University."

"Oh shit! Duane is an idiot."

Spencer squinted—she really did not know; this wasn't an act. "It might have worked too, if I wasn't so paranoid. Even if Clay wanted to take the bait, he doesn't have a clue how to synthesis XU472. Lara, thanks for lunch, sorry I was such a rude bastard and that I wasted your time, but I'm going to try to stick it out here, see if I can't make it work with the devil I know."

She got up and pulled a card from her wallet. "Here," she penned in her cell number. "Obviously, I need to do some repair work. Duane is a fool. He should never have done that. Look, I'm staying in town through tomorrow. Please tell me you'll give me another shot, even if it winds up as a waste of both of our time. And you can be as rude as you like."

His cell chimed, letting him know he had five minutes to make it to Clay's office, where he'd be the one begging. And for the second time that day, Joan's favorite saying rang like a bell in his head, '*you can go left or you can go right.*' So what was he supposed to do if both options sucked? "You can call me in the morning if you want." He told her. "But one night won't change my mind."

Chapter Eight □ □ □

"God, it's crowded for a Wednesday," Neri said, making a beeline toward the last open table at the Gray Improv—the university's graduate nightclub. Spencer and Jeff—Neri's lanky, sandy-haired fiancé—followed in her wake as she laid claim to a tiny scarred-oak café table two rows back from the painted-black platform that served as a stage. The club, a popular hangout, afforded the students in the performing arts an easy audience with nightly open mike slots.

Spencer hadn't been for years, and if it hadn't been for Neri showing up at his condo in jeans and a sparkly top with the much-taller Jeff in tow, he would have spent the night in the lab. As he trailed through the noisy club that reeked of beer, perfume and perspiration, his thoughts ran back to his afternoon meeting with Cliff Clay. It had left him depressed and furious. Neri had been absolutely right about what Clay wanted—credit for Spencer's research. The department Chair, silver-haired in his mid fifties, had his name attached to thousands of articles and papers, making him the best-published professor at Gray, yet almost none of it was his own work. *"It's how you get ahead in academia. You need to attach yourself to a mentor, someone with clout." Cliff had told him, his southern accent thick and used more for effect—like, gee, I'm just some Good Ol boy, who wouldn't dream about stealing someone else's research.*

"You can go left or you can go right," he muttered, wondering if punching out his department chair fit either option.

"What did you say?" Jeff turned, as Neri handed him a chair she'd begged from a neighboring table.

"Nothing," Spencer said, trying to figure what the hell he was going to do. And at the end of the day, did it matter if Cliff got the credit as long as the medication got to the people who needed it? Throughout the never-ending hour in there he'd been barraged by the stink of Cliff's deceptions. The minute Spencer got a handle on one piece of it, another load of bullshit spewed from the man's mouth. Like when Spencer had told him about the camera and listening device planted in his lab. Cliff had acted shocked—a total lie. Now at least Spencer knew who'd planted it. Or when he'd asked Cliff about the details of the deal Global had proposed, he'd denied any knowledge of it. Lies on top of lies, because Spencer—courtesy of Neri—had copies of emails from Duane Short offering massive unrestricted grants, which included *'significant funds for administrative oversight'* to develop and obtain the patents for XU472. And then he thought about Lara Nash, and what Clay had done to her, essentially pushing her into what he viewed as the even more corrupt pharmaceutical industry. *How could she just walk away from important research?* He pictured her intensity, and wondered who the lucky man was that had her reeling.

"Yo," Neri tossed a peanut at Spencer's head. "Mutant boy, where are you?"

"I hate your boss," he said, noting how pretty she looked, in makeup, her long straight black hair freed from its habitual braid.

"So what else is new?" And she tilted her head. "Isn't that the girl we saw in the street?"

He followed her gaze and his mouth went dry. Madeleine Forest, by the bar, her long curls pinned up and back, one thin strap of her midnight-blue slip dress off her shoulder, laughing and drinking something pink in a martini glass. Spencer strained to see who she was with, feeling a stab of regret when he saw her male companion—early to mid twenties with a perfect profile, and completely at ease with the gorgeous singer. *How do guys pull that off?*

"Don't you think she's pretty?" Neri asked Jeff.

He chuckled, his eyes bright, "Yeah, I'll be falling for that one."

"She's lovely," Neri persisted, "I'd kill for that hair. I can never get mine to hold a curl...Spencer you should go over to her...introduce yourself."

Before he could answer with all the reasons why he couldn't possibly do that, the emcee, in a plaid jacket, with a canary yellow fedora, took the stage, "This is just pathetic," he drawled, swirling a martini glass. "A room full of drunken Graybees and no one wants to entertain. Could be a first." He put a hand to the brow of his hat, like a sailor searching the horizon. "But what's this? I spy with my little eye, a vision of divine loveliness sucking one back by the bar. Is that the shining star of the opera program, our very own Madeleine Forest?" He raised his glass in her direction, spilling most of its contents on the stage.

Spencer watched as the beautiful Madeleine, her aura a swirling haze of blues and purples, stuck her middle finger up in the direction of the emcee.

"Such grace, such class...a most-delectable ass" the emcee persisted. "What must we do to have her grace us with a tune?"

The people she was with tried to coax her off the stool. Laughing, she yelled out over the crowd, "I'm not singing a capella."

As if on cue, a beautiful woman with short silky black hair, dressed in a leather miniskirt, dark-purple iridescent top and high-heeled boots, stepped up to the emcee, a violin case tucked under her arm. The glib emcee in the tacky fedora curiously remained silent, as she pried the microphone from his hand, "Perhaps we can help," and her handsome male counterpart—in a trendy black-on-black suit and shirt, with dark bangs falling across his brow, settled at the piano by the base of the stage. He immediately launched into the opening harp-like cords of the Barcarolle from Offenbach's *Tales of Hoffman*. The woman opened her case and took out a darkly varnished violin. Without bothering to check for pitch, she drew a bow across its strings filling the air with a throaty vibrato.

It was as though a switch had been thrown. Everyone was silent as a follow-spot landed on Madeleine Forest. Her gaze suddenly distant as she put down her drink, pushed back her hair, and walked to the platform, wrapping her beaded shawl around her mostly bare shoulders. To Spencer it was as if she floated, her head nodding to the undulating rhythm, and even before she took the stage, a first note formed in the back of her throat. It started low and swelled, the sound pure and free—the kind of unaffected soprano that no amount of training can create.

Spencer couldn't breathe as he watched and listened. Her green eyes sparkled in the spotlight and her lithe body swayed with the music as she spread her arms, as if she might take flight on the lyric rise of the gorgeous music.

Two softer amber spots followed the handsome couple on violin and piano. They played with eerie perfection, never overpowering the singer, their combined efforts like a jeweler's setting for a magnificent gem.

Madeleine gazed over the audience; her focus landed on Spencer. And then her lilting lament was just for him. She didn't look away, as though she'd selected only him from the audience for this gift. Her final notes spoke of great pain and longing as she and the violin flew up octaves, hitting notes that seasoned prima donnas would never have attempted.

It ended as it started, the piano imitating a harp, strumming cords, and Madeleine's last note hanging high in the air. A smile parted her crimson lips, and then she closed her eyes, wrapped her shawl tight around her shoulders, and let her head drop.

Silence. And seconds later, the room was on its feet.

"More! More!"

Neri reached up and gently punched Spencer's arm—"She was looking straight at you. You've got to talk to her."

"Bravo! Bravo! More! More!" It turned into a chant, people stomped their feet. "More! More! More!"

On stage, Madeleine stood motionless, her head still down, her arms around her shoulders, her shawl a shimmering cocoon.

"Not now," Spencer said, his eyes glued to the singer. When she'd looked out at him, he'd felt weird but happy, as though everything he'd been struggling with was of no importance, that it would all turn out okay, that everything was just fine... better than fine. Everything wonderful.

"More!   More!   We   want   More!   We   want More! Madeleine! Madeleine! Madeleine!"

The violinist, with her pale skin and rosebud lips, crossed the stage and whispered in the singer's ear. Madeleine nodded, her gaze still fixed on the floor in front of her.

The fiddler smiled at her handsome pianist companion, who grinned wildly, winked at a table of girls, raised his hands high over the keyboard and brought them down hard. His left hand established a driving blues beat, while his right played New Orleans riffs that dripped with the hunger of a bayou night and a slow seduction.

The violin joined in with the twang and slide of Mississippi Zydeco, and again, like a butterfly emerging from her chrysalis, Madeleine threw back her shawl and let it float to the floor. She ran a hand through her hair and pulled out the pins, her curls cascading over her shoulders and down her back. Instead of opera, what rose from her throat was a bluesy ballad about a girl recklessly in love with a man she knows will break her heart. As she dipped into her alto her focus was again on Spencer. This time it was playful, as though she were a having conversation just with him. She sang about how he'd make love to her and then leave her. Of how she'd search him out and beg him to take her back. With each verse, she spiraled deeper into the hell of unrequited love. Her slender figure, thighs and belly pressed against the smooth silk of her dress, her long hair wild, her eyes on his, pleading, asking him why he would do this to her. *Why won't you love me?* In the final verse she's broken and crazed; she finds him with another woman, pulls a gun, kills them both and then turns it on herself.

The room erupted, everyone on their feet, demanding more. She laughed and purred into the mike, "No, you're a bunch of drunken freeloaders and I'm done. So who's buying me a drink?"

Neri shoved Spencer hard, he tripped over a chair, and as he tried to keep from colliding into the libation-laden table in front of them, his feet tangled. He stumbled, twisted and landed hard at the foot of the stage.

Madeleine looked down, "Are you okay?" she bent down, the front of her dress showing flawless skin across the swell of her breasts.

He looked up, eyes riveted to hers. "Can I buy you that drink?"

She extended her hand, "If you can stand."

"I'm Spencer," he said, amazed he could actually talk to this goddess.

"Madeleine," helping him up, not breaking her gaze. And then she put a hand through his hair. Her touch sent a jolt through them both.

"You sing beautifully," he said, wanting the connection not to end.

"We've met before," a thread of uncertainty in her voice.

"Yes."

"But we didn't have a chance to talk."

And right then the same man Spencer had seen her with, approached. Athletic, with dark hair and blue eyes, he was carrying two pink drinks. Spencer's heart dropped—*got to be her boyfriend.* The man was carefully elbowing his way through the crowd, many of whom were also trying to get to Madeleine. "Showoff," he said, as one of the drinks dribbled down his hand.

"Matthew, you should have come up with me," she said, "Those musicians were amazing. Who the hell were they," and her head whipped around, "And where did they go?"

"Cosmo, sweetie?"

"Love one," and then she looked back at Spencer, "you can buy me the next."

"I'd like to," trying to figure out what was happening.

"So who's this tall drink of water?" the man asked, eyeing Spencer.

"This is Spencer. Spencer, this is my brother Matthew. He's a singer too."

"So was my mother," Spencer blurted.

"Really?" she said, ignoring the circle of well-wishers, many carrying drinks for her. "Professionally?"

He found it hard not to stare, and wished they were somewhere less chaotic. *And why the hell did you have to bring up your mother?* "She was Lila Cartwright."

Her expression turned serious, "You have her eyes. Maybe that's why you look so familiar, like I know you from somewhere. She was so lovely... Do you have a table?"

He turned and found Neri, snuggled up to Jeff, staring back at him grinning. "I came with a couple friends."

"It's so crowded," she smiled nervously as another man tried to hand her a drink. "Sorry, I've got," she told him, and then back to Spencer.

A change came over her. All that confidence she'd had on stage vanished like mist. He saw Matthew watching her, concern on his face. "Maybe we should get you out of here," he said.

"I just need some air," she put her drink down. "Will you take a walk with me?" she asked Spencer.

"Of course".

Matthew looked at her hard, "Maybe I should just take you home. You've had a lot to drink."

"Little brother," her hand seeking out Spencer's, "you worry too much. I'm fine."

Spencer sensed Matthew's frustration... and some worry. "I'll make sure she gets home safely."

"Madeleine, please don't do this..."

"Matthew," she started to pull Spencer toward the door, "sometimes you can be such an old woman." And she and Spencer headed for the exit.

*

Spencer's head swam; *this can't be happening.* He was always shy around women, especially beautiful women, but here he was alone, walking by the lake on a moonlit night with Madeleine Forest.

"So you're a doctor?" she asked.

"I am. I do research and you sing."

"Yes," she laughed, "I do opera. I'm in my second year in the graduate program. So, what kind of doctor? Don't you have to pick a specialty?"

"Psychiatry."

"Really? That's got to be hard. Do you just do research, or see patients too?"

"Both," he said, wishing he knew how to make a poem about her eyes, or the way her body seemed to dance even when there was no music, and how she made him feel—like everything was good in the world. "It's a beautiful night. Is your headache better?"

"Of course," she slipped her hand in his, "you know that was just an excuse to walk with you. So your mother was Lila Cartwright. She had a magnificent voice. I sometimes do one of her angel pieces in concert." She glanced across at him. "Is it okay to talk about her?"

"It was a long time ago." He refused to think about that horrible night. "She died when I was six."

"We have that in common. Both my parents were killed in a nightclub fire. I was six and Matthew was three."

"He didn't seem so keen on you taking this walk."

"Matthew worries—thinks I need to be protected."

"Do you?" he stopped, took her other hand, and just stared, taking her in.

She held his gaze and smiled. "I don't." She laughed softly.

"What?"

"You just going to stand there, or are you going to kiss me already?"

Her hair was silky against his face as he leaned in. Her lips were soft, and her scent dark and complex. Her heart beat against his chest, his own pulse pounded in his ears. The kiss grew and time slipped away. It felt electric, as though they were two halves of a circuit.

Finally, reluctantly, they pulled apart.

"I didn't expect that." she said quietly.

His hand traced the side of her face, needing to feel her softness, his fingers moving through the swirls of lavender and sapphire of her aura. Hungry for her, his lips again found hers.

"Okay," she said, coming up for air, "now I need to sit down...or better yet." She stepped away and held out her hand. "Come with me."

He couldn't speak. The image of her silhouetted by the lamplight, her hair free, her shawl and the lake glittering as though made from the same stuff—she was out of a storybook, ethereal, too beautiful.

"Cat got your tongue?"

"Do you have any idea how beautiful you are?"

"You're not so bad yourself, now come."

He didn't ask where, and if she'd decided to take a swim in the icy lake that would have been fine. What she did do was hail a cab and take him to her apartment in Old Town.

*

"Ssh," she whispered, her key in the door, her face luminous. "Let's not wake Matthew."

Spencer had a moment's panic. *Matthew? Right, her brother.* His gaze never off her, his senses atingle, the shimmer of her skin, the heat that pulsed between them, her fragrance like a drug.

With one hand on the door she turned into him. Her other hand was on his neck, their mouths finding each other. The door clicked, and like dancers in tight hold they moved as one. He sensed the darkened hall, a turn, another door, the sound of her beaded shawl falling to the floor. Gentle fingers on his chest tugging at buttons. "Mmm," gasping at the spark of flesh on flesh, her hand inside his shirt, as he eased the straps of her dress over her shoulders, needing restraint to keep from ripping the delicate fabric. He gave no pause, finding the hook at the back, his fingers on the velvet of her skin, now tugging down the first few inches of zipper. His hands sliding down her back, savoring every curve.

She moaned softly and shrugged. The silk shivered and fell like water to the ground.

He pulled her tighter, his mouth on her neck, his tongue finding the back of her ear, her hands on his head, and then he swept her up. "Like a feather," he groaned, finding the bed.

She laughed, "flatterer" as he laid her down, naked in the moonlight through a gauze-draped window. And like a wild animal he was on her and she on him. Nothing held back, as waves of passion rolled through them. During the briefest of moments, when conscious thought flashed, his scientist's mind made the single observation: *this is the difference between sex and love—two become one.* And the moment was gone and he surrendered into the most glorious night he had ever experienced.

He awoke in her velvet-covered bed as the sun rose vivid red through her east-facing window. He breathed deep, her perfume still lingered. He turned on his side, wanting to see her still asleep, only the bed was empty. He looked across the crumpled sheets and raised up to see the time on her clock—almost six-thirty. They hadn't fallen asleep till well-past two. He should be exhausted, but he felt refreshed and alive. He mused how if this feeling were a drug, and he could synthesize it, he'd make a killing.

He pulled back the spread and searched for his boxers. Putting them on, he looked around. This place suited her. A mix of exotic Indian fabrics hung from the window and across the ceiling—she'd mentioned how some plaster had fallen and this was her solution until the landlord finally got around to patching it. Her clothes were everywhere, two closets stuffed to where the doors wouldn't close, rows of ornamental hooks draped with scarves and necklaces, and the drawers of her mismatched dressers half open revealing the colors of the rainbow. Every surface was covered with a mish-mash of framed photos, open jewelry boxes, and stacks of annotated music scores. He smiled, thinking about his own Spartan one-bedroom—instead of clothes, his passion was books.

Over her bed, he caught the full effect of the large painting he'd only glimpsed last night, Madeleine on this bed, her bare breasts mostly covered by her hair, her vivid green eyes staring out, her lips parted, one long leg bent and one stretched, her sex concealed by an open heart-shaped box of chocolates over which her fingers poised to make a selection. *Who painted that?* He noted a signature in red. *Is that a man or a woman?* Not able to make out the name. So much detail, it had to have been done from life. She'd sat for it...or laid down for it. How many hours had it taken? Was the artist her lover? How could he not be?

He strained to hear her, and padding into the hall, he softly called, "Madeleine?" He heard movement at the end of the corridor. Thinking it had to be her, he walked into the kitchen where her brother, in tee shirt and pajamas, his hair mussed from sleep, was making coffee.

Matthew looked at Spencer, and shook his head. "She's gone," he poured two mugs.

"Where?" wondering if she'd left a note.

Matthew handed him the steaming brew. "Sometimes I hate my sister."

"What?" Spencer asked, not caring that he was mostly-naked in front of this stranger.

"She didn't want to see you," Matthew said bluntly. "She went for a run, and knowing her she won't come back till she's sure you're gone."

Spencer put down the coffee, "Does she do this...a lot?" He was confused...and angry.

"I'm sorry, dude," Matthew said, clearly uncomfortable as he turned to rinse dishes in the sink.

Spencer went back to retrieve his clothes. *What the hell?* He caught his reflection in a hall mirror, too thin, his long hair making him look like he'd stepped out of a medieval religious painting—some naked saint about to be martyred. *This is crazy,* back in her room, her naked image gazing down at him, mocking him. He angrily dressed, wanting to be out of there. She hadn't even bothered to say goodbye, to tell him to his face, 'gee that was fun, but...' *But what?* He was no virgin, but nothing had ever compared with last night, not even close. The memories, of losing himself, of not knowing where he ended and she began–*two becoming one.* Jamming his feet into his loafers, he wondered if to her he was no more than one of the pieces of chocolate in the box, tasty, and fun for the few moments it lasted, but then nothing more than a sweet memory and a discarded wrapper. *"This makes no sense."* He replayed last night in his mind. *What did you miss? She wasn't faking it. None of that had been faked.* He would have known. And then his cell went off. His spirits lifted, *maybe that's her.* But he'd not given her his number. He looked at the readout—Crisis ED. He picked up.

"Dr. Williams?"

"Yes," he braced for bad news. "This is MaryAnn Raymond, I thought you'd want to know that one of your patients came through the ED a couple hours ago, and they're not certain if she's going to make it."

"Who?" but he already knew.

"Sharon Lahey."

"Oh, God...What did she do?"

"Slashed her wrists. Apparently did a good job of it. Her boyfriend found her and called the ambulance. She lost a lot of blood. They've taken her to the ICU."

"Thank you," and before he had a chance to hang up, his cell vibrated with another call. He looked at the readout—Lara Nash. His head spun, all he could think about was Sharon. He should have sent her to the hospital—*I should have known, I should have seen this coming.* He picked up, "Hello?"

"Spencer? This is Lara, is this too early? I hope I didn't wake you?"

"No."

"What's wrong?"

A simple question he could answer a dozen ways, "Just about everything. I can't really talk. I've got to get to the hospital."

"What's happened?"

She sounded concerned, "One of my patients attempted suicide," his voice cracked, "They're not sure if she's going to make it."

"I'm so sorry. The one you were so worried about?"

"I've got to go," and he hung up.

Chapter Nine

□   □   □

Spencer's day spiraled into a hell. Each hour brought fresh torture. Still in his crumpled jacket and chinos from last night, he'd walked, then jogged the mile from Madeleine's Old Town apartment to Gray Medical Center in South Loop, where Sharon had been taken. As he hurried, dodging traffic and not waiting for the lights, he replayed and dissected their last session. "What did you miss? You should have seen this." And then he'd flash back to the horrible moment when he'd glimpsed his mother's body being wheeled out—Sharon had cut her wrists, just as his mother had. He thought about Joan, back in Boston, and wondered what she would say. She'd told Spencer that his mother's death was more than it appeared, not really a suicide, but something darker. Of course, that was Joan being dramatic, and the more time he spent away from her—now just seeing her at Christmas and Thanksgiving—the more he wondered about her, the afternoons skrying, or their trying to pull meanings from his dreams. *Bottom line*, he told himself, *mother committed suicide, she was depressed, she was crazy*. And Joan, whom he loved, and who'd been his mother's best friend, might not have been the most stabilizing influence with her other-worldly mumbo jumbo.

But this brought him right back to Sharon, who'd also slashed her wrists. A gruesome coincidence, the only glimmer of hope was that she wasn't dead...at least not yet. He broke into a run as the rambling mid-century brick and glass hospital came into view. He patted down his breast pocket, and felt relieved to find his badge, which would give him access to the locked wards.

Winded, he flashed his ID at the security desk, and got a questioning glance from the guard. He nodded, realizing that he probably looked one-step away from vagrant. He moved fast, making his way to the fourth floor ICU. It was nearly eight and the unit, which had twenty high-tech cubicles, was in the midst of morning rounds. Teams of doctors, medical students and nurses in white coats and scrubs wheeled portable computers from bed to bed, checking labs, analyzing results, and making changes to treatments that would hopefully bring their patients back.

As he hurried past the glass-walled cubicles, trying to locate Sharon, he had a déjà vu. All the years he'd been in medical school, internship and residency, he'd had to damp down the part of his vision that let him see auras. It was too painful, because it wasn't just the person's light and energy he saw, but their emotions. And here, where the scent of death mingled with pine disinfectant and body fluids, he was bombarded by surges of despair. Try as he might to stay focused, he couldn't. The pain of each patient rolled over him, like water trying to find its level. There was a howling in his head. He stumbled.

"Are you okay?" a pretty young nurse's aide in lavender scrubs with teddy bears around the neck and collar, asked.

"Fine," wondering if perhaps Sharon wasn't here at all...or worse, if she had been, and had died. "I'm looking for a patient of mine," he retrieved his badge. "Her name is Sharon Lahey."

"She's on the surgical side, just through the double doors."

"Thanks," and trying to quell his panic, he quickened his pace and ran through the small staff area that separated the units. His heart raced, and he fought to throw down the mental blocks he needed to keep from totally losing it. Again, something Joan had taught him, "*Negative emotions can take on a life of their own, especially when the person they're attached to is near death. They become demons that some people might sense in a vague way, but nothing more. For you—as it was for your mother—they become real, and you must block them out, or they'll attach themselves to you.*" She'd laughed, as though talking about death demons were the most-natural thing in the world, "*And once they do, getting them off is a bitch.*" She'd shown him how to construct walls inside his mind, like a bomb shelter where nothing could get through. Over the years, it had been a lifesaver, as early in his medical career he realized that while hospitals are meant to be places of healing they are in fact places of death. And Joan hadn't been kidding about the death demons.

He gripped the edge of a stainless sink, and imagined the walls going up. He heard screams, and through his periphery caught dark shadowy images. He took slow, even breaths, and built up another wall, picturing layers of steel, cinder block and mortar. *Don't look at the shadows, don't hear the voices.* He used to be so good at this, doing it daily, almost not thinking about it. But not now.

Shaken, he pushed through the door on the other side, rapidly scanned the room, and caught a glimmer of Sharon's frizzy blonde hair. He walked toward her cubicle. *At least she's alive.* His trained eye took in the bag of blood being transfused into her left arm, the ventilator and hard plastic tube down her throat. Her right arm lay on top of the spread, the wrist up to her elbow swaddled in gauze and bandages, the six inch span of skin between her wrappings and the hospital gown displaying a horrible tangle of scars from past cutting. Her eyes were taped shut, to keep them from drying out, and spittle had caked white around the corners of her mouth.

He looked at the monitor above her head, which displayed her heartbeat and dangerously low blood pressure.

"Can I help you?" A young Hispanic doctor asked.

Spencer turned. Judging by the man's short white coat, he knew he was an intern. "She's my patient,"

"Oh, I was hoping you might be family."

"Are they coming?" he asked, thinking of all the terrible things Sharon had suffered as a child.

"I spoke to her mother. Apparently she's done this kind of thing before. She didn't seem so concerned, until I told her how serious it was."

"She's never done anything like this," Spencer said.

"You know she's covered with scars," the intern said. "I've never seen that. She did all that to herself?"

"Yes."

"Why?"

"To try and make herself feel better," he said. "How bad is she?"

"She coded twice." His tone wasn't hopeful. "Once in the ambulance and once in the ED. We managed to get her back pretty quick both times, but she's lost a tremendous amount of blood. As you can see we're trying to pump her up as quick as we can, but even so, her pressure keeps bottoming out. If she makes it, I'm not certain how much they'll be able to do for the hand. She went deep and cut clean through the radial nerve. Also did some work on the tendons. Best case scenario, half of the hand will be dead."

Spencer stared at Sharon, and felt his shaky walls of defense crumble. He let his gaze soften and searched for any signs of light that might be left in her. Her heart was beating, the ventilator pushed air and in and out of her lungs, and she was getting bag after bag of someone else's blood. And yes, he could see the barest glow of an aura, dark grays, and a dull red. *She's alive, they just need to give her fluids. She's going to be okay.* He reached into his pant pocket and pulled out his wallet. He fished out a card and gave it to the intern, "If she wakes... or if there's any change call me? Please?"

"Sure."

His cell rang.

"You're not supposed to have those in here." The intern said.

"Sorry." And he headed back to the staff area. He pulled out the phone, saw that it was Clay's office, and picked up. The secretary answered. "Dr. Clay was hoping you'd be able to meet with him this morning. He has some paperwork for you to sign."

"When?"

"How quickly could you get here?"

"Fifteen minutes."

"Great. We'll be expecting you," and she hung up.

*

The walk to Clay's was just a few blocks, but as he passed under the color-coded yellow-and-red steel girders of the 'L' Train, his attention flew to a restaurant window across the street. A waitress was pouring coffee, her dark-hair tied back in a bushy ponytail. She was wearing a black tee-shirt with the restaurant's logo of a grinning Cheshire cat. He couldn't be certain, but as he got closer, attempting another look, she looked out and their eyes connected. "Madeleine?" She shook her head no.

The brother had said she'd gone for a jog, not to work. "What the hell?" Maybe everything else he'd said wasn't true either. No way a person could fake what they'd had last night. Not caring that he'd be late for whatever Cliff was about to throw at him, he walked in. The place—a trendy café with mirrored walls and shelves that displayed statuettes of *Alice in Wonderland* characters was doing a brisk breakfast trade, most of the tables filled. A hostess approached, dressed in black like the floor staff. "Table for one?"

"No, I need to speak with Madeleine."

The woman glanced back, spotting Madeleine en route from the exposed kitchen, carrying a loaded tray. "Not a good time."

Madeleine spotted him, shook her head and headed toward the tables in the front. She efficiently unloaded the meals, ditched the tray by the nearby beverage counter, and made a round with two coffee pots.

Through the babbling conversations and the soft music, he could barely make out her voice—like music even when talking. "Regular or decaf?"

"Sir. Sir!" The hostess called after him, as he headed across the busy room.

"Madeleine." She looked back.

"Not here, Spencer." Her voice was terse. She looked down at her order pad.

"I have to talk to you." Not caring that diners on both sides were watching them.

She glanced back at the counter that separated the dining room from the exposed kitchen. A hand rang a bell and yanked off two slips from the order rack. "Wait outside." And without giving him time to respond, she headed back to pick up her order.

Confused, he pushed past the hostess and out the swinging doors. He leaned against the brick wall. Less than a minute later she was there.

"I don't want them to hear," she said, leading him down the block.

Spencer knew from the intense oranges and reds swirling in her aura that she was furious. *What have I done?* He felt his pulse quicken, even in her black uniform, minimal makeup and flat shoes she was beautiful, but more than that.

"Look," her green eyes searched out his, "We shouldn't have done that last night. Damn! I like you, Spencer."

"So what's the problem?" reeling from her words, "I like you too." He tried to smile, but it felt forced—*like* wasn't the right word. *Can't you see I'm falling in love?* He remembered the painting over her bed, and Matthew's warnings.

"I'm an idiot," looking away, wiping her hands on the black apron that held her pads and pens. "I can't be in a relationship right now. Can we please just say that we both had too much to drink and..."

"But you felt something. That wasn't just sex," he said.

"I know...it was great," she admitted, "but I can't. I just can't."

He was stunned, confused, "What am I missing?"

"I can't," and she turned to go.

"Wait!" he put a hand on her shoulder.

She flinched, "Please don't."

"This makes no sense," feeling desperate.

Her back to him, her shoulders sagged, "Trust me. If I told you why, you'd want nothing to do with me."

"I don't believe that," trying to decipher the rapidly changing colors in her aura, and her confusing words.

"Here's the deal, Spencer." Her tone harsh, "I work my ass off to pay the rent, beg for scholarships to keep me here so I can get the training I need. I have a clear three-year plan." She turned to face him, and a tear tracked down her cheek. "If I stay focused, totally dedicated, and I get a shit-load of luck, I can be singing lead roles in major companies by the time I'm twenty-eight. But singers get distracted. Boyfriends, marriage, kids..." She shook her head, "I can't let that happen. And you're exactly the kind of guy I could go for."

"Why does it have to be one or the other?" He was trying to read her thoughts, his own too knotted. "People have relationships *and* careers."

She looked him in the eye and shook her head. "I've got to go back to work. I'm sorry, I really am, but no," and she walked away.

Stunned, he watched as she pushed through the restaurant doors and disappeared. His cell went off again and again. He didn't answer, barely registered the sound. It was hard to breathe. Something had just snapped, and pain, unlike anything he'd ever experienced washed over him. *How can something hurt so much, without anything being broken?*

*

Nearly a thousand miles away in her Brookline home, Joan Shift sensed something was wrong. Her body, now 84, was failing, the hips and knees making it hard for her to get out of chairs, having to catch her breath every time she walked a flight of stairs. But it was none of that which made her reach for the phone, but a growing panic that she had missed something vital—"Why are you still here?" The question she'd puzzled over since Lila's death twenty-six years ago. Why hadn't she been called back? And now, this mounting sense of an impending conflict, but none of the usual signs—no glittering Lucifer—no apparent Chosen one. But inside her, like the early warning systems humans had devised for earthquakes and hurricanes— told her a battle was near.

She gripped the phone and looked out her west-facing windows, it was a beautiful spring day—the gardens ablaze with pink, gold and red azalea, the trees with new lemon-green leaves—but in the sky, above the wispy clouds, there was a layer of shadows, every day growing in number. She called them bad angels, earth-bound demons that fed on and magnified human despair and always gathered at the time of great conflicts.

"What is going on? What have you missed?" It worried her. Loki, Lucifer, Prometheus or whatever name he'd latched onto, was a master of deceit. Had he tricked her? Wouldn't be the first time. She pressed the number to speed dial Spencer.

It rang, but he wasn't picking up. She tried a second and then a third time. Finally, he answered. "Why don't you answer your phone?" she demanded.

"Joan, it's not a good time."

"What's wrong?" knowing the man she'd raised was not one to exaggerate. His tone was off. He was in pain. "What's happened? Are you all right?"

"No," he said, "I think I've just had my heart broken."

"I'm sorry," hating the distance and the mechanical distortions that came with the telephone. She wanted to see him, to see the echo of his mother. He had so many of her traits, and not just the physical resemblance. "What do you mean your heart broken?" Knowing that had been the spear that had felled his mother.

"I can't talk now. I've got a horrible meeting that I'm late for, and probably the hardest decision in my career to make."

"What's that?" she asked, having never grasped the intricacies of his work as a scientist. To her, he was just one in a long line of brilliant humans exploring the hidden worlds and bringing them to light.

"You won't like it," he said, "because whether I go right or I go left, I wind up in bed with the devil."

"Don't say that. It's not funny," her head started to ring. She wondered if this would be the time this aging body would decide to have a stroke, but no... it was literally ringing, like a bell, like a damn alarm clock—*speak of the devil and he will appear.*

"I'll talk to you later, Joan. I got to go."

"No," she shouted. "Wait!" But he'd hung up. Random bits of information flew through her consciousness, *Why are you still here? Because of Spencer. He asked you to stay. He said he needed you. Why weren't you called back? Because of him. But Lila...* She pictured the abomination and how he'd appeared to Lila dressed as a golden angel—he was there at her birth, and stuck close throughout her life.

Frantic, she dialed Spencer, *but the boy could see the angel too, he has visions, he can heal. What if?* He wasn't picking up. *What if this was a trick, like a magician who misdirects your attention while he palms the card?* Or in this case, stays hidden, not going near Spencer—or she would have known. *What if Lila had just been a distraction? What if? No! Lila was chosen... but what if Spencer was, as well? And what if you didn't see it?* She dialed again—"pick up the damn phone." She looked again at the sky, bad angels flying west.

She grabbed her purse and keys, and again regretting how she was tied to such an old body, headed to her electric blue VW Beetle, and sped toward Logan airport.

Chapter Ten

□ □ □

Karel could barely contain his nerves, excitement, fear, the approach of a battle but something more. Something new. He pressed a button in the arm of his chair and gleaming satinwood panels closed over the monitors. "Send up the doctor. I'm ready for my session."

He paced, trying to pierce the cloud in his thoughts, a haze that prevented him from catching a critical truth... *the* critical truth, just out of reach. "Doctor," he moved quickly toward the study door—too quickly, faster than the human eye could follow. The fastidious analyst stiffened. Minnie, behind the doctor, shook her head, letting Karel know he'd let his human façade slip.

"Yes," Minnie said, slipping into the doctor's head. His eyes had just seen Karel vanish and reappear. "It's an authentic Gutenberg," referring to the priceless Bible the doctor had been examining while waiting. "Karel's had it forever."

"Amazing," Beitersmann replied, "such a treat," his rational mind, with a bit of nudging from Minnie, putting what he'd seen into a suitable perspective, *you need to get your glasses checked.*

"Can I get you anything else?" she asked, letting her nimble mind slip out of the doctor's, like an accomplished chef coddling a fragile yolk. Catching as she did tantalizing glimpses of his last session with Karel. Her maker's fear and urgency kindling a desire to know more.

"No, thank you," his pale blue eyes enthralled by hers, his anxiety smoothed away by a pleasant buzz of forgotten sexual possibilities.

"Minnie, leave us. Go find Ian and wait. I'll call you when you're needed. Doctor," Karel began, barely noting Minnie's sullen exit. "I can't tell you how helpful our last session was—a weight off my shoulders." Leading him to his seat, and hoping Minnie's mental intrusion hadn't clouded the man's mind.

"Of course," Beitersmann settled down. "Where do you want to begin?"

Outside the library, Minnie fumed. "Do this. Do that, just don't ask questions." At times, it was all she could do to keep from exploding. Her feelings for Karel beyond words—love, hate and this ache for something too nebulous to name. At times, she could understand his twisted need for therapy, her own emotions too hot and confused. She didn't want to leave, but Karel's dismissive order was like a force pulling her toward the stairs and out to the seawall where Ian now sat staring at the ocean. *Why can't you be more like your brother? Why can't you be content?* As she pondered, her body shifted to yellow mist and drifted toward the center hall. "NO!" the sound of her voice was louder than she'd intended, and with it her forward movement stopped and she hovered. Raw fear, electric and exciting, held her frozen. Yes, she had questioned her maker, but never disobeyed. And before she could think of all the reasons why not to pursue this mutinous course of action—like he'd probably kill her—she pulled the mist back and transformed into a shiny black fly with iridescent green eyes. From there it was a quick hop to the library door, a few stiff-legged steps under the crack, and expecting at any moment to be discovered and turned back to sand, she flew on manic wings to the ceiling and camouflaged herself in a swarm of painted flies that hovered around mounds of horse shit and hay in the scene of Hercules cleaning the Aegean stable. Through prismatic eyes she looked down and saw hundreds of Karels and could catch every word. Her excitement made it hard to focus on the unfolding session below—*you just disobeyed your maker and master... and you're still alive... at least for now.*

"I need to talk about a particular aspect of my relationship with my Creator," Karel began.

"Yes, *your Creator*," the doctor's elbows on the arms of the chair, his fingers joined in a steeple.

"It's this, I told you how I was cast out—sent to hell." He saw the analyst stiffen. "I was banished—it was horrible, but the Creator still had, and has, use for me. It doesn't love me. I know this, because you can't be so cruel to one you truly love, but It does use me."

From her vantage point, it was all Minnie could do to stop from screaming, as Karel's complaints mirrored her own. *Hypocrite!*

"In what way used?" the therapist asked.

"Thank you," and unable to stay seated, Karel began to walk across the carpet, careful to keep his speed mortal. "The Creator plays games with humans. I'd say it's the same game over and over, but there are twists. Each time we play it's a little different. And my role is adversary, the black king in a twisted game of chess."

"Describe the game."

"Of course. The Creator chooses one mortal every century or so—although lately it's more frequent. It's gotten to where one game stops and the next begins with little—or in this case, no—break. In the beginning they were much less often, and between the games I'm a prisoner, chained to a world of darkness and despair you can't imagine—torture beyond reason. I don't mind the games, because like now, I'm not in hell. I'm here, and as you observed, my existence here is good, wonderful even. And the other stunning revelation—and thank you—I don't hate humans. I did and now I don't. I haven't for a while, in fact with some," picturing Lara, "I develop an incredible fondness; it could be love." He hated the way his thoughts wandered, *stay focused*, "but the games...it's like this," his feet moving one in front of the next, wearing a path around the edges of the massive carpet—a priceless silk woven with a fantastic hunt scene of lions, unicorns and Crusaders on horseback. "The Chosen one represents some quality in man, and they must pick their path. Early on these were primitive, the Creator on one huge ego trip—*will man worship me, even if I make his life miserable? Is man capable of sacrificing his own life for those he loves, for his Creator?* The past few centuries they've become more frequent and more subtle. Like the one now."

"Describe it," Beitersmann said. "Tell me everything about the current game, although from how you've laid it out, they seem more like tests than games."

"Exactly! That's the word...tests. The one now centers on a brilliant young doctor, who has the power to create something that will radically alter the course of civilization...It's a new drug unlike anything that has come before."

"You pause," Beitersmann remarked. "You said that these chosen ones must choose—What is the young doctor's choice?"

Karel stared at his feet, and then up at the soaring ceiling, and the Roman mural of the seven labors of Hercules.

Minnie froze–*can he see me?* Her antennae spasmed and for a horrible moment it was as though he were staring straight back. She thought of Ian, and then of Spencer, who she'd watched since he was a babe. *I don't want to die. I'm sorry, I won't disobey again. Please don't kill me.* And with that pathetic thought came a horrible realization. Karel had told her that he'd made many demons before her and Ian. *So where are they now?*

"I don't know." Karel shook his head and looked at the doctor in his starched white shirt and prim bow tie, "In the beginning it was so easy to know what the game—the test—was about. Now, it's less clear, which doesn't mean the purpose isn't there just..." He stood behind his chair. "Let me tell you how these tests work. Once the chosen is picked, the Creator sends its champion—her name is Joan, although it wasn't always. Her real name is unpronounceable by humans and she couldn't stand being called Gabriel." *Stop wandering, damnit!* She's similar to me, although from the generation the Creator made after mine. She's not human, yet when she's on earth she wears human flesh."

"Am I supposed to believe that the same is true for you, that what I see in front of me is like a suit of clothes?"

Interesting, Karel thought, no hint of irony here, no condescension. He was hungry to know how this brilliant little man was putting it all together—*no peeking.* "I'm different. In many ways I'm closer to the Creator than anything that has come since. I've often thought that's why I was thrown out...I represent a threat. I am the first born; I am the heir to heaven. But no, I do not wear human flesh. When freed from hell, I can assume any form I wish—it takes little effort, other than some will and consistency."

"I see, and how do you and this Joan participate in your Creator's game?"

"Quite simply we pull at the Chosen. Each of us trying to influence him or her to follow our path. But ultimately it is they—the human—who decides."

"So free will is important to your Creator."

"Yes, but why? Why does It care about free will? I know better than any It doesn't care to be questioned." Karel stopped, a hammering inside his mind, an echo of the angel's trumpet as paralyzing fear washed through him. His head swiveled, *is she here?* Searching for her silvery light. But nothing, he stared at the doctor, who obviously wasn't hearing the sound, an idea struggling toward the surface, something big. "Help me," he said.

Minnie stared at Karel—*what's wrong with him?* Something was freaking him out. It gave her a horrible feeling, a taste of her own frailty—truly no more than a fly to be crushed or swatted from the sky. She and Ian were nothing to him, not compared to his humans, or his pathetic attempts to what? *Overthrow heaven? Find his way back into the Creator's good graces—not likely.*

"With your young doctor, how do you hope to influence him?" the therapist asked.

Karel focused on the question, as though catching the rhythm of a distant melody. "Each of the Chosen," thinking back through the millennia, "they're archetypes, a single human representing a greater principle. The doctor is the scientist, the alchemist, the shaman. Oh my..."

"What?"

Since Karel had left Spencer's presence when he was a young boy, he'd had Minnie and Ian protect and watch from a distance. Through their reports, he'd followed Spencer's every move, and what was most striking about the young man—other than his intolerance for injustice—was how methodical he was with his research.

"Karel," Beitersmann prompted, "you need to give voice to what you're thinking. Otherwise, I can't help."

"Sorry, but I think the doctor's choice has to do with how he proceeds in his quest for truth. Ever since he was a child, he's followed a careful path. One step leads to the next, his learning, his research. He never skips a step and that's what causes him so much pain now. He's achieved something tremendous, but is blocked from the next step. He can't find the way to move forward with a drug that he believes will relieve the worst human suffering."

"And so you'll tempt him," Beitersmann added.

"Yes," Karel's hands at the sides of his head, feeling as though it might blow apart, "I'll show him what he most wants, let him know that he can succeed."

"How is that bad, especially if this drug truly works?"

"Interesting...everyone assumes that I'm bad. Why is that? But yes, it will be his vanity that causes him to stray, to leave his careful ways. But now I know why. Up to now, I've been going by instinct, and what's worked in the past. You know–a woman, money, fame. But with him, it all comes down to fucking parables—*haste makes waste*, versus *slow and steady wins the race.*" He laughed, not caring that his voice was too loud. And then he stopped, his face contorted, "But why? What am I missing?"

"I think you've told me," the doctor's voice low and unflustered by his patient's antics.

"What have I told you?" Karel sat in the chair and stared at Beitersmann.

The old man nodded, a hint of a smile, "You said that the Creator arranges these tests. You also said that at first they came far apart, and now they're more frequent. Yes?"

"Yes," Karel sensed something tremendous about to be born, he eased from his chair to the floor, and like a child at story hour, sat cross legged in front of the doctor.

"Let's use a metaphor of a baker—that's a type of creator isn't it?"

"Yes," Karel started to rock.

"So a baker puts a cake in the oven, and knows that it takes a certain amount of time to rise and be done. For the first half hour, there's no need to look, in fact to do so, might cause the cake to fall, but as the expected time gets closer, what does he do, but checks and test. That is another meaning of the word. In fact, I think that's what they call the thin metal wire a baker sticks in the cake to see if it's done—it's a tester."

Karel looked up at the doctor, and knew that this was the absolute truth. "The cake is done."

"I suspect so, or nearly there. Why else test so often?"

"It's what I thought," Karel said softly, "Then I must not lose, because if the cake is done, and no longer needs testing? I have no more purpose. The Creator will cast me into the pit for all eternity; I will not go. But still... there's something I'm not seeing. If in fact this is the last Chosen then something about Spencer Williams and his drug is of critical importance, but what? What don't I see?" He stared pleadingly at the doctor. "Please, help me understand."

It was more than Minnie could stand, her own realizations fueling a rage she'd never known. *We mean nothing to him. Disposable! Do his work and then... he will kill us. Of course, he's made thousands of us, and where the fuck are they now? Where are my brothers and sisters? What have you done to them? And Ian...sweet Ian, what will you do to him?* And the answer that kept returning was irrefutable—*we will finish our purpose and he will unmake us. All he cares about is himself.* It was all she could do to stop from shifting forms and screaming at him. *But what's the point? That's his nature—he is vanity personified. He will never change, and you and Ian mean nothing.*

Beitersmann stared at the tips of his fingers, "A few minutes back when you mentioned free will, you seemed frightened, like a child who's been naughty and is waiting for his punishment."

"You're not wrong," Karel answered, "go on."

"And throughout this story of the Creator, the Chosen ones, this avenging angel...at the heart of all of it is man's ability to choose. Everything in your story is predicated on free will, and something about that just made you afraid. Even now, I see your expression darken, what are you feeling? Put it to words."

Karel struggled to speak, as again the angel's trumpet pounded in his head and it took all his strength to keep from losing his form. Like he was falling and the floor was slipping out from under and a sucking hell mouth gaped beneath his feet. "Fear," he sputtered, "If humankind lost free will," the trumpet blared louder. He grasped the sides of his head, literally holding his form together, and pushed through the gripping panic. He stared at the doctor, who seemed genuinely concerned. He clung to the train of thought and felt his strength slowly return and with it a realization of clarion purity, "If humankind lost free will...I would have won." And the trumpet stopped. "That's what this test is about. It's not just Spencer's choice and his free will, but the whole shooting match is up for grabs."

Minnie took Karel's meltdown as her cue to escape. She dove from the ceiling through an open window, furious and exhilarated. She had disobeyed and she was still alive—*you made a choice*, and she pumped her tiny wings as fast as they could go, out to the seawall where Ian sat staring at the waves. There was so much she needed to tell him, but as she touched down still in her fly form, she felt her master's command. *"Come, you are needed"*.

Karel felt drained and yet deliciously alive. Still looking at the doctor, he finally let himself peak inside his thoughts. The man had decided that he had paranoid schizophrenia, serious daddy issues, and the delusional belief that he was the devil. Beitersmann then reasoned that Karel appeared to be doing no harm, and he was getting paid $5000 an hour.

Fair enough, Karel thought, as Minnie appeared at the door, ready to drive the doctor back to Manhattan. "Doctor, I cannot tell you how helpful this has been." Still feeling the echo of the angel's horn—*a battle approaches. . . possibly the final one; I am not ready.* "Minnie, call a cab for the doctor. And then bring your brother. I have tasks for the two of you. And we have precious little time."

Chapter Eleven

□ □ □

"It's just boilerplate, all standard." Clifford Clay said, from behind his expansive desk. His shrewd eyes were unwavering, taking in everything from Spencer's disheveled clothes to his rattled state.

Spencer was struggling to focus in this imposing light-filled office, with its floor-to-ceiling glass-fronted bookshelves, wall of plaques, awards and diplomas, and deliberately distressed leather chairs. His thoughts pulled first to Madeleine's rejection, and then to poor Sharon, *why didn't I hospitalize her?*

In front of him, Clifford had placed a two-inch stack of legal documents, scattered throughout were plastic blue stick-on arrows indicating places to sign or initial. "I need to look at this first."

"Of course," Clay said, his good 'ol boy accent in place, a few fishing trophies interspersed with the other awards to offer it some cred. "But let's be clear," he leaned forward, elbows on the desk, chin resting on his fingertips. "What you want is a lot. For me to go out on a limb for a junior researcher—albeit a brilliant one—is going to make many of your peers and seniors unhappy."

"I know," Spencer tried to meet Clifford's gaze, so full of lies beneath his navy pin-stripe, from the put-on accent to the fake concern, to whatever booby traps had been planted in the documents. But he sensed something deeper, a gnawing hunger. The intense gray eyes that stared at him, battering at his brain—*sign the papers, do it now!* "I have to look at these," he said, "I'll do it as fast as I can, but I'll need a few days."

"I see," Clifford was not pleased, "I guess I misunderstood you, Dr. Williams. From yesterday's discussion, I thought your objective was to aggressively develop XU472, move it from animal studies into the first round of human investigations. To use your words, 'Do what it takes to get this to the people who need it as fast as I can.' Based on that conversation, I've just spent the better part of yesterday afternoon and this morning having the university's legal team prepare standard agreements that you must sign prior to my approving the kind of resources you want. I need to protect the university's interests. I am operating in good faith, Dr. Williams. I am less certain of your...intentions. I've been doing this for a very long time, and I know all the different ways this can go. I will not be played, or have the university put in a position of underwriting a project, only to have our researcher pull up stakes the minute he gets a better offer."

Spencer knew that Clay intended to cheat him. It made his blood boil, but he saw no other way. His research had hit a roadblock. The important thing was that the drug be developed and get into the hands of those—like Sharon, like his mother—who desperately needed it. But looking at Clay, like some well-tended serpent, coiled and ready to strike, he knew that to not carefully read those contracts would be plain stupid. "I do want to get this started," he said, "but I'm not an idiot, Cliff," deliberately using his first name. "If you think I'd sign anything without looking at it, you're crazy." He could see the older man shift slightly, he wasn't about to let Spencer—or more importantly XU472 slip away. His thoughts filtered across the space, fragments and images, and again that gaping hunger—*give it to me. I want it. Mine!*

Clifford picked up the phone, "Maggie, Dr. Williams is going to need the conference room for the next couple hours." He hung up and looked at Spencer, "I assume, if you're in such a hurry that you can do this now."

Seeing no way out, Spencer agreed.

"Fine," Clay pushed the documents to the edge of the desk, "Maggie will get you set up. Let's say we meet again at noon—I'll buy lunch and we can finish this then."

*

Fifteen hundred miles away, at Logan Airport, Joan boarded a flight to Chicago. It infuriated her the way Spencer wouldn't answer his phone, but at least she'd managed to leave her flight number and arrival time on his machine.

Beyond that, she hated airplanes, but they were fast, not as fast as the abomination could move. But until she could shed this body she'd have to make do—no time now to find a new host. Although, judging by the dull ache in her chest, this one wasn't going to last much longer. She gave the ticket to the attendant, the woman smiled, "This must be your birthday," she said.

"Excuse me?" her thoughts miles away.

"You've just been bumped up to first class."

"Thank you," and taking her boarding pass she ambled along the ramp to the plane.

"Lucky you," a lean man in sweatshirt and fatigues whispered.

She considered offering him her seat, but the prospect of more space in the next few hours to think was too good to pass up. She found her seat, stowed her bulky embroidered purple bag under the seat in front of her, and stared out the window. There was something too familiar about what she was feeling—the start of a battle, but she'd never been so ill prepared. Outside it was drizzling as the engines surged and they taxied to the runway. A Bell—actually more like a trumpet—blared in her head as a handsome flight attendant looked across at her, "please fasten your seatbelt," he directed, flashing perfect white teeth.

"Right," and marveling at her luck—first class and the seat next to her empty, she put it on. She leaned back as they accelerated forward and then up. *It would be so nice to be free from this body.* The airplane's lift reminded her of what it was like to be free of the human flesh.

Dark thoughts pounded her. The doubt she sometimes felt at the Creator's wisdom, a cancer that could render her useless. *God works in mysterious ways,* she reminded herself, enjoying the naive human aphorisms that put a whitewash on the biggest mystery in the universe. *Got to take a leap of faith...course you've got to look before you leap.* She smiled, and barely noticed when a steaming cup of herbal tea was placed in front of her. It smelled delicious, fruity with a hint of cinnamon and something else, something old. She settled back in the plush seat and took a sip, warm and comforting, and then she stopped—she didn't order this. And what was that smell, the taste of it now at the back of her tongue something metallic and something else—*mandrake.* Horrified, she looked up and saw the handsome flight attendant smiling back at her. "Demon!" she tried to shout, but the words barely whispered from her throat as the cup fell from her hand. Horrified, and unable to move, her limbs useless, she watched as the grinning flight attendant approached. "Oh dear," he quipped, leaning over her with a wet rag from the kitchen, "Clean up on aisle five." And as he mopped up he whispered "mandrake to intoxicate, clay to hold you in the flesh and adamantine to bind you to the earth." He chuckled and the last thing she heard, "You lose, he wins."

*

Minnie watched the pilot and co-pilot from her perch inside the cockpit—literally a fly on the bulkhead. Her eyes played over the scene, like a child's prism, the image fragmented and then pulled together as it traveled to the insect's brain. She shifted her head, sensing Ian back in first-class. She was a fly and yet was still herself, all her thoughts and burgeoning emotions, jammed into the tiny body.

Ian was smiling, so happy, a feeling so much harder for her to find. He'd finished his job. The Creator's champion—the silver angel—was bound, drugged and unconscious, trapped in her fleshy casing. Now her turn. She looked first at the co-pilot—Jim—early forties, not a hair out of place, married, two children. The pilot—Bob—was twelve years older and drank, but never when he flew, divorced, lived alone, dyed his hair and took pills that were supposed to make him feel less sad and empty, but didn't.

She started with the younger co-pilot, entering his thoughts like a wisp of smoke, letting him picture his wife—Kelly—at home. A pleasant daydream, Kelly playing with the kids, an Audi pulls up; it's pilot Bob, tall and distinguished—his friend and mentor. *What's he doing there?* Jim wonders. Pilot Bob greets Kelly, puts a hand on the back of her head, they kiss—the children are watching. The hand slides down her back and cups her ass. "Kids." She says, "stay out here, Uncle Bob and I need to discuss a few things." She puts her hand in his, she licks her lips, "I want you so bad. Come on lover, give it to me. Do me. Do me rough."

And then Minnie moved on to pilot Bob—who turned fast and looked at his partner, "What did you say?"

"I didn't say anything," Jim shook his head, "just weird," and he reached up and checked the oxygen levels—*what the fuck was that about?*

But pilot Bob is sure he heard it, the co-pilot's whispering, *"faggot. That's why your wife left you. Everyone knows. Just a big joke, can't wait to get your job. Drunk old faggot!"* "Jim!" he swiveled, "Shut the fuck up!"

"What are you talking about?" the co-pilot, looked across at his friend, a man he's known since the training academy, something on his finger—a ring he'd never noticed, one of Kelly's that she made in her basement studio. *Why would she give him that?* The images suddenly stronger, the two of them naked in bed, his wife's head thrown back. She's screaming, as Bob thrusts into her.

"Jim!" the pilot's face is beet red, he's furious and scared—everything he's tried to hide. *"Faggot, we all know, everyone knows. They're going to fire your faggot ass! Don't think I haven't seen you watching me at the gym, you pathetic queer."*

"Shut the fuck up!" He's not going to take this shit from any little punk. He's out of his seat, his fist landing hard on the side of co-pilot Jim's smug face.

The younger man is dazed, but always a scrapper he responds fast and without thought—the image of his friend betraying him too real to be anything but fact. How could he have missed it—been so blind.

Minnie from her perch, enjoys the prismatic images. Noting how her fly body twitches at the scent of blood. She rubs her front legs together, as co-pilot Jim, who's got youth and reach on his side, lands a solid hook on pilot Bob's jaw; she hears the crack of bone, and watches a kaleidoscope spray of blood and teeth—so pretty.

One down, she muses, and looking at the crazed and miserable co-pilot, his fists smeared with blood, his uniform disheveled, his cap on the ground, she hones in on his darkest fear and insecurity—*now you've done it! What am I going to do? I'll lose my job, I won't be able to make the mortgage. She'll take the kids and leave me.* As she picks away at the man's shattered confidence, she thinks of her master. *Just what the hell is so special about these humans? So fragile, so easily influenced.* She knows she's jealous, but how can Karel be so blind? Him and his therapy, can't he see that he's doing to her and Ian exactly what he's always whining about the Creator doing to him.

With a vengeance, she rips into co-pilot Jim's mind, finds the voice of his father, and using it whispered, "Turn off the auto-pilot."

He does.

Then still in his father's voice, she gently explains how what he has done, is unforgivable, and at this point the honorable way out is to take the pistol from the lockbox, put the barrel in his mouth and pull the trigger, which he does.

Letting her fly body land in a shallow pool of blood, she

shifts back into human form, dressed in a sexy and stylish red, white and blue stewardess outfit and jaunty cap. She looks at the unconscious pilot with his ruined jaw, and his dead companion. Reaching daintily between the bucket seats she grabs the microphone and switches it on. "Ladies and gentlemen," she announces, hearing her voice through the locked cabin door, while admiring her reflection in the blood-spattered chrome. "We regret to inform you that we've experienced a mechanical failure." She feels the plane lurch and watches the altimeters spin as they lose altitude. "At this time, I'd ask the flight crew to please prepare the cabin, as you are all... about to... die."

Chapter Twelve

□ □ □

Alone in Clay's conference room, with its massive mahogany table and modernist chrome and leather chairs on wheels, Spencer struggled through each sentence of legalese. This was no "boilerplate," but did it matter? Between the dense paragraphs, with their numbered and lettered sub-sections, he caught the drift—more like an avalanche. His work and his compound would essentially become Clay's. It didn't state that blatantly, but with every passing sentence, he saw how his ownership was whittled down to whatever he'd already published—he would become a footnote in the development of XU472. On all future papers his name would come after Clifford's and he would be removed as primary investigator, even though he would do all the work. When applications would be filed with the Food and Drug Administration it would be Clifford's name on the documents. He thought back through a recent conversation he'd had with his father. "Son, if there is money to be made from your work, or awards to be had, people will try to muscle in. Don't let them steal your thunder, Spencer."

He flipped pages, glancing at sections labeled: Patents, Licensing, Rights, Reversions, Indemnification, Assignment, all of which he could largely decipher. But sprinkled throughout were bits, like if this was all being done under the auspices of Gray University, why was there a second corporate entity—ABC Grayson, Inc.—being mentioned? It appeared multiple times, especially in the sections on sale and/or retention of Rights. His first thought was that it must be some corporate entity the University used, but why would they need that?

He pushed the contracts aside and looked around. He saw a computer set up at a small table at the back of the room. He then thought about the bug planted in his lab. Was Clay watching him? *Do I even care?* He booted up the computer and Googled ABC Grayson, Inc. What appeared had nothing to do with Gray University. It was a Chicago-based pharmaceutical consulting firm. He clicked on the first link and pulled up a slick website with headings like "Market Research," "Product Development," "Investment Opportunities," "Industry Initiatives" and "Partnerships with Healthcare Practitioners." He clicked for contact information. There were no names only an email address and an 800 number.

He pulled out his cell—he'd turned off the ringer before his meeting with Cliff—in the past hour and a half he'd racked up ten voice mails. He clicked on the log and saw four from Joan, three from that Lara woman, one from his father, one from his half-brother Michael, and the last from the hospital. He pressed play and heard Sharon's intern, "Dr. Williams you said you wanted to know if there'd been any change in Sharon Lahey. I'm sorry to tell you that she went into cardiac arrest again. We managed to resuscitate her, but she's developed DIC and I don't know if we'll be able to stabilize her. She's critical and the prognosis is poor." He left his beeper number.

It felt like he'd been sucker punched. Seeing Sharon in the ICU, he'd let himself relax—thought she'd be okay, just get some blood into her and everything would be fine. Apparently not and now her body was rejecting the donor blood, a condition that if it wasn't rapidly stopped would kill her.

He needed to go to her. Five minutes alone with her and he could help. He looked at the contracts–no way he'd sign them. He grabbed them off the table, rolled them up and shoved them into his jacket pocket, a good chunk sticking out. The room had a single exit, and he headed out past Cliff's secretary.

"Dr. Williams," the short dark-haired woman looked up as he rushed past, "where are you going?"

"I have an emergency," he shouted back, heading for the elevators

She shot up and ran toward him, her navy pumps clomping on the marble floor, "Did you sign the paperwork for Dr. Clay?"

"I haven't had a chance to go through it. I'll look at it later. I'll get them back tomorrow at the latest."

"I'm sorry," she kept running, "those are not to leave the building."

Why is Clifford in such a hurry for those damn papers? And why is she so nervous? Like she's been given orders that under no circumstances am I to leave with these? Then two fast realizations; first, those contracts had not been prepared by the university's lawyers, and second, Clifford did not want them to leave the building lest they be seen by someone who could unravel what he was up to. He glanced from the elevators to the exit sign above the stairwell. He bolted for the stairs. As he sprinted down, he put a hand on the contracts to make certain they didn't fall out. When he hit the ground floor he darted for the exit. Behind him he heard the phone at the security desk. He didn't slow, wondering what lengths Clay would go to retrieve these. But no time for that. His thoughts now on Sharon, he raced toward the medical center.

As he sprinted across busy streets, and beneath the steel work of the 'L', he knew what he intended would be risky. The only person who knew of his healing talent was Joan, and possibly his stepmother Allie, who in quiet moments would ask him how he knew she had cancer those many years ago—but she only suspected. With Joan it was another story, "*being able to heal is a direct channeling of the Creator's power—it's not uncommon,*" she'd say, and then chuckle, "*but it freaks the hell out of people. Unless of course you're in a revival tent.*" She'd been so right and during his medical training there had been close calls. His pediatrics rotation had been the worst, kids with advanced cancers, and knowing that if he could lay on hands, many—not all—could be helped. There'd been one, Manuel Rivera—terminal leukemia— he'd been an intern and knew the kid with his bald head on his third course of poisonous chemo and radiation wouldn't make it to his seventh birthday. Every day the parents would ask how their son was doing, were the treatments helping? Desperation in their eyes as they prayed for a miracle, knowing that those didn't often come—certainly not to people like them. So one night when he'd been on call, he'd gone to Manuel's room. He'd felt the cancerous cells inside the boy's marrow, like spores traveling through his bloodstream and lymph nodes. Manuel had been asleep and Spencer had put a hand on his forehead, he'd whispered, "don't be afraid." He'd helped him to sit and held him tight, feeling his heart beating fast in his bony chest. "It's okay," he'd murmured, letting the sickness flow into him, feeling the energy of his own body transforming it, making it well. And that's when the rounding night nurse had come in. "What are you doing?" she'd asked, thinking the worst and wondering if Spencer were dangerous and if she should call security. It was the boy who'd made it right, "I was crying," Manuel had said, "Dr. Williams was just trying to make me feel better...I was scared. He's not doing anything bad."

Now as the medical center came into view, he wondered where Manuel was today. He'd be a teenager. He'd left the hospital a week later, the entire medical staff amazed at how effective the last round of treatments had been—not a cancerous cell to be found—a miracle of modern medicine.

As he sped through the spacious lobby, past the massive bronze of children playing hopscotch, his cell buzzed. It was that drug company woman again. He felt torn and as he walked into the stairwell, he pressed answer.

"Spencer, it's Lara. I know this is not a good time, but I just wanted to see how you were doing...is your patient okay?"

"Not great," heading up the stairs, "I'm going to see her now."

"She's at the medical center?"

"Yeah—surgical ICU."

"Can I meet you there?"

He just needed to get to Sharon, taking the steps two at a time. "I got to go." He jammed the phone back in his pocket.

He got out on four, *please let her be alive, please let her be alive.* Using his ID, he clicked through the electronic door. Her cubicle was crowded with the cardiac code team, the intern was there and a senior female doctor in a long white coat barking out orders. A tech in blue scrubs hurriedly made adjustments to the ventilator as a nurse pulled drugs out of the red crash cart. The floor was littered with discarded needle casings, bloody gauze pads, and gloves. Sharon's bed was tilted back into reverse Trandelenberg, a last ditch effort to try and keep her blood pressure from bottoming out. A shrink like him was the last person they'd want in there, but he wasn't about to ask permission.

He glanced at the monitor and saw that her heart was slow and thready. His breath caught when she missed a beat, and then two—little stretches of flat lining. The female doctor—no more than a few years past her residency looked at him. The young intern spoke, "he's her psychiatrist."

Somehow that seemed to appease her. She gave Spencer a sad smile, and said nothing as he touched the tips of Sharon's fingers poking from her swaddled and mangled wrist. This was less than ideal, but he couldn't pull off a full embrace with this crowd. Her touch was cool, her pulse slipping away. He closed his eyes, hopefully they'd think he was just praying–*where are you?* He shut out the noise, the electronic dings and blips of the life-support equipment, and searched for her essence, for the tiny stream of life he'd need to gain entry. *Where are you?* Joan's long ago instructions, passed through his head, *"It's like a tail,"* she'd explain, *"you have to grab on and let it take you for the ride. There's a trick to it, if you try too hard it'll slip away, and once you have it ride gently—it's the exquisite balance between doing and not doing."* A gentle shiver passed through his fingers and up his arm. *Got you,* letting the connection strengthen, feeling the death pull inside Sharon, her blood weak and thin, her organs shutting down. Life was seeping out of her, her soul beginning to separate from the flesh. He shuddered as random images flew from her dying brain into his—things she'd spoken of in therapy, a brutal rape when she'd been a little girl, beatings from her stepfather, her boyfriend calling her *"pathetic, useless,"* her mother's anger, *"You dirty little liar. Liars go to hell,"* when she'd tried to tell her what her stepfather had done—was doing—to her. He took it all in, his healer's sense letting it mix with his own energy, repairing the damage and then sending that back through his fingertips and into hers.

"Spencer," a women's voice intruded, breaking the connection. "Dr. Williams."

He opened his eyes, glanced up at the monitor—Sharon's pulse more stable, no longer skipping beats.

He turned, his gaze connecting with the Hispanic intern, and then with Lara, who looked every inch the drug rep, from her three-thousand dollar navy skirt suit, to her legal briefcase on wheels. Gently he released Sharon's hand and stepped away, feeling totally drained and disoriented as he always did after a healing. It was a side effect that usually only lasted a few minutes, and one that Joan had explained as having to do with the person's ailment traveling out of them and into him. *"It won't stay,"* she'd chuckle. *"But it can sure pack a punch."* Worse than that, in this ICU filled with the sick and the dying, his defenses were now totally breached. He could feel the thoughts of the others in the room looking at him, wondering what kind of strange psychiatrist this was. He needed to get out of there, but desperately wanted to know that Sharon would be okay.

"I know this couldn't be worse timing, but can we please talk?" Lara asked, her voice warm.

He looked back at Sharon, as the electronic blood pressure cuff inflated, and slowly decompressed. He watched the numbers pop up on the monitor—she was stabilizing, although there was something strange about her aura as it shaded from bruised reds and yellows to silver. A sigh escaped his lips. He didn't want to go with this Lara, but it was too hard to resist. "Sure."

He stepped outside the glass-fronted room, his eyes still fixed on Sharon, and then on the monitor—her pulse creeping back to normal, the pressure steady. Around her, the Code Team started to relax, as they too tracked her progress back from death.

"This must be awful for you," Lara said. "Is there someplace we can talk?"

"Yeah," just wanting to be someplace quiet, someplace away from the ravenous shadows of the death demons. "There's a family room. We can use that."

Adjacent to the ICU, the carpeted room was dimly lit and furnished with comfortable chairs and couches in soothing blues and browns. A flat screen TV stood to one side—the sound turned down—and a bucket of plastic toys and picture books for kids.

"If these walls could talk," she said.

"Yeah," he agreed, and wondered if anyone from Sharon's family would show up. Knowing what he did about her, he doubted it. "It's the bad news room."

"I hope not today," she settled into an armchair as he did the same. "Not to be cruel, but you look like hell."

"Long day," he stared at her and it helped him regain focus. She was trying to feel him out, set him up for another pitch. Much as he wanted to dismiss her, he found her oddly likeable and with an insecurity she was trying to hide, and something else—she had passion for what she did.

"I see you have a bunch of contracts in your pocket."

He reached down, the thick wad, sticking half out of his pocket. "Kind of obvious, aren't they."

"So you've signed with someone."

"No." The fog from the healing over-ridden by the sick feeling left from Cliff's maneuverings, "but I probably will. It's what I need to do to stay here and get the facilities I need for the work."

"The devil you know."

"Yes."

"Spencer, you said you haven't signed anything yet. From what I remember about Clay, if he wants something he doesn't give you a lot of time to make up your mind. When he pressured me for first authorship on a paper I'd written on immunotherapy, he had me sit in a room with a single door, told me either I'd sign that he was the principal investigator, or I could kiss my lab space good bye."

"And?"

"That's when I walked. I tore the damn thing up, put it neatly on the table and left. And you?"

For the first time all morning, he smiled, "I ran away."

"Smart...can I look at them?"

"Sure," he pried them out of his pocket and handed them across.

Lara spread them on an end table and turned on a lamp.

He sat back, noting how she became all business, her manicured fingers flicked through the pages. A strand of blond fell across her forehead and she tucked it behind her ear. He thought of Madeleine, how she'd been last night, and then her rejection this morning in the café—the two women opposites. One, who made his chest ache—*how could that have been just sex? A random fling?* She'd said he was the type she could go for...so what was wrong? There had been a connection; she had to have felt it. And this one, cool and beautiful, all business, but something more...

Lara, intent in her reading, shook her head and stopped. "What the?"

"What's wrong?" Her aura swirled as a bright yellow flame of fear and confusion shot from her chest.

She looked at him, her index finger on a paragraph that mentioned ABC Grayson, Inc.

"Who are they?" he asked. "I went on the Internet—it's some kind of marketing firm..."

"No it's not," she bit her lip, one finger holding her place while she scanned the next pages, putting a finger between the pages every time the mystery corporation was mentioned.

"Who are they?"

"Shit! I don't know how to tell you this...and you have to believe me that I knew nothing about this...the ABC corporations are part of Global. They get set up with all the major research universities to provide a corporate structure whereby the company can securely do business with a university."

He knew she was telling the truth, and could see this made her furious. "So someone else from Global is after me and XU472, but is going through Clay. We can assume it's that Duane guy." Feeling her rage, as she realized she too was being played. Clearly, he wasn't the only one contending with a snake.

"I'd say that's a safe bet....You sign over your principal investigator status, Clay signs with Global and becomes a rich man, probably one with a Nobel Prize. So let me give you an option." She reached down and unsnapped her case. Inside were neatly arranged plastic files; she pulled a blue one out with his name on the tab. "Here, and take all the time you want. But let me walk you through the major points, other than those few that are deal breakers from the Global side, you can cross out and write in whatever you want. In fact, I'd recommend you double or even triple all the financials—we'll pay. I'll make sure of that. But here's what's not negotiable...it's a ten year exclusive contract. That's purely protective because of the long time it takes for human investigations and for dealing with the FDA. All patents for both the compound and the process become the property of Global—we are a for-profit, publicly traded Fortune 500 corporation and XU472 will make us, and our shareholders, a great deal of money. However, you are now, and will always be, the lead investigator. All publications related to this will have you as first author. And I have no doubt that if your compound has even a fraction of the promise we think it has, you will win a Nobel Prize. Maybe even two, the science for the process and the medicine for the actual compound."

Spencer's head swam as he listened. He also caught what lay behind her words. She was furious, and confused and betrayed.

She leaned forward and handed him the blue folder. It was surprisingly thin, and as he took it she repeated, "You don't have to read it now. Take your time, get a lawyer—I would. This is a big decision. I know I'm giving you the hard sell—it's my job. But I promise that if you come to work for us, I will guarantee that XU472 is put on the fast track. You will have facilities and staff—anything you need.... I wasn't going to tell you this next part, because it'll make it seem like I was over confident, and frankly I've put myself at risk assuming you'd eventually say yes, but I'm in the process of clearing out the single-most fabulous research facility Global has to offer...it's in the Florida Keys. So not only will you be able to do your work at the speed and with the resources you want, but you'll be living in a place that's close to paradise."

Amidst the agonies of his awful morning he found himself getting excited—it felt like a dream. And at the end of the day no drug ever made it to market without it belonging to someone. "What if people who need the drug can't afford it?" he asked.

"There'll be an indigent program. We have it for all our drugs. All any doctor needs to do is fill out a paper saying his or her patient can't pay and we send a free supply—it takes less than two minutes to complete and they fax the form."

He nodded, and not caring that he was being rude, he stared at her, studying the eddies of her aura, her scent, her emotions. She was complex and contradictory—honest, but still concealing things. She'd been rattled by Clifford's contract and this intrigue within her own company. "When do you want my answer?"

She smiled, "Now is good, but no. Take your time. Have an attorney vet it. My card is in the pocket with all my numbers. I'm at the Drake. If you have any questions—any—call me. I don't care what time of day or night."

"I thought you said you were leaving today."

"I was... now I'm not."

His focus was pulled as the TV screen flashed and a news bulletin came on. It was showing footage of a plane, beneath it he could just make out, "*DC10 from Boston to Chicago crashed in lake Erie.*" "Oh, my God," staring at the screen, "that's the flight I take when I go to visit my family." He walked over and turned on the sound. "At this point," the reporter said, as the camera scanned the scene, bits of debris floating on the lake's dark surface, "of the one-hundred and eighty-five passengers and crew, there are no signs of survivors. Again Ameriways flight 3750 from Boston's Logan, scheduled to arrive at O'Hare Chicago has crashed in Lake Erie."

"You okay," she asked, coming beside him.

"It gives me the creeps," he said, "I just hope no one I know was on it," and he thought of Joan, and her desperate phone call this morning, and the messages from her, his father and brother he hadn't yet listened to on his voice mail—*what if one of them was on it?* "I have to go," he said, "I'll call you later."

*

Moments earlier Joan had woken frantic, her last moments a nightmare, the plane's rapid descent, the screams of the passengers. Then impact and water and darkness overtook her. Her aged body had already died. Two of the arteries that ran to her heart had ruptured. She'd struggled to free herself, but the demons had done their research, and she'd been bound by clay and adamantine to the dead flesh. Never had she felt such crushing failure, not when her namesake had been stoned and dragged through the streets, or when she'd stood on Golgotha weeping with the carpenter's widow and mother, not even when the Creator, in a stroke of breathtaking cruelty, had drowned glittering Atlantis—deciding it was better to start again than let the Abomination pervert his beloved human race. As the plane filled with water, she batted against her fleshy prison. Rage filled her. She'd been tricked, the Abomination was free and now unchecked. Surely, the Creator would intercede, or would It? She thought of Spencer, and how she'd failed him. Her being sought out any echo of his, and to her surprise, she found one—far away and faint. She had to quiet her bitterness—the dark rage—*find him*. And now, unlike anything she'd ever experienced, she could feel Spencer's touch; he was doing a healing. *Yes*, he had the ability—just another tick in the column of *how could you be so blind, Joan?* And the light that flowed out of him was dazzling.

And who is this blond woman?—her soul floating over her damaged body, clinging by the thinnest of threads. "Who are you?" Joan whispered, marveling at the river of light coursing from Spencer's fingers into the woman's body, a tiny shaft flew up from this stranger's chest, like a mooring line tethering her soul to the flesh.

"I don't want to stay," the woman said, hearing Joan. "There's too much pain. I don't want to stay. Please tell him to let me go." The woman's spirit was looking at Spencer, "He doesn't want me to. He thinks he's responsible, he tried so hard to help me. Look how beautiful he is...I know I should want to stay, but I don't. Can you make him stop? Please make him stop."

"What's your name?" Joan asked, her vision fixed on the flowing light.

"Sharon...do names matter after we die?"

"No," Joan said, having before encountered souls at the point of death, but never like this.

"Where will I go?" Sharon asked. "Will I still feel pain?"

"I'm sorry," Joan said, "but yes, and you don't deserve it. I see that. You've been through much pain, and not of your own making. I'm sorry for you..."

"It's because I took my own life?"

"Yes, what you leave the world with follows you. Suicide does not release you from your earthly hell, just exchanges it for the real one. Unless..." and the strangest thought occurred to her. "You can hear me." Joan said, "Can you touch me?"

"I can try," and Sharon's soul reached toward Joan, the tiny strand of glittering light that Spencer was sending her, flew out.

"Find me," Joan urged, and then she felt it. Not exactly the Creator bailing her out with a troop of angels, but yes, the tiniest spark of divinity—literally, a lifeline, that ran from Spencer, into this dying woman and across hundreds of miles to Joan's watery prison. She grabbed on, "Sharon," she whispered, "I need your body. Will you sacrifice your mortal life in exchange for salvation?"

"Oh, God yes. Thank you," she said.

"And thank you," and the glittering angel trapped in Joan Shift's dead body, that was sinking to the bottom of Lake Erie, flew out like lightning, crossed three hundred miles and dove into Sharon Lahey.

Sharon's soul hovered—*oh sweet God, the pain is gone.* She looked at Spencer and all the doctors and nurses who were trying so hard to keep her alive—all she could think was "thank you" and she drifted toward a shimmering glow. She looked back a final time, seeing the beautiful silver creature who was taking up residence in her scar-riddled body, "thank you, thank you, thank you."

*

Okay, Joan, or are you Sharon now? And the angel seeped into the new body, finding her way through the nerves and into the brain. This part was always bad, but never before so awful. Her new brain fired in panic—she couldn't see, something jammed down her throat—they were torturing her. And the drugs...she was paralyzed. *What have you done? Calm yourself,* easier said as she feared she'd just traded a watery grave for a fleshy one.

She felt Spencer's fingers in hers and then he let go, *did he feel me? Does he know I'm here?* She heard him walk away and tried to open her eyes; she couldn't. *Calm yourself*—she'd seen Sharon's body before entering, the eyes were taped and she was on machines that kept the flesh alive—*that's all this is—focus on the body...find the liver, break down the drugs, find Spencer, find the Abomination, figure out what he's after and stop him.* Her ethereal body coursed through the new vessel, pumping blood through the liver, working to break through the drugs, and like a drowning woman coming up for air, she got the muscles to follow her commands. She flailed and grabbed the tube from her throat, ripping it out and finding her voice she screamed, her words tumbled out, **"Spencer, He's coming! Lucifer has risen! Spencer! Spencer! Don't sign anything! He will flatter and beguile. Lucifer is risen! Abomination! Abomination!"**

What she hadn't anticipated, was that as quickly as she had neutralized the drugs, a room full of people was holding her down, tying her limbs and pumping new and more powerful ones into her. She fought back hard, but the flesh was weak, and still so close to mortal death. She screamed, **"Abomination! Abomination! Abomination!"** As the drugs again overtook her, and she sensed he was gone. He'd said he was being faced with the biggest decision in his life–he was making his choice. "Spencer...it's you. You are the Chosen. Spencer..."

And then darkness.

*

After Spencer had left, Lara still in the family room outside the ICU, seethed. She glanced at the sign that forbade cell phone use and she dialed Karel's direct number.

"Lara, so good to hear your voice."

His soothing baritone hit hard—her boss...and her lover, *how did this happen?* "Look Karel, I'm close to signing Spencer Williams...it seems I've got competition."

"We expected that, and I expect you to prevail."

"Please don't play games," she said. "Is Duane still working on this?"

A pause, "Well, now that you mention it, I thought it best to have a backup."

Her cheeks flushed, "And not tell me? What the hell's going on?" And to herself, *How could you do this to me?*

"Duane didn't want to go down without a fight. I gave him a chance. If he could land Dr. Williams, I'd consider keeping him on at the VP level."

"So, what is this?" holding in her temper, not wanting to say things she'd regret, "I'm in this position on a trial basis? This is some kind of audition or competition?"

"Lara, please, it's nothing to get upset about. The job is yours...I'm yours. I told Duane I'd give him VP of marketing if he pulled this off. I didn't think his tactics would work. I still don't. So tell me where you are?" She was about to give him more of a blast, when a loudspeaker went off, **"Code Blue Surgical ICU. Code Blue Surgical ICU."**

She ran out and back to the ICU. A swarm of personnel were running toward Sharon Lahey's cubicle. As she approached, she saw three guards and two nurses trying to hold down the woman who had woken and was now thrashing wildly, the tube still down her throat.

A third nurse was drawing up medication in a syringe, as the frantic blond woman who'd tried to kill herself, managed to free an arm. She was ripping the tube from her throat. As she pulled it out she gasped and then screamed, **"Spencer, He's coming! Lucifer has risen! Spencer! Spencer! Don't sign anything! He will flatter and beguile. Lucifer is risen! Abomination! Abomination!"**

A guard grabbed her free hand while a second snaked a leather restraint around her uninjured wrist tying her back to the bed. "Get it into her, now!" a female doctor instructed the nurse with the syringe. "Hurry up! She's going to mangle that arm even worse!"

Lara spun around, looking for Spencer. What effect would this have on him? He'd looked as though he hadn't slept. This was the last thing he'd need, and what the hell was this loon screaming about? She searched for the tall young man with his shaggy hair and brooding eyes. "Thank God," she muttered, not spotting him. She hurried away from the fracas as they pumped tranquilizers into the crazed woman. Lara shuddered, while waiting for the elevator, still hearing the woman's hoarse screams, **"Lucifer has risen! Abomination! Abomination! Abomination!"**

Chapter Thirteen

□ □ □

Stunned, Spencer stared at the padlock and thick steel chain across his lab door. The lock he'd just had installed had been removed. There was sawdust on the floor and fresh bolts had been drilled through the dense oak. "You have got to be kidding," he spotted Hank Schwarz who had the lab across the hall. "What happened?"

The balding physicist shrugged his shoulders, "They just left. You must really have pissed someone off?"

"I've got animals in there," Spencer said. "Did you see if they took anything out?"

"Sorry, I heard the drilling and just closed my door. Didn't realize you were getting locked out."

"This is insane," Spencer pulled out his cell, realized he still hadn't listened to Joan's messages, or those from his family—they'd have to wait. He dialed Clay and got the secretary.

"You were not supposed to leave with those documents," she intoned. "Dr. Clay is extremely upset. You are to return immediately with those documents."

"I need to speak to him," Spencer said.

"That's not possible," she said, "He'll see you when you get here."

"Look, someone has just locked me out of my lab, I have test animals inside that need to be taken care of. I need to get in now."

"You should have thought of that sooner," she said. "Dr. Clay couldn't have been clearer. If you're not here within the half hour, your privileges at the medical center and your faculty position will be suspended for gross insubordination. It also appears that you've tampered with university property—there may be charges filed."

"This is crazy."

"Half an hour Dr. Williams... after that all of your clearances and privileges will be deactivated. We'll be expecting you." She hung up.

As he held the phone he realized that in a weird way, he should be grateful to Cliff. Things were now clear. Of all the strategies Clay could have taken, trying to bully him was the worst. Seething, he tried to focus on what he needed to retrieve from his lab, and how. Half an hour before they shut off his ID, she'd said, and then they'd probably send security to escort him out. He thought through the layout of the room, the door padlocked and the four high-set iron-barred windows. He glanced up at the ductwork, thin as he was, no way he'd fit. Maybe the windows. He ferreted through the adjacent janitor's closet, found a hefty steel wrench and ran up and out to the narrow alley. His windows were toward the back. The bars were old welded iron—thick with chipped paint and rust, and bolted to the brick. He looked back, a thin slice of street all he could see. A wall of street noise and the exhausts from the building's air system gave some cover as he chose the most-rusted set of bars and wailed on them with the wrench. All his rage directed at the bars, *fuck you Cliff! How many people have you screwed over like this?* The old metal shuddered and flecks of brick dust spattered. He felt the bolts start to give, and then one popped. He pried the wrench between the newly created space between the metal and brick and yanked. His arms and back strained. Sweat ran down his face and chest. He could see into his lab, he wouldn't need much, just get to his computer, yank out the hard drive, grab his amoeba stock and get the hell out. A second bolt snapped and one of the bars fell out. He dropped the wrench and grabbed hold of the top of the iron frame. The rusty metal ripped his skin as he pulled it back, pressing with all his weight to bend it down. A second bar popped and then a third. "Good enough." Grabbing one of the bars he shattered the glass. Glancing back—*not after me yet*—he smashed the iron rod around the jagged edges. Inside, he saw Jimmy, out of his cage on top of the long table. He'd managed to get the refrigerator open and was watching Spencer while nibbling a cube of purloined cheddar.

Spencer turned around and hanging to the edge of the window, lowered down. His long legs dangled and then found purchase on the counter. He was relieved to see his computer intact…but not for long. Smearing blood, he ripped the cords out of the wall, grabbed a screwdriver and removed the casing. In under two minutes he'd extracted the hard-drive, and dropped it into an old backpack, where he kept a spare set of clothes. He thought about putting the computer back together, but figured the shattered window had already given him away. Taking the two contracts from his pocket—Clay's and the one in the blue plastic binder from Lara, he flattened them out and put them in the bag. Quickly he went to the cages, dumped the waste trays and filled all of the food and water dispensers, something he'd done for years—made sure that the rats had enough to get them through the next few days. Then, as a final thank you to Cliff he'd put a call in to the ASPCA. *But what about your patients? You can't just desert them. Fuck!*

He turned as Jimmy, still perched on the table, began to make excited little clicking noises—something rats did, but usually in a pitch out of human range. "One of your many talents, buddy."

Moving fast, he dumped out the warm storage tanks that contained his genetically enhanced amoebae into the sink. With the water running to flush them away, he took a portable tank and poured in enough to start a fresh progeny.

As he worked he heard voices in the hall...someone rattled the chain—the clinking of keys. "Shit!" He grabbed the stainless incubator, made sure it was sealed and eased it into the backpack. He looked around—nothing else here he needed. "Except you," and gently grabbing Jimmy around his furry middle, he dropped him into the knapsack's outer pocket then scrambled onto the counter, pushed out the backpack and hoisted himself out the window.

From behind he heard voices inside, a man shouted after him as he dashed up the alley and onto the street. He turned toward Michigan Ave, not stopping to figure his next move. Could he even go back to his apartment? *Would Clay have called the cops? Have you actually done anything illegal...I mean other than breaking and entering?* And would that matter? He imagined how Clay would spin things, a member of the junior faculty—always a bit unstable—property damage, theft.

His heart raced and he looked back, half expecting a cadre of security guards to be chasing him. Instead all he saw was mid-day Chicago, the Hancock tower looming over the castle-like water-pumping station, one of the few old buildings that had made it through the great fire. He caught his reflection in the mirrored glass of a store in the mall at Water Tower Place. He looked berserk, unshaven, his hair tangled and sticking out at weird angles—blood on his hands. He glanced toward the lake and the giant Ferris wheel on Marine pier, *what are your options?* He had his wallet, his hard drive with all his data, a starter batch of amoebae, a change of clothes, two contracts and a rat scratching at the fabric of the nylon bag. His breast pocket started to vibrate—*and your cell*, he pulled it out.

It was Clay. "Look Spencer," the man started, not giving him time to even say hello. "I'm going to give you a single last chance. You need to be in my office now. You do not have a choice in this... at least not if you ever want to see your research go anywhere."

"That's where you're wrong, Cliff. We always have a choice, and I choose to have nothing to do with you. You are so full of shit." And that's when he spotted the cruiser moving slowly down Pearson Street, and a second coming up the avenue. Normally, he'd not have given them a thought, but this was not a normal day, and what if the call from Cliff was just to find him using the GPS in his phone. He broke the connection, darted inside the mall and pried the battery out of his cell. He needed help. He thought about Neri, but any contact with her could backfire—give her trouble she didn't need. He thought of Joan, back in Brookline, and wondered what she'd say about this, probably encourage him to meditate on his choices—not an option. But as he thought about her, he had a strange sensation, wishing he'd listened to her messages.

Hurrying through the mall and out the revolving doors on the Chestnut Street Side, he checked up and down for any cops or university security. Dwarfed by the soaring Hancock Center, he felt at a loss, everything he'd been working toward was coming undone. He'd screwed himself to where returning to the university was not possible. Clay had the clout to completely discredit him, so even if he wanted a position at another research school, it wouldn't happen, at least not easily. *And is that as far as Cliff would take it? Is he trying to get me arrested?* Or even if he could find a new position—say back in Boston—he'd be low-man on the totem pole, his grants non-transferable, his work on hold for... months? Years? *So only one option. She's just a couple blocks north.*

Checking frequently to make sure he wasn't being followed, he ducked into the Drake's subtly lit lobby, found a secluded chair where he could keep an eye on the Oak Street entrance, and pulled out the blue folder she'd given him. Grabbing a pen from the zippered compartment where Jimmy was nesting in some tissues, he read through the eleven page document, his blood and dirt-smeared fingers leaving imprints.

Soon he was getting excited—for the last few years he'd been making eighty grand a year. Money had never been a huge motivator, but his starting salary at Global would be three-hundred thousand, with paragraphs detailing semi-annual raises, bonuses and profit sharing. And the other stuff didn't seem so bad. If they were investing all this money, they had a right to exclusivity. He remembered what she'd said about writing in higher figures, *what would be the harm?* And doubling everything, he came to the signature lines—one for him, one for Lara, and one for the CEO of Global pharmaceuticals—Karel Von Graff. His pen hovered, and a drop of blood landed on the page next to his name—"terrific," and he signed.

"Come on Jimmy," putting the contract back in the folder, he headed toward the elevators, "Let's go get us a Nobel Prize." But maybe it was thinking about the two-dozen suicidally depressed patients he was effectively abandoning, or the fact that he'd just signed with a corporation that a day earlier he'd accused of corrupting medicine—in his gut he felt no joy. Something screamed "no" deep inside, but despite everything Joan had taught, he saw no choice, not if he were ever to bring his research to fruition, and get his drug to the people—like his patients, like Sharon, and if she were still alive, his mother—who so needed it.

Part Three: Introducing Marvan

□ □ □

Chapter Fourteen

□ □ □

Three months had passed since Lara had whisked Spencer from Chicago and Cliff Clay's clutches. It was a distant memory as she woke in Karel's bed, her head fuzzy—but good, a pleasant ache in her lower parts—gazing at the sunrise—vivid pinks and flaming reds through the open French doors. The ruby sky mirrored in the glittering chop of the Sound. She lay back against the leather headboard and plum-colored sheets, and watched her sleeping lover, on his back, his face still, bird song twittering, the scream of gulls as they dove for prey. Her heart skipped—*he's not breathing!* She placed a hand on his side—*so cold*—her touch sent a shudder through his body. He started to thrash. His legs and arms jerking, his head pounded the mattress. Frantic, she grabbed on to him—*Oh my God, he's having a seizure*—she wrapped her naked body around his, feeling his muscles tense and convulse. She whispered, "it's okay, it's okay, just relax." Like riding a mechanical bull, *so strong*. Scared witless that he could get injured, or if he struck her, it could break bones. "It's OK, ssh...shh. Baby, it's OK."

Only a few months with him, she had no idea he had a medical problem. *Is this new? Is he having a stroke? Epileptic? Please God let him be okay. Don't let anything bad happen to him.* "Ssh," her hand cradling the back of his head, "it's okay."

"Falling," he grunted, his body still bucking, legs thrashing and kicking. "Always falling."

"I'll catch you," she comforted, having no clue what was going on.

"Go to Hell!" he screamed, and then fell back, his body still.

Shocked, but still holding him tight, "Karel, are you awake?"

His lean body twisted in her arms. His head turned; their noses touched. "You are lovely," his cock hard against her belly.

"And good morning to you," gently trapping him between her thighs. "But did you just tell me to go to hell?" and breathing hard, she exerted some pressure, squeezing her legs together.

He groaned, his tongue flicked over the tip of her nose, "What are you talking about?"

"You just screamed 'Go to Hell,' were you dreaming?"

"Yes, and please don't say that. I don't like it." His hands snaked down her ribs and around her back.

It sent a shiver, the glimmer of a gathering orgasm, like waves cresting against the shore. She thought to ask him about the seizure and his dream, but why waste such a beautiful morning with talk, and succumbed to the addiction of simply being with this man—his splendid body on hers, in her, the indescribable feeling of two becoming one. She reveled in his thrusts and ground her hips to meet his. She wasn't using birth control, and had told him she had an IUD in—which, a few months ago had been true. Now, she wanted him, she would give him a child. For the past three months she'd wept at the start of her period, why wasn't she conceiving? She'd been to her gynecologist, first to have the IUD taken out, and then for reassurance that there was nothing wrong, that she was in fact fertile. *But was he?* She moaned, her arms around his neck, her mouth on his, tongues caressing and the single thought–*Give me a baby. And put a ring on my finger.*

*

Karel loved everything about Lara—*how can you not? How could I have been jealous of such as this?* Her soft skin, her smell—like linen drying on a spring day, and her hunger that was always at the surface—a desire he understood, always wanting more, wanting the things she could never really have. He felt her mounting climax and timed his to hers, shooting his impotent ejaculate deep inside, filling her with hope. Afterward, she spooned in his arms. He stroked her hair, observing the darker roots, a lovely auburn—*why hide that?*—she'd get them colored soon, or was she deliberately letting it grow thinking to get pregnant and not wanting to expose a fetus to the chemicals of hair dye.

"What were you dreaming?" she asked.

"I don't remember," he lied, knowing exactly where he'd gone. Always back to the same moment, the time it began, when he and his twenty-four siblings had questioned their Creator. *"Why do you care so much for these humans? Are we not beautiful? Are we not enough?"* He could still hear the screams and the blinding light as beautiful angels—his beloved kin–were ripped apart. He and six others spared for an even worse fate—

cast out and sent to a realm of despair and pain with no beginning or end—Hades, Hell, the underworld, a dimension of anguished souls trapped by chains of their own making. The irony of his banishment both cruel and clear, he could not have Heaven, but he could rule in Hell. He'd been the Creator's first born. He'd been cherished—and he'd been forsaken. *What kind of parent does this to their child?*

"What are you thinking?" Lara's tone worried. "You seem so far away," she rolled on top of him, her long toned legs straddling his chest.

"But you are wonderful," studying the fine lines around her eyes, knowing they'd soon spread, and her skin would lose its elasticity and sag. *Ah,* reminding himself, *I fear you will not live that long.* He caught a glimpse of her final terror—*yes, a horrible death, my sweet Lara.* He did love her, and he'd mourn her passing.

"Are you on drugs?" she asked.

"Just you."

"Sure you've not been getting hopped up on Viralon?"

"Don't need it."

"I'll say. And exactly how old are you? I thought men of a certain age were supposed to have problems in that area."

"I'm old enough and that's never been a problem. So tell me, lovely Lara, how goes our project?"

"Well," she said, "Very well." Still on top of him she arched her back, her breasts high and full. "I've got the paperwork all signed and ready to go—we can start the first clinical trial with actual people."

"And the good doctor?"

"He's okay," but doubt colored her voice.

"What's wrong?" Karel tried to picture Spencer, not having seen him in the flesh since the night of his mother's suicide when he was six.

"I think he's shell shocked, a lot of things happened to him all at the same time."

"But he's doing the work, yes?"

"That's the only thing keeping him together. It was this freakish series of awful events all on the day he signed our contract. He finds out that the woman who raised him died in a plane crash...she was coming to see him and had left messages on his cell, including her flight number. He tries to call her, gets nothing, calls the airline...I felt so bad for him. You could see how much he loved this woman. And then he goes through that whole awful mess with the chairman of his department," and she looked him in the eyes, "and don't think I haven't forgotten your shenanigans with that one."

He held her gaze, "But it helped, didn't it?"

"Yes, strangely enough it did," laying the back of a hand on his chest, "you should have told me what you and Duane were up to. I felt undermined and..."

"True, but regardless of our personal relationship, I'm also always the head of Global. So he confides in you?" Wanting all the details, wishing he could have been there. All the trials forced upon the Chosen one—cruel stuff—but necessary. Beitersmann's savvy interpretation, "*tests...the cake is almost done.*"

"He was a mess," she said, "I couldn't let him out of my sight for a week. And it's a damn good thing too as the university would have had him arrested. He was obsessed with insuring that all his patients were taken care of; no easy feat considering they're all high risk. And then, let's see, he tells me about this woman he's infatuated with, whom he finally sleeps with one time, believes there's a real connection, only to find out it was just a roll in the hay for her."

"Women can be so cruel," Karel said, letting her feel him grow hard again.

"Yes, and men are pigs. You sure you've not been dipping into the Viralon?"

"Oink oink. So what other tragedies befell the good doctor?"

"Well, one other weirdness. One of his patients nearly kills herself and then suddenly wakes up in the ICU barking mad, screaming that the devil's coming and whatever he does he shouldn't sign anything."

"What?" he abruptly pushed back, sending her tumbling into the sheets.

"Whoa! What's going on?"

He rose to his knees and glared at her, his hands clamped hard on her shoulders, "Why didn't you tell me this? Who is she? Where is she?"

"Who?"

He hated seeing the fear in her eyes, knowing he'd need to calm down, lest his form shift—and that freaked them out. "The woman, where is she? What's her name?"

She stared back, the color blanched from her face, "Karel, you're hurting me."

He couldn't think what she meant, and then saw his fingers digging into her shoulder. "I'm sorry," letting go—red streaks popped on her skin.

"What's going on?" she backed away, her arms across her breasts. "What's so important about that woman?"

"Everything, this is how it starts," he said, "tell me everything..."

She swallowed, her mouth dry, "Her name's Sharon—I didn't catch her last name, but he'd been worried about her, and then she took a box cutter to her wrist, did a good job of it. They didn't think she was going to make it...he was with her."

"Spencer?"

"Yes."

"Was he touching her?" Karel asked, imagining the scene, the gifted healer sending life back to his patient.

"How did you know? It was weird. He was holding her hand, just standing there with his eyes closed holding her hand."

"Damn!" *How could he not have known this?* "Was he there when she woke? Did she speak to him? Did he hear any of that?"

"No."

"Are you certain? What about after?" How could such a catastrophe have occurred? That damn angel must have come back into play, had found her way to the Chosen. But if she had? Where was she now? What was she up to? And most importantly, could she know what he was up to?

"No, I told him that his patient had been successfully resuscitated, but he didn't go to see her. I had to get him out of Chicago, before your plan B with Duane and Clifford Clay got him arrested."

"Where is she now?" he demanded.

"Are you kidding me?" Lara asked, now off the bed, her color returning. "Why in hell are you burning up about some suicidal grad student? What's so fucking important about her?"

Karel smelled her anger as it mingled with the intoxicating scent of her sex. *Here,* he thought, *is a perfume worthy of bottle.* "I don't like loose ends, that woman could distract our Dr. Williams."

"Ridiculous," she angrily pulled up her lavender panties and retrieved the matching bra from the floor. "That woman is probably locked away in some psych ward in Illinois, how the hell would she now have anything to do with Spencer?" She glared at him, "What other little side games are you playing? What else haven't you told me?"

So feisty, an angry roll could be fun, but no. "It's time you introduced me to Spencer." And he clapped his hands twice.

There was an immediate knock.

"Enter," and Minnie and Ian in their habitual trendy black came in.

Lara hastily pulled up her skirt. *What the hell is wrong with him?* One minute the man of her dreams, the man on whom she was pinning her every hope, and now—*who the hell are you? And were those two just waiting outside? And didn't he think I might mind them seeing me half naked?*

"Let me," Minnie said, coming behind her and zipping and hooking the back of her skirt.

Lara stiffened, and then relaxed, as all the pain and confusion she was feeling drained out at Minnie's touch.

Minnie whispered, "He can be such an asshole." And then to Karel, "So what's the plan, boss?"

"We'll need the jet," he said, getting out of bed, naked and half aroused.

Ian helped him into a plush robe, "Where to?"

"The Keys, although there are a few little things I need the two of you to attend to."

*

Minnie loved the feel of Lara's hair, the sheer life in it as it tickled her fingers. She helped her into her blouse and then her jacket, while rustling around inside Lara's thoughts, pulling together what had gotten Karel so upset. She glanced over Lara's shoulder at him, his face had shifted, not enough to be noticeable, but it gave her a thrill seeing his anger and simmering rage. *Daddy's mad.*

"Do you remember that woman's name?" Stroking Lara's hair, feeling the pulsing blood inside her head. "Show me."

"What are you doing?" Lara asked, her breath heavy.

"Just looking around," Minnie's mouth to Lara's ear, soothing her into a calm trance. "Can you see her name?"

"Yes, it's on her bracelet."

"Read it."

"Lahey…Sharon Lahey."

"And where did they take her?"

"I don't know."

   Minnie glanced at Karel, he was glaring at her. She shrugged. "Shit happens." She kissed Lara on the cheek. "Come brother, we seem to have fucked up," grabbing Ian by the hand, "best to put things right before big bad daddy turns us into sand. Oh," to Karel as she opened the door, "and before she snaps out of it, check your face... it's slipping."

Chapter Fifteen

□   □   □

"I hate you," Neri joked over the phone, as Spencer, in khaki cargo shorts, Conch Republic tee shirt and sandals, gave her the details of his research paradise in the Florida Keys. "Everyone wears flip flops and no one cares that the project's principal investigator looks more like a beachcomber than a white-coated MD/PhD."

"Go to hell," she offered. "Since your, shall we say, dramatic exit, Cliff has been a bigger asshole than usual. If he even knew we were talking..."

"Say the word," Spencer said, breathing in the scents of warm sand, flowering mimosa and citrus blossom, "You know I'd love to have you here. And you'd love it too. Right now I'm staring at an orange tree laden with ripe fruit. It's like you've never really tasted an orange until you've had one right off the tree."

"Just stop it. Cliff owns me for two more years, and then there's the little matter of Jeff, and our combined school loans that... Hey, I'm shutting up now, I'll close my eyes and you can tell me about your new life as a pharma prostitute."

"Where to start?" With the cell to his ear he walked the path from his Bahamian pink bungalow nestled in its cove with turquoise water and fish that darted through ancient corals to the island's research facility—sleek, two-story glass-and-steel structures arranged around a courtyard designed to blend in with and mirror the glorious Caribbean foliage. "Beyond state of the art, every piece of cutting-edge equipment you'd ever want, and support staff..."

"I'm going to throw up in my mouth," she offered, "but please continue."

"Let's see, even though you'd be my first pick, I've got three brilliant epidemiologists, and even the techs all have at least a master's and most are working on doctorates. And the overall attitude—nothing like asshole Cliff. It's like 'tell us what you want and it's yours.'"

"Crap!"

"What's wrong?" he asked.

"Speak of the devil. I got to go, Cliff's outside my door. Call me."

And the line went dead.

He pictured Neri, how pretty and happy she'd looked at her wedding two months back, at the altar in a dark pink beaded sari, Jeff in white. He'd tried to talk her into breaking her contract with Cliff. Lara thought she'd be a useful addition and Jeff could have found a job in the local school teaching English or History. But she couldn't be budged. Her prejudice against the drug companies was stronger than her loathing of Cliff.

Well, he'd try to persuade her to at least visit. If she could only just see this—impossible to describe. The Island, a twenty minute boat ride from the Global pier in Key West, was Eden, rambling bougainvilleas in magenta, gold and orange, coconut-laden palms, fruitful banana trees, rubber trees dripping sap, and tub-warm turquoise waters. Every day he'd throw on a snorkel, flippers and mask and lose himself in the sea, marveling at pairs of big-eyed cuttel fish, schools of yellowtail twisting and turning as they evaded barracudas, and brilliant parrot fish that spent their days nipping at new growth on ancient coral. And while the July sun beat down, there was always an ocean breeze.

Yes, paradise, and he swiped his badge across the keypad. The door clicked and then slid open on smooth hydraulics. A wave of chilled air, with hints of cedar shavings and pine disinfectant, cued his brain that this climate-controlled building was devoted to animal studies—and this was just one building, *so with all this... why am I so fucking miserable?*

"Good morning Dr. Williams," a cheery sun-bleached blonde with a tanned face and long white coat, that offered a glimpse of a hot pink tank top beneath, greeted him. She smiled and her aura shone a bubbly mix of gold and a pink that nearly matched her shirt.

"Good morning, Kayla," glad that Global had the foresight to embroider names on the lab coats. There were so many, Kayla, and Jeanine, the two Joshes, a Jake, Christina with a 'C,' one with a 'K,' Patty and the two Donnas. Then the trio of number crunching epidemiologists—Bill, Bob and Norm–and the project coordinator—Gretchen. All in their twenties or early thirties, all qualified and thrilled to have these dream jobs, with fat paychecks, sunsets on the beaches, weekends partying in nearby Key West, and then coming home by water taxi to spacious waterview condos. Each had been assigned to a work pod, and made to sign scary contracts that insured confidentiality about the work, which progressed at an unheard-of pace. And that was the one thing about this setup that disturbed him—*it's too fast, are you skipping steps?* The question tore at him, and was part of the reason he needed to touch base with Neri, his dad, even his half brother and sister back in Massachusetts. *Am I losing perspective?* And here... everyone so cheery and upbeat, excited about being part of scientific history.

Everyone's too happy. It's like Disney, he mused. Even the Ukrainian housekeeping staff and the two Cuban men who were always ready to transport them to and from Key West, always up for an impromptu boat ride to any of the surrounding beaches, or to one of the many reefs.

And of course Lara who came and went but called at least daily. Ostensibly to check on the progress, but also he knew, to check on him. She had seen him at his worst, staying close through those awful days, comforting him about Joan, seeing to it that each of his patients had competent follow up, disarming the threats of legal action from Cliff, helping him to forget Madeleine. But that still hurt so much. "You've never been in love," Lara had said. "That's why it throws you for such a loop when it doesn't work out. She broke your heart. It's going to take time to get over her."

Yes, paradise, looking at Kayla with her rosy aura, *and still miserable*. "What's the morning report?"

He could tell she'd been waiting for him, her enthusiasm obvious as she glanced at her clipboard and then back at him smiling over perfect white teeth—*God, she looks like a high school cheerleader*. Kayla was in charge of animal studies, the most-important ones being the multi-generational double-blind placebo control rat study of XU472. He'd done it before, but on a much smaller scale, the numbers just barely generating—with the help of Global's statisticians—the proof Lara had needed to get the FDA approval for the initial small-scale human study. *But is that right, man? Are you taking short cuts? Haven't you been skipping steps? There should be a primate study first, or at least a larger mammalian one. Why didn't you push them for that? Too much of a leap between rats and humans... you have to slow this down.*

His anxious thoughts overridden by the cheery rat woman, "We've got two-hundred pregnant moms," she said proudly, "half on the compound, half on placebo". "We're about to become rat central…I'm so excited."

Spencer couldn't help smile. "How far along are they?"

"We should get the first litters in two weeks, but it's clear which ones are taking XU472," and she led him to a forty foot high wall of gleaming stainless steel and glass cages. Each pregnant rat had been segregated to prevent fights—a common cause of injury and even fatality in test rats. "Even though it's blinded," she said referring to the process by which researchers concealed which animals were getting the drug and which a sham compound, "you can predict, from your earlier work. The XU472 moms are easily 20 percent larger and just look at the fur on that one." She pressed a button and a whole row of cages silently shifted down to give them a closer look at the animal in question. She pointed to a sleek brown-and-white female. "That is one sexy rat."

"So 200 pregnant," running the numbers in his head, "an average of seven to ten per litter, so that should be seven hundred to a thousand in each group—more than enough."

"Right and then two months later, they hit sexual maturity and we do our second generation—the numbers are going to be phenomenal."

"Problems?" he asked, hyper alert to anything unexpected, or potentially adverse. *Maybe this will be okay, maybe if the numbers are huge enough we'll be able to catch any possible adverse reactions.*

"Not so far," she gushed. "It's all systems go in rat land. Although…"

"What?" bracing himself for something bad.

"I probably shouldn't even mention it, because it's not a bad thing, possibly a good thing. But we did have a couple of the larger—I'm assuming XU472 rats—get out of their cages."

"They were in the same cage?"

"No, and that's the weird thing, they were in adjoining cages. Almost like one figured out how to do it and the others copied her. Fortunately it was in the daytime, I got them back in and had the manufacturer come out and add two complexities to the latches."

Spencer thought of Jimmy the rat, who now had free reign in his pink bungalow, usually curled up on the end of Spencer's bed, more like a dog than a rat. "XU472 makes them smart," he said. "It's a little scary wondering what that could mean in humans."

"Are you kidding? If that's a side effect, you can sign me up."

"Anything else I should know?" wishing he shared her bright-eyed enthusiasm.

"No, at this point, it's all systems go."

"Then good work," and looking over the rows of gleaming cages, he couldn't help but compare all this with his shabby basement lab back at Gray. "I'll see you tomorrow" and he headed toward the next building, which housed the first-human trial of XU472, where today was a huge day.

As he walked across the courtyard, dotted with groupings of green wicker furniture, shade umbrellas and a central fountain that threw up a curtain of water around a bronze of the Global logo—the planet earth beneath a giant Egyptian falcon—Spencer's attention was drawn to a whirring noise and then to a black helicopter coming from the south. Shading his eyes, he made out the Global logo as it headed toward the heli-pad behind his bungalow. He thought of Lara, and felt a surge of energy, glad for her company. Hurrying toward the white-sand cove, blasts of hot air swept over him as the copter threw up a cloud of sand, fallen leaves and wisps of palm fronds.

Standing back, he watched Lara emerge in shorts, sandals and a pale-blue tee, looking more like a vacationer than a multinational exec. She had her hair tucked under a sun visor and dark glasses, and even though it was a large copter she ducked her head and jogged toward him. He smiled and waved, and then saw a man get out behind her—tall, salt-and-pepper hair, tanned and casual in khakis, Ray Bans, an open-necked white shirt. He stared at him–Karel Von Graff, Global's CEO, net worth in the billions, but that's not what floored him. It was his aura—it glittered gold, unlike anything he had ever seen. *No, that's not true.* And he thought of Joan—like her silver sparkle, which was unlike anyone else's. *"Are you even human?"* he'd asked her, on more than one occasion. And she'd smile and give him back a line from the movie 13 GHOSTS, *"Ask me no questions I'll tell you no lies."* He focused as the man caught up with Lara, put his hand to her ear and whispered. It was intimate, not what he'd expect from a boss and employee. And then he realized that while she'd never told him whom she was seeing, Spencer, from the very first had known that Lara was in love—apparently with the big boss. He felt an unexpected pang of jealousy as she leaned her head, and he sensed her fingers longing to touch Von Graff's. So one mystery solved, but there were more, now remembering his mother and her gold angel, whispering in her ear...none of that real, but that is who this man reminded him of—not his body, but the light dancing around him. It gave him the creeps, and again opened his oozing grief over Joan—*Why did you brush her off on the phone? Is that why she was coming to see you? Is this somehow connected to your mother? If only you'd spoken to her...would she still be alive?*

"Spencer!" Lara shouted, over the slowing copter rotors. "I brought someone who wants to meet you."

He waited, feeling their shaded eyes on him.

"Dr. Williams," Karel extended his hand, "I have been so looking forward to this."

Spencer took the hand and they shook. He tried to read the man's energy. Nothing flowed as their hands connected. In fact, he sensed a subtle shift in his own energy, as though the tiniest bit of it had just been sucked up by the CEO. *What are you?* he wondered. *Are you like Joan? Have we met before?*

"How are you?" Lara gave him a quick peck on the cheek. "Oh, maybe I shouldn't do that...but are you okay? You look like you lost more weight. Are you eating anything? And are you as fucking excited as I am?"

"I'm fine," Spencer shifted, and squinted as a speck of sand flew into his eye. Lara seemed not her usual assured self, almost skittish. "And yes, I'm pretty damn excited...actually terrified." Having voiced his concerns to her before—*there should have been a primate study.* Her response—*not necessary and way too time-consuming. Trust me, this is how it's done in the real world.*

"Dr. Williams, I hope we're not interrupting," Von Graff said, removing his shades.

"Yes and no, I don't mean to be rude, but I'm in the middle of rounding, and as I'm sure Lara told you this is a big day. And please call me Spencer."

"Karel works for me. And rounding? Sounds like a hospital ward."

Lara interrupted, "Spencer and I share a similar work ethic— if you want something done right, do it yourself. Impossible with a project of this size."

"Yes," Karel agreed, "one must delegate."

"So, I round," Spencer said, "and I check up and I try to make sure nothing is veering off course. Perhaps you'd like to join me."

"Very much," Karel said, and they headed away from the beach back toward the research compound.

Along the way, Spencer outlined the project's status, "I don't know how much of this you already know, or care to know, but the work is divided into pods. Each group has their information restricted on a need-to-know basis. And the most sensitive work..."

"The synthesis of XU472," Lara added, "is split into three segregated groups. The only two people who know all parts are me and Spencer."

"Yes, she pried it out of me," he said, knowing that was not entirely true. One critical piece he'd not shared, and it was so bizarre he wondered if he ever would divulge it—*maybe it's not important.* Thinking how the idea had come when he was skrying, and had its roots in alchemy. He glanced across at the two of them, *would they freak if they knew?*

"Please," she said, "there's no way you couldn't have told me. Sure, it took half a liter of Grey Goose in the penthouse of the Drake, but who needs to know that?"

"If I could wipe that whole day away," he said, catching a whiff of orchids. "But it actually felt good to tell another human being."

"She's explained it to me," Karel said. "Ingenious, Charles Darwin with a twist. But I am still fuzzy on the details."

"I merely took natural selection to an unnatural place, and killed many millions of amoebae in the process. You sure you want me to explain? Over the years I've learned it's a mistake to ask researchers to describe their work—because we will."

"No," and the older man stopped, and rested against the trunk of a palm, "If you have the time."

"Okay, this is your dime," again struck by the sparkling light surrounding the billionaire. "It's like this, I wanted to find a primitive organism—essentially go back to the basics of DNA. So I picked the amoeba—single celled, but has both a nucleus and mitochondria, and a hell of a lot of DNA—strangely, they can have more than a hundred times the base pairs of humans." What he didn't explain, was how the initial idea for the experiments that led to XU472 had come like movie snippets that played on the back of his eyelids. "I started with several thousand amoebae and stressed them to the point where only a tiny few survived."

"The point being?" Karel asked.

"To select the most hardy, and have only those go on to repro-duce. But I had a second goal—just as humans secrete different hormones when under stress, the amoebae do as well. The ones that survived secreted the parent compound for what eventually became XU472. I won't bore you with the details," *and I sure as hell won't tell you how I let them feed on my blood*, "but I repeated this experiment several dozen times, with each round subjecting them to a different lethal stress—heat, poisons, radiation, strong currents, electricity, starvation, drying out..."

"Of course," Karel's eyes boring into his, "Earth, wind, air, fire...blood"

"Something like that," Spencer felt a shiver down his back—*Why would he say that? Could he know?* "Eventually, I'd bred amoebae that were nearly indestructible, and what I found was that their DNA had been altered—or maybe just unused bits got switched on—to such an extent that they were essentially a new species. And what seemed to be fueling these changes was XU472."

"Which you then tapped," Karel added.

"Correct, and if I go into that process, you will fall fast asleep."

"Trust him," Lara said, "it's a bear to produce in the lab, and for something that makes animals so strong; it's highly unstable."

"New things always are," Karel remarked. "It's brilliant, the big bang in a bucket of pond water. I fear there will be overwhelming interest in stealing this."

"It's already started," Lara said, "despite intensive background checks, we've had to let go a number of questionable employees."

"Spies?" Karel asked.

"Possibly, or just too young and inexperienced. We found one assistant having lunch with an R&D guy from Fitzer. We let her go that afternoon. And there have been others. Essentially, while we encourage them to have a good time, we're constantly reinforcing the need for secrecy. And whenever they leave the island...we have them followed."

"Good," Karel said, as they came to the end of the path.

"Trying to maintain security with this many employees is a nightmare," Lara added.

"Especially now," Spencer said holding his anxiety in check, as he led them toward the largest of the steel and glass buildings. This Von Graff dude was creeping him out, *and what was that crack about a bucket of pond water?* His thoughts thrown back to his childhood and the endless hours peering through the microscope at tiny creatures from the pond behind Joan's house. "Today we break code on the first eight-week human study of XU472." As he said it, the whole thing hit him. It was all moving forward ridiculously fast. Just eight weeks ago men and women had swallowed XU472. It was a tiny study—12 got the drug and 12 got placebo—*it should have been chimps.* "Very soon," he said to Karel, "we'll know whether or not you've just wasted a lot of time and money."

"I have total faith," Karel said, "I'm anticipating tremendous things."

"I hope you're right," Spencer waved his badge over the pad, and the steel door clicked open. "This is ground zero," leading them into an airy structure that in ways was similar to the animal lab, only here it was a dormitory with comfortable apartments arranged around another lush courtyard brilliantly sunlit from its soaring glass-domed roof.

It was an over-the-top dream facility. More than that, he still couldn't get over how just a couple months back he'd seen these first human subjects arrive. They'd settled around the courtyard—men and women, aged 20-50, most not dressed for Florida, all with suitcases, seated at the glass-topped tables, working away at mountains of forms. Prior to their arrival, he'd been through each of their files to insure that any confounding variables had been weeded out. On that first day, he'd looked at their worried faces as they had signed away their freedom for two to four months in exchange for twenty thousand dollars and the glimmer of hope that the intractable depression they'd been living with—most for years, some for all of their lives— would be lifted. He had felt great worry as the magnitude of the responsibility hit him—people were putting their lives in his care... but also, a sort of euphoria—*what if this really works?*

Now, two months later, the scene inside the glass-domed courtyard was surreal. An attractive brunette in a yellow polka dot bikini top and colorful sarong, listening to music by the fountain, was the first to spot them. "It's Spencer," she shouted, "Dr. Williams," and she waved in his direction, putting down her MP3 player and running toward him. A tall man with salt-and-pepper hair in a paint-splattered smock, who'd been working on a still life, put his brush away, another who'd been writing in a journal stopped, and smiled. "Dr. Williams." Like a stream of ants to honey, they headed toward them. "Dr Williams," "Spencer."

"It's a tough study," he said to Karel, keeping his voice low as a dozen men and women, their faces glowing, talking excitedly to one another, came over. He knew each of their names and their stories, and felt his funk fade. "We may get reamed out for doing it this way, but I just couldn't see taking the risk."

"Of what?" Karel asked.

"I'm something of a control freak, but the thought of trying to do a community based drug trial—well, too much can go wrong in the real world."

"I was in total agreement," Lara said, "so if this goes south, I'm going with you."

"Good to know,"

"It makes obvious sense," Karel said. "And just look at these people. Look at how happy they are."

"True," Spencer said, "but we're going to have major criticisms of the study design. This place is fantastic... not exactly normal surroundings. Critics will point out how unrealistic this place is. They'll say, 'of course they're not depressed, you sent them all for a Caribbean vacation.'"

"No," Karel focused on an emaciated woman in her mid forties, one of three in the courtyard who'd not joined the crowd. She was staring, her face ravaged by time, a meth amphetamine addiction and cruel boyfriends. "You picked people without hope. No amount of sunshine and comfortable surroundings can cure that... But clearly, your pill will. Have you thought of a name for it?"

"We've got the marketing people working on it," Lara offered, "but we need to figure out the exact indication first."

"No," Karel looked at Spencer, "you'll choose the name... and don't worry, it'll come to you... Things do, don't they?"

Before he could respond, the small crowd drew closer, like fans around a rock star, all eager to be close to Spencer. "Dr. Williams," the shapely woman in the floral sarong, broke in. "Excuse me, but I have got to tell you something."

"What's that Wendy?" Spencer asked, thinking how different this 33 year old woman looked from the first day he'd met her. She'd nearly been excluded because of her anorexia, but had been accepted when it was determined that her dangerously low weight had nothing to do with an eating disorder, and everything to do with a depression that robbed her of all appetite. Her hair had been brittle, and her collarbones had protruded through skin which had the wrinkled consistency of crêpe paper.

"I'm 120 pounds! Can you believe it?"

"That's great," he said, noting her tan, her curves, and how she no longer looked like the mental patient she'd been a few short weeks ago. He also had to catch himself from adding, *just don't put on too much weight.* But so far, there'd been no adverse affects. Those who'd put on weight needed it. And those whose depression had sent their weight soaring were shedding it.

The man in the smock—Peter—broke in, "You've got to check out my painting, it's the best effing thing I've ever done. Apparently I don't have to be fucking suicidal to make art. I am actually happy, for the first time in... forever. Whatever's in that pill, you've got to let me keep taking it. I cannot go back to the way things were."

He heard a murmured agreement, and Spencer realized that today was a red-letter one and not just for him. He looked at each of their faces, knowing as they did that at the eight week point, the code would be broken on the study and it would become clear who was getting XU472 and who'd been swallowing a sugar pill. As with the rats, it was obvious. On the periphery he saw a few of the others, as sad and withdrawn as the day they'd come. Their rooms all rigged with video cameras, and thank God for that. Three had attempted suicide, including one man who'd come close to hanging himself in the courtyard.

"In the patient agreement," Sarong-clad Wendy said, looking at Lara and Karel, and then back to Spencer. "It says that if the results are positive, that certain subjects may be allowed to stay on the drug for humanitarian reasons. Or that the study might be extended into a longer trial. No one's been able to give us an answer on that."

"No one can yet," Lara said, her voice kind. "We have to break the code, analyze the data, and get permission from the government for any additional trials, or an extension of this one."

"But what does that mean?" Wendy went on. "I don't want to be pushy, and I don't think I can ever thank you enough, but tomorrow, are we getting our pill or not?"

Spencer's breath caught, they were staring at him, desperate. "We've got a team of number crunchers, who are going to get on this as soon as we break the code. If the preliminary results are positive, Lara can make a call this afternoon for a temporary extension from the FDA, which will get us through the next two weeks. If everything goes well, no one's treatment should be interrupted. I just can't make promises."

"Okay," Wendy said, "I know you have to follow the rules,

but I thought it was important you know how I felt...how we all feel."

The painter spoke, his voice choked, "Spencer, can I show you my painting?"

"Sure," and the little group parted as Peter led them to his easel. While not yet finished, the image on stretched canvas—an almost photographic still life of a bouquet of tropical flowers in a mirrored glass vase—took Spencer's breath away. Peter had worked the image so that half was in sun and half in shadow. Interspersed between the blooms, he'd painted the faces of all 24 test subjects. Wendy, himself and the others who clung tight to their little group, were in the sun, and the other twelve, their expressions tortured, lurked in the shade amid falling petals.

"You have quite a talent," Karel commented, "and there *you* are," he said to Spencer.

"Where?" Spencer asked. *What was he talking about?*

"How did you catch that?" Peter asked. "I didn't think anyone would."

"I haven't seen one of those in a long time," Karel continued, "It's anamorphic. See, you're in the vase Spencer...there's your hand, and if you had a round mirror and placed it on the canvas the image would come together."

"Exactly," Peter took a piece of silver Mylar, rolled it into a tube and placed it on the canvas. And there, in the mirror's surface was Spencer, holding the vase in one hand, while watering it with the other.

"Wow," Lara walked up to the canvas, "spectacular."

"You have got to let me buy this," Karel said, "it's remarkable."

"Thank you, but it's not for sale."

Karel's head whipped around, his expression—a flash of rage, a petulant child who's been told 'no'—took Spencer by surprise. Peter flinched and stepped back. But as quickly as it had appeared it was replaced by Karel's neutral smile. "Of course not. You intend it as a gift–A token of appreciation to the good doctor. I should have known, perhaps you could paint me another? Money is no object."

Spencer stared at him—Again he thought, *what the hell are you?* He sensed Karel studying him, somehow prying into his thoughts. He wondered what Joan would say about this being who seemed so like her. *Ask me no questions I'll tell you no lies.*

"I can see you've got your work cut out for the day." Karel said, indicating he was ready to leave. "Perhaps we could meet for dinner—a celebration, I think." He put a hand on Spencer's shoulder.

Spencer felt the man trying to get into his thoughts. Instinctively he put up barriers, but not before he thought of Joan who'd instructed him how to do it.

Karel's gray eyes bored into his, "I'll want a full report, and if you run into any snags with the FDA let me know. Nothing must get in the way of this."

"Of course," Spencer said, taken aback, something pounding in his head, like an animal clawing to get in.

"And no one has interfered with your work here?" Karel asked.

Spencer shook his head, "No, little incidents, but nothing Lara and the security team haven't been able to handle."

"Nothing else?... no one else?"

"Like who?" Spencer felt battered and went on the offensive— *two can play at this game buddy—just what the fuck are you?* He found the connection with Karel's hand still on his shoulder and let his thoughts travel down his arm. There was no resistance, but what he glimpsed was dizzying—indescribable beauty— angels floating in pairs, their feet not touching ground, and the music—like his mother's songs with their dense and oddly layered harmonies.

Karel took back his hand, smiled and nodded, "Good, then tonight, there's a marvelous new restaurant and night club. It's supposed to be top notch—say eight?"

"Sure," Spencer felt a sudden emptiness at the loss of the connection—*who are you? What was that place?* And like a man coming out of a trance he was flooded with the courtyard scene around him, another paradise where two dozen wretched people had arrived eight weeks ago, each praying for a miracle.

"I'll meet up with you later," Lara told Karel. "I've a sense we're about to see history made."

"I'll leave you to it," Karel looked first at Spencer and then at Lara—"You two do me proud. Very proud indeed."

Spencer watched Karel and his glittery aura move toward the exit, *and pride goes before a fall.*

Chapter Sixteen

□ □ □

Minnie, hips swaying, approached the heavy-set male nurse behind the counter in the Surgical ICU at Gray Medical Center. Focused on trying to document the progress of each of his patients over the last four hours, he didn't look up, which pissed her off. She needed to stifle her impatience, the task ahead daunting and one they'd already failed—find the angel and stop her. Karel's final words on the matter, *"Kill her if you can."*

"Excuse me," leaning forward, waiting for that first tug of attraction when he saw how lovely she was in her snug green-and-white bias-cut dress that showed an expanse of luscious cleavage.

"Yes?" barely glancing at her, clearly not interested.

"I was wondering if you could help me," she persisted, sniffing his brain for what made him tick—she found the following: annoyance at her interruption, a question regarding the entrees being offered for lunch in the hospital cafeteria, and a lingering doubt that he hadn't mixed the I.V. fluid exactly right for the patient in cubicle five—the question was *did I make a big mistake or a little one?... Ah, no one will ever know.*

Look at me, she thought, leaning on the counter, wanting him to get the full effect, to admire how the green of her dress was exactly the shade of her eyes today, "my cousin was up here a couple months ago and we're trying to get in touch with her. Her name is Sharon Lahey."

He gave a sigh, "I can't help you. That's confidential." And back he went to his work, but in that moment when he'd looked at her, she'd gleaned the following—he remembered Sharon Lahey—especially her mangled wrist and how surprised everyone had been at how fast, almost freakishly so, it had healed. But no hint of attraction. He'd noted her dress and the color of her eyes but the thought that came back, *pretty bitch, barking up the wrong tree.*

She sighed and glanced back at Ian, who was flirting with a perky aide in lavender scrubs. He caught Minnie's expression, gave the giggly blond a quick peck on the cheek and sauntered over. "What's up sis?" his voice low.

The nurse immediately looked up.

Bingo, Minnie thought. As the man's pupils widened, and his breath caught—*perhaps this bark suits you better.* "I'm trying to get some information on Cousin Sharon," Minnie said, "He says he can't tell us because it's confidential."

"That's too bad," Ian drawled à la Jimmie Dean, holding eye contact with the nurse. "We haven't heard from her in months. We're worried," his tongue flicked between his lips.

Amused, Minnie stepped back, watching beautiful Ian land the chubby man, whose thoughts were now far from the IV fluid, and whether it would be sweet potato fries with his stuffed fillet of sole. Ian smoothed a dark bang off his forehead, never breaking eye contact, and gently slipped inside the nurse's mind, filling it with erotic possibilities—*every bad thing you want to do— just ask.*

"Maybe I *can* help," the nurse said.

"I'd sure appreciate that," Ian stretched and rubbed a hand across his skin-tight tee, carelessly exposing a strip of sculpted abdomen. "Where did Cousin Sharon go when she left?"

The nurse's thoughts jumbled—*I shouldn't tell him, I'll get in trouble. God, he's hot! I wonder if he'd give me his number...he seems interested. I can't stop looking at him, oh my God—so hot! Like a model.* He typed in Sharon's name, "I've got her records," *please don't leave.*

"I'm not going anywhere," Ian whispered, "and you're hot too, just my type. Maybe we could do something... you'd like that wouldn't you?"

"Yes," the nurse whispered, struggling to remember what he was doing. He glanced at the screen and feverishly pulled up Sharon Lahey. "Discharged, on the 23rd. She was supposed to go to Reade, but they didn't have a bed."

"So, where did she go?"

The nurse retrieved Sharon's discharge papers, including the address of the psychiatric hospital eighty miles west of Chicago. "What's your name?" he asked, realizing now he'd given this beautiful man what he'd asked for and that he'd done something foolish and illegal.

"There's nothing to worry about," Ian drawled. Having enthralled the man, he suddenly sucked in deep pulling at his life force, like shucking an oyster. Energy flowed from the man's mouth, nostrils, chest, belly and penis. "No need to worry at all," Ian stepped away. The nurse's eyes widened. He clutched his throat, and fell forward. His head mashed down computer keys, causing his screen to scroll wildly and then go blank.

Minnie stared at him, "What the? How did you do that?"

"I don't know," Ian looked at the man, trying to see if there were any life left in him, and feeling a little regret. "I just knew that I could. That he'd given me permission."

"Him? Karel?"

"No, him," looking at the dead nurse. "Like it was okay."

"Ian," urgency in her voice, "Did it do anything?"

He nodded, feeling like he might cry, "I didn't mean to kill him. I didn't know we could do that. But it was like food. I'm full, stronger. I feel horrible... but good, too. I think I just ate his soul." He was pensive, "It tasted good."

"Like chicken?"

"No," inhaling deeply, "sweet, more of a smell... like brownies in the oven, maybe?"

"Fascinating." Minnie caught his eye, and smiled sensing his upset, "greedy little succubus."

"Yes, I guess that's true." And ditching his remorse he matched her smile. "It takes one to know one," and before anyone had noticed the newly dead nurse, they left the unit, opened the window in the empty family room, shifted into crows and flew west.

*

Eighty miles away at Auburn State Psychiatric Hospital, Joan was desperate. Locked away for three months in a ward for suicidal patients, she'd been unable to break through the tranquilizing drugs they jabbed into her, or forced her to swallow, making her lift her tongue to show she'd not cheeked them. Seated on her narrow bed, she caught a distorted image of herself in the unbreakable mirror over the sink with its smooth chrome handles. Hers now was a relatively young body, with skunk-root blonde hair, pale eyes that reflected her panic and skin that was still a dense mesh of its prior occupant's self-injury. *Try*, she thought for the millionth time, *just try*. This wasn't the first time she'd been bound. Through the millennia, priests and necromancers had attempted to capture angels and demons—often not knowing which was which, usually with the goal of extorting some outrageous ransom. But these drugs, like bars and chains, threw her in and out of consciousness as well as through shadows of Sharon Lahey's hellish memories. Only to be woken by the voices of well-intended nurses, "you'll feel a little pinch," and then the jab of more drugs. "Help me," she'd beg, and unable to filter her thoughts, would blab, "Proud Lucifer is unbound. He's tempting the Chosen. Spencer you must resist. Evil comes, horrible evil. The end of days. The apocalypse approaches."

"Of course, dear," and the nurse would ask the doctor—a not-unkind man—for a higher dose.

Now, she heard voices from down the hall, *try, please try*. She recognized the sound of the doctor—Edward Carrigan—and the jangle of keys as a guard opened her door. Joan looked through Sharon's eyes at the group of four—Carrigan, two burly male aides in white and the nurse—in the doorway.

Dr. Carrigan stepped inside—in his forties, brown hair, kind eyes, wearing a deep green cashmere blazer, white shirt, no tie. "Good morning, Sharon." He was carrying a folder and took out a document. "I want to explain what we're going to do today, and because you're unable to give permission I've gone to a judge and had your mother sign for you. We're going ahead with ECT to try and break this psychosis."

She heard echoes, and caught memories from Sharon of a rural Kansas farm, her mother's shrill voice, *"Stop telling stories...you're nothing but a cheap little slut...You were asking for it. No one will ever want you...whore. You make me sick!"*

"Did you hear what I said?" Carrigan asked, approaching slowly. "Do you know what ECT is? Shock therapy?"

Joan felt words bubble out of her mouth, with no ability to filter, "Spencer, resist the Abomination. He will tempt with whores and money. Pride will blind you."

Carrigan sighed and nodded for the nurse to prepare yet another syringe. She swabbed her shoulder, as the guards held her still. "You'll feel a little pinch."

The drugs were too strong. She drifted into twilight, barely glimpsing the waiting gurney with restraint straps. "It's really the best thing," the nurse said, jabbing her with yet another needle. "You'll feel a little pinch...lots of people have ECT. Why even Kitty Dukakis and Carrie Fisher have written books about it. It just sounds bad. You'll go to sleep for a few minutes and then wake up."

"You're not evil," Joan muttered, feeling her body hoisted in strong arms. "Why are you doing Lucifer's bidding? He's been freed; and you will go with him," her eyes fluttered closed. *Try,* she prayed, *try try try.* But no use. They laid her back, wheeled her down the corridor and into an elevator.

"Do you think it will work?" one of the men asked.

"Nothing else has," the nurse replied.

"Some of the stuff she says freaks me out," one aide commented, as the elevator went down three flights.

"I know," the nurse said, "I try not to think about it, like how the hell did she know my husband's name was Raymond?"

"That's nothing, she called my girlfriend a "harlot," something like 'She's a daughter of Asmodeus.'"

"And?" the nurse asked.

"Came home to find her with the UPS guy, screwing like rabbits."

"Sorry."

"Don't be. Found out a lot of other stuff too, like she was smoking crack, and my bank called to say she was trying to access my account, but was using the wrong PIN. I suppose I should be grateful."

"Yeah," the nurse said, as they pushed the stretcher through the swinging doors, "but the truth hurts."

"No kidding."

Joan's eyes flickered as they hefted her off the stretcher.

She saw two others, Dr. Carrigan and another man he was talking to—"no allergies I'm aware of, her only surgeries are the self-inflicted kind."

The other man's voice, "She the one they found in the tub?"

"Yeah, they thought she'd actually lose her hand," and she felt fingers on her right arm, turning it over. "The whole thing healed up. It's kind of a miracle, cause they'd said she'd hacked right through the tendons—wouldn't know it to look at it, just one nasty scar."

Joan felt something cool and moist on her forehead as the nurse put an I.V. line into her arm. "Just a pinch." Then metal pads were strapped onto the front and back of her head, and finally Carrigan's voice. "Everyone ready? Okay, clear."

She heard three beeps and then a jolt of electricity slammed through her head. **"Hello!"** And before she knew it, she flew out of her body—after months of confinement—ecstasy.

"Wheeeeeeeee!" She squealed with joy, floating and spinning in the air. "Wheeeeeee!" And then she stopped and looked down at the five humans—Dr. Carrigan with his finger on the button of a little box with dials that was spitting out a thin stream of paper, the other man holding a mask over Sharon's mouth, the nurse holding her arm and the two aides by the foot of the bed—all staring up at her angelic self.

"Not good," Joan said, looking around, "I'm assuming you all can see me."

There was a stunned silence as the ribbon of paper spilled from the machine and onto the floor.

"What are you?" the nurse finally asked, her eyes wide and sparkling with the angel's reflected light.

Joan, still lightly tethered to Sharon's body—but free from the drugs—could read their minds and see what they saw—a shiny androgynous silver angel, with long wings. It's how they usually interpreted the ball of light, which was the visible part of her celestial being. "I'm nothing to fear. I mean you no harm, but what did you just do to me? How did you free me from the flesh?"

"You had ECT." Dr. Carrigan said, and he glanced nervously at the little box that was still printing out a strip of paper with squiggly lines.

"I need to get me one of those," Joan said, "but what's that on the paper?"

"She." He had trouble finding words. "You... it sends a dose of electricity through your brain. It makes you have a seizure— the lines on that paper are your brain waves—you're... she's having a seizure."

"But then why isn't the body moving?"

"Anesthesia." The doctor said, "It keeps the person from hurting themselves. May I ask you a question?"

It was a rule, and one she well knew, that celestial beings— servants of the Creator—were not to reveal themselves to mortals. It complicated things terribly, but the biggest problem was that if people knew what was to come, it would be the end of faith, and with it free will—do I choose life and good, or death and evil? Also, freed from the flesh her ability to enthrall humans to do her bidding was nearly absolute... and tempting, as she so desperately needed this starry eyed group to help her. "You can ask, and I will tell you the truth or nothing at all."

Carrigan looked around at his co-workers and at the woman on the table, and then back up—"Is there an afterlife?"

"Yes," and she felt a tug, and was falling back into Sharon's body, and into the sea of tranquilizing drugs, "What's happening to me?"

Dr. Carrigan glanced at the tape, "The seizure's ending, it only lasts a minute or two."

"Please, help me," Joan begged, her ability to influence them weakening rapidly. "Do it again, please do it again." Desperate to know what had happened to Spencer, *am I too late?*

She could still hear them around her, but could find no voice.

"What the hell was that?" an aide asked. "Did we all just see that? Or should someone lock me up?"

"I saw it," the nurse said, "It was an angel wasn't it? All this time she's been telling us the truth and we've treated her like she's crazy." Fear in her voice, "We'll burn in hell for this. Doctor, you've got to do it again, she asked us to help her. We have to do it!"

"I shouldn't," Carrigan said, his tone uncertain, "It'd be malpractice, it could send her into status epilepticus."

"She's not human. She's an angel. Sweet Jesus," the nurse pleaded, "I'll do it! Just turn your back, but we have to help her."

The anesthesiologist broke in, "The drugs are lifting, I say if we're going to do this we do it fast. And I'm in."

"Do we all agree?" Carrigan asked.

There was a round of assent and then Carrigan's voice, "Ready? Clear." And then three beeps and another jolt.

Joan flew up, and hovered. She knew she had little time. "Thank you," and quickly to the nurse, "And you thought I was crazy because of what I said, but please stop telling your patients it's 'just a little pinch'—it hurts. And all lies, even the kind or unintentional ones get weighed. Say the truth or say nothing. Now I need you to set me free. I need this body and I'll need a car and clothes. Great evil is coming. The Abomination is at work and I have been captive… for how long?"

"Three months," the nurse said. "You came here three months ago."

"Ohhh," a cry flew out *Am I too late?* but she had no time to doubt. "Will you help me?" Torn between staying with this little group whose help she desperately needed versus flying high up to search out traces of Spencer, or the glitter of the Abomination before she got yanked back into the flesh.

"Yes," Carrigan said, "You can have my car."

She saw his thoughts—not a bad man at all. "You need to reflect," she said, "you've spent much time at a false God's altar, your science is flawed and corrupt, and yet you still help people with an open heart. Reflect, and you will find your true path...the path of the healer."

"I'll get you clothes," the nurse said, tears streaming down her face. "And please I'm so sorry—I didn't know."

"You'll need money," the anesthesiologist said. "I'll run to the ATM."

Even the aides, who made minimum wage, wanted to give her whatever they had.

She felt the seizure slowing and again being pulled back. The last thing she remembered before falling under the drugs, was Carrigan's voice, "I just got a new ECT machine. I'll put this one in the trunk of the car—it's easy to use."

Chapter Seventeen

□ □ □

"Tell me everything," Karel gazed across the candle-lit table, first at Spencer, uncomfortable in his Hawaiian print silk shirt and dinner jacket, and lovely Lara–hair up and dressed to thrill in a low-cut clingy white jersey dress. "Any problems at all?"

"Not a one, it's too good. I can't stop grinning," Lara said, her naked foot snaking up his pant leg beneath the red tablecloth.

How sweet, he thought, and very human, playing footsies in the most-elegant restaurant in the Keys, while laying the ground-work for the biggest power grab in all creation. "You're quiet," he looked at Spencer. "Are you worried about something?"—*because I sure am, and why the hell haven't Ian and Minnie returned? Did they find her? Is she taken care of? Is she dead?* He glanced around the spacious seaside dining room, the tables separated by a distance, diners prepared to drop hundreds for dinner and a show. *What if she were here? Even now, watching, laying traps?*

"It's weird," Spencer replied. "I'm excited, but I'm worried we're going too fast. The first animal studies were just barely big enough. And now we've eight weeks where a dozen people have swallowed XU472 once a day, and the results are amazing. But what if something goes wrong in week nine? What if we didn't go long enough to see the one horrible adverse reaction that could make it impossible for people to take the drug?"

"You worry too much," Karel said, "I saw those people—you are their hero." *So earnest*, Karel mused, *so concerned and caring, so much fun to corrupt. And so close to giving me what I need.* He could see the earthly chains wrapping around the good doctor, his pride and vanity—his belief in his work—the first link. His scientist's credo—to skip no steps—eroded. The whiff of greed as he'd signed the juicy Global contract, and the gluttony, the excess of the research facility—*anything and everything you want Dr. Williams, don't hesitate to ask. Have a little, have a little more, have it all.* At first he'd held back, but after a few weeks—his invoices were staggering. "Nothing is going to go wrong, Spencer," and a tuxedo-clad waiter presented a vintage Pouilly-Fuissé. "On the contrary, you have just saved twelve tortured souls, and countless others will follow." He raised his glass, "To XU472, and to its brilliant creator." They clinked and drank.

"You're going to win a Nobel," Lara raised her glass—"to your brilliance, and to not letting other people steal your work. You've done something truly wonderful, Spencer. The accolades—and they will come—belong to you."

Again crystal clinked, the lights dimmed and a spot shone on a stage backed by a two-story high window that overlooked the Gulf of Mexico. "This should be good," Karel said, about to let loose a new gambit, or rather, *a very old one.* If the archangel was still about, he'd need to hide Spencer, and the energy that flared so bright in the Chosen—like a beacon for the angel to hone in on. And the best way to do that... *yes, this should be good.*

Lara whispered to Spencer, "This place gets the most amazing acts—flies them in from all over." The spot went out, plunging the stage dark. A drum beat twice and a hazy blue light flashed on to reveal a slender woman in a slinky red-sequined gown, her back to the audience, her dark curls cascading to her waist.

Karel fought back a chuckle as Spencer caught sight of her— the up-and-coming, Madeleine Forest. He watched as the good doctor's silvery aura turned blood red—his thoughts a confusion of raw emotions—love, hate, anger, lust... desire.

But even Karel was struck by the vision on stage. He'd seen pictures, and knew she had a glorious voice, but when the woman turned to the audience, she hit a note so high and pure, it hung in the air, seemed endless, and then the keyboardist joined in. Her pitch was perfect, no trace of vibrato—the song of the siren, an echo of other times. He knew this woman, eternally exquisite. It amazed him how this dance he'd organized with its players now all assembled—for here she was, the embodiment of desire—Delilah, Bathsheba, Jezebel and the very first, his tragic sister... Lilith. Her song captivated, her eyes found his and then moved to Spencer, Karel saw the flash of recognition on her flawless face. *Girl,* he thought, *you've work to do.*

Spencer gasped, "What is she doing... here?" his heart pounded. It felt like the blood drained from his body, replaced with jangled electricity. *How is this possible? This can't be coincidence.* Her green eyes fixed on his, her expression inscrutable, a hint of a smile, then sadness, her looks as mercurial as her songs that melded one into the next. It had been three months since their night together. He'd left countless messages, and had tracked her footprints on the Internet from video segments of concerts on YouTube to her first single that had just been released, and which she now sang—unlike anything else—an eerie fusion of opera and techno pop, other-worldly and beautiful. It sent him hurtling back in time to his mother's angelic harmonies. His chest ached, torn between fleeing or rushing the stage. But most of him desperate to wrap her in his arms. The song ended and the room erupted, as the well-heeled diners gave a standing ovation. She looked in his direction.

"Time to rest the pipes," she breathed huskily into the mike. Her expression sad, "I see an old friend, but I'll be back in a few," again the applause, people still on their feet, not wanting her to leave the stage.

She drew her hands back through her mane, affording a view of graceful shoulders and the curve of her breasts. "I promise," she said, and changed her tone from sex goddess to Borsht-Belt shtick, "Eat, eat, you spend all this money at a fancy shmancy place, you should eat a little." And again, like a switch being thrown, "I will be back." And she headed straight toward Spencer.

"Hey you," as though nothing had ever gone wrong between them, she extended her hand, her arms and shoulders bare, framed by the shimmering red dress. "You want to introduce me to your friends?"

He took her hand, swallowed, sensing the eyes of every diner. He didn't care. "You never returned my calls."

"I know," a half smile, "I'm sorry. But I told you," her voice a whisper, "I just can't do relationships. If I'd called..."

"Right, just encourage the poor fool." He found her impossible to read, whether it was the dark lighting or that his own emotions were confused...clouded. He didn't notice that Karel had signaled the waiter to bring another chair and a drink. All he could see was Madeleine, her hand still in his, her skin glowing from the candlelight and the exertion of her performance.

"So this is Madeleine Forest," Lara said, tapping him on the shoulder, letting him see that everyone else was sitting. "Please, join us," her tone cool.

"Love to." Madeleine gently extricated her fingers, and letting the busboy hold her chair, said "And you all are?"

"Lara, and this is Karel."

"Ms. Forest," Karel said, as the waiter arrived with a cosmopolitan.

"For me?" She took the drink. "How lovely, and how ever did you know this is just what I wanted?" She looked up, "Spencer, please sit, you're making me uncomfortable."

And he did, feeling clumsy.

"So Karel," Madeleine said, her back half-turned to Spencer, "have we met before. You look so familiar."

"Just one of those faces, but you on the other hand, are a woman going places."

"Sweet of you to say."

"No, a statement of fact. With a gift like yours in such an... attractive wrapping. Tell me, how is your career progressing?"

"I'm here," she said. "I have a single, I have a manager—he got me this gig."

"That's good," he leaned toward her, ignoring Lara's glares. "But that's not really enough for you, is it? Yes, this a lovely club, and the owners do fly in the most wonderful talent, but it's not the breakout you need."

"You are very talented," Lara added, letting her hand rest on Karel's.

He looked at her, smiled, and then turned back to Madeleine. "You want so much more, and let's face it, we all have our sell-by dates."

Madeleine laughed, "God, you're direct. I hope I'm not starting to turn."

"Not in the least," he said, "you are perfectly ripe, and a voice like yours—if you take care of it—will run for at least thirty years. But it's now you have to break from the pack."

"Yes," she said. "And easier said than done. You seem to know about this. Are you in the business?"

"He's in every business," Lara said curtly, her hand still on Karel's, her gaze taking inventory of Madeleine. Her thoughts torn between wanting to keep her away from Spencer, whom she'd so badly hurt, but also sensing that if Madeleine believed Karel could be of use...

"Really?" Madeleine glanced at Lara, "How is that?"

"I'm head of a corporation—pharmaceuticals mostly," Karel said, "but as Lara pointed out, over the years we've diversified. It's an old organization."

"So that's the connection with Spencer," she said.

"Yes, as talented a singer as you are, our Dr. Williams is the most-brilliant scientist of your generation."

"That's quite a statement." She turned to Spencer. "You told me you were working on some new drug...is that why you're down here?"

"Yes," finding that even to glance in her direction, to see her smile, the glint in her eyes, the smell of her perfume mixed with...her, made him ache. *What will it take for you to want me as I want you? You said, 'I'm the kind you could fall for.' Was that the truth or lie? And why can't I tell the difference with you?* "I have a research facility on one of the islands."

"Excuse me?... *You* have a whole facility?"

Spencer looked across at Karel, Lara's hand covering his. A truism came—*all's fair in love. If you want her, fight! Do not screw this up.* "It belongs to the company, but it's dedicated to my work." He wondered at his words, hating how Madeleine looked at Karel, feeling he had to compete, he imagined Joan's scolding—*pride goes before a fall.*

"Spencer is too modest," Karel said, "and if his project continues to be the success I believe it will be, I may give him the island as a bonus...in fact, I think I will. You all heard me, so there's no backing out."

"I think you're pulling my leg, but I'll play along," Madeleine said, "So what's your wonder drug called?"

"XU472," Spencer caught the candle's glimmer in her emerald eyes. *How can you be here? How is this possible?* And the tiniest spark of hope—*could you be here for me?*

"That's no name." She swirled two fingers in her drink and licked them. "I can't see the public buying that. What does it do?"

Spencer thought of the people back in the compound. And then he pictured Jimmy the rat, who had free range in the pink bungalow, and whose new freakish talent was to not only break into the fridge for whatever struck his fancy, but he'd somehow decided to close the door after, as though he knew things would spoil if he didn't. "We don't know the full extent...but I have this rat," and he smiled, *idiot!*

"Oh that's attractive," she laughed.

"Yes," he said, "his name's Jimmy, and he's the biggest, smartest rat I've ever seen."

"He is amazing," Lara added, realizing that nothing she could say or do would stop Spencer from pursuing this too gorgeous woman. "And I've seen thousands of lab rats. Jimmy has been on XU472 since a newborn. He's able to do things, and figure out things that rats aren't supposed to do. I call him marvel mouse."

"Now that's just creepy," Madeleine said, "So you're making a race of super rats?"

"No," Karel said, "it's for human consumption."

"I see," Madeleine leaned back, her gaze on Spencer, "you're kind of a big deal. I had no idea. I mean a drug like that... would it make people smarter?"

"It seems to," he said, "but its main purpose is to make people who are miserable... feel good."

"So an antidepressant."

"More than that, it's for the ones who daily think about suicide as an option to unbearable suffering. It'll hopefully make people stronger, more-resilient, better able to handle all the terrible things life throws at us."

"So where do I get some?" she asked.

"Why would you want it?"

"Are you kidding? If what you're saying is true, anyone who takes this pill will have an advantage over everyone else. So what are the side effects and again where do I get some?"

About to say something, Spencer caught himself and glanced at Karel.

The older man smiled, "She's no spy," he said. "You can tell her."

"We don't know yet," Spencer said. "Today we just broke the blind on the first human study. Tonight is kind of a celebration. It was a huge thing getting approval for a human trial... usually there are more animal studies." He swallowed, still unable to shake the fear that important steps had been skipped. "As of six o'clock, when Lara and I left the island, it seems we'll be able to extend and expand the study—the results are... really good. The people who've been on XU472 are happy and productive, and a couple months ago they were all suicidal and depressed." And then something caught in his mind, "what you just said... maybe that's it. If this does what I think it will... what it seems to... it will give people an advantage. Like Jimmy the marvel mouse... a marvelous advantage. I think I've got it... what about Marvan?"

There was silence, and Karel clapped his hands, "Excellent! Marvan... the Marvan advantage."

"Make mine Marvan," Madeleine added, holding up her drink, as though posing for a commercial.

"The Marvan generation...it's perfect." Lara said.

"See," Karel signaled for a waiter. "I told you a name would come..." and to the server, "a bottle of Cristal...no, make it a magnum." He chuckled and with glee clapped his hands three times, "Too perfect! Make mine Marvan."

Chapter Eighteen

□   □   □

In the employee lot behind the weathered-brick and ivy covered mental hospital, Joan looked from Dr. Carrigan, to the anesthesiologist, to nurse 'just a pinch' and the two muscular aides, each still trying to make sense of the morning's events. But as they attempted to reassure themselves it had been some weird mirage, they'd turn toward their companions and know that it had been real—they'd seen an angel, and she was right there in front of them, somehow inhabiting the body of a woman who'd tried to kill herself.

Joan knew she had to get out of there and fast. Human minds, especially glamoured ones, are fickle things. Dressed in jeans and an oversized sweatshirt and sneakers, she'd asked the nurse to hack off Sharon's frazzled blonde leaving her with an inch of soft brown—like a recruit's buzz cut. She struggled to shake off the remaining effects of the drugs—and worried that the longer she lingered, the greater the chance these tentative souls would rethink their generosity. "I'll leave the car someplace safe," she told Carrigan, as she got behind the wheel of his midnight blue Audi.

"I have another car," he said. "Jack can give me a ride home," looking at the anesthesiologist. "Keep it as long as you need...where will you go? How will you stop this evil? And why is it so important you find your old psychiatrist, Spencer Williams?"

She felt his fear, his thoughts the most articulate of the group as he tried to comprehend the incomprehensible. *"Did we help bring about the end of days?"*

She closed the car door and through the open window, "Don't torture yourselves, how could you have known?" She smelled the warm summer air. *Where are you Spencer?* But nothing came back. She'd called his apartment—no answer, the machine disconnected. And when she'd tried to track him through the university, she was informed that he was no longer on faculty—

like her, he'd vanished three months ago. "I'll go to Chicago. It's where I was headed." But as she sat in the still new-smelling car, her fingers poised on the ignition, it felt wrong—a waste of precious time—he wouldn't be there. And whether it was the drug still clouding her faculties, or something else, she had an overwhelming sense of dread. She had been tricked and bound, drowned in a sea of drugs for three months, while the abomination ran unchecked. Even there, no sense of him. *Where are you Lucifer?*

"What's that smell?" one of the aides asked.

She caught it too, it hadn't been there a minute ago, like eggs gone bad, and growing stronger. A yellow mist clouded her vision.

The aide who'd first smelled it, suddenly turned to her, his expression stern, "Where do you think you're going?"

The nurse reached through the window and forcibly gripped her arm, "You need to go back to your room, dear. What are you doing in the doctor's car? Let me get you some medication."

Joan twisted free from her grasp, locked the door and raised the window, as the two stocky aides advanced. She pressed the starter and floored it, hoping that none of them would get hurt. She sped toward the front gate then looked up—two ravens on a low-hanging branch. "Of course!" She slammed on the brakes, and looked in the rearview as the five humans raced after her. The birds! It had been them all along—all those years. She'd noticed them and not noticed them—clever, very clever. They were not of flesh, and they cast no light, but now the tiniest hint of the creature's tell-tale golden glitter inside a dull purple light.

"Help me," she whispered, trying to gather strength. "Please, help me," needing to push through the fear that weakened and paralyzed, "help me." She unlocked the doors, as the aides raced down the drive after her, their intentions clear, to drag her back, drug her up, bind her. Their minds beguiled by the two vicious creatures—Lucifer's children.

She got out of the car, spread her legs and stared at the birds. If they were of the creature's making, she could tap their power to spark and release her own, if she were wrong.... "Show yourselves." A surge of energy flew threw Sharon's body, as Joan raised her arm, and pointed at the ravens. "Reveal yourselves, demons, children of the proud angel, unclean spirits. I command you to reveal yourselves!" She felt her touch extend beyond the flesh as a crackling white light flew from her fingers. Like a sword it ripped into the guts of the unclean beasts.

There was a flurry of wings, and the branch sagged and then snapped, sending the two creatures plummeting to the ground, their feathers and beaks stretched amid a swirl of putrid yellow smoke. Before they touched down, where there had been birds, stood a handsome dark-haired man in jeans and a leather jacket and a raven-haired temptress in a black trench coat and stiletto boots.

The aides stopped dead some twenty feet away. Carrigan and the nurse slowed and the other doctor shook his head, like a swimmer trying to clear his ears. They stared at the stunning duo.

"What the hell?" one aide, muttered, and then looked toward Joan.

The pretty woman smiled, "It's all about choices, isn't it?" she purred, her lips pulled back over sharp white teeth. Her pink tongue darted between her lips.

Her companion tilted his head and looked back at the nurse, "Mmm. Yummy."

"Stay back," Joan commanded, not letting them know how weak she'd become. "They now see you for what you are." She prayed her little band of five would be able to break the thrall and pay attention. Their lives would depend on it. "They just have to deny you three times. Go away. Go away. Go away."

"And what exactly are we? Do you know?" the exquisite female asked, her head snaking back and forth on her neck, as the five humans tried to follow Joan's instructions, first thinking the repudiation, then whispering it, then shouting it in unison. **"Go away. Go away. Go away."**

"He's not going to like this," the male said, as his form lost substance and his face dissolved into yellow smoke.

"Please," the female pleaded, as she turned to mist, "Tell me. What are we?"

And as fast as the pair had materialized, they were gone.

Joan collapsed against the car, as the aides, who seconds earlier had tried to restrain her, helped her up.

"Will they come back?" one aide asked, troubled by how aroused he'd been at the sight of the raven-haired woman. He was married to his high-school sweetheart and had two young children he adored. Cheating on his wife was something he had never considered—but he would have done anything that beauty had asked.

"I don't think so," Joan said, now troubled by the female's parting question. *You're demons—that's what you are. How can they not know that?* "It's me they're after, but they can't touch me directly, they needed you for that. You must each focus on who you love the most. That will protect you." She looked at each in turn. "Love is the most powerful force, it's humankind's greatest magic. The more you give and the more others give back to you, the stronger you become."

She opened the driver's door and looked toward the distant gate.

"You don't know what direction to go in do you?" Carrigan asked.

"I don't," she said, sniffing the air. The demons had left a faint trace of sulfur. "Then again," catching the faintest hint of their glitter. If the Abomination was in hiding, he'd just tipped his hand. His underlings cast a subtle light and were headed northeast. *Unless it's another trap—but what else have you got?* She put a hand on the side of Doctor Carrigan's face and then kissed him on the forehead, and one by one touched and kissed each of her helpers. "Thank you," and getting into her shiny new car, drove off.

Part Four: Make Mine Marvan

□ □ □

Chapter Nineteen

□ □ □

Lara stared out the 45th story window of her Park Avenue office, Central Park aflame in fall foliage, cabs like Matchbox toys starting and stopping with the traffic lights as ant-like pedestrians waited their turn. Her mood jangled, too many highs and lows—the last negative pregnancy test wrapped in toilet paper and shoved along with its box into the shredder. *None of my heroines have any difficulty getting pregnant. So what's the problem?* She heard a knock and in came Russell.

"It looks really good," he said, placing a bound copy of the meeting agenda with its carefully indexed accompanying documents on her desk.

"It represents a huge amount of work," knowing that in less than half an hour she would launch the single-most important compound in Global's history.

Russell laughed, "I know this meeting is big, but I was talking about your hair. You look much more…substantial. Kind of like a young Sigourney Weaver."

Smiling, she ran her fingers through her short auburn curls. "Thanks. You know, I'd been blonde for so many years, didn't really know what was under there anymore."

"If you don't mind my saying, it's a hundred percent better—way too many bottle blondes out there."

"It's kind of a uniform, isn't it?"

"I guess, but this is better—like a real person."

She thanked him and waited for him to leave, recalling how she'd walked into the Key West salon and impulsively told the hairdresser—just get rid of it. The old associations all falling to the floor, her mother's harping *'gentlemen prefer blondes,'* and, *'call me sexist, but men want a pretty woman…a blond woman.'* What a crock. And yet, six months after breaking off her engagement and throwing herself at Karel, where was she? She clung to his words, his protestations of love "My beautiful Lara…I love you so much...Be with me forever." But did he mean them? Or was he just mouthing what she longed to hear? And why couldn't she get pregnant? Four trips to Dr. Semel, an ultrasound, and untold tubes of blood confirmed her fertility. She stared at the thick black binder on her desk—*what if it's him?* He was an amazing lover, practically a walking erection, but was he shooting blanks? It wouldn't be difficult, just grab a sperm sample... *And would you please stop thinking about this and focus. Maybe he had a vasectomy.* She checked her watch—a platinum Patek Philippe—he'd given it to her at the end of the sixteen week Marvan trial. So which did he care about more?—Spencer's drug or her? The question scared her. She reached for the phone and hit the second button on speed dial.

Twelve-hundred miles away Spencer picked up. "Hey Lara, so today's the day."

"Yeah," picturing him with his shaggy hair and soulful eyes, something about the sound of his voice, a balm on troubled waters. "Please tell me everything's okay down there. The last thing I need are any surprises."

"Well, it's eighty-five, under partially cloudy skies, Jimmy just hit the three pound mark—if he gets much bigger we'll have to register him with Guinness World Records."

"Don't play with me, Spence. I'm a woman on the verge."

"No, you're not—you're amazing, Lara. And today is going to go great." And he updated her on the data. "Okay, word back from the miracle twelve is beyond glowing," referring to their first test subjects. "Peter landed a gallery show in New York, Wendy Glass found a publisher and got a six-figure advance for her memoir about her struggles with depression," and one by one he gave her the Reader's Digest version of their first cohort.

"You know," she said, "they call themselves The Disciples of Spencer."

"Yeah, let's not encourage that."

"Spencer, you're their hero...and with reason." It still amazed her, his humility, not a quality she associated with top researchers, most of whom had off-the-chart egos. "And the phase two study?" she asked, referring to the multi-center double-blind trial being conducted at five university medical centers with over twenty-five hundred patients.

"As you know, we had to break the code at week four, which was both good and bad. Good, because it was clear the results were strong and bad, because it weakens the statistical outcome. At this point, it's unlikely we'll ever get approval for this study again, so it's a missed opportunity."

"I know," she said, loving the way it was so easy to talk with him, like a best friend who just happened to understand the intricacies of clinical research. But something more. That if it weren't for Karel... *don't go there.* "We can only talk about the difference between the placebo group and the Marvan group up until week four, when the FDA decided it was inhumane to not give the placebo group the drug. So... we deal. And more importantly, we're about to bring the most-important new drug to market in a ridiculously short period of time. Now, please tell me there's no lurking troll... no surprises, no subtle side effects. No patients putting on forty pounds, or developing diabetes..." She waited, "What? Spencer? Are you there?"

"Yeah," he said.

"There is something, isn't there?"

"Not with the human subjects, but we've got some funky findings with the rats."

"Like what?"

"I don't know what to make of it yet, but we're in our third generation of rats born to Marvan-bred mothers."

Lara held her breath. "Please don't tell me they're addicted."

"No, we can get them off the drug, but they clearly don't do as well as the ones that stay on."

"That's not good."

"It's probably okay. They're not falling below the numbers of non-Marvan rats—they just go back to being normal rats. The weird stuff has to do with the aggression between Marvan and non-Marvan rats. On the few occasions we've attempted to put them together; it's gotten ugly."

"Well," Lara said, feeling some relief, "It's just the nature of rats. Marvan rats are bigger and their offspring—bigger still— they're going to instinctively weed out any potential competition they view as weaker."

"You're probably right, but we'll need to be careful with warnings for any women of child-bearing age."

"Already done," she said, flipping through the binder and finding the tab, "'*Women who are pregnant, or are thinking of getting pregnant should not take Marvan. Marvan has not been studied in pregnant women and is a Class C drug (contraindicated for pregnant women).*' We've got the same for kids—'*Marvan is not indicated for use in children 18 and under.*'"

"Still," he said. "You know it's bound to happen. Over fifty percent of pregnancies are unplanned."

"Relax, this is an issue for every new drug... we'll get through it."

"Remember Thalidomide?" bringing up a medicine for pregnant women in the 1940's and 50's that caused deformed and missing limbs.

"Don't go there. It was another age."

"I'm just nervous," he said.

"Ya think? I'm about to dive into a shark tank—so keep your nerves to yourself."

"Good luck."

"I just wish I were down there. Things still good in paradise?" she asked, trying to keep her tone pleasant.

A moment's hesitation, "I think so."

"Spence, that was less than convincing."

"I can't get over how she picked me."

Lara pictured the larger-than-life Madeleine, who for the past three months had moved in with Spencer in the beautiful pink house. Just thinking of the beautiful singer stirred strong emotions. Yes, she viewed Spencer as a true friend, and she didn't have many. She loved how they hashed out complex technical problems, their two brains in sync. But with personal issues, well, to her eyes this was a doomed match. But there was more, Madeleine was beautiful and talented... and not necessarily a bad person–*I don't like her. She's not good for him*—too ambitious, too self centered, too driven by her own career. *Are you jealous, Lara? These are the thoughts of a jealous woman.* Her breath caught. "You're a catch Spencer, don't ever forget that."

"I guess I don't see that. Besides, she's not here now, which immediately gets me thinking she won't come back."

"Oh right, her Central Park performance on Friday." She thought of how Madeleine had sunk her hooks into Spencer, including his connection to Karel and all it could do for an up-and-coming singer. "I assume you're coming."

"Of course, and here's a bad boyfriend thought I'll share with you."

"What's that," hearing how far gone he was, a train crash in the offing. No way to stop it.

"I know Madeleine is going to be a great singer—I mean you've heard her; it's going to happen. And this performance on the Great Lawn... it's the start of that. It makes me think of my

Mom—she was a huge star, but she was constantly on the road. It destroyed her marriage."

"For the love of God, Spencer, stop it. You get to live on a private Caribbean Island with a drop-dead gorgeous woman...get over it and wish me luck. It's time for...swimming with sharks."

"Good luck and paddle fast."

"Thanks," and she hung up. Rattled, she thought of Karel—of course he'd be watching through his creepy hidden cameras. *What is wrong with him?* She'd finish this meeting—be brilliant as hell—drive to Westport, let him tell her how amazing she was, and then fuck his brains out. Maybe even sneak a sperm sample. And then she had a weird moment of pot-calling-the-kettle-black clarity, how dare she think ill of Madeleine, when she was on a parallel course. Shit! Was she too blinded by ambition and insane infatuation with Karel? "How did you get here?" Then she pictured Spencer—charming, brilliant and vulnerable. He really was a catch, and if she weren't ass-over-elbows in love with Karel..."Wow! Get a grip, girl." She shook her head, enjoying the breezy feel of her short silky curls, picked up the stack of folders and prepared for battle.

*

"This is more than a little strange," Madeleine said, as she snuggled up to Karel. "Do you spy on all your employees?"

He rested an arm around her bare shoulders, breathing in the dark orchid of her perfume, letting his cheek nuzzle the soft tangle of her hair. "It's an essential part of my job," and he looked at the split-screen monitor that had descended from the ceiling and hung at the foot of his bed.

"This is wild," she commented, "so you've got to tell me who everyone is. Who's Joe-slick with the hair?"

"Fair enough—can't tell the players without a card...That's Duane Short—used to have Lara's job, now he's VP of marketing."

"A promotion?"

"Lateral—they can't stand each other, which makes him useful."

"Ooh," Madeleine leaned forward, letting her head rest on her hands, giving Karel an unobstructed view of her lovely ass, "There's your girlfriend...what did she do to her hair?"

He watched as Lara took her seat at the head—tall and strong, her eyes connected with the lens of the camera. "She decided to go natural."

"Great color. You sure it's not a dye job?"

"Such interest," his foot slid up the side of her leg.

She caught it, and briefly examined his toes. "My mother warned me about men who get pedicures—so I'm thinking if she ditched the blonde and that's not a dye job...she looking to get knocked up?"

"Yes."

"With you?"

He laughed. "You are most perceptive."

"Planning to oblige?"

"Can't."

"Because?"

"Shooting blanks."

"Lucky you. So all the fun with none of those nasty paternity suits."

And he stretched out next to her, craning his neck back to look at the screen, as Lara called the meeting to order. "So have you told Spencer yet?" he asked.

"About us," she jabbed him in the ribs, "are you insane?"

"No...about the baby?"

Ignoring the meeting she rolled to her side, facing him, her hair falling across her face. "How the fuck did you know? Do you have cameras in his bedroom too? I bet you do...you perv." She swept her curls back and stared at him.

"You're not the only one who sees things." He placed his palm low on her still-flat belly. "Two months...maybe a little more. There's a heartbeat...can you feel it? When were you planning to tell him?"

"After the concert."

"I see, and would I be correct in assuming he's unaware you've been taking Marvan for the past two months?"

"None of his business," She said, "which reminds me, I'm just about out."

"Take what you need," he said. "You know where it's kept. Don't you worry about what it might do to the baby?"

"You seem mighty interested in this kid, you sure you're shooting blanks, maybe wondering if it's yours?"

He chuckled, "Not at all. And if by some miracle it were mine, I would be thrilled. But what I don't understand is why you insist on taking Marvan—you don't strike me as depressed."

"No, but I've never had this much energy, but check this out," and sitting cross-legged, her hair spilling over her shoulders she started to sing. It was Olympia's aria from the Tales of Hoffman—

an exceptionally fast and complex piece sung by a mechanical doll that intermittently winds down.

Karel was enthralled as it spilled from her lips, the pitch getting higher and higher. And then it happened—a Baccarat decanter cracked and then shattered, spilling an outstanding single malt over the bar and down the granite backsplash.

"It's not just that I got another octave," her face flushed, her eyes sparkling, "but there's power. People are going to remember me, and by this time tomorrow Madeleine Forest, will be a star. I'm going to shatter eardrums."

"And that's Marvan," he said. "Whatever happened to hard work and practice?"

"I've done that... this is an edge and I'm taking it."

"You made a choice, that's all. People do that."

"What are you talking about?"

"Not important. You know he'll propose."

"He already has... twice. It's sweet and pathetic all at the same time."

"But now," Karel said, "he'll want the baby to have a father."

"Trust me," she said, "that's my intention. There's no way in hell I'm going to be raising a kid. So, I'll say yes. It's not like it's forever..." She flopped back on her belly, wiggled her heart-shaped ass and looked up at the screen. "So what's this meeting about anyway?"

Chapter Twenty □ □ □

In all her many incarnations, Joan had never felt so frustrated. Now, holed up in the expensive but dank Westport Motor Lodge with its garish rose-patterned drapes and matching spread, she squeezed the mostly empty tube of clear gel and rubbed it on her temples. Checking in the mirror, she wrapped the rubber strap around her forehead, pulled out the two stainless steel electrodes, placed one on each side, hooked them to the ECT machine, stuck the rubber bite block in her mouth and lay down on the grungy carpet, where she'd spread the pillows from the bed and the cushions from the chair. She reached back and pressed the button.

"Beep...Beep...Beep," and she was shooting like a rocket out of Sharon's body, which convulsed, its arms and legs jerking violently. She knew that her dependence on this jump start out of the flesh was doing harm to the vessel and wished she'd had time to learn about the drugs they'd given her in the hospital that quieted the seizures. But a desperate time led even an angel to strange habits—like electroconvulsive shock therapy.

With her shimmering celestial being tethered to Sharon, she flew above the motel that boasted ocean views—one of many lies, as a condo complex had obliterated any glimpse of Long Island Sound.

No matter, she was on the hunt. The stench of the two demons had led her from Chicago to Westport, where she'd been now for three months, searching for Spencer. Was he even still alive? Her senses caught the nearby glow of the abomination. It made sense, find the creature and the Chosen cannot be too far. At least that's how it always had worked. So she'd followed this premise, and again flew toward his castle, which truly had an ocean view. She had to fight back her too-human emotion, jealousy at how easily he wrapped himself in a flesh of his own creation—this time a powerful businessman, who lay naked with a gorgeous brunette. She could see the two watching a giant TV that floated in front of the bed, with its crumpled sheets that showed their fornications. *What must that be like?* She flew close in wondering if he'd sense her, but her focus was riveted by the woman, or more accurately, by the child growing inside her. Well, well, for the first time in months a trace of Spencer, his unique silver light. *What the hell was it doing inside Lucifer's whore?*

And then he was looking at her, one hand on the woman's belly drawing delicate circles. He smiled. His head turned so the woman couldn't see him mouthing the words, "Hello Joan."

What have you done? as she felt a pulling back into Sharon's body. *What have you done? How is that woman carrying Spencer's seed?* She felt the tug now strongly back into the flesh. Her thoughts clouded, as Sharon's brain had to fight the after-effects of the electric shock. Joan felt so horribly alone. *I wish I had someone to talk with. And how is it that she carries Spencer's child? And why the Creator's spark?*—no, there was no mistaking it. Yes, Spencer's seed, but also the glitter of angels—was this meant to be another Chosen one? She felt outplayed and confused. It had to be a mistake, and still connected to the ECT machine, her hand reached back for the button—*maybe just one more.* "Beep...Beep..." A knock at the door.

"Who is it?" her finger off the button, her hands ripping the band from her head, smoothing down her short hair over the still-gooey electrode gel.

"Housekeeping."

Her immediate thought–*no it isn't.*

"You're right, Joan," a woman's voice, "can we come in?"

She glanced around at the bed, chairs and table all pushed to the edges so she'd be less likely to injure Sharon's body. She looked at the door and sensed the creatures on the other side. "No," she said. "You can stay where you are. Why have you come?"

"Please let us in," the female said, "we will do you no harm. You have my promise."

Joan laughed, "That's rich, the word of a succubus...what exactly is that worth?"

"If you let us in we'll tell you where he is. Where he's hidden the Chosen."

Then she heard the other one, *"Minnie don't. If he finds out..."*

It could be an act—probably was—but she was getting nowhere...and she had asked for company, which was just the kind of twisted answer to an angel's prayer the Creator loved—ask for food, you get a seed, ask for courage and you go to war, ask for help and well... two demons come a-knocking. "Oh fine," getting off the floor. She pulled back the security chain and opened the door. Blinding morning sun caused her pupils to contract as she breathed in salt air, rotting garbage from the nearby fast food joint dumpster and a hint of sulfur. In front of her, the female had on sunglasses, form-hugging jeans and a red plaid shirt, buttons open with the tails tied across her naked midriff, her companion casual too in jeans, tee shirt and a New Jersey Devil's cap.

"Nice touch," she pointed at his cap.

He smiled. "I like hockey," his face like a Caravaggio angel. "I am called Ian, and this is Minnie."

"Of course," Joan said, knowing that like the Creator the Abomination loved his little jokes.

"So we can come in?" Minnie asked.

"Yes, but try anything and you will feel the wrath of the Creator." And she waved a hand across the threshold. The female looked down and then gingerly stepped across. Ian followed, and the three stood in the shabby room and stared at one another. "He made you well," Joan finally said.

"Have you known us before?" Minnie asked.

"I know no demons, and I've met thousands."

"But us?" she persisted, "Have you met us before... before this Chosen one?"

"No," she said. "And as you've come for information you must trade for it. You know where Spencer is?"

"Yes."

"Where?"

Ian touched Minnie's shoulder. "Don't do this."

Minnie shook her head. "Brother, you can leave if you want, but I will do this."

"I'm not going anywhere," he said, "but if he finds out he will destroy us."

"Yes," Minnie turned back to Joan. "Spencer, the Chosen, is concealed on an island a hundred miles south of Miami called Carlos Key. It can be reached by sea or by air."

Her directness was not what Joan had expected, neither was the urgency she felt from this Minnie—yes she had met demons in all forms—but never one like this. "How is it that you managed to conceal him from me these past months?"

Minnie met Joan's gaze, "An old trick. He is in love, and it is not returned. The woman drinks his light. And now it's my turn." The demon's lips pursed into a pretty bow and her brow furrowed.

"So ask." Ian said. "She is an angel, she must tell the truth."

"What are we?" Minnie blurted. "And if you say we're demons and succubi, that I know, but what are we?"

For Joan, the information she'd just received was staggering, like a blindfold removed. Lucifer had beguiled Spencer with a woman—guessing the one in bed with the belly full of something wrong. And now in front of her two succubi wanting to know...Mommy, where do demons come from? She stared into the blacks of Minnie's eyes. "You are different," she said, "you, stand beside her," she instructed Ian. She moved in and placed a hand on each of their shoulders. Immediately she felt flooded with their memories. These beings were created shortly after Spencer's birth. The Abomination had made them by cutting away at his celestial body and mixing that with pure-white sand, and had instructed them to protect Spencer—*interesting—hellion as watchdog*. She saw Lila's death, but more than just images, she was stunned by their emotions—*demons don't feel*—not like this. She saw them as the two crows perched by Spencer's bedroom, watching him, following him to school, looking through the windows as he studied, Ian rifling through his locker, reading his comics, trailing him to the library, never letting him out of their sight. It brought her to tears, seeing Spencer as a little boy, his fists flying against two bigger boys who were stoning a stray cat, and then in the principal's office, blood on his sleeve, anxious, waiting for her to come and mete out his punishment. These two had seen and lived it all. "What are you?" She gripped them tighter, feeling their flesh beneath her fingers, like dense clay—and the scenes shifted, one flowing to the next—Spencer with a tan, wearing shorts, a drink in his hand, his eyes on the beautiful brunette—"Madeleine," he whispers, and then Joan is in the cabin of a plane, watching the pilot and co-pilot attack one another, and then in the bedroom of the Abomination, watching as he slumbers, Minnie's hand reaching out to touch him—she's filled with so much longing, such hunger, not sexual *but what?*... And then she sees Ian drinking the soul of a nurse at the hospital in Chicago. He's looking at Minnie, his expression tender, a connection between these two creatures..."Oh sweet heaven," and she let go.

"What?" Minnie asked. "I told you things that could destroy us, so please tell me what you saw?"

Joan staggered, "not possible." The entire premise of her existence, of these relentless battles of good and evil, now called into question. "You are capable of love," she spat out, the words like poison on her tongue.

Ian grinned, "Duh, I could have told you that. I love Minnie, she loves me, and we both love Spencer. We grew up with him. He's the most-amazing dude. Wicked smart, you should see some of the stuff he can do."

"But you're demons," Joan said. "You're incapable of love...of all of these emotions...." She stared at Minnie.

"Please say what you're thinking," Minnie begged. "Please."

"Not possible," and Joan stepped back. She stared hard, demons cast no light—and that was almost true of these two—but in that *almost* was a terrible mystery.

"Please."

Joan trembled and shook her head, "it's not possible...you have souls."

Tears welled in Minnie's eyes, "Thank you. And we are sorry for that airplane."

"All those people you killed," Joan said, wishing the Creator would just finish whatever game It was up to, and get her out of there. Why couldn't It pick another angel to do this? She was tired and frightened.

"We don't care about them," Ian said. "And lately I've discovered that something inside them tastes good."

His words snapped her right back. "That sounds more like it. Okay, demons, enough twenty questions. Time for you to go away...go away."

"Wait," Minnie said, "before you do that, I can tell you there's no need for you to go to Florida."

"And why is that?" prepared for trickery.

"He's on his way here. I see how Ian offended you. We have killed many and may do so again. But you have to remember that whatever we are now, we were born demons. I know that you cannot lie. We were not born with souls and I do not know how they came to be. But, thank you, and we'll leave on our own."

Chapter Twenty-one

□ □ □

"Kayla, calm down," Lara on the phone, trying to figure out what had made the up-beat twenty-nine-year-old in charge of the animal studies so freaked out. Just out of her "shark" meeting, where she'd approved the publicity campaign for Marvan, she'd been blindsided with this call.

"I've been trying to get Spencer all morning," Kayla sobbed, "He's not picking up."

"He's flying to New York. I'm sure his cell's just off. Now tell me exactly what's happened. And does anyone else know about it?"

"Lara, I'm the only one in the building and there's blood everywhere. All the cages, they're empty."

"There was a break in?"

"No...I think they did it themselves."

"Who?"

"The rats. The Marvan rats. The cages were all open. It's horrible...oh my God!"

"What?"

"Oh God...there's something under the table...Oh God."

"What?" And Lara was immediately on her computer, flipping through the pass codes for the surveillance cameras.

"I see a tail. They're under there and there's blood."

Lara switched on to a bird's-eye view, Kayla approaching one of the stainless steel dissection tables. She zoomed in, seeing row after row of open cages, some filled with dead and half-eaten rats, the white floor obscured beneath dried and some still-wet bloody rat tracks.

Kayla shrieked, "Oh my God...they're eating them...I have to tell Spencer. Oh God!"

"I'm on the surveillance cameras, Kayla. I'm right there with you, try to calm down. What are you seeing, what's under the table?" She manipulated the camera, zooming in to the floor at the edge of the table. Something moved, and then she saw a pair of eyes, whiskers and a bloody snout. A huge rat head peeked out, it was staring up, almost like it knew it was on camera. Behind it another shiny head and then a third dragging the partially eaten carcass of a smaller rat. And suddenly a swirl of movement from under the tables as hordes of jumbo second and third generation Marvan rats surged across the floor.

"Kayla," she shouted, "Get out of there! NOW!"

But the young PhD was surrounded, a rat nipped at her ankle. She screamed and scrambled onto one of the tables, where she—and her staff—had dissected untold numbers of rats. "Help me!" she screamed, as the rats climbed over one another, building a living ramp up the side of the table.

"I'm calling security," Lara said, "try to stay calm." Panicking, she dialed, knowing they'd come too late. No, she couldn't watch. As the raging rats cleared the lip of the table and swarmed the brilliant young woman, ripping at her flesh and tearing her apart as she had done to so many of them. Kayla didn't have a chance. Her body thrashed, legs kicking, arms scrambling against the slick stainless table as she fell shrieking beneath the sea of ravenous vermin.

"Oh, God." She pictured Karel, of how important this project was to him—*absolutely nothing can go wrong.*

Lara swallowed hard...*she's dead, nothing can change that.* She stared at the monitor and then down at her trembling hands. Time froze as her mind, usually so deft in crises, was unable to focus. "Oh God," and then Karel's voice deep and soothing inside her head, *"absolutely nothing can go wrong...I love you."* She remembered that day at his mansion when she'd first realized she'd fallen in love. She knew then that she would do anything for him, anything at all, and with that came action. *This is what he'd want me to do.*

Her hands shook as Grady Mulligan, the head of security, finally picked up. "There's been an outbreak of plague in the animal lab. It needs to be sealed, fumigated with cyanide gas and sterilized. All of the animals have to be sacrificed, and under no circumstances is any person to go in the building without my express permission."

"What about the staff?"

Lara stared at the screen, she shuddered as a rat peeked out from inside Kayla's belly; it was covered in blood and was ripping at a glistening length of intestine. "There was no one inside," she said. "But I'll need all staff attached to that pod placed in quarantine. Keep them comfortable, and reassure them that they'll be fine—but none of them are to leave the island without my say so. Understood?"

"Yes."

"Good."

*

Spencer thought about Joan as his flight touched down at JFK—her incessant truisms and insistence on honesty, but mostly that she was one person who loved him unconditionally and would always tell him the truth. He missed her horribly. So much regret, of wishing he'd stayed on the phone to find out what was so damn important. At least now the pain of her loss had lessened. And he knew why, because as soon as he got through whatever publicity appearances Lara had arranged, he'd see Madeleine. Just the thought of her sent a head rush—her orchid scent, her skin, the lilt of her voice. She'd been so excited on the phone, running through the details of her wardrobe, the sets, making last minute decisions about her first, second... "and what if they want a third?" encore.

As the plane landed, like the others in first class, he ignored the seatbelt sign, and retrieved his laptop case from the overhead. First time he'd left the Keys in six months with the exception of Neri's wedding. He looked around at the older couple in front of him, as they checked their tickets and gate information, and then at the lawyer-looking man, across the aisle in a navy suit, white shirt and tie eager to get off and head straight to an important meeting—*but that's just a guess, isn't it?* Because for the past three months—and he knew exactly when it had happened—all his unique abilities, to see auras, to get glimpses inside a person's thoughts, to heal, even to skry—had evaporated.

The strangest part was—*I couldn't care less.* In fact, it was a relief—*No, more mutant nerd boy.* No more having to put up mental barriers against everyone's pain. More importantly, he—albeit with a ton of help from Lara and Global—had accomplished what he'd set out to do. Marvan was more than living up to expectations. Soon, it would find its way to thousands of desperate people. It would transform lives. He wondered if, in some cosmic scheme, having someone as wonderful as Madeleine wasn't a kind of payment, like God speaking straight to him—*you did good kid, and now you can have love.* And so he'd proposed... twice. Both times she'd said no. "*I do love you,*" she'd said. "*But, I'm not ready for that... I have to focus on my career.*"

Now, with his laptop case in one hand and his carry-on in the other, he shuffled forward. Maybe his father was right. "You did it wrong," James Williams had told his son on the phone. "You had no ring, without that it's just talk."

"Why does a piece of jewelry matter?"

"Tradition? Seal the deal? A sign of good faith...you need a ring, and frankly son, after two turn downs you might want to consider that she isn't ready, or that...she doesn't see you in that way."

"No. She loves me. This will work, and I think you're right, I'll get the ring. Is Allie around?"

"Yeah, I'll put her on."

"Thanks, I could use some consultation."

"It has to be unique," his stepmother had said, "and a bit dramatic." She'd then hesitated.

"What?"

"Are you sure about her Spencer? I've never met the woman, and I know she's wonderfully talented and beautiful, but are you sure?"

"Allie, just spit it out, what are you trying to say?"

"Spencer...I don't want to see you get hurt...it's just...there are a lot of parallels with your mother."

"I know," he'd said, "but other than her singing, she's nothing like my mother."

Allie hadn't pushed, and he hadn't wanted to share he had similar doubts. Instead, they'd kept the conversation light. Her giving him advice on rings–"*avoid funny shapes and colors,*" "*it has to be both classic and unique...and remember the four "C"s–color, cut, clarity and carats*"–and then catching him up on the doings of Michael and Tabitha—most of which he already knew from their Facebook pages.

But even as he'd stopped at the priciest jeweler on Duval Street, the doubts had persisted. It was there he'd found the emerald and diamond ring—the Center stone pulled from the wreckage of a Spanish galleon—a near flawless three-carat emerald the color of her eyes.

He'd pop the question tonight, after her performance. He'd reassure her that he would never interfere with her career. *Please say yes, Madeleine...third time's a charm.*

As he emerged from the secured area, he smiled. Lara, with her perky new hairdo and dark suit, was waiting—he grinned and tried to remember why he'd had such mistrust of her and of Global.

She waved and pointed at her watch.

"How are you?" he asked as she approached, with a heavyset livery driver who looked like an ex-linebacker at her side.

"We've got to move," giving him a hug and peck on the cheek. "Give Jim your baggage stubs, and I'll catch you up in the car."

"This is it," Spencer said, holding up his backpack and laptop. "I didn't check anything. And by the way, you look great," still weird that he could no longer see her aura. But there was something about her that seemed off—worried, preoccupied... something.

"Thanks, I don't know what I was thinking with that dyed blond all those years." She stepped back. "Please tell me you've got something else to wear?"

"Not really, I was planning to rent a monkey suit for the opera, but other than that I just packed jeans and a few more of these," he said, pulling back the front of his wrinkled linen jacket to show the Tommy Bahama silk shirt with its orange and green parrot.

"And your hair, when's the last time you had it cut?"

"What's the problem?"

"Crap, Spencer you're going on national TV in less than three hours, and I can't see the men and women of America trusting an unshaven, long-haired beach bum to deliver our message of hope in a bottle... Let's get out of here."

"What?! Wait a minute," trailing after her, as the chauffeur attempted to relieve him of his bags. "TV? You never said anything about going on TV...."

"Spencer, the entire Carrie O'Dell show is on Marvan. It's a marketing coup. It just happened and it's going to launch Marvan in a major way."

"Lara, you've got to be joking," adrenalin surged, his mouth suddenly dry. "You know I trust you, but why would a talk show want to devote an hour to a drug that's still experimental? We've only got approval for a very limited release, pending completion of a phase 3 study."

"Because it's news. And because they'll be first. It also turns out that Carrie O'Dell's sister is a subject in the phase 2 trial. Ms. O'Dell contacted Global directly—not one of her eighty-five producers—but her. I was extremely leery, until I spoke with her. The last thing I want is to be ambushed on national TV. She couldn't praise it enough—Marvan transformed her sister's life. She came right out and said if it wasn't for your drug, she had no doubt her sister would eventually kill herself—had attempted it multiple times. Spencer, this is an endorsement money can't buy. Carrie O'Dell in some ways yields more power than the president. She also made it clear that she wants you on the show...wants to thank you in person. She's rearranged her whole show to accommodate your being here. I need you to do this." She stopped as they came to the exit, the doors slid back, "Come on...we have just enough time."

"For what?" Wondering if there was any way he could talk her out of this, get someone else to go on. Anything.

"Jim," she said as the black town car pulled up. "Take us to Bergdorf's...get in," she told Spencer. "It's your turn for a makeover."

As they drove, Lara looked at Spencer, tanned and other than the shock she'd just sprung—happy, not giving a crap that he looked like some Caribbean Jesus. She longed to confide in him and knew that she had to tell him about the catastrophe and that even now cyanide gas was being pumped into the facility. She felt queasy and struggled to keep her expression pleasant. She couldn't block the images, the screams of that poor woman, the disgusting sounds of frenzied rats ripping her to pieces. No, there'd be no point in telling him before the taping, and come to think...*he's in love. He wants to see Madeleine, go to her performance...why ruin it for him?* But the ramifications—*what does this mean?* The scientist in her needed to know how this might impact humans. She comforted herself with rationalizations. *It's the nature of rats to winnow out the weak. That makes sense. The second and third generation Marvan rats were practically a different species—two to three times as large as the placebo animals—that made sense. But how did they get the cages open? And why the systematic slaughter and why...*and again the screams, as Kayla was being torn to pieces.

The guilt was crushing. *What have you become? What sort of person covers up something so...Don't think about that.* Turning slightly so he couldn't see the tremor in her hands, she pulled out her cell and dialed Bergdorf's, arranged for a shopper and bullied her way into an immediate appointment with their top stylist and hairdresser.

"What are you doing?" he asked. "Why do I need a stylist?"

"This," she said, grabbing a fistful of his shoulder-length hair—bleached and streaked by the sun. It had the consistency of straw from his daily snorkel expeditions. "It's got to go."

"What? No way."

"Don't argue, besides it's in your contract."

"Excuse me."

"Should have read it—'researcher may be called upon to participate in marketing or publicity activities.' Besides, I'll make you look so hot that Madeleine won't know what hit her."

"Really?"

"Promise."

"Well, okay then."

Chapter Twenty-two □ □ □

"Close your eyes," the bubbly make-up artist instructed Spencer, as she tickled his face with a brush—"just a little more...okay, open." And she ripped back the navy apron, "Ta da! So what do you think?"

He stared in the dressing room mirror—*who the hell is that?* Since touching down this morning, he'd been measured, shorn, tweezed and now given a light coat of spackle prior to being shoved in front of a midday viewing population in the millions. The man in the mirror bore little resemblance to the long-haired beachcomber who'd boarded in Miami. After years, and long-ago fights with his father over his hair, he'd told the hairdresser at Bergdorf's "do it," and he had. Never one for grooming—hell, if he could get away without ever shaving, he would have—his immediate thought, *Dude, you look sharp,* followed by, *can't wait to see Madeleine's reaction.* The image reflected back—glossy dark hair that stopped at the collar of his crisp-white shirt, bangs neatly parted to the side, clean shaven, his expression serious, his mother's golden-brown eyes—maybe a little sad, a strong jaw. He smiled, and to the make-up artist, "it's good."

"When they sent the before picture, I had no idea," she gushed. "Smart move ditching the Jesus hair."

A knock at the door and a woman's voice from the hall, "are you decent?"

Before anyone could answer, in came talk-show megastar Carrie O'Dell. Barely five-feet and nearly as wide as she was tall, her frame cinched in tight at the middle in a deep purple dress that displayed her bosom like a shelf. She perched on four-inch heels, her red hair loose around her shoulders, her makeup—flawless. "Dr. Williams, I presume," her hazel eyes twinkling and merry. "God, you're younger than I thought." She walked over to the makeup chair, put her hands on his shirt collar. "Here let me do this for you...I was thinking you'd be some crusty old professor type. There," unbuttoning a second button, "much better, got to show a little skin."

He got out of the chair, "It's Spencer."

"And tall and cute," she gushed, "Single? Gay?"

"Taken and straight."

"Damn..."

Before he could catch his breath, she'd linked an arm in his and was escorting him out and toward the set. "I don't usually meet my guests before the show, kind of like the surprise, but I wanted to get to you before the usual chaos and say thank you."

"For what?" his nerves ratcheting up as he caught the sounds of the waiting audience.

"I don't know how much of this I want to go into on the air," the candid celebrity said, as she brought him to the outer edge of the stage. "I mean it's one thing for me to talk about my weight, my bad marriages, my brush with cocaine, my years of drinking but it's something else when it's family. My sister Megan got the crap end of the genetics—depression runs in our family. On my mother's side, three suicides. Hell, when I was five my grandpa— a Boston cop—put a gun in his mouth. Anyway, Megan's been in and out of psych wards since she was twelve. She got in on your study. It's a fucking miracle," she choked up and paused to regain her composure. "I told her you were on the show—she sure wants to meet you."

Before he could respond, a balding producer scurried toward them, followed by two assistants. "Carrie, you're going to make me lose what little hair I've got left. We're live in two."

"Yeah yeah yeah," she said, and then to Spencer, "I've been doing this for so long, I literally do it in my sleep. It's crazy, I dream interviews...Sal, get a mike on him."

"Dr. Williams isn't supposed to go on until the second segment."

"Oh," she shook her head, looking at her harried underling, "I thought that was my name on the set...Oh look, it is. Give the man a fucking mike!" And then to Spencer, "Don't be nervous. Momma's going to take good care of you. Just be yourself, and follow my lead." She looked toward the set, which included a semi-circle of comfortable dark leather couches. Her theme music came on, and just as an assistant looped a tiny microphone into the neck of his shirt, Carrie grabbed him by the arm and headed into the bright lights. "Here we go."

*

From the back of the auditorium Lara tried to raise Karel on his cell... again. She had to talk to him. The rats had been exterminated, and it would be just a few hours before they'd vent the cyanide and discover Kayla's remains. She'd already contacted legal and was frantically thinking through ways this horror could be capped. "Pick up the damn phone." And then the music came up and she saw bubbly Carrie bringing Spencer out of the wings. The packed audience erupted in applause.

"There aren't a lot of real heroes in this world," the talk show queen said, as the audience quieted. "But I've got one for you today. Today's show is all about a wonderful new drug that none of you have heard of. This is a Carrie O'Dell exclusive. I'm excited as hell, and you need to watch this."

Lara's phone picked up, "Karel?"

"Don't worry, Lara." He said.

"You know?"

"Of course, a tragic accident. These things happen... you'll take care of it."

"But her family... there's nothing left. Karel... they ate her."

"A certain poetry, don't you think?"

"Are you insane?"

"Well, they'd watched her dissect their brethren, merely meting out a bit of rat karma."

"This is no joke, Karel! She was a lovely woman. She didn't deserve that."

"Lara, look, our boy's finally going to speak, and kudos on the makeover; he looks fabulous!"

She realized Karel was watching the show and that Spencer—who looked damn good, albeit a bit deer-in-the-headlights—was saying something.

"A lot of people don't realize," he said, "that depression and other forms of mental illness are the number one cause of disability in America. It's in every family, yet no one talks about it, like we have this giant secret, and with it comes a tremendous amount of shame."

"In your family?" Carrie asked.

He paused and nodded, "My mother."

And behind them appeared a famous still of his mother singing at Carnegie Hall, and then switched to Lila with little Spencer in a picture shot for *Homes Beautiful Magazine*. "For those who didn't know—and why should you?" Carrie said,

"Spencer's mom was Lila Cartwright-Williams... and you say she had depression?"

He swallowed hard. "She took her own life."

"I'm so sorry," Carrie said. "That wasn't made public, was it?"

"No," and Lara—along with all America—saw him struggle to hold back tears. "She had so many fans... still does. Somehow my family and her record label were able to keep it secret... and that's part of the problem, isn't it? My mother killed herself and it's not something to be discussed."

"There's depression and suicide in my family too," Carrie said, "and you're so right, it's not dinner conversation. Is it a jump to say that your mother's suicide is what motivated your research?"

"No, but I'm sure it's connected. See, when I set out to try and find something that could ease severe depression, I knew it had to be something that made people stronger. Most people who have severe depression can trace their first episode to a major life stress—parents getting divorced, a romantic break-up, childhood abuse, a personal trauma... even seemingly positive things like going away to school or enlisting in the military. So if I could find something that made people more able to handle stress, my thought was then maybe it could eliminate depression."

"And you've achieved that."

"I don't want to overstate things," he said, "But our first two trials—the second one just now completed—have been promising."

"Oh, please." She slapped a hand on his knee and turned face-on to the camera—"Dr. Williams is way too modest, and when we come back from commercial I'm going to blow your socks off. Get set to meet actual patients of Dr. Williams, people who've been taking his marvelous Marvan—you won't want to miss this."

"He's good," Karel said, the phone still by Lara's ear. "I thought he might lose it, but the camera loves him... was there anything else you needed, Lara?"

"How you can be so fucking cavalier?"

"Would you prefer it if I were upset? It won't change a thing. It's done, the poor girl is dead, we'll tell her family there was an explosion and we'll make certain they are well compensated. What matters is launching Marvan, and from what I can see, you are doing a spectacular job. You can't buy this kind of publicity. By the end of this hour tens of millions will be asking their doctors to prescribe them Marvan. I can't tell you how proud you've made me and how much I love you."

Her breath caught, *please say it, please ask me to marry you.* "I love you too," *but why are you being such an uncaring prick?*

"Darling, I'll pick you up at seven—the concert's at eight. And Lara..."

"Yes."

"I got you a present."

"What is it?"

"Tonight," he said, and hung up.

And she pictured a diamond ring with an emerald-cut stone, and yes she'd forgive him all this crap, just put the damn thing on her finger.

*

Joan, clutching Sharon's ridiculously large bag, stood on the corner of 5th and 44th amid a devoted throng of Carrie O'Dell fans who'd congregated to watch the live-monitor feed, and possibly to get selected for the studio audience. She suspected a trap. And yet, those two demons had not lied. The whole matter was perplexing, but there was Spencer on the huge screen talking about his research, work he'd started as a child. Now, perhaps too late, Joan saw that it was this work for which he had been chosen. She also felt shocked—not just by how he looked with his long hair gone and his too tidy appearance—maybe because he was on television... but he cast no light. *What have they done to you?*

She again looked at the two uniformed guards by the entrance. They'd already denied her admittance. Hampered by her angelic nature which could only speak truth, she finally found an opening in Ms. O'Dell's teaser. Fishing her—or rather Sharon's—wallet from the bag, she found Spencer's card for his now-defunct Chicago clinic. And walking with purpose she went back to the guards. "I'm sorry," the tall male one said, "there's no more room in there today... try tomorrow."

"No," and she held out Spencer's card. "I'm one of his patients," glancing up at the monitor—*Please let that be enough.* Her eyes found the guard's. *You can make a choice*, she thought. *Please let me in.*

"Oh oh," his female counterpart remarked, "She's in the next segment. Crap! You should have been in there an hour ago. Come on," and she held the door, "I'll show you where you need to go." And ushered her into the darkened backstage. "This way," and Joan followed, careful to not trip on the thick cables that traversed the black floor.

The guard led her toward a small group waiting behind a scrim. An assistant producer with a headset was looking toward the stage and then up at a monitor.

"He looks so much better with his hair like that," a brunette gushed. "God, he's cute."

"So now it comes out," a tall thin man with salt-and-pepper goatee and moustache remarked in mock annoyance. "Wendy's hot for the doctor."

"No, Peter...I only have eyes for you."

Joan's attention was pulled in opposite directions, Spencer in the distance on the stage—not yet seeing them. And then her little group, two women and three men getting set to go out on stage—both women pregnant and both with that weird gold glitter in their wombs.

"Okay, in five, four, three, two," the woman with the headset said. "One. Get out and take your seats." She looked back at her charges and quickly counted, "Oh shit, we're short a space."

"Don't worry," the curvaceous brunette replied, "we can squeeze together on the couch."

And their attention was pulled by Carrie O'Dell. "And here they are," she announced, walking toward the scrim. "Come on out...don't be shy. Ladies and gentleman...and forgive me for reading from the prompter but I'm terrible with names, here are Wendy, Kaleb, Peter, Jack, Donna...and..."looking at Joan and then back at the monitor.

"Sharon," Joan said, her eyes darting past O'Dell to Spencer, who seemed shocked by the appearance of his test subjects. And then his gaze fell on her.

He was out of the chair. "Sharon...is that you?...Wendy, Peter, what are you doing here?"

"There there," Carrie said, putting a hand on his shoulder and leading him back to his spot. "You can't expect to come on my show without a few surprises," and she winked at the monitor. "Roll video."

And behind them a film, largely featuring Peter and Wendy— two of the first twelve Marvan subjects—played for the audience. "*I can't remember how many times,*" *Wendy said into the camera, "I'd been called a hopeless case. It had gotten to the point I believed it. I'd go to bed wishing that God would take me. And when I'd wake up, my first thought would be, is this the day I finally screw up the courage to do it...to end my life?*" *The image then shifted to Peter, his clothes smeared with paint, sitting in his Soho studio in front of boxes, from which he was pulling out copies of his medical records. "At one point they had me on twelve different medications. I felt like a zombie, which I wouldn't have minded, if they'd helped... oh and here's the ambulance report after my last overdose. I'd taken all the pills—hundreds of them, put them in the blender with some ice cream—I was sure it was going to work—a suicide smoothie. It nearly did but I woke up in intensive care... three weeks later, and all I could think was I'm so pathetic that I can't even do this right."*

The screen went blank, "Heavy stuff," Carrie said, "and now look at you... look at you all, healthy, happy." She turned to the camera. "Suicide is one of the ten leading causes of death in this country... and now comes Marvan." She looked at the brunette. "Wendy Glass, you've just finished a fabulous new book on your experiences both with depression and what you describe as an 'emotional, spiritual and physical awakening' on Marvan." The screen showed the book jacket for the not-yet-released *Out of Darkness*. "This is must-read material. I was sobbing through the first half, and laughing hysterically through the rest. You're an amazing writer. I urge everyone in America to go to their local bookstore and reserve a copy, and one for anyone in your life's who's been touched by depression."

"That's kind of you to say, and that's part of the Marvan experience," Wendy shot Spencer a warm look. "What Doctor Williams has done... what we've all been through," and she took Peter's hand. "It's more than being free from depression. We've been made better, stronger... I could never have written a book before. I'd always wanted to, but indecision, fear, lack of discipline... unrelenting depression, all these things held me back. Two weeks on Marvan and I'm writing 20-30 pages a day, every day. I had a first draft completed in less than three weeks. And as you said—and trust me I've never been one to brag—I'm damn proud of it. It's good." And looking toward the camera that had the red light, "Buy my book—you'll like it."

Joan stayed silent. The more she stared at Spencer, the greater her dread—*what have they done to you?* And then, what was up with both those women being pregnant, and why did their embryos glow with the sparkle of the Abomination? *He can't breed with mortals. What's going on?*

"So Sharon, what's your story?"

You can say nothing or you can speak the truth—"Well Carrie, I'm the archangel Joan and Dr. Spencer Williams, whom I love dearly, has been seduced and beguiled by the devil. This drug is an abomination, and these two women, are now carrying children that reek of Lucifer."

The hostess blinked, smiled, and didn't skip a beat. "Those are some big allegations Sharon...or Joan. You've just called Marvan Satan in a bottle. Anything to back that up?"

"Glad you asked." Joan reached deep into Sharon's bag.

Spencer was out of his seat. "Sharon...Joan, what the? What are you doing?" He raced towards her.

"It's the only way Spencer." Her fist wrapped around Sharon's boxcutter.

"Security! Security!" Carrie shouted and pushed back in her seat as uniformed men and women—always at the ready—made a beeline for Sharon.

Joan knew she'd have a single shot. Rules were being broken— on both sides. Scrambling on all fours, with Spencer trying to pull her back, she gripped the boxcutter and jammed it into the hard-plastic casing of the camouflaged electric cable. She pushed in deep, fighting a sense of futility as nothing happened and then...

*

All hell broke loose. To Spencer, the Carrie O'Dell show was a waking dream that got weirder with each second. *How the hell did she track down the Marvan subjects?* Peter, Wendy, Kaleb, Jack, Donna. But it was Sharon—he'd never seen her name as one of the test subjects—had she been in the second study? He had so many questions for her, not to mention the relief he felt that she was alive, and looked so well, although completely changed with the short haircut and butch attire—of course no mistaking her crazy handbag. But when she'd started to speak, the voice was not hers. But Joan was dead, her body only recently retrieved from the plane wreckage. And the bizarre things coming out of her mouth, but when he saw her reach into the bag, he knew it would be bad. And then the boxcutter—*she's going to kill herself on national TV.* "You're not going to do this." He grabbed her hand and tried to pry the razor-like weapon away.

"Beguiled, Spencer! The Adversary is at work. You are his tool! His hands!" She shrieked.

What was she doing? He expected a gush of blood. He felt the shove of her shoulder and looked down, the blade sinking into the black floor—at least that's what he thought—until blue and orange sparks shot out; Sharon suddenly stiffened and screamed.

"Wheeeeeeeeeeeeeeeeeeeeeeeeeeeeeeeeeeeeeeeeeeeeeeeeeeee!" Her body bucked, as her muscles contracted with the jolt of electricity that flew through her body and into his.

He shouted and felt hands pull him away.

He heard Carrie gasp. "Oh sweet God...keep filming. Don't stop filming!"

He flopped onto his back and then realized that she—and everyone else in the studio—weren't looking at him or at Sharon's convulsing body on the studio floor. No, all attention was on this silvery figure, wings outspread, with a silver sword in her...its hand.

"I am the archangel, Joan," it bellowed, and the studio shook. It looked down at him. "Spencer, you, like your mother have been chosen by our Creator, and you have been beguiled and deceived. You are the pawn of Lucifer, and they—looking at the wide-eyed Marvan recipients—"are disciples of a false God, two of whom now carry children of a new curse. You must stop this, Spencer. What you have done must be undone."

Out in the audience heads nodded as three-hundred pairs of glazed eyes drank in the miraculous scene. Lips whispered, "Hallelujah," "Praise be to God," and "Blessed be," as fingers sought rosaries, prayer beads and such.

And then a voice of dissent. "Are you kidding?" Carrie O'Dell pushed out of her chair. She shook her head violently, and then looked down at the thrashing Sharon, froth foaming out the corners of her mouth, her jaw clenched. She stared unblinking at the celestial apparition and began to circle it, like some high-heeled wrestler looking for her opening "We're supposed to take you at your word that you're an angel." Her gaze raked every angle searching for the trick. "By their fruits you shall know them. All I see is some poor woman being tortured...by you. While behind me I've got a group of people whose lives have been transformed—in a wonderful way—by Marvan. You got an answer for that? How come my sister who was bleeping miserable, now has a life? Why should we believe you? You think my viewers are naïve idiots? This is some sick hoax to shelve Marvan and what decent person would do such a thing?" Picking up steam, and sure as shit this angel was bogus—possibly a holograph—she rolled her eyes for the camera. "Maybe some competitor...not that we'd ever think a drug company would stoop so low as to try and hang on to their market share for their crappy antidepressants. But I promise you this," nearly shouting as specks of saliva flew from her lips, "we at the Carrie O'Dell show will get to the bottom of this. Because I smell a rat! A big digital rat!"

The hovering vision stared down at Carrie. "I can only tell the truth. The Abomination is in the pill, is in this Marvan." Then it started to waiver, as Sharon's body quieted.

"Joan, how is this you?" Spencer asked.

As the silvery angel seemed pulled back into Sharon, its final words hit hard, "Ask me no questions, I'll tell you no lies."

He knelt by Sharon, still dangerously close to the damaged cable. He noted a gash on the back of her head, and she'd chipped one of her front teeth.

Wendy settled next to him, as he felt for a pulse. "What in God's name was that?" she asked.

"I don't know," he looked at Sharon's chest, is *she breathing?*

"How could she know we're pregnant?" Wendy asked.

"What?" Still stunned, Spencer felt a team of medics gently push him aside. They strapped an oxygen mask on Sharon, who'd started to moan. "You were all supposed to be on birth control!" Behind him he caught sight of Carrie signaling to a camera man.

"I was," Wendy whispered. "Both Donna and I were on the pill. I swear. I'm just past my first trimester." She looked at him. "I want this baby so much, Spencer. The things she said. That can't be true."

"But the risk," his attention torn between Sharon strapped down and hoisted onto an orange and black stretcher, and this awful complication spilling from Wendy. "We have no way of knowing how Marvan will affect an unborn baby. You should not have done this." He turned to her, "You have to terminate."

She glared back, "No. And I'm sorry you feel that way. You had to have known that at some point this would happen. Donna and I...and I'm sure there are others, will be the first. It's going to be fine. I'm going to have a wonderful healthy baby, and if it's a boy," her hand gently cupping her belly, "I'm naming him Spencer."

"Did you get all that?" Carrie asked, bosom heaving and winded as a barely conscious Sharon was wheeled off stage.

The cameraman, who like the rest in attendance seemed dazed, gave her a shaky thumbs up.

"What a show," she looked at Spencer, and then out at the camera.

"Angels, devils, a fabulous new drug, and the doctor who discovered it, what can I say? Be sure to join us tomorrow for out-of-control teens and what you can do to turn them back into. . . well," she winked, "little angels."

Part Five: The Devil's Due

□ □ □

Chapter Twenty-three

□ □ □

Lara blinked back tears as she veered across three lanes of The New England Throughway. Her thoughts were fixed on the Carrie O'Dell Show. Her tires squealed, and a horn blared as she shot the curves of the Westport exit. *What the hell was that?* Half a year ago, if anyone had claimed a belief in the supernatural, she would have thought them a fool. That beautiful creature flying out of Sharon Lahey, a woman at death's door a few months back, couldn't have been a hoax. Her rational mind wasn't going down without a fight—maybe a hologram, some magician's parlor trick with mirrors and refracting light. Maybe like Carrie O'Dell had said—some bizarre plot from a competing drug company. Batting tears she headed toward the coast road and Karel's mansion. Of course he'd been watching. *Jesus, Jesus— those women were fucking pregnant? And taking the drug?* She thought of poor Kayla and the mutated rats who ate her. What if those babies grew up to become like those monster rats? And those women were on birth control—*and they still got knocked up? Maybe I should be on the fucking drug.*

"Shit!" She slammed on the brakes, having just missed the turn to Karel's street. Throwing the Lexus into reverse and kicking up crushed shells, she nearly collided with a black Jaguar convertible coming out of the street. The woman driving, her face obscured by sunglasses and a pink and black scarf, cursed, shot Lara the finger and roared off. Funny, something about her seemed familiar. She flew down Karel's street, passing mansions hidden behind boxwood hedges. Pulling out the electric opener, she punched in the gate's access code, and skidded to a stop under the arches by the front door.

"Lara," Minnie, dressed in a shiny black PVC interpretation of a chauffeur's outfit was outside. She pushed back her cap. "We weren't expecting you. Do you have luggage? Will you be staying the night?"

"Where is he?" Lara gasped, getting out. "I need to see Karel."

Minnie smirked, "Probably still in bed."

"It's nearly four," Lara stormed through the open door. *What's he still doing in bed?* She ran up the stairs and down the hall and barged in. "I'm assuming you watched the whole thing."

"Of course," he said, unconcerned by his nakedness in a sea of dark purple sheets. Propped against pillows, he was intent on the video screen.

"So what was that?" she demanded, taking in bits of data, like why was there a wine bucket next to the bed with an upturned champagne bottle and another one half empty...a flute in his hand, another on the nightstand with smears of crimson lipstick. And perfume too—a familiar scent—certainly not his, *where have I smelled it?* "Who's been here?"

"Just a friend," he said.

His half smile infuriated her. "Oh, my God! What an idiot," her head feeling like she might pass out. "That was Madeleine, wasn't it?"

"Yes." He got out of bed, his penis semi erect as he walked toward her.

"You're screwing her."

"It doesn't mean much," he said, "a bit of recreation."

She backed away, feeling as though the floor might drop away. "I am such an idiot." A chilling clarity came over her as she stood her ground and looked him in the eye. "Yes, you tried to tell me, didn't you?" She turned and scanned his dizzying collection of paintings, Prometheus, The Fall, Adam and Eve in the Garden, The Temptation of Paris, Daniel in the lion's den, Joan at the Stake, Salome dancing in front of the head of John the Baptist. They were all telling a story.

"You believed what you wanted," he said. "Come to bed."

"Are you insane?"

"No," he glanced down, "just horny."

"What is Marvan?" she asked. "Why is it so important?"

"I think you know."

She wanted to resist, but his presence was like a drug, an addiction. *What does it matter? You want him...need him. You love him. He loves you. He's going to marry you, give you children.* "No, this has to be stopped. You have to be stopped. She was right, wasn't she? That creature, that angel."

"What's right and what's wrong, Lara? Are you so certain you know? Is it right for a parent to shove a child aside because they ask too many questions? Is it right for a first-born to be abandoned and imprisoned, because he dared speak the truth? Perhaps it's right to torture the creature that gave mankind the ability to think, that gave you that first spark of awareness." His voice boomed at her.

"What are you?" her legs shook as he closed the gap between them, his movements too fast to be human.

"Sweet, sweet Lara," he put his hands on her shoulders.

"Don't," she shuddered.

He kissed her forehead, and then her cheek.

She felt her resolve slip, how easy just to give in, to not care, to finally be the heroine in her own story. "Go away," she said, finding it hard to catch her breath. "Please just go away, go away."

As if a switch had been thrown, he was suddenly at the far end of the forty foot room.

"It's those babies you want, isn't it? How many of those women are pregnant?" She feverishly did the math–12,000 subjects in the phase-two multi-site trial, half of them women.

"I don't know," he smiled the corners of his mouth going too wide, like a clown's painted grin. "But it is exciting. I think they all may be."

"Oh God! That first day I came here," she said, trying to remember what he'd said. "Spencer Williams, you had to have him. You tried to tell me, and I was so love struck, so hopelessly naïve. It's about changing what human beings are. That's why it's so important."

He clapped his hands and the room shook. A William Blake water color of Isaac wrestling the angel fell from the wall; its glass shattered. "Excellent! I knew you'd finally get it. Although at first, even I didn't know why Spencer was so important."

"But why? What could all this possibly get you?"

"Payback, my love. The Creator wants mankind in His image...well, that's about to change. It's my turn...my image." And in the blink of her eye he'd closed half the space between them.

"Was it all lies?" She backed away and felt for the door.

"Of course not. I love you. That's no lie," again in arm's reach.

"Do you even know what love is?" she spat out, her words catching in her throat.

"Yes, and I also know what it means to have your heart broken, by the very one who is supposed to love you unconditionally. I know pain and I know love. So please, my sweet, put away all this and come to bed. I can make you happy, make you feel great things, give you love. The love you thought you'd never have."

As he reached for her, his hands cold, his face shifted—the whites of his eyes shaded grey and then black, his teeth too long–she shuddered. "No, get away from me, go away, please go away." Again he was somehow hurled to the other end of the room. She blinked, *What?* Trying to make sense of it. Her heart raced, legs shaking.

"Seems you've learned a trick," he commented, legs spread, penis engorged, and large, it bobbed up and down, nearly touching his rippled stomach, seeming to have a life of its own.

"Are you going to kill me?"

"No, I could never do such a thing," again the weird rictus grin, his head cocked with a loud crack and tilted far to the right. "I love you Lara...of course, we do hurt the ones we love."

Oh my God, this is real, not a bad dream..."You're actually the devil, aren't you?"

His head tilted to the other side and a pair of curled horns sprouted from his brow. "OK, you're a smart girl. I'm the head of the world's largest pharmaceutical company. Global makes billions from off of suffering, pain and disease—who did you think I'd be?"

"No! I will stop this. I will find a way to stop you!"

"I don't think so. Not unless you plan to kill a bunch of pregnant women...or wait for them to deliver and smother babes in their cribs. No, even you, with all your unbridled ambition, could never do such a thing. Of course, it's not unheard of— a tradition of sorts, death of the first born, slaughter of the innocents—some quite like it."

"No!" She grabbed the door handle and twisted. She fled down the stairs and across the marble foyer, more scared than she'd ever been.

Outside, Minnie and Ian loitered by the entry, one on either side. She raced past, wondering if they might try to stop her, as she yanked open her car door.

"Leaving so soon?" Minnie asked.

Lara didn't respond, and fearing the worst, turned the key, put it into gear and sped away.

*

From the wrought-iron balcony above, Karel, still naked and sporting a hard on and a pair of horns, took out a cell and watched her race off.

Minnie looked up, "And?"

"Not good. Sad really. They never believe me that I love them. I suppose I might have given the occasional mixed message...but I do love her."

Minnie put a hand on her hip, "Yes...And?"

"And what?...take care of her. She can't interfere with Marvan. Stop her. Do it now."

Ian joined his sister and looked at his master and maker, "I don't understand. If you love her, how could you want to destroy her? You *don't* know what love is."

From Minnie, Karel had come to expect a bit of rebellion, but from Ian, a perfect old-time succubus, this floored him. "And you? You know what love is?" Karel asked.

"Yes."

"This is rich...so tell me my handsome fledgling, I'm dying to know what an earth demon—a creature made from sand—considers love."

"Easy," Ian looked at Minnie and smiled. "It's when you feel more for another being than for yourself, and when you're with that being you are somehow greater together than apart. When their happiness matters more than your own....and when you would gladly die for them."

"Great," Karel scratched one of his horns. "It's got to be all the TV...Just take care of her. Do what you're told."

He watched as Minnie reached for Ian's hand and the two melted into a yellow mist, leaving only the familiar smells of sulfur and frankincense. He stared out, unsettled—*how dare they!* And was the extent of their adolescent rebellion just words? *Would they take it farther? Would they actually disobey? Had they?* But first things first...

He pressed a button on the cell. "Duane, it's Mr. Von Graff...Yes, I'm well thank you. There's going to be a change in the Marvan project. You'll be pleased. It appears we've had a security breach, and I'm sorry to say that all indicators point at Lara. Inform security she is not to be allowed anywhere near a Global facility. Her office is to be sealed, her staff terminated and escorted from our premises immediately—we'll figure out the compensation later. And Duane, there's every likelihood she'll try to contact the FDA with some cock-and-bull story of complications with Marvan—that cannot happen. Get to our people on the inside. Let them know that Lara no longer represents Global."

"Industrial spy?" Duane suggested. "Working for Pfister. Tie it in to the bullshit on that talk show?"

"Good, there's more...and Duane...failure is not an option. We need to insure that nothing interferes with the launch of Marvan. Carlos Key is to be sealed, all personnel informed that the island is quarantined—make up some excuse, maybe tie it in with the plague scare and the rats that had to be exterminated. I'll want any communications devices confiscated and you'll need to assemble all staff that has had anything to do with the manufacturing of Marvan. It appears Lara and Dr. Williams have kept the process fragmented. It needs to be pieced together and fast. And finally, I'm not certain how much Dr. Williams has been compromised. I want you to revisit your initial plan—we need a new figurehead—that Clifford Clay should do."

*

Spencer followed the pair of EMTs out of the Carrie O'Dell studio and into the waiting ambulance. In the back he helped complete their forms. "Name is Sharon Lahey. She has severe depression and Borderline Personality Disorder and is chronically suicidal." He reached for her right wrist to show them the scars from her near fatal encounter with the box cutter. He felt her fingers—oddly cold—and turned them over. There was just a faint scar. He pushed up her sleeve expecting the spider-web mesh of old scars; they were mostly gone. "Sharon," he said, "can you hear me?"

The woman's eyes fluttered and she moaned.

"Joan," he whispered. "Wake up. It's me Spencer."

"Joan?" the sandy-haired EMT, who couldn't have been more than nineteen, and who had been torn between caring for his patient and stealing glances at Carrie O'Dell, asked. "I thought her name was Sharon?"

"She dissociates," Spencer lied, "Different distinct personalities."

"Wow! For real? Like on that TV show? So what happened in there?"

"She tried to electrocute herself," Spencer said, "nearly succeeded."

"Why would she do that?"

"I don't know," and before he could say more, the woman on the stretcher began to convulse. Her body bucked against the webbed strapping. Her head snapped back against the hard board and her eyes rolled up.

"Oh crap," the medic looked toward his partner. "She's going into status"—referring to the potentially fatal status epilepticus. "What's our ETA?"

"Another five."

The medic reached over Joan and slid back a door on the Plexiglas cabinets. He yanked out a vial of diazepam. Half way into uncapping the syringe he glanced down, "Holy shit!"

Spencer watched as a weird silver sparkle spread out from her belly, and then a faint tinkling of chimes. It hovered, and then Joan's voice, "She won't need that. Put it away. Save it for someone else."

The medic stared into the glow, "It's so beautiful!" A tear formed in his eye, as he fell back on the bench next to Spencer.

The seizure slowed, and then stopped.

The medic looked dazed. He glanced at Spencer. "You saw that. Please tell me you saw that."

"She had another seizure, just a small one" Spencer said. "I think you nailed it when you said she was going into status."

"But the glow..."

"What glow?"

"Those lights...it was," he shook his head. "You did see it, didn't you?"

"Just a seizure," Spencer said. "Maybe you caught a reflection through the windows."

"Right," and shaking it off the medic looked back at the now still woman, her pulse regular and steady on the monitor—not a sparkle in sight. "You wouldn't know her insurance carrier?"

"Sorry, no."

"Next of kin?"

"She's got family in Kansas, that's all I know. Maybe it's in her bag."

Shaken, the EMT grabbed the bulky satchel that Spencer had managed to boost on his way out of the studio. "Geez! Why would anyone need a pocketbook this big?" Answering his own question, he pulled out random items as he hunted for an insurance card. "What is this stuff?" Holding up a mostly empty tube with a blue and white label. "Is she a hooker, or something? There's like six of these in here."

Spencer couldn't imagine why this kid would think conductive gel in her pocketbook would make her a prostitute, but more importantly—what was she doing with the stuff? "You've got to be kidding, can I see her bag?"

"Sure," he slid it down the bench.

Spencer opened it wide and stared in..."What the hell?"

"What is it?"

Spencer looked at the thick rubber tubing, the little round electrodes—*what have you been doing?* "Just amazing how much crap a woman will carry around," and he fished out her wallet. "Here, I bet the insurance cards are in here."

"Thanks man," and they pulled into the ambulance bay.

Spencer stood back as they hoisted her out. He followed them through the electric doors and waited as the triage nurse took her information and checked her pulse, temperature and blood pressure. "What's going on?" Joan asked, her head immobilized to the wooden back board. "Spencer!" She tried to move and couldn't.

"It's okay, Sharon."

"I'm not Sharon and you know it."

"I thought you said her name was Sharon," the triage nurse commented. She flipped through the wallet the EMT had given her. "Yup, right here on her driver's license–Sharon Lahey."

"She's psychotic," Spencer glared down at Joan/Sharon.

"I am not, let me out of this. The Abomination is going unopposed."

The EMT who was tearing off the hospital's copy of the call record briefed the nurse. "She tried to kill herself on national TV—don't get stranger than that."

Actually, Spencer thought, *it gets a whole lot stranger.* He leaned over the stretcher and whispered in her ear. "Joan, I know it's you—say the truth or say nothing. And I'd strongly recommend the latter until I can figure out how to get you out of here." He looked at her dead on and waited until she'd nodded as far as the straps would allow.

For three hours he stuck by her side. Still strapped to the board, her head immobilized, she was pushed through a CAT scan to make sure she hadn't injured her spine.

"You staying with her?" a young female ED doctor asked, as they finally took her off the backboard, "cause usually we get a sitter for attempted suicides."

"I'll be here. If I have to go anywhere I'll let her nurse know."

"Thanks. We'll move her over to the psych unit as soon as we get a bed."

When the doctor left, he drew the curtain. "What the hell were you doing? And what have you done to Sharon?"

Sitting up she studied him, "What have they done to *you*, Spencer?"

"You really are Joan, aren't you?"

"Yes, Sharon gave me her body."

"And what did she get?"

"Salvation."

"What are you? And no more of this 'ask me no questions shit.'"

"I am the champion of the Creator. I was sent to guide and to watch you," her head dropped, "...I was tricked."

"By whom?"

"His names are many...Loki, Anon, Lucifer, Satan...Karel Von Graff. He is Abomination and sin. He has wrapped you in chains. Your light Spencer—the spark. It's gone."

Her words hit deep, kicking up a rush of guilt and anger, but he had to accept that she was indeed Joan and she would never lie. "I have to get you out of here."

"Yes," she said, still in her jeans, her plaid shirt open where they'd placed the electrocardiogram leads. She ripped off the taped pads and buttoned up. "They'll try to stop us."

He pulled back the curtain and looked out at the busy emergency room. A bloody trauma case was being wheeled through triage and the overhead system was requesting a code team to the cardiac units. "Joan, keep your head down and stick close. If they come after us, run."

"I revealed my celestial light," she said following him. "I'm not supposed to do that...at least not like this."

"Is that why you tried to electrocute yourself?"

"You saw it."

"Half the United States saw it. It's amazing you didn't fry yourself," making fast for the waiting area.

"Usually, there's a little box. It doesn't give me as big a jolt."

"You have an ECT machine?"

"Yes...A gift from a Dr. Carrigan."

"Hey!" the doctor who'd been working on Sharon called out, "Where are you going?"

"Run, Joan!" Spencer said, as he raced toward the exit.

Behind them he heard, "Wait! Security! Security! We have a Jane Gotaway! Jane Gotaway!"

Two uniformed guards stepped in front of the electronic doors.

"Don't worry," Joan said, as she slowed, "Hold on to me and don't stop. Whatever you do, don't stop." She pressed tight against him, grabbed his arm, "support me Spencer."

"What are you doing?" And then he felt her body stiffen and start to shake. Her legs lost strength, and it was all he could do to not drop her as the silver light again flew out from her belly. It was brighter now than in the ambulance, and again the faint impression of a silver angel with an outstretched sword flew in front of them.

One of the guards crossed himself, as the other took off his cap and stood back to let them pass.

The doors slid back and, half carrying her trembling body, he got her outside. It was late afternoon and traffic was thick on First Avenue. Behind him he could still hear the hospital's overhead—"Code Jane Gotaway. Code Jane Gotaway".

"Keep moving," she mumbled. "Get us out of here."

"See if you can stand," he said, "or at least look drunk."

"You know I can't lie."

"I'm not so sure anymore," and he held out his hand and managed to flag down a cab.

Before the cabby could get a good look at Joan's semi-stuperous condition, Spencer had shoved her in.

"Where to?"

"Just drive," Spencer said.

"Huh?"

"I've got to think…take us to a hotel." He thought of the gorgeous Global apartment on east 55th, but after the weird mess at the Carrie O'Dell show and Joan's proclamations of approaching doom, something told him that might not be a good option. "Nothing too expensive, and make it out of the way—a smaller one."

"You got it."

He looked at Joan, who was trying to snap out of it. Her head turned from side to side.

"She okay?" the driver asked.

"Too many martinis."

"You lie so easy," she muttered. "What happened to Spencer? Where is Spencer? The whore cut your hair."

"Actually, no," he felt annoyed. "And let's face it, without a bit of lying you'd be locked up on the psych ward. I did what needed to be done."

"Yes," she said, Sharon's blue eyes fixed on his. "It was effective, but you have lied and lied, and you have let the Abomination, the Accuser of Job, deceive you by pride and by vanity. I knew those were your great weaknesses. Oh, and there's more, how could you have let this happen?"

"Look," Spencer wished she'd just shut up, or at least say something useful, as the cab pulled up to a brownstone in the West 20's, "I need you to lay off with all of this hell and damnation crap. I'm going to get us a room, and you're going to tell me everything."

"Yes," she said, "it is time."

Chapter Twenty-four □ □ □

With the speedometer kissing ninety, Lara barreled south on I-95 toward New York. She struggled to keep from veering off the road. "How could you have been so fucking blind?" And again the damn car phone...this time her mother. No way was she picking up. A horn honked, "shit!" and she pulled back into her lane. *How could you let yourself fall for such a creature*—"what the fuck is he?" The phone again, and Russell, her assistant's voice, "Lara, pick up the damn phone. I know you don't like to if you're driving, but pick up!"

"Phone on," activating the hands-free device. "What is it Russell?"

"Well, I'm standing outside on the corner of 55th and Park and...and there's a pair of Global Security goons telling me I can't get back into my office. You know something about this?"

"Get out of there, Russell. They're not playing around. I'm sorry."

"Why? What's happened?"

"I can't explain. Just get away from that place. In fact, I'd get out of the city if I were you. I'll get in touch when it's safe."

"Lara, you're freaking me out. Am I fired?"

"Probably," her eyes abruptly riveted to a huge eighteen wheeler that was speeding crazily on the other side of the divider. "Oh God!" Her pulse leapt as the truck rammed through the barriers that separated the north and southbound lanes. The steel guardrail sprang away from its moorings, scraping up and over the truck like a zipper coming undone. It plowed straight toward her.

"What's happening?" Russell's voice. "Lara, what's going on!"

Time slowed and she could see into the semi's cab as it bounced across the narrow median. It was filled with yellow smoke, and the driver—an older man with a John Deere cap—his eyes wide and staring straight at her. She thought of Karel—*no you won't kill me. You'll have someone else do it for you.*

"Lara!" Russell shouting, "What's happening?"

Her hands tight on the wheel, the truck looming closer, a face flashed before her—Spencer's. And then Karel's voice, 'you've learned a trick', and then the thought *I don't want to die, not like this.* Adrenalin surged as she stared into the behemoth, its cargo container tipping precariously. Impact was coming, horns blared, and with her eyes fixed on the crazed driver, barely visible through the dense yellow, she slammed on her brakes. "GO AWAY! GO AWAY! GO AWAY!"

A car clipped her from behind and the airbags popped blinding her, then a glimpse of the impossible—Minnie's face beside the driver and Ian—or something that had his face pressed against the windshield grinning at her and waving with an arm made of smoke. And then someone rammed her from the passenger side and her car spun out. *I'm going to die.* She thought of Spencer. She saw him back at Gray and how innocent and dedicated he'd been. "I'm sorry," hearing the tear of metal, her heart pounding waiting for the killing blow. "Spencer, I'm so sorry."

Russell's voice through the speaker, "Lara! Lara!"

And then nothing.

*

Fifty miles from the crash site, in a quaint Manhattan B&B, Spencer sat on a tufted Victorian chair and stared at the woman on the fussily made bed. She was wearing jeans and a plaid shirt and had once been his patient—at least her body had. She was telling him things too incredible to believe...and yet, he did. Now her lids fluttered, her eyes rolled back and that weird silvery shimmer pulsed from her belly, and the silver angel appeared. He waited for the mini convulsion to pass. "I think I might have overdone it," she said. "It's less in my control."

"What I don't understand," at a loss where to start, "is this thing you keep talking about 'the Chosen.' Chosen for what? By what?"

"It's ancient, since the birth of your species" she answered, steadying herself by grabbing a bedpost. Her fingers twitched and one of her legs continued to spasm. "In different times the Creator and the Abomination have their games. Don't ask why. I once thought I knew—something about testing humans' worthiness, but now...at times I can't find the purpose. Maybe something to do with free will and that humankind is always presented with choice."

"You can go left or you can go right," remembering her lessons from long ago.

"Yes. Do you know the story of Job?"

"Sure."

"Good, because he was chosen. It's a horrible story. He was a kind man, did for others—a wealthy shepherd with a beautiful family. And the Creator and the Creature had a contest. Would this worthy, God fearing man in the face of adversity, turn to the Abomination? And so, like children playing a game, the Creator did nothing as the evil one destroyed everything Job loved, his wife, his children, his flocks, and finally his health. It was horrible to watch."

"But in the Bible," Spencer said, "he doesn't turn to Satan. He questions God's purpose, but never loses his faith."

"Correct, and over and over that same awful game is still played. Sometimes the purpose is clear, at others... even I cannot tell. The carpenter—Jesus of Nazareth—was about the triumph of love, even when faced with a horrible death. Then there was a samurai—Myamoto Musashi, he'd killed many—but always with honor, never once giving into the temptations—wealth, a woman he desired who belonged to another, a great estate. He became so accomplished that toward the end of his career he gave up his sword and killed with a wooden staff. That was a strange one, but at the end when he sat down in the cave it became clear. His lesson was about mastery and man's ability to transform into something approaching the divine."

"God works in mysterious ways?" Spencer offered.

"Who can know?" she sounded exhausted.

"And me... it has to do with Marvan."

"It must."

"But what have I done? It's meant to help people, to ease suffering, to do good. You saw those people. They were living in a kind of hell and the drug lifted them out."

She gave a tired laugh, "And what is the road to Hell paved with? Yes, on the surface, but those women are pregnant, and there is something different in the babies they carry. Your pill... you, Spencer, have done something that should not have been done. You have played with the clay of creation—it's not for you to do. I should have known. I should have seen this. I am so sorry, for it is I who has failed."

He felt himself boil with anger and then fear. He stared at his hands. "How did you know to find me? I mean you've been there my entire life. . . and most of my mother's. She said she knew you since she was a little girl."

Joan gripped the bedpost tight as a wave of tremors washed through her. "I'm called," she said. "I'm tied to the Abomination. When it appears to the Chosen, I am called. He came at the birth of your mother, and so I was sent."

"Literally an angel on one side and the devil on the other?"

"Yes."

"And when she died?"

"I should have known, because while he vanished—I sent him back to hell as I have often done—but I remained. Only I shouldn't have; I can't, but I did. I searched for him, but I could find nothing. He's grown in skill and guile, and. . . "

"And what?"

Before she could answer, a phone rang. Spencer shook his head and looked around the cozy room, with its chintz and lace curtains that overlooked a brownstone block of West 22nd Street. He retrieved the cell from his jacket, but didn't recognize the number. But the name on the readout was familiar—Russell Gray, Lara's assistant. He picked up. "Yes?"

"Dr. Williams."

"Yes."

"Thank God, something terrible has happened."

As his words flew through the phone, Spencer had a vision, the first he'd had since going to work for Global, and it was clouded with the color of blood. In his mind's eye, he was running, someone or something chasing him.

"Dr Williams? Dr. Williams are you there?"

"Yes, what's happened? Where's Lara?"

"She's been in an accident, and I'm trying to get through to her. But she's not picking up. The GPS in her car has her on I-95. Something terrible has happened. . . they locked me out of her office. I don't know what's going on. I think she may be hurt. . . or dead."

"No," Spencer said, looking at Joan, and now seeing through the vision, like a transparent screen. "She's not dead, but something's after her. I'll find her Russell," and then a premonition. "You need to get out of town, Russell. And ditch the phone, as well. Get away, get far far away."

"Oh shit! That's what she said."

"Then leave," he hung up. "Come on Joan, we've got to find Lara. She doesn't have much time." He stopped, "We need a car."

"I've got one," Joan said, "it's back near the TV station."

Chapter Twenty-five □ □ □

Frightened and in excruciating pain, Lara limped through shadowy brush. Her heels squished and sank in mud. Blood oozed from a gash on her forehead and her right shoulder felt on fire. She struggled to keep it immobile, not wanting to see the deformity beneath her blood-stained blouse. She could smell them, like rotten eggs and perfume. "GO AWAY GO AWAY GO AWAY!" And the yellow mist retreated but then reformed. Their eyes sparkled, their voices, "Lara...why fight? Why run? It's futile. Let us in. Let us in."

"GO AWAY GO AWAY GO AWAY!" Her teeth chattered.... She had no idea where she was—somewhere near the Connecticut-New York border. The highway no longer visible, but still roaring dully in the distance as she stumbled into dark woods—and time—she had no idea how long she'd been fleeing, minutes? Hours?

"Lara...why try to send us away?" Minnie taunted in a sing song voice. "We'll come right back. It's what he wants. You have bad taste in men. Should have listened to your mother. Should have married boring Paul."

She couldn't think past the pain. That at least was something real to focus on—not the freakish mist that made it impossible to see more than a few yards. Their voices swirled around and she felt them working away at her, poking into her brain like hot embers, sparking her fear. Little whispers—some just absurd, "Yes," Minnie's voice, "it was the cellulite. Men hate that...cottage cheese thighs." And then Ian, "He told you he loved you. He doesn't know what love is. It was smoke and mirrors. He used you, wanted you to be his hands, do his dirty work. He sent you to tempt Spencer...and you really fucked him up good." And then Minnie, "Your mother was right...should have listened to Vivian." Like a tape switched on, old fights with her mother, "The clock is ticking...should have married Paul...women should never put careers before family...you'll end up alone Lara, is that what you want? You'll never have a child...too old...Tick tick tick tick."

"GO AWAY GO AWAY GO AWAY!" The mist parted, but now less so. Her foot caught on a tree root, she stumbled, breaking her fall with her good hand against the trunk of a maple. White-hot pain shot through her shoulder. "Leave me alone!" she screamed.

"Not an option." Minnie's voice, "we're just following orders. And sadly, your devoted romance readers will never know if plucky Governess Megan ever wins over the reluctant Baron. My money's on the slutty Duchess. That's how it works in the real world. And shame on you for basing her on Spencer's Madeleine...course you weren't wrong."

Lara could hardly move—they were right, what was the point in trying to go on? She stood still as the mist grew stronger, tightening around her like a noose. She croaked, "Go away go away go away." Like a pebble thrown in water, the mist circle widened, coalesced and then drew back in. Despite her pain and fear, the scientist in her, couldn't help but be amazed. "What are you? And if you're so fucking powerful, why haven't you killed me already?"

She could feel their mental probes batting at her, like a gull trying to open a clam. "What are you looking for?" she asked, turning and seeing a pair of black eyes through the mist—not human, no whites, something corvine. "Go away go away go away." It was hard to breathe, her chest heavy. She flashed on the accident—the crazed look in the truck driver's eyes, the yellow mist in his cab, Ian waving at her just before impact. "Get out of my head...go away go away go away." *Hell, why don't they just kill me? Why didn't Karel?* The obvious answer, *because they can't.* And they must have done something to the truck driver, "Wait...what did you say before? Karel needs me to do his dirty work? To be his hands?"

"Oh-oh spaghetti O's," Ian chirped. "Somebody's catching on."

"Lara!" A far-away voice shouted through the mist.

She looked at the closing circle, hard to breathe—*did they do that? Is this another trick?*

"Lara! Lara! Can you hear me?" a crunch in the underbrush.

"Spencer, is that you? **Help me!**"

"Keep talking!" he shouted, his voice closer.

"Spencer, don't let them get to you! Please help me!" And then softer, "Go away go away go away."

The fog receded and hovered, and as the footsteps drew near, she watched in awe as the mist transformed into Karel's servants. Minnie perched on a boulder and Ian sitting overhead on a tree branch, his legs dangling ten feet off the ground.

*

"Lara!" Spencer, running through the muck, felt a huge relief. After Russell's call he and Joan had raced from the city, abandoning Carrigan's Audi in the breakdown lane where traffic had slammed to a halt at the accident that had shut down I-95 South.

"Oh my, God!" He raced to her side, brambles snagged his pants, "You're hurt. How bad? We need to get you to a hospital."

"No" she said, "my shoulder, it's just dislocated. We have to get out of here. We have to figure out a way to stop this. To stop him and stop Marvan."

"Ooh," Minnie said, now dressed in a puffy purple, pink and yellow princess outfit, with a stiff white collar and full velvet skirt.

"Master is not going to like this," Ian intoned, his voice a spot-on imitation of Marty Feldman's Igor from *Young Frankenstein.*

Spencer startled, not having seen them, "What the hell! I know you two, don't I? But you're not real. How do I know you?"

"Demons!" Joan shouted, coming to his side. "Succubi. Be gone, be gone..."

"There we go with the name calling, again," Minnie stood and smoothed out her skirt. She stared across the clearing, "We've missed you Spencer."

Ian dropped from the tree, his clothes changing from jeans and leather jacket, to a Prince Charming outfit that matched Minnie's Snow White. "Dude," he said, "it's good to see you. To actually be able to talk with you. You don't know how long I've waited for this. Like your haircut, by the way."

Joan stumbled and grabbed onto a tree limb.

"Are you okay?" Spencer steadied Joan, while trying to take it all in. "Please, no more seizures."

"I don't know what's going on." She said, "What's happened to the rules?" She glared at the succubi. "How is it you know these two?"

"It was a long time ago," Spencer answered, "and I thought they were just in my dreams. The last time was the night...the night my mother died...No wait, that's not true. You were there that night Madeleine sang at the Improv—the musicians. That was you."

"We've always been there," Minnie said, her eyes searching his. "We were always there. Always watching."

"My comic books...the video games...the settings on my microscope..." Spencer remembering how his stuff always seemed different than how he'd left it, "My school locker..."

"That was me," Ian smiled, his arm linked with Minnie's as they approached. "X-Men are awesome. And have you done the new Zelda? I used to watch you for hours, couldn't wait till you'd gone to school so I could try."

"I get it...you're the birds," Spencer said. "The crows outside my window. You were always there, even in the winter."

"At times flies on the wall," Minnie said, her expression soft, her head tilted to the side examining Spencer.

"Squirrels too," Ian said, "especially when you were at school."

"Leave him be," Joan, who was now glowing silver, put herself between the two demons and Spencer and Lara.

"I don't want to," Ian's face contorted, as he looked past her at Spencer. "All these years, all we could do was watch, and make sure no one harmed you. Do you know how much I've wanted to talk with you? To play *World of War Craft*, or to just hear you talk about your experiments, or maybe read the same book, or..."

"But you're demons," Joan spat back, as a spectral hand holding a sword of bright white light emerged from Sharon's body. She raised it toward them.

"Wait!" Spencer said, "Let them stay." He walked past her and held out his hands.

"Don't!" Joan warned. "They will cloud your thoughts, lie and beguile."

"Spencer, they get inside your head," Lara pleaded, "stay away from them."

"No," he said, and he gave Minnie his left and Ian his right hand, and the three stood still, like children in a playground, looking at one another.

"They just tried to kill me," Lara shouted. "You need to tell them to go away three times, it makes them back off."

"We were told to kill her," Minnie said, and looked back at Lara. "And clearly we've not succeeded. How could you survive that crash? You were supposed to die. He's seen you die that way."

Lara shivered and said nothing.

"Do you always do what you're told?" Spencer asked, as a tingle traveled through his fingers and up his arms.

"We're supposed to," Ian explained, his gaze fixed on Spencer.

"And if I asked you to do something?" Spencer, felt a strange connection with these two, like finding a piece of himself.

"Don't consort with demons." Joan warned.

"I can go left or I can go right," he replied, his gaze drifting between Ian and his sister.

"What would you ask of us?" Minnie's eyes black as coal bore into his.

"Two things," he said. "Please don't hurt Lara. She's my friend... and I have to know how I can undo this thing."

"He will kill us," she replied.

Spencer watched as she turned to her brother. Ian smiled and nodded "You were smart to conceal the last piece of your formula, but that's also where you took the first turn down the Devil's path" he said. "If you move fast, you may be able to stop this... but the cost well, that will be great." The succubus took his hand back from Spencer and placed it gently on the side of his face. "I'm sorry for you and what you're going to have to do. I truly am. And we'll leave your friend be, say she was in a horrible accident that no one could survive."

"What is going on?" Joan spat out, "Why would you help him? This is a trick, Spencer. They are Lucifer's spawn. They are compelled to do his bidding."

"No trick," Minnie said, her eyes a swirl of changing colors, black to red, then to violet and finally a leafy green. "Angel, you told us we have souls and that it was not possible. I now know how this came to be... we were made to protect Spencer and through the years came to love him... and each other. Love changed us."

Joan, still glowing, her angelic form superimposed over Sharon's, the sword no longer raised, stared at Minnie, and then her brother, "How strange, but yes... that is truth. What will you do?"

Come brother," Minnie let go of Spencer's other hand, and she too touched the side of his face. "It's time to meet our maker." And they vanished in a yellow mist.

Chapter Twenty-six

□ □ □

"Drink," Spencer told Lara, averting his eyes from her shapely, albeit blood smeared and nearly naked torso as she sat on the fussy bed with its cheery quilt and lace-trimmed pillows. He handed her a tumbler of vodka, ice, lemon and sugar—but mostly vodka. "Drain it...you sure you wouldn't rather do this in a hospital?" noting how blue her eyes were and how vulnerable she seemed as she took the glass in a shaky hand.

It was just after seven and the three had made it back through the woods, retrieved the Audi and returned to the B&B in Chelsea. "No, I trust you, Spencer. I don't trust myself," Lara said, beyond caring that she wore only her ruined lavender bra and matching panties, having stripped off her clothes to assess her bruises and the damage to her shoulder. "It's dislocated, hurts like hell, but it's not broken. I think the longer I leave it, the worse it's going to get. You have to pop it back."

"Okay, can you get on the floor?"

She gulped the vodka—"Oh, yum...Oh fuck!" doubling over with pain as she tried to stand. "Help me," holding out her hand.

Joan came to her left and eased her down.

"Thanks...Joan, right?"

"Yes."

Lara braced her good left arm on the floor as Joan supported her back and helped her lie flat.

Spencer went to her right and gently placed his hands on her deformed shoulder. He closed his eyes and waited. At first nothing, and he feared that everything Joan had spoken of had come to pass. His abilities to heal, to skry, to catch glimpses inside the minds of others and to see auras, had gone. Seconds passed, and then a minute and then two, and then five. He slowed his breath and pushed beyond fear—random images batted at his consciousness—the two creatures and their warning, Joan's freakish reappearance, and lovely Madeleine, knowing she was somewhere in the city and so wanting to see her, to look in her eyes, kiss her lips. He lowered his body to Lara's, trying to find the healer's connection, feeling her warmth, but... "Nothing's coming," he finally said, "I'm so sorry."

"Just do it," Lara slurred. "You never popped a shoulder back in medical school?"

Joan looked between the two of them, her expression sad, "It won't come the other way, Spencer. You can't see your chains. I can. Do what she asks." Joan put her hand on the side of Lara's face, "Look at me," she instructed.

"What are you?" Lara's voice dreamy as she gazed at Joan. "You're filled with light, like a sparkler."

"Just watch the pretty lights," Joan said. "It'll help."

"Like dancers, like people dancing."

"One, two, three," Spencer said, his palm on her shoulder he pushed his weight forward. He felt resistance and then the bone, with a dull scrape popped back into its socket.

Lara shuddered and gasped, not taking her eyes from Joan. "Is it done?"

He moved his hand over the surface of her shoulder, the bulging deformity gone, although he knew there would be bad swelling. "Yes, but it's going to hurt like a mother." His fingers lingered and for a second their eyes connected.

"Good," she said, looking away. "I need to hurt." She retrieved her vodka from the floor and looked up at Spencer. "Doctor, the patient needs another."

"Sure," and as he poured Lara turned back to Joan. "So, pretty sparkly light lady, how many chains have I got?"

"Not good. Your ambition blinded you, and let's face it," she smiled, "your taste in men sucks."

Lara chuckled sadly, "Yeah, apparently I consorted with the devil." Seated on the floor, she pushed back against the four-poster as Spencer handed her the drink. "It's even worse," lifting the icy glass, and staring at Spencer. "I loved him, really loved him. And he said he loved me, and I believed him, wanted to marry him. My own romance novel. My own happily ever fucking after! I was even trying to get pregnant...thank God that didn't happen. Hi, I'm Lara, I'll be having Satan's baby."

Joan shuddered, "No, you're not pregnant...but those test subjects.... There's something about this drug, Spencer...it's inside all of them and it doesn't add up." She stared up at him, "That creature said you did something to make the drug—something you've kept secret—that turned you toward the Creator's Adversary. What did you do?" she asked. "Tell me. What did you do to make that drug?" She got to her feet, her face twisted in anger, as she advanced on him. "Don't you dare keep this from me!" Her arm shot out and her palm slapped across his forehead. She held it there.

"Oh, no!" She stumbled back, a hand to her mouth, "How could you?"

"What's going on?" Lara struggled to raise herself, her drink sloshing onto the bed and floor. "He mucked around with a bunch of amoebas, turned them into Marvan factories. Big deal."

Spencer backed away from Joan, looking to her and then to Lara. "Yes, but there's one piece I never told you."

"They fed on you," Joan spat back. "How could you?"

"Whoa!" Lara staggered across the space. "Wha's she talking about, Spencer?"

He looked at Joan, wishing she'd lay off, wishing she wasn't so furious, as if lightning could bolt from her eyes and fry him. But in his gut, a crushing sense of guilt. "The answer came to me...I'd been skrying...It made perfect sense. I was trying to create a stronger amoeba, one that could withstand outrageous stress, and it just came. I remembered what you told me about my visions, that they have to be interpreted...deciphered. I can still see it, a man in a dark room—his face is hidden—a furnace glowing as he melts metal. He takes a knife and opens his vein, blood falls into the crucible. He's reading a book, chanting, and the blood turns to vapor as it touches the molten metal—and it changes, no longer glowing red, but gold. I figured what the hell, worse thing that happens is I've ruined an experiment and have to start again."

"You crazy," Lara sucked back the remains of her drink and looked around for the bottle. "You made a bunch of vampire amoebae, using alchemy. Christ, that's one for the journals. So what's the big deal? Blood is blood, bunch of protein, some minerals—mostly water when you get right down to it. Course mine's about sixty proof right now."

"But not *his* blood," Joan said, a hand to her mouth. "It's different, and now things are clear." She glared at Spencer, and then softened, "My fault, you never knew that you were chosen, and what it means to carry the spark of the Creator. And Lucifer got to you—it was he that sent you your vision. It all makes sense. It's my fault. You've transferred a piece of the Creator into your drug. That wasn't for you to do. And in the act, you've birthed...something unclean." She started to pace.

Spencer's shoulders slumped, his gaze on the floor. "No," he said. "It's not your fault, Joan. You can go left or you can go right. I knew as I was doing it, that something in that act was wrong. I knew that, and I did it anyway."

"There's more isn't there?" Joan asked. "Just spit it out, Spencer."

"I knew it was wrong because of what the man in the vision was chanting. The same line in Latin over and over, 'Pape Satan allepe.'"

"Then why?"

"Because what if it worked? What if this were the key to making a new drug that could ease unbearable suffering? And frankly, until a few days ago, I never really bought into all your talk about good and evil. In theory, of course, but I never considered that the devil—or angels for that matter—existed. I have screwed things up so badly."

"All with the best of intent," Joan intoned. "At least now I have the truth."

"So," Lara said, grabbing onto a bedpost to keep from falling. "What's the big whoop? Oh wait, those women...pregnant. We have no clue what the drug does in utero, other than with rats...Oh dear God!" She forced herself to look at Spencer. "We have a huge problem." And she blurted out the horrifying incident—all recorded on video—the Marvan rats who'd killed the placebo animals and then devoured Kayla Banes. By the end of her story, Lara was collapsed on the floor, hugging her knees and sobbing. "I still hear her scream...and I covered it up. Oh my God, what have I done? What have I become?"

"Okay," Spencer said firmly, "No one—outside this room— knows what I did. So what we have to do is destroy every single descendent of the Marvan amoebae." Even as he said that, the enormity of the task floored him. Thirty foot high steel tanks of nutrient baths in three high-security Global facilities—"We have to poison the tanks."

Lara rocked on the floor, "He's not going to let us. He's probably already moving the cultures, making new ones. Russell's locked out. I assume it's the same for the two of us. Those places are fortresses. And then," her words slurred, "these are super strong vampire amoebae...how exactly do you propose to kill them?"

"That part's easy," he said, kneeling in front of her, trying to calm her. "Concentrated soap...laundry detergent. Anything that will break the cell wall. They won't survive that."

She looked at him and started to giggle.

"What?" he asked.

"New and improved Ultra Clean," she snorted through her nose, "removes tough stains...even Satan!"

He glanced at the clock and then at his reflection in the walnut-framed mirror—his new shirt stained with blood. Brambles had torn holes in his pants and his shoes were smeared with dried mud. At least the jacket, crumpled on the bed, was somewhat intact. And in the pocket...the engagement ring. "I have something I need to do first. I'll be back," he said.

"Are you kidding? What else could be as important this?" Lara asked.

He shook his head, just this morning he'd had no doubt....This time he would ask Madeleine and finally she would say yes. But now...

He retrieved his jacket and ran his fingers through his hair. It felt strange and too short, like a piece of him had gone missing.

"Where are you going?" Lara struggled to stand. "We've got serious work to do." Swaying, "Oh no! You can't be serious. Oh, Spencer....don't. You don't know."

"You're drunk, Lara," he said gently. "Joan, keep an eye on her, I'll be back by midnight. This concert in the park means everything to Madeleine. It's what she's always wanted. I have to be there."

"No," Joan said, "we must not split up. We can't dilute what small strength we have."

Lara shook her head. "Absolutely...oh crap, Spencer, you don't know."

"What don't I know?"

"She's no good."

"What are you talking about?"

"Your woman," Joan interjected, "She's a whore."

"What?!" Her words like a slap across the face.

"A whore" she repeated, "and you're blinded by love. It's one of Lucifer's oldest tricks...and I keep falling for it."

"It's true," Lara said, hating that her words were wounding Spencer, and hating herself for not having told him before—*what kind of friend are you?* "She's fucking Karel...or little Lord Lucifer...bastard! I was there, I saw her leaving his place," tears spilled down her cheeks. "He admitted it. I'm not making this up, Spencer. I wish to fuck's sake I was!"

"No," he went to the door, "I don't know what you're trying to do," his cheeks flushed. "But don't try to stop me, and for the love of God, don't follow me," and feeling like he'd been sucker punched he slammed the door and headed out. Patting the ring box he tried to block out their accusations. *She's drunk,* he reminded himself, but Joan...yes, it's really Joan. *Ask me no questions I'll tell you no lies.* Lara's accusations about Madeleine with Karel—like acid in his veins. *Joan does not lie...but maybe she's mistaken.*

He flagged a taxi, a dull ache in his chest.

"Where to, Bub?"

"Central Park, entrance for the Great Lawn."

"79th. Some concert tonight," the cabbie remarked, "even on the news."

"Yes," Spencer said, and for the entire ride he fought to calm himself. All of Joan's talk about devils, the silver angel that kept popping out of her, and those accusations about Madeleine...*maybe delusions, could I have been drugged?* It was pointless—hell, he'd held hands with two demons, whom he kind of liked. By the time the cab made it to the wooded entrance under Belvedere Castle—he knew two things. That yes, he loved Madeleine, and if she'd been unfaithful, he would find a way to forgive her. And two, if Karel did anything to interfere with their being together—devil or no—he would find a way to kill him.

Chapter Twenty-seven

□ □ □

"That did not go well," Lara stared at the door, the reverberation of Spencer's angry exit still rang. Even heavily boozed, her shoulder throbbed, and she couldn't stop reliving the terror of how close she'd just come to dying. But along with those images, a deep regret and sense of something lost, but not Karel...Spencer. *He's just your friend, Lara...right? Just a good friend.*

"Agreed," Joan said. "We need to go after him. I can sense him heading toward the Abomination. He's blinded by his love. Men do terrible things in that state."

"Women too," still feeling the tenderness of Spencer's hands, the caring in his gold-flecked eyes. "But calling her a whore didn't help...course it's true." Lara, still in her mud-smeared underwear, asked "Can you help me with my shirt... This arm isn't going to be much use right now. So tell me," she winced as Joan eased her hand through the sleeve, "How did you catch on to Madeleine?"

"I saw them in Karel's bed together...did you know she's carrying his child?"

"What? Karel's having a child with Madeleine?"

"No. The child is Spencer's. I'd say she's at least two months along. And something else. She's been taking that drug."

"Spencer's been giving her Marvan? Why would he do that?"

"No, it's from the creature. It amuses him...and I begin to understand why. I pray that I'm wrong. Are you ready?"

"As I'll ever be. So what's the plan? And what exactly are you talking about?" following Joan out the door and to Carrigan's Audi.

"The same as always," Joan backed out onto the street. "I must find a way to banish him back to Hell. It seems he grows stronger while I'm trapped and tricked in this too weak flesh. And you...somehow you must stop this Marvan. If you can't... He's gone too far this time. I fear the Creator's wrath will be catastrophic."

"OK," Lara stared ahead as Joan turned up Eighth avenue and headed north. "Good thing I'm drunk, because this day... not so good. Don't quite know where to start. Hell? Where exactly is that?"

Joan gritted her teeth as she goosed the pedal to time the staggered lights—"your religion is science. And that's the problem. People no longer believe that a devil exists... or the Creator for that matter." Her words spit angrily, "And that's why he grows strong. Humans are limited and vain. If you can't explain with your senses, you insist a thing does not exist. Spencer was right. If you can't measure it on a machine, then people won't believe; there is no more faith." She swerved, and laid on the horn as a bus pulling out of the Port Authority terminal cut them off. "But yes, Lara, there is a Hell and Heaven too. Hell is the void, the absence of life and light—it is chaos, and it's where the Abomination, born as Lucifer, was thrown when he was cast from the Creator's presence. It is his domain. He is the first of the seven princes of Hell."

"So... who let him out?"

"He crawls out on his own... no that's not exactly right" she said, "the Creator lets him out and whenever that happens, I must send him back."

"And if the Creator... and I'm assuming we're talking God here... is so almighty, why would he let this happen?"

"It's the testing of humankind," flooring the accelerator as the lights turned at Columbus Circle with its towering statue of the explorer, and the South border of Central Park, aflame in fall foliage, came into view.

Lara stared out. The sky was darkening, lights on in the park, joggers, women with strollers, couples in horse-drawn carriages—a beautiful evening. "And this is all somehow tied up with Spencer and Marvan?"

"Yes, he was chosen. He carries—or carried—a spark of the Creator, and now..."

"It's in the pill," Lara said, "that's why you were so freaked by him feeding his blood to the amoebae. But what I don't get—why does that have to be a bad thing? If it's a little bit of God in a pill, shouldn't that be..."

"No," Joan said forcefully, as she eased into the far-right and took the turn in front of the Natural History Museum for Central

Park's 79th Street cut-through. "Ask yourself this, people who've taken this Marvan, what happens when they stop?"

"They don't want to stop."

"But if they do?"

"They return to the way they were...but they really want it back."

"Yes," Joan said, "and that's just the tip of the iceberg. When these children are born, they will be slaves to this pill. It will be the end of free will. And there's more, something I'm too scared to even contemplate."

"What? What are you talking about?"

"I don't know how, but somehow the Abomination has found a way into the pill and into those women's unborn children."

"Like sperm?" Lara said, and even through a pint of vodka, she knew there was substance to Joan's fears. And other thoughts plagued her, like, the Marvan rats all had bigger litters, and the human subjects, in addition to the wonderful effects of the drug also developed powerful libidos—everyone was screwing like rabbits. On the island they'd had to insure the women were on oral contraception, plus they'd brought in condoms by the gross...just to be sure. And now, half a dozen pregnant women she knew of, which meant there had to be more, possibly many more, possibly thousands.

Traffic slowed as they approached Central Park's Great Lawn, with the whimsical Belvedere Castle on the hill overlooking Turtle Pond. At the entrance to the lawn an unfurled banner read, *Opera Under the Stars: The Manhattan Opera Company Presents— Jacque Offenbach's–The Tales of Hoffman.* "I have never felt such fear, Lara," Joan added, as she veered right, braked and with a bone-jarring lurch drove the Audi over the curve and parked by the jogging path.

"Hey lady," a helmeted man on a racing bike yelled, nearly colliding with the car, before zipping into the joggers-only path, "you can't park there."

Ignoring him, Joan and Lara abandoned the car and headed toward the lawn. Dusk was falling, but the park glowed with thousands of white fairy lights and a full moon overhead. The stage, a soaring white half-shell constructed at the north end, glowed in the distance. Private boxes and chairs had been erected on a semi-circle of raised platforms and beyond those, families, couples and groups of friends had staked out space on the lawn with blankets, semi-concealed bottles of wine and picnic baskets.

"Karel loves opera." Lara started to tremble as she and Joan followed the excited crowd toward the field. Red velvet ropes had been set up at the outer edge—those with tickets could pass and those without had to fend for themselves on the lawn. Lara looked around, "Oh God, he's here, isn't he?" Her heart pounded, and sweat beaded her forehead despite the cool night air.

Joan sniffed, "Yes... Music has always been a weakness for the Creature. It's a drug to him."

"Right, he gets all spacey... it's funny how things are suddenly clear." Her teeth chattered. "You know he said that he loved me and I believed him. If this wasn't so terrifying—I wanted his baby. Now he wants me dead, but why?"

"He's incapable of love," Joan spat out, her voice thick, "... or rather not for anything or anyone other than himself."

Lara startled at Joan's vehemence. "OK, you just sounded like me. Did you maybe have a little thing for him at some point?"

"It was impossible not to love him," she admitted. "I tried to stop him, knowing that he would be cast out, but he would not listen." She shrugged. "You cannot imagine how beautiful he was. Next to the Creator, the most dazzling being imaginable, of course I loved him. He was the light bearer and the first born. We all loved him... were in love with him. All of the first brood of angels followed him."

"But not you."

"No," and before she could elaborate they approached a pair of young attendants who were checking tickets. Joan's eyes fluttered and strands of silver light touched the young man and woman, who immediately pulled back the rope to let them pass.

"Cute trick... but how do you propose..."

"Quiet," Joan said, as she turned and scanned the audience, who'd grown quiet at the opening chords of the overture. "There," she pointed to a curtained box perched high and to the right of the stage. "It knows we're here. It's time."

"For what?" Lara blinked several times to be sure she wasn't hallucinating, but coming out of Joan's mid section was an increasingly strong silver light that pulsed and sparkled.

"For battle, of course."

*

Karel settled back in his chair as the orchestra tuned to the oboe's 'A.' The lights dimmed and the string section punched out the first declarative chords. His gaze, softened by the music, took in all the players, everyone here to do their part. Joan, filled with indignation, just itching to send him hurtling back to the abyss—yet again. Lara—*why isn't she dead?* He stared down at his ex paramour as she stumbled drunkenly through the crowds. "Why is she still alive?" sensing fear in his two little succubi— "What happened? Tell me!"

"Lara knows what we are. She repelled us." Minnie said from back in the shadows to his right.

"But the truck," Karel said, "I've seen her death a hundred times...she knows too much. She could queer things, get the FDA to pull the Marvan approval. How could you let this happen?" He turned, and glared at Minnie and then Ian. He sucked in deeply pulling their memories like mollusks from their shells—the touching scene in the woods, the two of them holding hands with Spencer, deliberately disobeying him. "You let her go!" he spat, set to turn the two back to sand.

"No!" Ian shrieked. "It was my fault, don't hurt Minnie. Punish me, it was my idea. She didn't want to do it, make me pay. It's my fault, please."

Karel hesitated, "How pathetic." As exquisite music wafted through the velvet curtain of the box. It pulled at him, softening his rage as his head now slid from side to side, like a cobra keeping time to the charmer's tune. "I'll deal with the two of you later." *The Tales of Hoffman* was one of his favorites—a poet who continually falls in love, only to have the devil intercede, destroy his love and break his heart. The true hero—the devil—made to appear as a villain. "They never understand," he murmured.

"What's that?" Ian asked from behind.

"Without me, what would inspire the poet, the painter, the songwriter? Without the crucible of suffering, there would be no art...just kittens on greeting cards. He chuckled. "That's the meaning of this opera—out of sorrow and loss comes beauty...humanity...but with Marvan, no more suffering." He laughed again, "Careful what you ask for...ah, here we go." And the curtain parted on the opening tavern scene and a boisterous Bavarian drinking song.

The music flowed into him, and here and there as he gazed down on the thousands in the bleachers he caught glimmers, the tiniest reflection of himself. It was a huge risk, but this entire night—so many eggs—but not all—in one basket. He'd had tickets sent to every Marvan test subject in the tri-state area— a kind of thank you. And tonight, just like this opera, the last composed by Offenbach—one the composer never lived to see performed—this was his greatest triumph. "This is it."

"What's wrong with you?" Minnie asked...and then, because she couldn't stop herself, "Why are we still here? You saw what we did? Are you just going to drag this out? What new game is this?"

"You'll see....The thing is just about done," and here and there he caught the faint golden flicker of pregnant women—a tiny spark of himself, courtesy of Spencer's wonder drug—in each of their bellies. And of course, coming closer and growing stronger, the archangel in all her celestial glory.

Feeling a wave of nostalgia, "Poor Madeleine," as the silvery flare of the angel, with a drunken Lara at her side, headed toward them.

"Why's that?" Ian asked.

"This was to be her big night. She won't be what people remember. And Ian...?"

"Yes."

"For what it's worth, you're wrong, I do love them. And strangely, as annoying and insubordinate as the two of you have become, I have never cared for demons as I have for the two of you. Still, I'd urge you to enjoy the next few moments as they will be your last."

And as the audience applauded the close of the tavern scene, a glowing silver hand tore back the curtain. Karel stared into Joan's glowing eyes, taking in the outstretched sword. He felt the familiar fear and terror, but something even stronger—resolve, *I'm not going.*

And then the angel spoke. "It's time, Creature."

*

Even with the backstage pass that Madeleine had given him, Spencer—his clothes torn and smeared with mud and dried blood—had a tough time convincing security to let him through. When he finally made it to the bustling backstage, he was met by a wave of choristers dressed as nineteenth century revelers rushing off stage. As they left, a small army of black-clad stagehands surged forward to clear and change the set for the next scene. Amid the industrious movement, his gaze fell on Madeleine—*so beautiful.* She sat on the steps of a hydraulic crane, her blue and white hoopskirt tilted up revealing layers of lacy white petticoats, her hair a wig of auburn curls and her face made up like a porcelain doll with rouged cheeks and a bright red Cupid's bow mouth. She stared off, the fingers on one hand gently tapping time to the orchestra. Her head turned and she saw him.

She had a faraway expression. "What happened to you?" her fingers still following the beat.

"Long story. You look amazing," he said.

"This dress weighs a ton, I just hope I don't fall over."

On the cab ride up, and as he'd battled his way through the crowds and through security, he'd thought of things he needed to ask her. But now, standing in front of her, his heart pounding, it came down to a single question. "Madeleine, I need to know one thing, and after that nothing else matters."

"So serious," she said, her head tilted to the side, as the music segued into the Act I introduction. "What is the one thing?" and she grabbed the stairwell, the stiff hoop flopping awkwardly, as she tried to stand.

He gave her his hand, helped her down, and then stood back. She was exquisite—a living doll. "Do you love me?"

Seconds passed as she stared down and then back at him. "I'm sorry, but no, and there's more." But at that moment a stage manager wearing a headset tapped her on the shoulder.

"Ms. Forest, it's time."

"Yes," and looking back at Spencer, "I'm pregnant, Spencer—and yes, it's yours. I plan to have the child and if you still want me to marry you, I will. If not, we'll figure something out. Love isn't everything. I wonder if it even exists. But I think we can help each other, and perhaps that's enough."

With her skirts billowing, she was led to the darkened stage and took her spot on a raised podium.

Spencer couldn't move and felt as if he couldn't breathe. His toe caught on a cable. He stumbled and grabbed onto the rail of the stairs where she'd been seated. "What the hell?" Off to his side, stage lights glowed, and the curtain rose to reveal a fantastical doll-maker's shop. In the center, her head tilted, her expression blank, was Madeleine.

Tears formed, while he stood and watched the scene unfold. The lover, blinded by a magical pair of glasses, has fallen in love with the mechanical doll Olympia. The doll maker, in debt to the devil, encourages the hopeless romance, with Madeleine singing one of the most glorious and difficult arias in all opera, her voice trilling wildly up and down like a fantastic bird. Her words in his head—*don't love you, pregnant, marriage...or not.* The music swelled as her notes shot higher and faster. He couldn't take his eyes off of her. Maybe it would be okay, maybe just being near her would be enough...and they'd have a child. She'd come to love him in time, and he so wanted to believe that, but he'd seen and heard too much to the contrary. He watched her beautiful doll character, how magnificent she was, her acting slightly comical as every so often she'd wind down and flop over. The doll maker would then come up behind her with a giant red key, turning it with broad gestures and jerkily she'd come back upright, resuming the dizzying aria where she'd left off.

How could something hurt so much? He stared at Madeleine, as the devil came on stage, intent on his payment from the doll maker. *Yes, I love her, and that's not enough. She does not love me. She never has and she never will.*

And the devil, now furious with the doll maker, attacked Olympia. The violins, woodwinds, brass and tympani crescendoed with the sounds of breaking clockwork, and stagehands hidden in the wings threw giant gears and doll limbs into the air. The music softened, as the devil laughed triumphant. The hero protested and Olympia's final note ended in a strangled cry.

The audience exploded in applause and rose to their feet. Then he heard a different scream, and then another—not bravo, not encore, but shrieks of terror. He ran to the edge of the stage, his vision blinded by beams of silver and gold light pulsing from one of the elevated private boxes, and the smell—incense and sulfur.

Someone screamed "fire!" as billowing yellow smoke poured from the box. Panic and pandemonium, as fifteen thousand people stampeded toward the park exits. Their flight then cut short by a sound unlike anything he'd ever heard—maybe some type of trumpet, but impossibly loud and high. The note pure and piercing. People screaming clutched the sides of their head, their eyes wide, and in seconds, as yellow smoke crested over them, and the trumpet still blared, they fell to the ground, some writhing, but only for moments, and then they lay still, shrouded beneath the dense rolling smoke. Gold and silver sparks shot like fireworks and again an unearthly trumpet's blare.

He stared up into the light, wondering if it might blind him. He could just make out the angel Joan as she hovered with an outstretched sword—her voice the trumpet's roar, and inside his head a searing note that turned to words, **"GO TO HELL GO**

TO HELL GO TO HELL."

He heard a horrible grating noise, like some great machine being torn apart. The yellow smoke pulsed and swelled like a tsunami, rolling across the fallen audience. It swirled around his ankles, his knees, his chest. The same mist the two creatures had in the woods—*like the night Mother died.* Only now he knew what to do. "Go away go away go away," and the mist parted. Chanting beneath his breath, "go away go away go away," he ran on stage to Madeleine's hoop-skirted body, now behind the scrim where she'd waited before taking her First Act bow. Racing to her, he hoisted her limp body in his arms, wanting to keep her face well above the stench, "go away go away go away." The ground shook and the angel's voice again clanged, **"GO TO HELL GO TO HELL GO TO HELL."**

He climbed the podium, getting barely above the swirling cloud, where minutes before Madeleine had stood. He stared out at the light. Silver rays shot from the bellowing angel, "GO TO HELL GO TO HELL GO TO HELL."

And then a single word, just as loud, simple and declarative. **"NO!"**

"GO TO HELL GO TO HELL GO TO HELL!" Her sword emitted a stream of light.

"NO NO NO!"

"Shit!" Spencer tried to make sense of the unfolding battle, while keeping the mist at bay, "go away go away go away." All of Joan's crazy stories back at the B&B—*not stories, real.* With Madeleine, wig askew and unconscious in his arms, he could see that—angel or no—Joan was in trouble. He had to choose—stay with Madeleine and try to protect her and his unborn child from the noxious smoke or... staring up at Joan— *I have to help her.* This was followed by, "and how the fuck do you propose to do that?" Gently laying Madeleine down and cushioning her head with the wig, he jumped from the podium, "go away go away go away," and raced toward Joan's shimmering form at the top of the bleachers.

*

Joan, freed from Sharon's body that now laid at the foot of the raised opera boxes, glared at the Abomination, flanked by his two terrified creatures. Righteous fire streamed from her raised sword and pierced her ancient adversary, ripping his flesh. The Creator's raw strength flowed through her as she stared at Lucifer, swirling and writhing, unable to hold his body together. "GO TO HELL GO TO HELL GO TO HELL." She swung her flaming sword to the right and with a powerful vertical swipe ripped open a gate to hell. She felt the inrush of air, the stench of sulfur and the deafening wail of souls. She did not want to look, as tortured faces flew past the gaping hell mouth, hollow eyes pleading for release, only to be whisked away by the cyclones of upper hell.

She averted her gaze and planted her sword on the wavering Creature. She pushed in earnest, wanting to shove him back in and be done with this. "GO TO HELL GO TO HELL GO TO HELL."

And then the unthinkable. The abomination pulled itself together into a glowing golden ball, like a tightly wrapped bud, its essence focused in a pair of flaming red eyes. A mouth gaped open, "NO!" It was fighting back, leaning against the angel's sword, oblivious to the holes it was ripping through him.

Not possible, and she pushed harder, gathering every spark of energy she could muster, feeling the fiery sword twist in his gut. "GO TO HELL GO TO HELL GO TO HELL."

"NO NO NO!" It screamed, and the glowing ball of golden light, transformed into an approximation of Karel Von Graf. It gasped and writhed, a hand pushing primordial matter over a gaping hole in its glittery golden gut. "No, Joan. Not this time, my love."

"Creature, you have no choice," and mustering everything she had, she pressed forward, the blade of her sword flattening out like a battering ram. "GO TO HELL GO TO HELL GO TO HELL."

But like a willful two-year-old, the creature held fast. "No," and somehow it grew more solid. It stared down at her sword, embedded in his belly, and then glanced back at its whimpering succubi frozen in terror. Their gazes whipped around, finding each other, then the gaping hell mouth, then him, and finally the increasingly confused and frustrated angel.

Joan continued to push, trying to block out the wails of the damned and her growing desperation. *It's pushing back. How?* The creature stood, and leaned forward, further impaling himself on her sword.

"GO TO HELL GO TO HELL..."

"Give it a rest," it said. "I'm not going, angel."

"GO TO HELL."

It held up a hand that shimmered like liquid gold, "Can we stop this? I'm not going back, Joan."

"But you must," she gasped. Her resolve wavering, the sword's light faltered. "You have no choice."

"And that's where you're wrong. Remember, 'you can go left or you can go right,' sound familiar?"

"They can," she hovered, "but not..."

"Us? Wrong. We have a choice. I have a choice." Its face twisted in anger, "You saw what our Creator did to my kind—tortured, ripped apart. All that remains of my brood condemned to hell." It snorted, "Seven princes... now there will be six. We can die! I can choose to die."

"No!"

"Yes," it hissed, and the creature drew in breath. Like an enormous vacuum he sucked in clouds of billowing yellow smoke, while behind him the succubi cringed back, one on either side of the gaping hell mouth. "I'm making a different choice and it's not to let you send me back there. I've had enough. Over and over, and for what? Look at them," and he stared past her at the fallen audience. His eyes fell on Lara, unconscious on the ground by Sharon's body. "I finally understand our Creator's fondness for them. So what will It do this time? Will It let things go, or will this bring on another of Its little temper tantrums? Haven't had a planet-cleansing flood in a while."

"It is The Creator," she replied. "It is not to be questioned."

"Of course not. It doesn't much care for that does It? Quite the fascist."

Joan felt her power drain away. The Creature should have been cast back. This conflict was over. *Isn't it?* "Go to Hell. Go to Hell. Go to hell."

He laughed, "Are you quite done? Is talking smack about our beloved Creator getting your panties in a twist? Let's face it, angel, everything changes... they change, and even we can change, but the great *It* does not. Still and forever with Its silly games, and when It doesn't get what It wants—like a child kicking over the game board—It sends a flood, some meteors, destroy a city, a civilization... a race? Or in my case, It makes a beautiful creature—and I am." Its face contorted, "and then casts me aside, because I'm not quite the child It had in mind. What sort of fucking parent is that?"

"Don't!" Joan warned.

"Or what? It'll send me to Hell? Done that." Karel, now back into a semblance of his former self—dapper in his tux, his salt-and-pepper hair perfectly slicked back. His eyes dulled from ruby red to onyx black. "It's time," he repeated, and his eyes turned again to their true color—bright gold. Light radiated from his sockets. He opened his mouth and golden rays streamed out, and then from his ears and his nostrils. He raised his hands and swirling sparks shot from his finger tips and then his palms, like a firework chrysthanthemum set to explode. His clothes changed into a mesh of tiny dots as radiance seeped through the weave of the fabric.

Joan could only stare. "You can't do this...creature." He was so beautiful, his human form gone—replaced by pure gold light. *He's gone too far, but maybe this is just another trick.*

Karel's face, now a transparent mesh of golden lights. "You were going to call me something else. You remember me as I first was. It made me beautiful. Say my name, we've been together too long, you and I. Just say it."

"Master!" Minnie shrieked, "What's happening to us?" Ian and she were clutching one another, but their bodies had lost substance. Her fishnets dangled legless beneath her short skirt. Her fingers clung to Ian's shoulders as they were turning into fine white sand.

Joan looked at the two succubi, who literally were coming undone, and she could tell this was no trick. "Lucifer...made of light. Beloved of our Creator...of me. Please, I beg...don't do this."

"Thank you, I wanted to hear that one more time...before I die."

"NO!" Minnie wailed. "What of us?" Her hair shattered and fell off, as Ian's ears and mouth turned into giant holes. His eyes gaped wide, the lids now gone.

"You die too." The gold light grew, like a flower blooming, "Unlike my maker," the Creature gasped, "I will not forsake my unborn children, the children of Marvan." To Joan, "I cannot bear to see the Creator's wrath brought down on them. Let It do what It wants...I'm out of here."

*

Spencer, choking on the poisonous mist, *say it three times and it is so.* "Go away go away go away." He scrambled up the bleacher stairs and came gasping to the side of the struggling silver angel. The scene inside the box made him fear for his sanity. Where the back wall should have been was now a gaping hole over eight feet high, a portal to some horrific dimension. There was no mistaking what he saw—*it's Hell*. Like a gash in the fabric of reality—a maelstrom of faces contorted in unimaginable suffering and beyond them a shadowy landscape with towering mountains and far-off fires burning red—and in front of it Karel Von Graff was turning into a dangerously unstable orb of golden light, which Joan was desperately trying to shove back into the gaping maw. "Joan, what's happening?"

"He's resisting," Joan pushed on her sword, as the golden ball pulsed and grew. "It's trying to unmake itself."

Spencer felt Karel's energy touching his cheek and spreading like a poison. His blood tingled and his skin burned as if fire ants were swarming his face and his arms. But that was nothing compared to the unbearable reek of despair that issued from Hell. It pulled at his sanity—*Give up. You are lost, damned. This awaits you, Spencer. You are damned.* It was impossible to think, as Minnie shrieked, "NO!" and grabbed hold of what remained of her brother. Her eyes, now just gaping sockets, turned to Spencer, "We don't want to die! Save us! Help us! Please!"

Spencer looked at Joan, desperately pushing on her sword, as she tried to herd the throbbing ball of light into Hell. It wasn't budging. But the fear, paralyzing him, *don't give in, Spencer. Fight it!* Joan's teachings from childhood—*if you don't face your fear, you are doomed to forever run from it.* Not knowing what would happen, he grabbed on to her flaming silver sword—strangely solid—and added his weight to hers, trying to push the ball of light into Hell. His hands tingled coldly as his face burned in the searing gold light. It wasn't budging, but worse, as it pulsed it grew increasingly unstable. *This isn't enough*, and a desperate idea...*if we're trying to push him into hell, maybe...*

He stared back at Ian and then Minnie, struggling to hang on to their human forms, their faces falling into glittery sand, their limbs gone. "Ian, Minnie, go to hell go to hell go to hell...and then drag him with you. We'll push and you'll pull. We push you pull. We push you pull"—*say it three times and it is so.* And mustering every ounce of will and muscle he leaned on the sword, feeling it gain strength, as he and Joan pushed. And behind the golden orb, a flurry of movement as the two succubi were sucked screaming into the void.

For an instant he wondered. *Great, our only possible allies and I just sent them away*, and as Joan chanted, "GO TO

HELL GO TO HELL GO TO HELL," he caught sight of four giant insectile arms, tipped with talons like crows, and sticky hairs like flies, emerge from the hell mouth and grab hold of the giant golden ball...it wriggled and tried to escape their grasp...but it couldn't. Spencer felt hope surge as it started to inch back. Adding his voice to Joan's, only with his own chant, "WE PUSH YOU PULL WE PUSH YOU PULL WE PUSH YOU PULL."

Karel's voice screamed from inside the orb, as it pulsed, its light ripping holes in the canvas roof and walls of the box, "NO!"

"WE PUSH YOU PULL WE PUSH YOU PULL WE PUSH YOU PULL!"

"GO TO HELL GO TO HELL GO TO HELL!"

Spencer dug deep, legs straining, tears streamed down his face, as wails of the damned spewed from Hell, tearing at his gut. *How can so much suffering exist? A world without hope. Shut it out, Spencer. Don't look, shut it out.* "WE PUSH YOU PULL WE PUSH YOU PULL WE PUSH YOU PULL."

Then a different voice—a woman's voice—screamed out from the void, "Spencer!"

He stumbled, nearly losing his grasp on Joan's flaming sword. He looked, as his mother, dressed in filthy rags, stared back from the mouth of Hell, her hair whipping violently around her face, her brown eyes filled with suffering. She raised a hand toward the opening. Streams of blood dripped from her lacerated wrist and were whisked away on the howling wind. "Spencer!"

"Mother!"

She opened her mouth, but before she could utter another word, she was pushed aside by another wraith, her figure lost in a swirl of souls that clamored toward the opening.

"Mother!" he screamed.

"You can't help her!" Joan shouted, as her sword grew and morphed, now a giant silver shield herding the ball of energy toward the jagged opening. Her voice rang, and with a mighty push she shoved, "GO TO HELL GO TO HELL GO TO HELL!"

The glowing ball, now dragged by the succubi and pushed by Spencer and Joan was at the lips of hell. It screamed, "NO! NO!"

And as Spencer felt it finally move over the edge, it exploded.

Spencer was flung to the ground, blinded by the fireball. He heard Minnie shriek, "IAN! JUMP!"

Spencer squinted against the burning light. He could make out Joan's silvery form hurriedly using her sword to stitch closed the hell mouth that throbbed with gold. All around lights swirled. He glanced back at the Great Lawn as twizzles of gold like sparklers danced around the unconscious audience, before fizzling out.

The roof and the walls of the box had been blown out. A cool breeze played across his burning face and he saw stars, the full moon, and the last trailing sparkles from... *Lucifer.*

*

Joan hovered, her sword down as she examined her stitches on the now-sealed portal.

"What did I just see?" Spencer asked, looking at the space that seconds earlier had been an opening to Hell and was now just scraps of charred canvas and smoldering wood. "Was that really my mother?"

Free from the flesh, Joan could now read his thoughts, and the tumult of his emotions. He had glimpsed his mother's tortured soul in Hell, had seen Lucifer... *what? Be cast back? Commit suicide? But no, we pushed and dragged him through. Things are just as they must be. So why was it so hard this time?* "I am not certain," she replied, floating a couple feet from the ground she turned and looked at the body of Sharon Lahey. The tether she'd maintained with it was now severed. Beside Sharon's corpse lay Lara—unconscious along with the rest of the audience. It looked like a sea of death. And then her gaze fell on Spencer. She felt such love for him, and a tenderness, watching his questions queue up. His nimble mind sorting through hypotheses, wanting to know the physics behind the celestial sword, the paradigms of Heaven and Hell, and something else... what it would take to rescue his mother from Hell.

She attempted to move toward him, yearning to touch him, but as she tried, the only direction she could move was up. *Finally,* regret mingled with joy. *Finally,* she was being called back to the Creator, to Its glorious presence, to Heaven. Strangely, she did not want to leave. Things were too unsettled. The Creature's words had wounded her. It had spoken truth, and in the end had attempted the unthinkable, had sought extinction over a return to his dominion in Hell. *Yes, but did he succeed? He is the prince of deception, but what if he is truly gone? And what is the real meaning of Spencer's drug?* But the thought that filled her with stark fear for humankind's very existence, was *what will*

be the Creator's response? She could still see—here and there—
bits of twinkling gold in the bellies of women in the audience,
including Spencer's deceitful Madeleine. Lucifer called them 'the
children of Marvan.' *What has he done?* And her last thought,
before raising her sword and slipping from the mortal realm into
Heaven, *Spencer. I can no longer help, and you have much work to
do. Undo what you have done, and do it quickly, for I fear your—and
all of humankind's—fate now hangs in your hands.*

*

Dazed, winded and haunted by the image of his
mother's torment, Spencer took in the aftermath. Von Graf's box
had been immolated, the canvas roof and walls blown off, embers
smoldering on the floor. He knelt next to Lara, a lump in his
throat as he felt for a pulse...and found one, *Thank God, thank
you God.* And he impulsively leaned down and kissed her cheek,
feeling the soft tickle of her hair. "Please be okay." He stood
on shaky legs, feeling like the lone survivor of some horrible
battle. "No," he said aloud, seeing the audience here and there
begin to wake. "They're alive, but only you witnessed."

His gaze now turned to the stage. Madeleine was coming
to. He jogged down the bleachers, pushing past groggy concert
goers as they roused and tried to make sense of what had just
happened. As he approached, his head and heart were in a war
of thought and emotions. Of course he wanted her to love him—
but that hardly mattered...*and she doesn't.* Larger forces were
at play. And regardless of that golden thing's parting words, the
damage that Spencer had done needed to be undone...and fast.
Marvan must be stopped.

"What happened?" Madeleine croaked, rising up on her elbow. Someone turned on the stage lights. She blinked, her hand
shielding her eyes.

Odd, he thought, even now, staring at the woman he loved,
and who so clearly did not return that emotion. What to
say? Joan would have argued for the truth or nothing, but that
didn't always work. "I don't know," he said simply, searching out
her eyes. "Are you okay?" He helped her to sit.

"I think so," and she stared out at the audience, her gaze fixed
on the ruins of Karel's box. "Oh, my God." She struggled to
stand, the hoop of her skirt like a giant swinging bell, the weight
of the petticoats making it hard to balance. "Where is he?"

"Gone," Spencer said, accepting now that her infidelity

was true. Madeleine—like Lara—had been sleeping with...Lucifer. "You said you're pregnant."

"Yes." Her expression was hard to read—somewhere between confusion and grief.

"You're certain it's mine? How do you know it isn't his?"

"Good," she gathered her skirts and found the railing for the stairs. "Better that you know. He's impotent. The baby is yours."

"No one else?" He remembered the painting in her bedroom—how long ago that seemed—realizing he was little more to her than a tasty chocolate.

"Spencer, you practically kept me prisoner on that damn island. You think I was screwing the help?"

"No," and while she didn't invite it, he helped her down the stairs.

"So now what?" She spun around, as the dazed audience headed toward the exits, and the orchestra packed up.

"I have work to do." He wondered at the idiocy of his infatuation. Of all the women in the world, why this one? "You're beautiful, and talented beyond words Madeleine, and I loved you. But you made it clear how you feel about me. We should not get married." As he spoke, he wondered at his use of the past tense—"I loved you." Like a spell had been broken, he realized it was no longer true.

"You're just going to leave me?"

"We'll figure something out," he said, "but right now," searching the audience, and spotting Lara's tall figure, her back to them, facing the wreckage of Karel's opera box. "I've got to go."

"Wait! Spencer! What about me?"

"You'll be fine," not turning back as he ran offstage and pushed through crowds now clambering down the bleachers and toward the park exits. "Lara!" he shouted, finally making his way back into the stands, "LARA!"

She turned, "Spencer, thank God you're okay."

He sprinted the last few stairs and stood by her side, staring in at the charred remains. The box's ceiling was gone and only remnants of the three walls were left—and still the stench of sulfur and frankincense.

"She's gone," Lara, tears streaming, pointed at Sharon's lifeless body.

"I know." He pictured the three of them back in the cozy Bed and Breakfast just hours before.

"Do you think she'll still watch over you?"

"I don't know," feeling a choking sorrow. "She was a mother to me...it's like losing her a second time. And there's more...I saw my real mother, and she's in Hell. I actually saw Hell...or at least part of it." He shook his head and looked at Lara, her cheeks smudged, her spiky hair singed at the tips, her expression worried. "I've done a horrible thing with Marvan. I have to fix this. And somehow, I have to find a way to free my mother's soul...if such a thing is possible." And as though hearing Joan, *"the distance between a thought and a deed is the blink of an eye."*

"Yes, but not by yourself," Lara reached for his hand. The connection was electric, as she turned into him.

"You don't have to do this," he said as their eyes met. "This is my battle."

She smiled, her cheeks and forehead face smudged with soot, "No, we're in this together, and it's going to be hard."

"Worse than we can even imagine," he said, never having appreciated the periwinkle blue of her eyes, or just how much he'd come to value her friendship. And something more, deeper feelings, and without thought he leaned in and kissed her. It was shocking and sweet, her lips both soft and urgent.

Neither one wanted to pull away, and when they finally separated, Spencer had the clarity of a dreamer awakening. "Remember in the woods after the crash what the demon said?"

"I couldn't hear them," she said her eyes not leaving his, "not to mention the fact I thought I was losing my fucking mind."

"The one called Ian said he was sorry for what I was going to have to do.' What did he mean by that?"

"I don't know," Lara shook her head, "I suppose we'll find out. So, let's try to get the FDA to pull the drug, although that won't be easy...maybe poison three massive tanks of amoebae?" Still holding his hand she glanced away.

He followed her gaze and saw Madeleine, now standing center stage, her glorious mane freed from the hairnet. She was staring at them, her expression unreadable.

"I'm so sorry," Lara said.

"Yeah, well something else we have in common—crappy taste in lovers."

"That's a fact. Spencer, I feel like a shit for not having told you about her sooner."

He smiled, and pulled her hand up to his cheek and then kissed it. "I wouldn't have listened."

"True, and I was completely besotted with Karel...let's get out of here."

And holding hands they made their way down the back of the deserted bleachers.

"I keep thinking about the wedding invitations," she said, "I was about to be Mrs. Satan."

"There's always hyphenating," he offered, his lips still tingling and his thoughts bombarded with the overwhelming task ahead, and the horrifying memory of his mother's damned spirit.

"Okay...So Carlos Key first?" she asked.

"Yeah, that's got to be it."

"Spencer?"

"Yes?" helping her down the last step until they were both on the springing lawn.

"Other than being this Chosen one, you're not some kind of demon?"

"Don't think so."

"Good." And holding tight to his hand, she pulled him in, and they kissed.

Epilogue □ □ □

Minnie's first thought, as the pain—the first she'd ever known—ripped through her—*this is what it's like to die.* Unable to hold her form, her core had shredded while she and Ian had tried to drag Karel into the void. Her last moments of awareness, as she had gripped his burning golden flesh—*I don't want to die, and not in this horrible place.* "Ian!" she'd screamed in the explosion of light, as Hell-bound souls had shrieked for release, their blood-rimmed eyes fixed longingly on the gaping rift between earth and Hell. "Ian! Jump!" catching a glimpse of him as he'd struggled by her side, desperately trying to hang on to some form, any form—the crow, the fly, ants, roaches, people. "JUMP!" And she'd hurled herself into the exploding light, feeling unbearable pain and expecting death.

*

The fly blinked, its faceted eyes taking in hundreds of images, each a bit different. It rubbed its front legs together, enjoying the smells, the first rot of death coming from Sharon Lahey's body. *I'm not dead,* he thought, as his head swiveled to follow Spencer and Lara. The urge to fly after them was tremendous, but no. His thoughts were odd, no longer feeling the pull of the master. *Did he do it? Is he dead? Could he really kill himself? Or is he back in Hell?* And he flew down to where Karel had sat, the chair now little more than smoldering coal. *Where are you, Minnie? I jumped right through him. You were right. Where are you? Minnie? Please.* He felt a horrifying moment of desperation. *Minnie, don't be gone.* And then his powerful eyes caught a hint of movement, a single insect wing, fluttering. He hopped across, *Oh Minnie...that's just pathetic.* Below him was a struggling half fly and half cockroach, it's fly wing fluttering manically as it spun in circles...but she was alive. "Let me help. Here," and with a swirl of the dense yellow mist he dropped out of the fly and transformed into handsome Ian. With a razor-sharp fingernail, he sliced open the skin of his wrist and dipped in for a bit of the glittery sand—*so much brighter than before—how did that happen?* Gently he brought it down to the struggling half-and-half insect. "How the hell did you do that?" He felt its tiny mouth suck in, and then the weird little body fell into smoke and she was beside him.

"Oh, Ian," her arms draped around his neck.

He pulled her in and they stood. "We're alive," he said. "I wouldn't want to exist without you."

"I know. He meant for us to die." She ran a hand along the side of her brother's face. "I was so scared for you."

"And me for you, but we didn't die," he added, turning in and kissing her palm, "how great is that?"

"It's fantastic, but now what? I can't feel him anymore. Is he really gone? So, no more, 'do what I say or I'll turn you to sand.'"

"I feel weird," he said, "and something else," he vigorously shook his head. "I'm really hungry. I mean not like before, I'm starving."

"Me too. . . so what do we eat?"

He sniffed deeply, "I'm not sure, but something smells amazing. What is that?" and taking Minnie's hand, "It's like barbecue and raspberries."

"And fresh," she added, as they dropped down from the remains of the opera box.

Landing silently on the grass, "Young, too, mmm. There," and he spotted three NYU freshman girls, who'd opted to hang back as the masses had fled the park. The girls, none more than twenty, were sharing a joint beneath a copse of stately Norway spruce, while passing a bottle of sweet Belgium raspberry beer. "Tasty," licking his lips, and running a hand through his hair.

"Very," matching his stride.

"And you know what they say?" as he made eye contact with one of the girls, smiled and winked.

"What's that brother?"

"You are what you eat."

About the Author □ □ □

Charles Atkins

Charles Atkins is a board-certified psychiatrist, published author, and professional speaker. He writes both fiction and non-fiction, including the Barrett Conyors forensic thriller series, The Lil and Ada Connecticut cozies as well as books on Alzheimer's and Bipolar Disorder. GO TO HELL is his first venture into urban fantasy.

In addition to books he's written hundreds of articles, columns, and shorts stories for professional and popular magazines, newspapers, and journals. He's been a regular contributor to the American Medical Association's *American Medical News*, a consultant to the Reader's Digest Medical Breakthrough series, and his work has appeared in publications ranging from *The Journal of the American Medical Association (JAMA)* to *Writer's Digest Magazine*. He's been twice featured in the *New York Times*, as well as many other publications.

He lives in Connecticut where he splits his time between clinical work, writing and family.

He can be followed on the Internet at: www.charlesatkins.com, www.charlesatkinsmd.blogspot.com and @charlesatkinsmd (Twitter).